THE SANDWICH MAN

BY

BOB JOHNSON

COPYRIGHT

ACKNOWLEDGEMENTS

"Thanks to Harvey and Matthew from Hexa Publishing and all the unknown editors, writers, book cover designers, and all those who have helped me over the time it has taken me to achieve my goal of getting this book published."

DEDICATION

To my wife Angela who has always been here for me.

ABOUT THE AUTHOR

"Bob Johnson is 74 years old and is married to Angela and lives in Wales. He is a retired Police Officer and has used his experience and imagination in writing this book. This is his first book of fiction since he started writing during the Covid Lockdown."

Table of Contents

PROLOGUE

He was always told to go for the weakest first, the innocent ones. He had lain there for almost two hours when he saw them. The young couple with a small girl skipping around them. The couple just walked slowly hand in hand, unaware that within a few moments, the world was going to change and not for the better. He had no idea who they were, nor did he care. To him, they were just practice for bigger things to come.

He looked through the scope of his long-range sniper rifle. The gap between him and the family did not appear anything like the 400 yds distance it actually was. The little girl was smiling as she skipped along, and he could see her parents laughing as they walked behind her. He set his rifle and slowly squeezed the trigger.

Before he had a chance to blink again, he saw a fountain of blood erupt from the little girl's head as she fell to the floor. Everyone stood still and a loud, piercing scream emanated from the mother. But before she even finished, a bullet went through her head and her blood and gore sprayed over her husband. An instant later, his head exploded, and his brains covered his wife and daughter as he fell beside them.

There was complete silence and then suddenly people started to scream and run in all directions, or stood still like statues, not comprehending what has taken place. Unbeknown to anyone and even himself, he had set a chain of events in motion that no one could have expected.

Satisfied with his work, he bagged his rifle, and the three spent bullets and walked back to his car, parked 300 yards away next to the local village green. As he drove away, he heard the distant sounds of sirens and watched as they sped past. He thought to himself a good day's work, I'm hungry, I fancy a nice BLT sarnie.

CHAPTER 1

Detective Inspector Sarah James sat at her desk in the noisy, busy office she had called "home" for the last 20 yrs. She looked at all the younger officers, some so young she thought they should still be at school. Others like her sergeant, Ken Matthews, grey before his time, shoulders stooped, the effects of too many years of long hours at work and in the pub.

She consoled herself with the promise that in three weeks, she would be starting her leave, and getting ready to go on that cruise she always promised herself. She looked down at what passed for coffee and reminded herself that last night was not going to be repeated, how many whiskies had she drank?

The phone suddenly roused her, and as she picked it up, she heard the deep rasping voice of her boss, Walter Edwards, shouting "Get your ass to my office now!" What the hell have I done wrong now she thought, can't be about last night can it?

She looked across at her Sergeant, he shrugged his shoulders, and she walked into her boss's office. He sat behind a table piled high with files and looked shocked and pale. "What's up Guv?" she asked, "You look as though you have seen a ghost." He whispered, "I wish that was all it was."

"There's been a shooting in the park, 3 dead, a man, woman and girl. It's chaos there, get your team down there now and see what the hell happened." Sarah looked at him, "Have they got it right? Not a prank, is it?"

"Go"! He shouted, "Let me know what is going on, before we hear it on the television."

Sarah ran out of the room, everyone staring at her, "Grab your stuff, we've a nasty one. Helen start up the Incident room and Geoff find out who is the HOLMES (Home Office Large Enquiry System) staff on today and get them on standby."

Within ten minutes they had pulled up inside the park and saw that there were several vehicles already there and a large white tent in the middle of the path.

Sarah looked around and saw with a heavy heart that the Crime scene manager, Detective Sergeant Grace Meadows was walking towards them. Meadows had the face of an angel, but a heart like a gin trap and was feared by everyone who ever crossed her.

"Hello Inspector," she smiled in her own, tight-lipped way, "Didn't realise they were going to send out their golden oldie for this one."

Sarah replied, "I Might be old Grace, but remember I am in charge here, you do your job and I'll do mine." She growled and walked to the tent, the team following and silently cheering Sarah on for facing her out.

DS Meadows had already made a start with her Scenes of Crime officers, all civilians, and everyone experts in their own right. They were waiting on the pathologist, before being able to get too close to the bodies. Sarah saw them lying as if in a huddle, dark blood everywhere and congealing, their pale unseeing faces distorted and shattered. What the hell has happened here she wondered, why I am here, I am on leave soon! She turned to her Sergeant and told him to talk to all the witnesses left at the scene and try and find out how and what this is about.

At that moment, the pathologist, Dr Graham Webster walked down the path and Meadows went to greet him. Sarah couldn't help but notice how she approached the doc, almost purring, but of course Grace would never admit her feelings for the older, widowed guy. She smiled to herself as she escorted him to the tent, looking at Sarah as if to say, he is not for you!

Sarah followed the pathologist and Meadows to the back of the tent. Nothing could be truly started until he had examined the bodies and given the go ahead to remove them once he had given them his verdict.

"Has anyone touched the bodies?" he asked, almost certain in the knowledge with what was lying there, no one would have wanted to get anywhere close. DS Meadows replied, "It's as it was when the shots were fired." He looked down at each of the three bodies and looked up to Sarah and told her to extend the search area another 200 yards. He said, "The kill shots are through and through. Whoever did this have some heavy kit and training." He continued, "Any ideas who they are?"

"We're waiting on you to have a quick look at their pockets to help us." Grace said as she smiled at him. Sarah winced but kept her mouth shut. He searched the pockets of the dead male but found nothing. "Sorry ladies, can't help you here, have to wait till we get them back to the mortuary, might tell us more."

He looked around and got his staff to bag their heads and hands. He walked around them while they were being photographed, thinking to himself that whoever did this was one hell of a cold-hearted killer.

The paramedics lifted the bodies onto the stretchers and wheeled them out. Everyone stopped as the little girl was taken out and more than one officer had tears in their eyes and a very steely determination to get the animal who had done this.

While Grace barked out orders to her staff, Sarah told her team to go over to the edge of the park, about 60 yards away and see if they could find any trace of the bullets.

She looked around and the silence was deafening. It was as if the sounds of the town had switched off in sympathy. There were pockets of people being spoken to by police officers. Before they wandered away seemingly in a daze, not fully understanding what had taken place less than an hour ago. The ambulances drove away, now the hard work was just starting.

Sarah went across to Grace and asked, "Anything which might help yet?"

"Give me a chance," she snapped back, "I want this asshole as much as you do!!"

She looked at the scene. Her team were searching the edges of the park. Uniformed bobbies taking details from the stragglers and Grace's team were on their hands and knees in the immediate kill area, taking samples of blood, body gore or anything that might help them reason why this abomination had taken place. Grace and Sarah stood together, trying to envisage what may have happened.

Grace said, "From my time in the army, those shots came from that clump up there, I know it's a distance, but new rifles can easily shoot 1000 yards and even more with a trained sniper." They both looked across to where she had pointed and Sarah said, "Fancy a walk"?

Grace shouted to one of the white suited officials, "Jack, I'm going up the slope with the Inspector, look after things will you"? He nodded and got back down to photographing whatever he had seen.

They walked together, exchanging polite talk, but both knew that there never had been or was ever going to be any form of personal friendships. It was all about business. As they got near to a bench, Grace told Sarah to stop and went to a small patch of ground about 20 feet away. She knelt down and stayed perfectly still for about 30 seconds. "This is where the gunman was, see the flattened grass and outline of a mat or blanket? She remarked, "Come here, let me show you."

Sarah followed Grace's line and saw what Grace has told her, "Damn, he was invisible here!" Grace got on her phone and told Jack to extend the scene to include this spot too. Sarah did the same and heard Ken swearing to the others, "We need more men," he told her. We can barely cover what we have now." "Leave it with me", she told him, "you just get on with what you can."

Grace told Sarah she will stay at the spot, while more manpower was gathered and able to do a wider search. Sarah stood back and dialled her boss's number, he answered almost immediately. "Yeah, what's going on? We have a shitstorm going on here," he shouted. Sarah commented "Not much fun here either boss, we need loads more uniforms to lockdown the scene, the death shots were well over 400 yards from where they hit, through and through, they never had a chance. We'll be here for several more hours yet, so get it done."

CHAPTER 2

It had taken him just 25 minutes to drive home. As he approached his detached, suburban house he pressed the remote on his Audi and drove straight inside, the door closing behind him. He sat in the car for a few minutes, gathering his thoughts before removing his bag and walking into his kitchen. He switched on the radio and listened to hear what, if anything, was being told about his little piece of work.

He put the kettle on for his obligatory coffee and, like all disciplined officers, removed his gun and stripped it down completely. His years in the army had served him well. He sipped his coffee and took the rifle to pieces. He laid it out, piece by piece in order. His cleaning cloth and oil at his elbow. He thought back on the previous hours. Could he have done it any different, any better? He was sure the police had found his lair, but he was confident that he had left nothing to chance there.

His bullets would have disintegrated into a thousand pieces on impact and exit. They were never going to be able to trace those again. He smiled to himself thinking of them trying to search for something which was not there anymore. He ran his hands over his trusted and well used rifle a legacy from his army days. He had “lost” it in a firefight in Iraq, the situation was so chaotic, that his word was accepted and allocated a new rifle.

He sat for a few minutes until his phone pinged. He was expecting it, but perhaps a little later, he had only just proved himself to his prospective employer. He just said "Yes?"

The male on the other end replied, "You did very well, better than anyone else who could have managed it."

He just said, "I am the best, that's why you want me so badly, so what do you want?" The other party answered, "Wait by the phone, in 30 minutes you will get a call, then you will know. Your money will be deposited on contact with the other party, that's all you need to know at the moment." The line went dead, he shrugged and thought to himself, as long as the money goes in when he said it would, then I'll be happy.

He went to the fridge, looked inside and took out a lump of cheese, beetroot and piccalilli, and spread a thick slice of bread with butter and made himself a sandwich, one that he has always enjoyed since he was a boy in Yorkshire.

He reassembled his gun, placed it back into its holdall, and then went about making his special bullets, taught to him by his old mentor when he first started Sniper School. He sat eating his sandwich, at peace with himself, breathing calmly and slowly, drawing himself back into his world of evil.

Thirty minutes later, his phone rang. He looked at his watch, opened his laptop and typed in his password to his bank and saw that his money had gone in. He picked up his phone and pressed the answer button. "You've paid, what do you need doing?" he said before the other end had a chance to say anything.

The answer came back, "In your letter box you will find your instructions. Yes, we know where you live and that you would have passed your assessment." The voice was deep and resonant.

He looked at the screen, 'unavailable, out of area' was displayed, as he had expected. He said, "Do that again and you will never see another day, do you understand me?"

A guttural laugh rang in his ears, "Touche. Let's cut the niceties and get on with what needs doing. You have 48 hours." The phone went dead. He sat at his table eating his sandwich and contemplated both the contract and his punishment for the temerity imposed on him. He undressed, put all his used clothes into a black bin bag and went for a shower, scrubbing himself clean, no traces of any residue on him. He dried off, put his new clothes on and went back downstairs. He placed the bin bag in his garage, ready to take to the local dump later with all the household rubbish he had kept back for this time.

He wandered through to the hall and lifted his letter box, and as promised a large brown envelope nestled inside. He returned to the kitchen, checked his laptop to make sure he hadn't been double crossed, saw the money still there and immediately transferred it to another account in another bank in another country.

He made himself another coffee and as he sipped it, he opened the envelope which revealed a folder of approximately 5 pages of information and most crucially several photographs. He read it slowly, understanding the complexity and ramifications of what he was expected to do.

This was not going to be as simple as earlier, it was going to need a little more planning. At least he didn't have to travel far. It was even less than he did this time, but the location could be a little problematic. He read the files again, saw what he needed to do and got back into sniper mode again.

CHAPTER 3

It was almost dusk by the time they had finished with the scene. They had no immediate clues nor evidence and were relying on the expertise of the Crime Scene officers to find even the tiniest shred which might help. It had been a sombre drive back to the office, only stopping off for pizzas and burgers. It was going to be a long night!

Sarah went across to Helen, she had surrounded herself with whiteboards, pens and enough paper to keep a school in supply for a year. Helen said she was already collating the info but still no idea on the identification of the victims. "Damn," Sarah swore under breath, "keep trying, let's hope Doc Webster has any more luck. Do we have any DNA or prints yet?"

"Not yet boss." She looked apologetically at Sarah, "I am just trying to sort out groups of witnesses. Any chance of some help?" Sarah replied, without much conviction "Let me speak to the big boss, and see who is available, maybe a couple of uniforms. I guess all our team are going to be interviewing well into the night." She walked over to Geoff. He had been busy, and his tables were covered in computers, monitors and phones, all connected to a main server. There were two others seated nearby, an elder guy, who Sarah vaguely recognised and a young Asian girl who was looking very intently at her monitor.

Geoff stood and introduced Brian Davies to Sarah, who said "Ah, you are the guy who broke the IRA team a few years ago, I thought I recognised you, welcome to the team." He smiled and shook her hand, "That's a few years back now, but let's get this bastard before he does any more damage." He turned back to his monitor and his fingers flew across the keyboard.

Geoff moved over to the girl, she looked up, but didn't bother to acknowledge Sarah, He said "This is Jackie Ling, she is a tech wizard, and knows HOLMES inside out. Any questions just ask her." Sarah said, "Nice to meet you Jackie, thanks for being here." She shrugged and said, "It's my job." and turned back to the monitor.

Sarah looked at Geoff as if to say good luck with her and went over to the main room, where her team were all now congregating. Grace and her boss, DCI Edwards, who was sat to the side, holding his folder, anxious for the meeting to start, so he could report to his bosses before he could even consider going home. Sarah introduced everyone in the room, and asked the Crime Scene Manager, Grace Meadows, for anything she might have on the scene and if they had been lucky enough to get any evidence.

Grace took out her I-pad and gave an illustration of what they had so far, which was very little. The only positive facts she was able to give was that they had found his lair, which had been 369 yards from the killing zone. That didn't give up a single clue which suggested that the shooter was a very highly trained individual. While Grace was giving her news, Sarah reminded herself to get hold of all the CCTV coverage within a four hundred yard radius of the park for the relevant times.

DS Matthews gave a synopsis of what the team had done. They had traced 112 persons who had been in the park at the moment of the shooting. Statements were in the process of being taken. A forensic search of the trees and shrubbery behind the bodies came up blank, not even a scrap of anything resembling a bullet.

Grace grimaced, “That sounds like the special bullets popular among the SAS and Special Forces during their times in Iraq and Afghanistan.” Everyone looked at each other and DCI Edwards stood and told Sarah, Grace and everyone else, including HOLMES, to search the records and see if anything of a similar nature has happened in the last few years, going backwards if necessary.

As the meeting broke up, Helen interrupted them and shouted, “We have an ID on the victims!” Everyone turned to her as she said, “They were reported as missing late this afternoon by a Mr and Mrs Jacobs, their son, daughter in law and granddaughter. The were out for the morning to go shopping for the little girl’s birthday, but never came back. They heard the news about the incident and rang the hotline.”

“Where do they live?” asked Sarah with a heavy heart. “Fulham, ma’am, responded Helen, about 15 minutes from the park, the little girls favourite place to visit and play.”

CHAPTER 4

He had read the dossier fully, memorised the identity and location and schedule of his mark. He had googled street views, maps, both satellite and roads until he was fully satisfied, he knew every inch.

He had checked for CCTV cameras and ANPR (Automatic Number Plate Recognition) cameras too. The route he had worked out meant he could be home within 11 minutes of completing his task.

According to the report he had a window of around 12 minutes to do what was needed. That was more than enough time, one shot at 500 yards was well within his capabilities. He had no worries as to where he was going to be sited. He thought to himself that he was being paid a lot of money for what appeared to be a straightforward job.

He copied everything onto a stick, then ripped the folder into several pieces before lighting it in the bin. Within seconds nothing remained. He placed the stick into an envelope, addressed to a PO Box, in another area, and settled down to have a coffee and sandwich.

He went over the plan in his mind several times, before going to his bedroom and changing into his cycling outfit, a dark Lycra ensemble, which fitted him very snugly. He went out through his back door to the shed in his garden, which he unlocked before taking out his state of the art bike. Putting his helmet on he went out through his back gate and started to cycle down his chosen route, meeting another couple of cyclists and blending in with them. His helmet cam recorded every step of the way. He moved his head from side to side, picking up all the road signs and junctions and more importantly the cameras atop the traffic lights.

He was suddenly aware of the high pitch sounds of sirens and horns rapidly closing behind him, and within seconds an unmarked police car with its lights flashing and horn sounding shot past and disappeared into the distance. He took no further notice and continue his ride with the others taking in all he needed to know.

The occupants of the speeding police car were DI Sarah James together with her DS, Ken Matthews, both were sitting in the back as the uniformed driver moved through the lanes at a speed which, quite frankly, terrified Sarah. She observed a small group of cyclists ahead. Bloody pests she thought to herself, but noticed one was in black as opposed to all the others in their multicolour Lycra. She thought to herself that he was a bit more professional as they raced past the bikes and onto their destination.

Within ten minutes they had reached their stop. Sarah took a few moments to compose herself. She was both glad they had got there, but also not so happy with what was about to come next. “Ready Ken?” she whispered, “I truly hate these moments, and this one is one from hell.”

They got out of the car, walked through a wooden 5 bar gate into a garden filled with roses, foxgloves and dahlias.

In the corner a toy house, swing and toys lay scattered around. Sarah wiped her eyes, trying hard to concentrate on what was needed next. As they approached the front door a tall, slim man opened it and stood there. He looked for all intents and purposes as though the world had come crashing down on him.

Sarah produced her warrant card and introduced herself and DS Matthews. He looked at them and said, “Simon Jacobs, please come in.” He led them into a large hallway, and Sarah felt the comfort and opulence with the fittings and carpet underfoot. He led them into a large room, through double doors and into a room dominated by a huge wall to ceiling glass front, overlooking immaculate lawns and a swimming pool. Sitting on a huge white leather settee was a beautiful, slender lady, who was obviously in distress. Her eyes were red from crying and her body shook and she just kept wringing her hands.

She was in her late 50’s, had blonde hair, and her clothing would have cost a year’s salary Sarah thought to herself as she walked across to meet her. She introduced herself and the lady, who identified herself as Barbara Jacobs, invited her to sit down. She pressed a bell beside her and immediately a young, dark haired woman stepped into the room. “Can we offer you drinks?” she asked throatily. Sarah looked across to Ken, who nodded, and she replied, “Coffee would be fine thanks.”

She continued, “We are very sorry for your loss, but unfortunately we need someone to formally identify the victims before we can go further.” she explained. Mr Jacobs stood and said, "Of course I'll do it, I cannot expect Barbara to see anything of this." Sarah explained what was going to happen, and Mrs Jacobs just stared straight ahead, not comprehending the enormity of what had taken place. She looked at her husband, and with a barely noticeable nod, she stood and walked out of the room.

The overwhelming atmosphere of sorrow and grief was eating into Sarah. She stood and asked Mr Jacobs if he was ready. He nodded and walked out of the room to the door. Not a word was exchanged.

During the drive to the mortuary, Sarah noticed the black clad cyclist again. she looked over at him, seeing a rather swarthy looking man in his mid to late 30s. He looked every inch a fitness guy, legs like pistons and his black helmet, fitted with the ubiquitous camera moving side to side as if he was observing the warm spring day. In a moment she had passed him, in a few moments more he was forgotten. Her quietness was interrupted when Mr Jacobs said, "Did they suffer at all do you know? It's hard enough thinking they are gone. I don't know how I would manage if they had suffered in any way. We loved them so much, they had everything going for them. The had no enemies. Did you know they had found out she was pregnant again?"

He couldn't contain himself and buried his hands in his face and burst into tears. Sarah and Ken looked at each other aghast and Sarah was almost ready to be sick. This was another level of depravity by the bastard who had taken them away in their prime of life.

The car drew up to the back gate of the mortuary, avoiding the press who were standing around outside the front doors, like a pack of vultures they all seemed to have become in the past few years in the chase for the "scoop" or "the big one."

Sarah said, "I must warn you Mr Jacobs that this is not going to be very pleasant at all. Besides that, you might find the smells rather overpowering too, unfortunately there is nothing we can do about that." He replied "That's ok, I am a consultant surgeon, so I know all the ins and out of what is needed Inspector. It's the other bit I am dreading." They walked through the double doors, down a long corridor, offices either side, where they could see white coated staff looking through various scopes, slicing god knows what, and others working on their computers.

They entered a little room off the corridor marked private. Inside were DS Grace Meadows and Graham Webster standing together looking out into the viewing room. Webster turned around and saw Jacobs. He looked horrified knowing who they were and what had to be done. He walked over, and offered his hand, "Hello Simon, I am so sorry, I never realised for a moment that it might be Raymond and family." Jacobs responded, "Hello Graham, I am glad it's you here and not some other cutter who would have no concept of who they might be." His eyes were full of tears.

Sarah and Grace looked at one another, not knowing what to say or do at this moment. Graham looked to them and said "Me and Simon were at medical school together, although Simon was by then very well known for his cardiac knowledge. We spent many a long hour discussing the intricacies of the heart, he led me to being who I am today." Jacobs smiled but it was not a genuine smile, just an appreciative one for his old friend.

Sarah introduced Grace to Jacobs, and she nodded said "I am very sorry for your loss." Jacobs retorted "Keep the sympathies until after I have made sure it is them." Grace was taken aback and stood aside, seething at his lack of manners, even in this awful time.

The pathologist knocked on the window and three gurneys were wheeled in and placed before the window. Three white sheets covered the bodies underneath.

Webster looked directly at Jacobs and said "I have to be direct, what you are about to see is pretty awful, but it needs to be done. Just tell me if you cannot proceed." Jacobs just said, "Get on with it, the quicker it's done the quicker I can get out of this hell hole."

Everyone looked at one another, then Webster nodded his head, and the attendant pulled the sheet down on the male body. Even though they had seen the damage before, they were not prepared for the almost total left side of the face missing. Jacobs put his hands to his mouth, eyes wide open and barely moved, he nodded and said "Yes, that's Raymond, my son." Webster nodded again and the covering was placed back over.

"I am sorry Simon, but the next two are no better, the shyster who did this was a pro and he never considered who he was ruining." This time Jacobs said nothing, looked to

Webster and went to the window. The attendant lifted the sheet to reveal a head with the top that was virtually missing. He whispered "Good god!! How could anyone do this to another human being?" He turned to Sarah and said, "Yes, that's Anne, with an e."

Everyone knew the worst was yet to come. A chill ran through the room. Sarah asked Jacobs if he was ok still to carry on. This time he didn't say anything. He was totally beaten and a shell of his former self from when he had entered the room. He just turned and stared into the window, the sheet was pulled back and Jacobs vomited over himself and let out an anguished cry. The little girl lay on the gurney, facing to the window. Eyes closed, but everyone could see that her face was the only part left of her head. He turned away, and barely audibly said, "That's Charlie, sorry Charlotte, we always called her Charlie, she was just seven, her whole life in front of her." He slid down the wall, not the famous Dr Jacobs, but a man who would never recover from what he has just seen.

Sarah took the pathologist aside and said, "To make matters worse, Anne was pregnant." He looked at her aghast and muttered "As if my day could not get any worse than it already is."

She went back to the stricken Mr Jacobs and said, "Let's get you out of here, no words can express my feelings to you and your wife. We need to let Dr Webster and DS Meadows get on with their work." He rose and with a barely audible voice "I don't know how you do this sort of work, it would have driven me crazy." Sarah thought to herself, you don't know the half it.

They left the mortuary the same way as they entered and drove Mr Jacobs home. Sarah asked if he would like her to go in with him, but he declined stating this was something he had to do himself. He shook hands and turned and went inside. Sarah thought that what he was about to do must be one of the worst moments of his life.

They drove back to the office with what information they had and were ready to brief the team as to what would happen next.

The teams were seated at various desks in front of the video screens and whiteboards which had been erected and readied whilst they had been out with their enquiries. DCI Edwards opened the briefing, and with great gusto announced additional manpower with effect from the next day. Sarah looked across and mouthed thank you to him. He smiled and continued to express his wishes for a speedy conclusion to the case and that overtime and funding had been released by Headquarters in view of the seriousness of the matter.

He nodded to Sarah and then sat down at the side of the room. Sarah stood and said to everyone, "We all now know who was murdered, a devoted husband and pregnant wife and their 7-year-old daughter. One shot to the head for each of them and estimated time for the 3 shots was less than 2 seconds. We are not dealing with a wannabe cowboy, this person, and I'll go with being a male until we know different, is a very highly skilled individual. No doubt military trained, which is one lead we are pursuing, and he will strike again."

She continued, “Geoff, anything on HOLMES which may suggest anything?” He replied, “No gov, but we are waiting on Interpol and FBI for anything similar.” Sarah continued, “We believe the bullets used to kill the victims were self-destructing on impact, hence the damage, and the fact we have not been able to find any trace of them despite fingertip searches.”

She asked, “Helen, how many statements have we taken now and into the system?” She replied, “103 to date, 63 from people in the park, and others from officers attending and local responses.” Sarah thanked her and warned her that it will get busier over the forthcoming hours, but with the additional manpower, she should be able to get help.

The postmortem results had not been included in the briefing, but hopefully by tomorrow the details would be available to them, not that anyone was under any misconception of what had taken place.

Sarah concluded by telling Ken to liaise with the MOD and hopefully they might give some guide as to the method and know-how of the sniper.

She ended with, “The night shift are on telephone and data duty. The rest of you go home and try and get some rest. I have a feeling tomorrow is going to be another long day.”

CHAPTER 5

He finished watching the latest disc of Band of Brothers, his mind wandering back to those simpler times when you knew who the enemy was. Even before joining the army, he had always been fascinated by the tactics of battles through the ages. He had lost count of the number of films he had seen, documentaries he had visually digested over the past 30 yrs. In his own mind he was now the complete strategist, able to make decisions quickly, amend them instantly if he felt that something was missing or not to his standards. Tomorrow would be another step towards his goal of attaining his promised total of kills, with the equivalent financial reward being enough for him to retire on. He switched the tv off and went and had the first of his showers he would have before leaving home next day.

At 6am he woke, he had never needed an alarm clock since he joined the army. He then did his 45 minute workout in his improvised gym in the garage. He felt alive again, his body and mind melded as one. He showered and dressed in an all-black coverall, soft military boots and fingerless leather gloves. He wore his black silk snood around his neck, and he had his dark cotton baseball cap in his bag for when he left home.

He checked his action bag. His rifle was broken down, oiled and the scope was already set, with just a slight calibration for the wind if needed. His six home-made bullets were in their airlocked case. He certainly did not want them to start to become obsolete before the job. He would select which bullet to use at the last moment.

He sat down and brewed a Columbian coffee from his machine. He made himself a ham and egg sandwich with a good lashing of HP sauce, his favourite. He sat quietly while he consumed both and went through his plan for the day. He washed his dishes and walked through to the garage. He flicked on the automatic door opener and got into his alternate car, a dark blue Hyundai SUV, one of the many thousands that had been sold and used every day by families and workers. He stored his bag in the compartment under the seat which he had made especially for his equipment. He drove out at 7:48am and joined the traffic heading into London.

He drove carefully, he wore his baseball cap low over his eyes. His dark frame glasses shielding his eyes from any cameras, although the glass in them was just plain and served no purpose. He drove direct to where he needed to go. Anyone driving in circles and around areas for any length of time always raised flags with the authorities. He parked his car in a parking yard. It was basically a spare piece of land and used by motorists who paid cash to the operators on a daily basis. He parked his car at 8:24am.

He removed his bag and carried it into the adjacent building, an old shopping centre. He knew there was no CCTV cameras anywhere. Most of the shops were boarded up, and the ones that were still operating had iron grills in front to protect whatever goods they might be selling, legal or otherwise. He turned down the underpass and came out behind the building he had selected. Anonymous but functional, 3 stories high with stair cases at either end of the building.

He entered the 3rd floor, and opened an office door, which he had checked beforehand, unoccupied and safe. He placed his kit on the desk in front of the window, walked over to the tinted glass and looked down at the street below. Already it was busy with people walking through the market stalls, looking for the early bargains before the tourists and the well-heeled took over. He looked at his watch, 8:46am, he had a few more minutes to wait before it was time to do what was needed to be done. He laid his rifle on the desk, selected 2 bullets from the case and loaded them into the stock. He took out the diamond cutter and made a circle in the window, just big enough to let the silenced barrel through.

He went through the routine in his mind once more and was satisfied that everything was set and that within 2 minutes of the completion of his task he would be back in his car. He would not be leaving, just stashing his equipment. He would go to the market and wander as if looking for the fruit and vegetables. At 8:59am he looked out of the window, saw his target walking slowly down the market street, surrounded by several large men who made sure his passage was not being obstructed by mere mortals.

He took his rifle and positioned himself comfortably and then took the man in his sights. He was about to pull the trigger, when the man's head exploded in a mass of red, as if a watermelon had blown up. He was stunned. He had nowhere to look. He immediately broke his rifle down and packed his bag. His mind was racing, someone else had the same contract, was he being set up? He left the room, locked it secure and went down the farthest set of stairs. He walked through the centre to his car. He hid the bag in the boot under the spare tyre, removed his hat and put on a brown fleece jacket, took out a brief case and walked away into the market area. He heard the sirens in the distance, he neared a stall and stood there, watching what was going on. His eyes were on the surrounding buildings but could not see anything or anyone untoward.

The police and emergency services rushed past and everyone stood by. He tried to see what had occurred, but it was too crowded. All he knew was that his target had been shot in exactly the same way he had shot the others and he was not happy about that at all. He tried to think who could have done what he did, but at the moment he came up with a blank.

The uniformed police started to walk towards the stalls and were putting up the blue tape to keep everyone at bay. He decided there was no reason to stay there any longer. He walked down the road adjacent to the market and walked through to the underground station. He joined the thousands still making their way to work, oblivious of what had taken place close by. He got a seat, and his mind was racing, he was going to have to make a call soon, but not here, not close.

He chose his stop 6 stations away and entered the main street. Trafalgar Square was full of tourists, the traffic chaotic as he walked into the British museum and mingled with the crowds inside. He was in no hurry to leave any more. The longer he was not in the vicinity of the shooting, within reason, the better. He looked at his watch, it was 10:36am. He needed to make his phone call, he walked into an internet café and paid for a terminal and sat and logged on.

Within five seconds the call was answered. He just said, "Did you put out another contract on the target"? The other end responded "No, why?" He said, "Because some other guy blew the marks head off at exactly the same time as I had planned and in the same manner!" The other end said, "Be assured we only trust you. We will find out more and get back to you, in the meantime you'll still get paid as agreed. We will be in touch." The line went dead. He sat back in his chair. He googled to see if any news of the shooting has been broadcast yet. There was some breaking news of a shooting in Peckham, but no further details were available.

He ordered a club sandwich and coffee. He idled his time, googling, news feeds and other insignificant matter before leaving. He walked back out, and moved with the crowds, still with his briefcase before catching the tube back to his original station. He still wore his glasses and walked slowly along the street, seeing the uniformed and obviously CID at the scene. He made his way to his car. He was stopped by a uniformed officer and asked for his details. He asked why and was told about the shooting and that they needed to check on everyone who might have been in the vicinity at the time. He knew exactly why and gave his details, there was no way that he could not have done so. The constable told him that someone would be in touch and get his statement.

He thanked the officer, reversed out of the plot and drove home. There were several road blocks and diversions, but no one seemed to be particularly interested. Their main concern was keeping the traffic moving and away from the crime scene. He arrived back home at 1:19pm, mentally exhausted after the day's events. He went through his normal procedures and locked everything away in the underground safe in the garage underneath the shower cabin.

He went to the kitchen, removed his clothes and put them into the washing machine, not having to worry about any residue from his weapon. He showered and changed into jeans, t shirt and slippers and walked through to his lounge. He sat down in his recliner, closed his eyes and relived every moment of the time leading up to the moment that someone else had taken his shot.

He could not fathom how it could have happened, too much of a coincidence with the day, time, and location. He was confident that his employer would find out who was responsible and that he was still getting paid. That at least allayed some of his anger.

He laid back and fell into a fitful sleep. His brain working out all the angles and the whys and wherefores of the shooting. He had a sudden realisation and leapt up and went to his filing cabinet in the dining room, which he used as an office and where he kept his personal documents.

He went straight to his photo album and to the photos of his colleagues at Bradbury Lines, Hereford. He scanned through them until he found the one he was looking for. "Son of a bitch" he exclaimed. "Where are you now?"

CHAPTER 6

Sarah was at her desk when the news came in of another shooting in the next district. She was briefed on the details within a few minutes and told her team was on standby to help with both cases. This had gone well beyond a single incident. She entered the command centre and told her team, by now expanded with the additional manpower the situation. They were to ensure that everything they had on their case was entered into the HOLMES system and given to Helen and her staff in the incident room. She established that Grace Meadows had been requested to attend the second scene, based on her experience with the killings on her patch.

Her phone shook her out of her thoughts, "DI James." she said. "Ms James, Commander John Freeman, Major Incident Team co-ordinator. You have been dealing with the Jacobs killings?" She replied, "Yes sir, well my boss DCI Edwards is technically in charge of course."

He said "Yes, I know. I have already spoken with him and told him you and your team will join the other team dealing with the new shooting from now on. Obviously, you will have responsibility overall for the Jacobs killings, but will work in tandem with DI Jason Kings team, I believe you know him?" Sarah smiled, "Oh yes sir, we go way back together, since training school in fact. We have been keeping tabs on each other ever since, he is a great guy and I know a very able DI." He said, "Well get your skates on, get to the scene and start working and keeping tabs on each other even closer than normal." With that he put the phone down.

She went to Ken Matthews and told him to get his team together and that they were going to the new shooting. It was now officially a joint enterprise from now onwards. She reminded the others to stay on standby but to ensure they continued their enquiries as instructed.

They drove fast, with lights flashing, until they got to the scene. They parked their car in an old yard, normally used for day parking and on a cash only basis, now though it was full of emergency vehicles of all descriptions, as well as other vehicles obviously parked earlier. They walked the 200 yards to the scene, uniformed officers guarding all the side paths and entrances. Sarah looked about and eyed the old shopping centre, a sign of the decay in a once vibrant area. Her head instinctively looked up based on the previous shooting, a few old offices, a couple of stories high. As they walked into the street, she could see that both sides of the stalls were surrounded by buildings up and on top of them.

She saw Jason and walked up to him, shook his hand and joked "Hello Kingy, got yourself a nasty one here." He laughed and said, "At least the shit who got it deserved it, not like yours from yesterday." Sarah asked who it was, and he said "Constantine Burlov, a real nasty Albanian head honcho. We can expect all sorts of retaliation after this one." "So why are we here?" asked Sarah, "This sounds like a gang slaying not a slaughter of innocents."

"Come with me," he nodded over to the end stall. "This might change your mind." They walked 20 yards and Sarah saw Grace and the pathologist, Graham Webster, huddled together looking down at a male who had no skull or any facial feature attached to his body. The surrounding area was covered in blood and gore and the forensic teams were on their hands and knees scraping anything they could find and bagging it. Sarah couldn't help noticing that Grace was as close to Graham as she could possibly get.

Sarah asked, "What have we got Grace?" she turned around and said, "Well there is no bullet. It's a head shot and whoever did it knew what he was doing, sounds like our guy." Sarah swore inwardly, "Any idea where it came from?"

Grace answered, "Looking at what is left of the head, it appears the shot came from around 150 yards from that office block, and from the angle he was quite high. We have teams going through all the buildings now."

Jason and Sarah stood aside while the work around them was being completed and before the body could be taken away. "Get as many witnesses as you can Jason, anyone who heard or saw anything, my bet is that no one saw nothing and heard nothing. No one will want to get involved in any form."

He replied, "Just my luck. I swapped holidays with my pal and got caught. He is going to have to pay me back spades loads on his return." Sarah laughed, "At least we have each other." and dug him in the ribs. At that moment, one of his officers came over to him "Sir, we have a problem." "What is it?" he asked, "We have found 2 sites, one on each side of the street", came back the reply.

Sarah said, "You take one, and I'll take the other." Jason told his officer, "Take DS Singh and the team with DI James and I'll go to the other site with DS Mason and his team." With that they split up and went to the two locations which Sarah found very odd. This was not a classic sniper mode of operation.

They walked through the old centre. As they walked Sarah was envisaging the direction of travel the sniper might have taken. They went through the office entrance and up three flights of stairs. She noticed that both ends had staircases, but no lifts. They walked slowly along the corridor until they met the officer at the opening to the small room. He pointed across the floor to the window. Sarah could see that there was a little hole, no larger than the size of a saucer cut out of the glass. Sarah looked around without going in, the floor was clean, no visible prints, and certainly no glass disc lying around anywhere.

She asked when the forensics would be arriving, the officer told her they were still in the street, going to the other scene and then to here. Sarah shrugged and got on the phone. Commander Freeman answered on the second ring, "Sir, DI James here, we are struggling with forensics teams, can you arrange for at least one other team to be called in and assist. We have potentially two snipers' nests."

He sounded shocked, "Haven't heard of twin nests for a long time, not since Afghanistan. This is serious, I'll get the teams and make some calls. Leave it with me."

Sarah rang to Jason and told him of the update. He replied that his was definitely the site, a quick search of the roof top had found two footprints just outside a door leading from the internal staircase. They too were waiting on forensics. Sarah told him of her call with the commander. They agreed to meet down on the street. Sarah left DS Singh at the scene and instructed him to use his team to do any enquiries, find anyone nearby who might have seen or heard anything.

Sarah went back out into the street, re tracing her steps. She took about 30 seconds to enter the street and a further 20 seconds to arrive at the scene.

Jason told Sarah that Burlov was like clockwork. Every morning at the same time he would enter the market. He'd walk along the stalls with his 3 henchmen, collect the daily "rent" from the stall holders, take his daily supplies from them and exit at the far end. He never varied his day, everyone was too shit scared to resist, or their stalls ceased to be stalls.

Sarah kept looking up at both the nests. This was crazy, two shooters, one fails, the other takes over, a whole new ball game to their case. In the park there was definitely only one site. The search of the park confirmed that. This was too easy, no attempt to hide them. Grace came over to them. She said, "This was different, we have a bullet fragment in the wood about 30 yards beyond the killing point. Maybe he was trying a new method. We'll get the lab guys to see what it is." She smiled and said, "See you later boss and new boss." and walked away.

"You'll have to excuse her, "Sarah said, "She is a brilliant scene manager, but she lives in a different world to the rest of us." She saw Jason looking at her as she walked away and laughed quietly, another man under her spell.

CHAPTER 7

The teams were deployed around the market and in an area of 400 yards to try and find any witnesses. It was amazing that a crowded market produced so few witnesses when it became known who the victim was. CCTV cameras were located, and a team was directed to collect any film from any of the cameras that may have possibly been working. Another team were instructed to check all car parks in the vicinity, including the one where they were all parked.

Sarah's phone rang, it was the Commander. He told her another forensics team would be seconded to the unit for as long as they wanted. He had also been in touch with a friend, he did not say who, and that he might be able to give some assistance. It would not be for a few days as the guy was on leave.

Freeman told her that both teams were now going to be housed in one office, an old station. It was used for anti-terrorist teams, but room enough to fit their investigation groups on the lower floors. Sarah related the news to Jason and they both set about discussing what was best for them and how they could deploy each team effectively.

The pathologist signalled for the ambulance to take away Burlov and came over. He said, "That was a hell of a calibre that blew his top off, maybe the others were just target practice. If that's the case, we do not need more if he is moving up in the world. You'll have my report in the morning, ask Grace to nip over and collect it." He smiled at Sarah and walked away with a broad grin on his face.

By mid-afternoon, Sarah and Jason had finished all they could do at the scene. They left their teams and officers to complete the enquiries. The blue and white tape was down, remnants just blowing in the wind. The traders had all long gone home and only a few onlookers remained, what they hoped to see, no one knew.

They drove to the old station on Edward Street, showed their cards to the armed uniformed officer at the gate. He let them in and they drove down into the car park, level 3, which was going to be their parking for the foreseeable future.

The walked up to another door, went through the same procedure as at the entrance, given a pass key and instructed to go through a door at the end of a corridor. They did as they were told, aware of the cameras following their every move. They each inserted their pass keys into the key holder and the door opened into a room. One room, the size of a football field it seemed. The looked at each other, laughed and both were making mental notes of what they required for their team's needs.

They wandered around the room. Assessing all the points, telephone sites, measuring how much space would be needed if everyone was going to be housed in there. The door buzzer sounded, and Jason went and answered.

Standing in the doorway was the Commissioner, Commander Freeman and a number of other officers, none of them he recognised. He stood aside as they entered, and the Commissioner in her typically blunt manner said, "We have a real shit-storm here, don't we?" Jason didn't know what to say, he just said, "Yes ma'am, and where is the shit going to stop"?

They walked into the room, and Jason was surprised to see a whole gaggle of others following behind, pushing trolleys, carrying boxes and cartons of computer terminals, phone lines and what looked like a trailer full of desks and chairs. "Don't worry, said the Commissioner, we have already stripped your offices and brought everything over here."

Sarah looked over at Jason and said, "Ma'am, exactly what is going on here, for you to be so involved and all the other senior officers here, it's not just a shooting is it?" She looked at them both, "Be patient, get settled in and do what you are doing, as soon as its possible we will let you know." She replied.

Sarah said, "Are we going still going to be in charge, or get swallowed up by the big boys, and consigned to doing all the donkey work while they sit and talk tactics all day?" She responded, "Well DI James, I am going to take personal charge of this case, Commander Freeman is my second, but as far as day to day running of the case, it's you two. We are at your disposal and always available to you."

The Commissioner continued, "Your reputation proceeds you. This is going to be quite an experience. Ensure that this room is up and running by 9:00am tomorrow when we will be back. Hopefully we can then give you further information."

The party turned and left the room. All around them people were busy fixing phones, placing desks and chairs into small groups with computer terminals on each. Jason noted that all the cables went into the floor, this old station was more high tech than anyone would admit.

They noticed that a couple of the staff had already got their priorities right and had installed a large coffee machine which was already full and steaming. They walked across and poured themselves a mug of coffee each, black and strong, as they would need it to keep going.

They made calls to their teams in the field and told them to brief all the others to report to the new location as soon as they had finished their enquiries. They watched as Geoff and his team walked over to their new base, a cluster of six desks and terminals.

A big HOLMES unit being installed. It looks as though we are going to get a whole load of new information soon enough Sarah thought to herself. Geoff grinned and gave her the thumbs up sign as he supervised several new staff members installing and setting up the new equipment. Jackie Ling was sorting her own terminal out, but Sarah did detect a slight smile on her face as she opened her new equipment.

As they drank their coffee, an armed uniform officer approached them with a large carton box. He put it on the table and told them that they were their entry cards to the station. Everyone had to go to the main entrance and get them validated. If they didn't, they don't get entry. He walked away through the doors.

"Friendly types aren't they." said Jason. Sarah opened the carton and saw that there were probably 200 cards inside. "Are we expecting the whole force on this?" she exclaimed.

Over the next few hours, the teams drifted into their new office. Quite a few were just dumbstruck at the size of the place and the facilities they had suddenly acquired. They all received their entry cards and went off to get them validated, before setting up their own team areas and desks. All information they had obtained so far was given to Helen and her team, who were situated adjacent to the HOLMES desks.

Whilst they all settled into their new home, pizzas and burgers were ordered in. By late evening it seemed they were now ready to be one team dealing with what appeared to be two different shootings, but hopefully this would be confirmed by next morning.

At 8pm Sarah called it a night for everyone except for the incident room and HOLMES night teams. They still had a lot of work to do. She also reminded them to be back in the office by 8am for briefings.

CHAPTER 8

He sat at his desk, going through the records of all the men who had gone through sniper school, and who he had served with over the 20 years he had been in the army. He had already had two piles of folders, one for the men who had died, either in combat or from other means during their lives. The other much smaller list was of potential and capable men who might have carried out the attack.

He looked at all the photographs of his different squads. He had always memorised his team members and knew who to trust and who not to truly trust. He started making notes, mentally listing the pros and cons of anyone who could have been responsible. He felt as if he was back at army school, selecting applicants who wanted to go to sniper school and examining their military records for any clue as to how they would adapt.

His home phone rang, rousing him from his concentration. He had not given his home number to anyone, the only people who knew were ones who needed to know.

He answered on the third ring, "Captain Brown, you are required to attend Head Office now." the caller rang off. He sat there, wondering what was going on, he was on leave for another six days and if they wanted him back now, there must be a big op about to take place.

He had no need to take any of the kit he had at home, everything regular was at Head Office. What he had at home was legacy of many years collecting and hiding. He closed everything up, placed them into a large envelope and opened up the floorboards in the conservatory, placed the package and all his equipment inside. He replaced the boarding and covered it up with the carpet and placed the chair on top. He changed into a suit and tie, took his overnight bag and closed up his home after taking his car out of the garage.

He drove into the imposing Whitehall office block, found his parking spot, parked and went through the double doors. He passed security by handing in his personal issue Glock to the security staff and showing his clearance card. He picked up his weapon, holstered it and took the lift to the seventh floor, where he was met by his senior officer, Major Lawrence Ellis. They walked through to his office and was met by Commander John Freeman. He discovered that he was from Scotland Yard. Introductions were made and they sat down.

Major Ellis opened up the proceeding by saying, "The Met have a problem, there have been two shootings within the last 24 hours and they need our assistance. I know you are on leave Kevin, but you are my most trusted and senior adviser and operative." Freeman looked across but said nothing.

Ellis continued, "It seems that we have at least 2 professional snipers operating in the city and that's not good for anyone." He looked across at Freeman and said, "For operational reasons I am not obliged or will say anything about our Department. I hope you that you honour that." Freeman responded and said, "The same applies with yourselves, but we have to work as a team."

Brown sat without any expression, but inside was trying to work out what was going on and how it affected him and the department. Everything that he and they did was covered under the Official Secrets Act and more.

Ellis turned to Brown and said to him "You are being seconded to the murder investigation teams working directly under Commander Freeman. You are purely there in an advisory capacity and to assist them in any way you can. If there is any blurring of lines between the police and us, then you will contact me before proceeding, understood?"

"Yes sir, of course, when do I start?" he replied, stunned at the manner in which this was all heading. He would be at the very heart of the investigations and he was going to benefit in so many ways from this.

Commander Freeman responded, "Report at 0800 hours tomorrow at Edwards Road police station. Here is your entry card, wear it at all times. Sorry but you will have to leave your weapon behind, but for what you are doing, you won't need it."

Brown looked across at Ellis who said, "Sorry John, he is on 24 hours on call for duty. He could leave at any time if he is called upon. The gun stays, please ensure that everyone is aware of the situation."

Brown could not believe what was going on, talk about being a fox in the chicken run. Freeman nodded his agreement, Ellis than said, "You will have access to all files that are necessary to identify the perpetrator of the attacks. Do not disclose anything which may endanger any operations we may have ongoing. I understand the police will want as much information as possible, but again clear that with me."

He answered, "Yes sir. Commander, who do I report to in the morning?"

Freeman said, "DI Sarah James will be expecting you, she is looking after the park atrocity, and you will be attached to her team, but you will also be working with a DI Jason King on the market shooting."

"Thank you, sir." He stood and went to leave, Ellis said, "It's going to mean looking into your old teammates. I am sorry, but we do need to root out whoever it is."

Brown smiled inwardly. He thought to himself that he needed to know who had taken the shot too, so I can keep an eye on what's good and what's bad. I think I am going to enjoy this.

As Brown left, Freeman said, "He looks a good man." Ellis replied, "The best. He will find out all manner of things and he is studious in his studies and investigations." They shook hands and Freeman left the office.

On his way-out Freeman rang the Commissioner and told him they had the cooperation from the

MOD, but with strings attached. Even so it was more than they had hoped for.

Brown did not leave the building, but went over to another office, spoke with a friend and she gave him access to the records pertaining to the Metropolitan Police. He found the records of DI Sarah James and Jason King. He read them at length and reminded himself he would have to be careful, particularly around the attractive Ms James. He tried to gain entry to the HOLMES system, but without success. He had used a tor address to disguise his attempt, so he was not worried. He was a patient man and would be able to check out more tomorrow. He went into his own office, checked for any official correspondence that needed completing and signed the two reports on his desk. He went to his safe, removed two data sticks and put them in his pocket. He was going to need all the information he could get and do it before he fed the cops their scraps. They would get just enough to keep him indispensable.

He locked his office, walked down into the car park and drove out and drove to his favourite eating spot, Subway. He felt alive and hungry and as he walked in. His taste buds were assailed by cooked meats and fresh bread. He walked up to the waitress and order two beef, tomato and Mexican chillies on a seven seeded bun. The girl asked if he wanted the normal six inch sandwich or the big one. He replied the big one, and he'd take two blueberry muffins as well. He picked them up, paid the bill and went home, locking up as soon as he entered. He felt mixed emotions, being both for and against the law, but he had been ordered to assist and that was what he had to do.

He made himself a pot of coffee, poured himself a mug of the Columbian mix he was so fond of, and sat at his chair in the lounge watching a rerun of The Shooter whilst he ate his sandwiches. He sat quietly, as he watched the film through, always enjoying the ending most. He watched the late news, catching up on the events in the market. There was not much detail except that one man was dead having been shot by an unknown assailant. He finished his muffins, cleaned the crumbs up and washed the dishes before getting ready for bed. He was both shocked and elated as to how this day had gone. He knew he had to be careful around the police, the ones in charge were not idiots. But then again, neither was he.

He was up early as normal next morning. He finalised his exercises and then had his breakfast of pain au chocolate and oranges, and the luxury of a mug of cappuccino. He felt he was able to take on anything now. He dressed in his blue suit, white shirt and striped tie. He fixed his Glock into his shoulder holster, slid the two tiny thumb drives into the recess in the holster, and left home.

CHAPTER 9

He arrived at the station at 7:40am and showed his identity to the armed officer on duty. He was directed to the lower floor car park where there were about 50 vehicles of all descriptions parked. He found an empty bay, locked his car and walked to the entrance. He went through the same procedure, but as he entered the corridor, an alarm was sounded. Immediately he was surrounded by three armed officers, all pointing their weapons at his face. He was told to get on the floor, hands behind head and cross his ankles. He complied, and said, "In my jacket pocket, is a letter, it will explain everything."

He was somewhat surprised by the level of security. He had not seen any obvious detectors. He thought that this was a place similar to Bradbury Lines and that impressed him. The sergeant removed the paper from his jacket, looked at it, folded it and gave it back to him and nodded to his colleagues to release him. He stood, and the sergeant said, "As you have now discovered, we have to be very careful as to who enters here and under what circumstances." Brown replied, "Its ok, I'd have done the same under the circumstances. Can you tell me which way to the major incident room please?"

The sergeant said, "I'll get my officer to show you, as you have not yet validated your entry card, you will be stopped every thirty seconds otherwise." He smiled and said, "Have a good day, Captain Brown."

Within a few minutes he arrived at a very secure steel double door, with a keypad and scanner to the side. As he could not gain entry he was forced to knock on the door. A light came on above him and he showed his card to the light and the door clicked open. He entered and was met by DI Jason King, who shook his hand and said, “Welcome to the bear pit.”

He looked over the room, saw that there must have been fifty to sixty persons in there, all looking busy at computers, checking with others. A woman who he knew to be DI James came across to them. She smiled at him, introduced herself and said that he will primarily be liaising with the two of them, and hopefully they would be able to access his expertise too.

She said, “Well Captain Brown, what do we call you, I am Sarah, and this is Jason, I hope you aren’t going to be all military on us.” He laughed, “No, my name is Kevin, I am not fully in the military anymore, but unfortunately I cannot tell you exactly who I work for unless your Commander Freeman gets permission, I am still operational in certain matters, and if called upon I will leave here immediately.”

She responded, “We have been briefed Kevin. Let’s hope that we can keep you as long as it takes to get this bastard. The Commissioner is here at 9:00am to give us an overall briefing. When she is finished the three of us can sit down and we’ll go through what we know.” He felt his pulse race, but just said, “Yes of course.”

She continued, "Help yourself to coffee, and your desk is over there." pointing to a desk which did not have a terminal attached to it. "We'll get you a terminal, but we are needing to organise the settings. Unfortunately, we cannot give you unlimited access, it's the same for many others, but you will have what is needed."

He said it was not important, providing he had access to his records which might assist them in their investigations. Sarah replied of course, and then said, "We have a few minutes. Go and validate your card and come back and we'll have coffee."

At 9:00am The Commissioner and her team entered the room and sat at the tables prepared for them. Among them was another person who Brown did not recognise. He was not introduced either, but he held a file in his hands and read slowly. He looked at him, he would have to find out more later.

The Commissioner then briefed the teams about both cases, including the fact that two sites had been found at the second scene. No bullet fragments at the first scene, whereas at the market shooting, several tiny shards had been found. She went on to describe what they had so far. She admitted it was not a lot, but with the help of the new liaison officer, looking at Captain Brown, they should start to narrow individuals down.

After twenty minutes the briefing concluded. The Senior officers left, but not before Commander Freeman had a quick word with Sarah. She nodded and turned back to the assembled team. She introduced Brown to the team. She said that if anything is required out of the ordinary or if he requests anything it has to go through her in the proper channels for HOLMES.

She said to him, "Sorry, its procedure, we have to get it right or we can have problems further down the road." He replied, "Of course, I understand, all disciplined services have protocols and regulations."

The three of them sat in a corner of the room. Sarah and Jason went through the cases as were known to them. Brown listened intently to each of them and when they both mentioned that the second scene appeared to have two nests, he asked, "So you think that it is a team working together?"

Sarah responded, "Not sure, the first scene was definitely the work of one, but whether the second scene was a distraction we don't know at this stage. Our Scenes of Crime officers are still working both sites."

Brown responded, "In the army it was not uncommon for having two teams working a target, for the want of a better word. If one failed, the other was usually in a position where he would finish the task. But both teams knew who was the principal shooter."

Jason asked, "Do you have records of who are trained snipers. Anyone who is capable of this, either from here or abroad?"

Brown stayed silent a moment and then answered, "The military and other organisations around the world keep records of many officers who have expertise in one field or another. However, without higher authority many records are sealed for a lifetime, as you must appreciate."

They looked at each other, "Do you have knowledge of anyone who may be capable of this, we assume that's why you are with us, not just a pretty face." Sarah smiled at him. He smiled back, "Yes I am here to help in any way I can of course."

She continued, "Thank you, from what you now know, how do you think this case has panned out? One shooter or two, anyone with known methods?"

He replied "You are obviously unaware of my background. I am ex SAS based at Bradbury Lines in Hereford, home of the 22nd Regiment SAS, the premier fighting team in the world. My rank is still Captain and I have retained that for my present role, which is very definitely covered by the Official Secrets Act."

He continued, "Whilst there I was on operational duties, both within the United Kingdom and outside. I was trained for a specific duty, hence my being here. Later I became an instructor at sniper schools in United Kingdom and overseas. I cannot go into how they were trained, but I can say that they were the best of the best. I have a feeling that the ones you are looking for may well be in that bracket too."

Sarah felt deflated, how on earth were they going to trace those bastards. She looked at Brown, suddenly thinking to herself, I recognise him!! She laughed out loud and said,

"You don't happen to be a cyclist by any chance?" He looked at her "Yes, in my down time."

She responded, "And wear a black Lycra outfit?" He was shocked and replied "Yes, how would you know?" She smiled and said, "You won't believe this but two days ago I was going to the scene of the first shooting and passed a group of cyclists. The others were in that awful multi-coloured gear, making them look idiotic, but there was one man, in black who looked professional. I only had a glimpse and now I have a feeling that it was you, could it be?"

His mind was in turmoil, he was going to have to be very, very careful around this lady, however attractive she was. He replied, "I have been on leave this week, until called in yesterday, and yes, I do cycle. Maybe I was in a group, sometimes it's safer to be with others, but I don't take much notice when I am out on my bike."

She retorted, "I thought you looked very professional." She smiled and then said, "Sorry if I embarrassed you, but it just came out, excuse my manners."

She then said, "Jason can you take Kevin to his desk, make sure he has everything he needs. Give him the password into his computer and sit with him and try and go over any initial thoughts."

They walked away. Sarah had a nagging feeling that she was not being told everything about this case and went to her desk and logged into HOLMES and the Scotland Yard data base. Her concentration was interrupted by DS Meadows tapping her on the shoulder. She spun around and saw

Grace looking across at Brown and almost drooling, "Who's the hunk?" she whispered. Sarah told her, "Captain Kevin Brown, military I think, and also I think he is as dark and secretive as anyone I have ever met." Grace smiled and purred, "All the better to get to know then." and walked off to where Brown and Jason were sitting.

Sarah shook her head and read the latest reports which had been fed into HOLMES. The causes of death were not in dispute. Already over two hundred statements had been taken. CCTV had produced film from twenty eight cameras in the areas around both scenes. The checks on all the car parks and parking areas had logged over three hundred car registrations. The SOCO's had finished with scene one and were finishing off on scene two. They had recovered scraps from the second scene, but nothing from the first scene.

Sarah looked across at Kevin Brown and thought that they were pinning a lot on him. How much useful info will be released to us? Just what has he done in his life?

CHAPTER 10

Across town, Hans Schmeir was sitting comfortably in his newly acquired apartment. The original and true owners were lying dead, already wrapped in the thick plastic coverings. He did not know them and he did not care. It was a convenient place to stay while he completed his next mission. He had just walked to the door, pressed the bell, and naturally some one answered, their last act on this earth. As he fell to the floor, another man came out of a side room, but before he could do or say anything, he suffered the same fate. Now he was at his "new" home, anonymous and ready to take control of his next contract.

The one the previous day had gone well, a perfect location and a perfect shot. The idiot walking down the street did not know what hit him, and then seeing everyone running round like headless chickens made his heart sing with joy. The English think they are the best in the world at everything, they are children in his eyes.

He did wonder about the shooting of the three in the park. He admitted to himself that not many could have conducted such precision. He knew of the reputation of the SAS and the Navy Seals, but they were nothing compared to his regiment. But it would not harm to make some enquiries through his overseas contacts.

He removed the phone from his pocket. He dialled a number which connected and then he disconnected immediately. Within thirty seconds his phone rang, he answered and waited. He heard the electronic crackle, then he was asked for his code. He gave it and waited another twenty seconds before he was put through to another individual.

He briefed his contact, asked them find out more of what the shooting of the three people in the park was about. He did not feel comfortable with a potential rival in the same city. He told them he had his new instructions and would contact them again in 2 hours. He rang off.

He rang another number and asked them to come the address as he had two carpets for cleaning. He was told that they would be there in fifteen minutes.

He switched on the tv and channel hopped until he got bored and switched over to Classic FM, the only decent radio station in this country as far as he was concerned. Wagner was playing, he tuned in and felt the Germanic theme flow through his veins. Although technically he was not German, he considered them to be the premier race, and had adopted the honorary nationality of being German.

His reverie was disturbed by the sound of the door being knocked as per instructions and coded sequence. He opened the door, four men entered, he pointed to the two bodies. They wrapped them into proper carpets and walked out. Not a word was said, and it was in and out within sixty seconds.

He downloaded the data required for the next assignment. There was no chance any of the encrypted message ever being cracked. His personal log in and decryption code stretched to 21 letters and numbers. Even NASA and the fools at GHQ would never be able to get anywhere near it. He studied the information, made notes on his notebook, and then closed down the data file.

He did not know who the new target was. He had always known about who the thug Burlov was. As far as he was concerned the man deserved everything that had been coming to him.

He opened a new page in Google and typed in the name Sir Jeremy Morgan. Immediately a whole slew of entries came on screen. This was no ordinary target. He was a senior Civil Servant, more commonly known as the Intelligence Secretary, responsible for the security of all Government buildings and agencies within the United Kingdom and holder of many of the secrets to the inner workings of the present Government.

This was not going to be easy, but from the amount of money he was being paid, they were serious about it and there was no turning down such an order. He had been given a schedule of the daily meetings Morgan attended. Of course, that could change at short notice. He knew where he lived and his route into work, where his official car was parked and the entrance in which he entered Downing Street.

He had seventy-two hours to complete his assignment. If he needed any assistance, it was available to him for the duration. He had no need, they were not up to his standards, they were just there for the dirty work. He would be up early tomorrow and be there when Morgan arrived for work. He would be there when he left work and he'd also be in place when Morgan arrived home A motorcycle was much more efficient in London. He was already formulating his plan as he listened to his favourite Wagner music.

CHAPTER 11

Across in London, Brown was going through the records of any one he could recollect as being able to commit such precision shots. He was putting as much space between himself and anyone remotely possible who could be called a suspect. He had given them around twenty five names, including one Hans Schmeir. He was also aware that the names he had given were the least likely to be able to do the job. Some were dead, some were on active service overseas and some were just experts in their own mind or just plain crazy.

Jason asked Brown why his name was not on the list? He looked at him and said, “All you need to know about me is to ask the Prime Minister, she will vouch for me, remind her of 2016.” He smiled outwardly, thinking that’s a good one to keep the dogs at bay.

Jason looked across, he was suitably impressed by his answer, thinking I must tell Sarah later. He gave the list to one of his team and told them to start looking at HOLMES and the other data bases they had access to and try and find out who and where the named individuals were.

Sarah was reading the various reports on her monitor, when a memo popped up. She read it and saw that is was an advisory bulletin warning of the possibility of a terror attack in UK. There was nothing specific at this stage, but all Forces needed to be aware.

He continued, "Can you give me a minute, I do have to ring my boss as a matter of protocol and might find something out". He walked away and took out his mobile, he pressed a speed dial and a few moments later his boss, Ellis answered, "How's it going Kevin, not bored yet?"

He laughed. "It's ok boss, a lot more involved than what we were led to believe when asked to assist. But it's a challenge." He went on "Do you know about a possible terrorism threat that the police have just received?"

He responded, "Nothing here yet, so must be very low level, I'll keep you informed if anything more comes of it." "Thanks boss," he replied, clicked off the phone and speed dialled another number. Within a few seconds it was answered, he gave his code to the other end of the line and it was acknowledged. He asked about the threat. "What is going on, do you have someone else working the targets besides me? Don't you trust me anymore?"

The voice at the other end responded, "This other shooter is part of an international overseas group we believe. We don't know why he was involved with the Bulgarian. But we suspect he is planning another shoot. I'll try and get the details, give you a head start with the police. I'll call you."

Brown walked back to the desk where Sarah had joined Jason, he said, "There is something vague, but no details. Just a little gossip on some chatlines emanating out of the middle east. It's being monitored by GCHQ and MI6. If there are any updates, you will be the first to know after me."

Sarah looked at him and smiled, "Thanks Kevin, it's always a pleasure to have a head start on others. Just keep us informed if anything happens and if you can disclose any of it." He smiled to himself and thought let's see what happens and where we go next.

Over the next three hours, officers came and went. Statements were taken and they gave their reports to the incident room manager, Helen crunched the details into HOLMES, collated anything that might have looked connected and sent the details on to the relevant team.

The information on the marksmen that Brown supplied came back fairly quickly. Of the twenty-five names, thirteen were still serving in the armed forces, and their details and whereabouts were presently classified to the current level of searching. Seven others were dead, three from non-military deaths, the others, again subject to classified levels. The remaining 5 names were still being searched.

Interestingly, Hans Schmeir was also a person of interest in Germany and France. The file was secret and For Authorised Eyes only. It was going to take a very senior officer to gain access to that one.

Brown was instantly alert. He considered him a crazy braggart over the years, full of his own self-importance and disdain for anyone else. He was not even convinced he was a German, there was something about him that did not fit right. Now he might be finding out why.

"Do you know him?" asked Sarah, "People in your line of work are not exactly two a penny, no disrespect to you." He laughed “None taken, the name has cropped up now and again. In Iraq and Afghanistan fairly often, but in all seriousness, he was considered a fool and full of his own ego by members of the various Forces around the world. No one seems to have had him in their ranks, certainly not the Germans or EU Forces.”

He continued, “I think we have to take the name Schmeir with a pinch of salt too, but until we know what’s in the records, we cannot be sure.”

Sarah responded and said, “Leave it with me, I’ll see what I can do.” She walked away and at her desk she called Commander Freeman with what she knew so far. He told her he was one step ahead of her and was requesting a meeting with the Foreign Office and will get back to her. He told her that no one else was to know of this conversation, no one, not even her team members. She sat there confused. How was he getting all this information before them and why in hell was the Foreign Office involved.

She went back to Jason and Kevin. She told them that she had asked for any information on Schmeir that maybe available elsewhere and her source would get back to her.

Brown eyed her, sensing she was hiding something. He knew he was going to have to be patient for the time being.

Jason looked at his watch, “Hey folks its lunch time, what does everyone want?” Sarah stuck her hand up and said, “Salad roll on wholemeal please.” Brown said, “A pastrami and horseradish sandwich on multigrain bread.” Jason looked at them both, “That was quick, hungry, are we?”

They took out ten pound notes, gave them to him and he said, “Give me ten minutes, I am a BLT man myself.”

He walked through the doors and away. Sarah turned to Brown, and asked him about his life before the military. He replied that he had been brought up in Harrogate, one of 4 siblings. He had never been a scholar but enjoyed being outdoors. He told Sarah of the military camp just outside Harrogate for boy soldiers. He had met some of them in town and was impressed by their lifestyle and discipline. As soon as he could, he left school and joined up, and never regretted a moment of it. Sarah listened quietly, understanding the intensity of him. He was letting her know what she needed to know, but that was logical given his background.

Just as she was about to give him some background, hoping that he would relax more, Jason walked in with a bag of sandwiches. He spilled them on to the desk and they selected their own and ate in an amical silence. Brown went to the coffee machine and brought three mugs back. “This will keep us going for the day, it’s thick enough.” He smiled and sat eating his sandwich in silence.

CHAPTER 12

Schmeir left home early and rode his motorcycle along the country lanes to where Morgan lived. He soon found his house, a large mansion in its own grounds, surrounded by hedges and walls. The only visual opportunity was the large metal gates which closed off the grounds leading down to the house. He rode around the whole area but found there was not much chance of finding a good spot to be able to shoot into the property.

He parked his bike in the road leading away from the house. He waited until he saw Morgan leave his home, in the back of his chauffer driven car. He drove slowly out, and the gates closed behind him. He was not accompanied by any other vehicle or personnel. The car picked up speed and drove down the lane onto the A3 into London. He followed them at a safe distance and watched as the car drove into Downing street, and immediately came under the protection of the armed police who were there in numbers.

He drove around Westminster and back out of the immediate area. He would wait until Morgan left his office later and then be there at his house when he arrived home.

He had already formulated an idea as to how it would go down but needed to see him arrive home today to finalise his plans and tactics.

He parked his bike and walked around St James Park, saw Buckingham Palace and the changing of the guard, to which he was not impressed.

Later in the afternoon he took his bike back to Westminster and saw Morgan leave. He took the same route as he had done in the morning. He passed him on the A3 and was parked up as he drove up the lane slowly and the gate opened for him to enter. The gate closed behind him and the car drove down to the house where he alighted and entered.

Schmeir watched and timed it all taking place. There had been one minute, twenty-eight seconds from leaving the A3 to the gate closing behind him. He worked out what the most vulnerable place he would be. Tomorrow he would be there early and in position.

At 6:30am the following morning, as the sun rose, he closed the door to the acquired apartment for the last time. The clean-up crew would attend, and an unfortunate fire would break out, destroying everything inside the premises.

He took an alternative route to where his lair was going to be for the next hour. He left his motorcycle behind the hedge under some foliage. He donned his camouflage suit and settled down and waited for the target to leave his drive.

At 7:25am, a vehicle drove up to the gates and entered. He recognised the car, a BMW series eight. German supremacy he smiled to himself, but this time the number plate was different. He scoffed, that they were so cheap that even he had to use a pool car.

At 7:30am the door to the house opened and Morgan left and entered the car in the back in behind the driver as normal. Schmeir settled down, the last few seconds were spent looking down his scope as it arrived at the gate. It opened, and the car drove out slowly. As it turned the driver and his passenger were side on to him and he squeezed the trigger. As normal there was no kickback from his weapon. However, instead of his bullet ripping through the car, all that happened was that there was a loud crunching sound and the rear passenger window had a slight craze in it. His mind could not believe it, he fired another round at the same spot, but the same happened.

The car suddenly accelerated away and down the lane and onto the main A3.

He lay there for a few moments before picking up his rifle and blanket and bagging it. He retrieved his motorcycle and drove away in the opposite direction getting as far away as possible from the scene. His mind was in turmoil. He had never experienced this before, how was it possible? There was no mention of this in his brief to even suggest that the car might be armoured. Why would it, he was just a civil servant, a senior one, but still a servant. He had to get away fast, back to his beloved motherland and his mentor in the Kremlin.

CHAPTER 13

Within fifteen minutes the scene had been locked down, Sarah and the teams had been informed and were heading to the location. A three mile exclusion zone had been placed around the house, causing huge traffic jams in and out of London. Captain Brown was the only non-police official allowed at the scene in the first instance, although later other agencies would be permitted.

As soon as they arrived, DS Meadows called them to a small patch to the front of the main gate. She pointed out where the shooter had lain, saying, "You can see the boot marks in the soft earth. Behind the hedge there was obviously a vehicle, probably a motorcycle and the tipping point is that we have already found one cartridge to the left hand side of the smoothed out area. Whoever it was, left in a hurry." She could hardly contain her excitement, and everyone felt their spirits rise at last.

They stood back as the SOCO's commenced their detailed examination of the scene and surrounding area. Sarah told Ken to find out what CCTV there might have been in the area, and the security arrangements for the Civil Servant. They could hear the hum of the traffic on the main road as well and all the sounding of the horns now much to the frustrations of the drivers.

She turned to Jason and said, "We need to track the route of Morgan for the last three days. It should be fairly easy with the GPS in the vehicles and then we can use the cameras on route, see if there is any pattern to any one during that time."

She turned to Brown, "Any thoughts?" she asked. He looked at the scene, "This was not thought out enough, he was arrogant and foolish thinking it was going to be an easy kill."

He took in what information they had been given. He speculated to himself that he should have suspected that such a high ranking civil servant would have had some security in place, however discreet. "When we get back to the office, check for any unusual occurrences which has happened this morning, before and after the time of the shooting."

Sarah looked at him and said, "What do you know Kevin? you seem to have an idea here."

He responded "Schmeir, he fits this, thinks he is perfect and untouchable. Too many mistakes for a homegrown sniper. Get on to the airports as quick as possible or he will be gone. You have to get his details through the Foreign Office now, and under the circumstances I don't think there will be a problem." He said, "Give me a minute and I'll get onto Ellis."

He walked about 20 yards away and pressed his speed dialler, Ellis answered and affirmed he had heard of the incident. He also said that as a matter of routine, senior government officials are given secure vehicles when there is a terrorist possibility. Brown mentioned Schmeir. He was told that his details were already on the wire throughout Europe. He told Brown he will keep in touch as and when further information was available. He disconnected.

He made another call. He relayed the information he had established and was told that Schmeir had no record of being alive before his 19th birthday. He was suspected of being a member of Russian Special Forces and had been integrated into the German army at 20 due to his linguistic and weaponry skills. He told them he would be in touch and in a better position to do what was required by them.

He walked back to Sarah and Jason and informed them that he had established some facts and was waiting on others before definitively being able to brief them. He told them about the security arrangements for Morgan. Sarah said she hadn't heard that the terrorist warning had been raised. She would find out why not and someone was going to get a lashing in spades!

A few minutes later Commander Freeman arrived with a number of other officials and time was spent showing them the scene from a distance. They were briefed on what was known and found. Grace Meadows was in the forefront of telling Freeman what was going on.

Freeman told the team that there was to be no press publicity at all on this shooting. If anyone asked it was in relation to a body being found in unusual circumstances. He wanted a briefing at 2:00pm in the office. There would be officials from the Government and other agencies too, but they were still leading the overt aspects of the investigation.

Brown was beginning to realise that he was going to have to be much more careful in what he did in the future. He could not plan anything soon, not until this had blown over for a while. His handler would have to accept the situation. He would be kept informed of any progress or any weak links in any enquiry. So far there had been none and he needed to be seen to be on their side.

They all left the scene together, going their different ways back to Scotland Yard and to their office. Jason said he felt hungry and there was a McDonalds down the road and was anyone up for it? Both Brown and Sarah shot their hands in the air, Sarah going for a Big Mac Meal, large size, with a Fanta orange, Kevin for a cheeseburger and fries with a strawberry milkshake and Jason opted for a double hamburger, wedges and diet coke.

They sat in the car eating their meal, not sure how this case was going to pan out. Nothing seemed right. The two scenes at the market, the botched shooting, only the first murderous shooting was what Sarah called a classic 'whodunit'.

Back at the office, they congregated together and all the information known about the recent attempt was collated and fed into HOLMES.

Brown was shocked to see his boss, Ellis, enter the room with Freeman and several others, including the unknown man from before. They sat together and opened what was obviously a number of files which they had brought with them. Freeman opened the briefing by thanking all of them for what they were doing, and he would be requiring the officers leading the enquiry to give him an update. But first he was handing over to Ellis saying he had been able to access certain records. This was hot off the press and he apologised for not being able to give them the information earlier.

Brown was amazed. He looked at his boss, who eyed him and gave a shake of his head. He had no idea what was coming and that disturbed him. Ellis stood and introduced himself, and mentioned that Captain Brown was on his staff, but seconded for the duration of the enquiry. Many eyes turned to Brown, he smiled and sat with his coffee in his hand. Ellis then said that the shooter this morning had been identified by a finger print left on a cartridge which had not been picked up. The person was Schmeir.

Brown sat up rigid. He had always guessed it was the crazy one but was surprised to find out it had been discovered so quickly. Ellis looked over at the unknown man who stood, looked around the room and said, "What I am about to tell you now is for your ears and eyes only. Nothing, and I repeat nothing will leave this room. He continued, "Schmeir is just an alias." There was a murmur around the room. "He is actually Viktor Gregorov, a Russian Special Forces operative, specialising in assassinations all over Europe and beyond. Up to now we have not been able to track him closely. He has multiple aliases and support teams here and elsewhere."

Freeman took over and said, "We believe that he was responsible for the Bulgarian's shooting and the attempt this morning, but not the first. It may be that there are two teams working together, but that is not usual with Gregorov. He is a lone wolf, a very dangerous lone wolf, who is arrogant enough to think he can go anywhere and not be found."

"Ladies and gentlemen, today he will be found and stopped. We traced him to a flat in Stepney, burnt out but again not carefully enough cleaned."

He continued, "All ports and airports have been closed for 24 hours, for reasons I will not bore you with. This will give us time to get as much manpower, from as many organisations as possible to find this man. Captain Brown, you will be returned to your unit immediately until we find him, then you will report back here, we still have another shooting to solve."

Freeman then told the assembled officers that specific instructions would be sent to them within the hour. In the meantime, they were to clear what they had done so far, have a tea break, and be ready to move when instructed.

CHAPTER 14

Brown said his farewell to Sarah and Jason and left the office, retaining his security card for when he would be returning to the team. He returned home, collected his uniform and equipment and drove the short distance to Aldershot, where his unit and office was based. He stopped at Fleet, found a call box and made a call. On the fourth ring it was answered. He gave his ID and password and was forwarded to another line, and a voice he knew answered.

"Have you heard?" Brown asked, "Of course," came the response, "Who do you think it was who passed on the information in the first place. We don't need the damn Russians causing trouble in this country. Get rid of him and perhaps we can get on with our next assignment."

"The details are in your usual drop box, you have five days for this one. As you are not with the police, you have a little bit more room to manoeuvre." He added, "Ensure the police get some distracting leads and keep Schmeir, or whatever his names is, from being arrested or shot too soon, keep the water muddied." The line went dead.

Brown knew he would have to wait until later before he could collect his brief. His priority was reporting to Ellis as soon as possible and not give anyone cause for concern.

He drove into the barracks, and parked behind a non-descript shed, in the middle of a car park full of military lorries, jeeps and other personnel carriers. He entered the code into a thick door. It swung open and at the entrance was an armed soldier who checked his ID against a computer behind the desk. He presented his eye to a scanner which verified his identity and he was given his ID back. The guard pressed a buzzer under his desk and a door opened into a lift. There were no floor buttons, just one to close. He pressed his index finger onto the switch and felt the lift descend as it had done for the last twenty years

A few seconds later, the door opened automatically, and he entered a room, about the size of a football pitch. Inside it was all bright and very business orientated. There were around 40 army officers inside the room, double the normal number when he had been there on many occasions previously. The two conference rooms which could house ten easily when seated around the table were both full. Both uniformed and civilian dressed individuals were looking at monitors which had obviously been recently installed.

He saw Ellis in Conference Room One. He pointed to him and he was signalled to go and join him.

There was very little conversation going on in the main room. People were typing into their computers and as images came up, being expanded and looked at closely. He tried to get close to the desks, but he could see Ellis looking at him and decided it was not worth the risk.

He entered and joined him, sat in a chair and listened to what was being discussed. A man, he knew as Colonel Francis was giving the assembled officers information on a known Russian syndicate operating in the United Kingdom. It appeared that it was more military than criminal, but the Russians wanted to make it look a criminal organisation in order to be able to distance themselves from it.

He briefed the attendees that Schmeir, alias Gregorov, was suspected of being part of the syndicate, but that had never been confirmed. Intelligence reports indicated that some members of the unit were involved in assisting one particular shooter, cleaning properties and getting rid of incriminating evidence and residual matters. Again, it pointed to Gregorov, but there was known to be at least three shooters in this unit, and all believed active here and in Europe.

Brown had heard rumours of this unit, but not of so many shooters. He knew one was a Ukrainian Sergeant, Yuri Belenko, and darknet chatter of maybe another, but never a name mentioned. He waited for a pause and then said "I have heard rumours of one, a Ukrainian, who I worked with way back. He went freelance, but it had been said he was killed during a mission in Africa a few years back."

He went on to say that he knew of Schmeir, aka Gregorov, who he considered to be an arrogant and over hyped. A decent shot but not that technically savvy. Since he had been with the police as a liaison officer for the past 2 days, he felt that from all that he had seen and talked about with the Senior Officers, it was Gregorov who had carried out these attacks.

They were told by Ellis that all airports and shipping terminals had been closed down for 48 hours. This was a direction from the Prime Minister, shrouded in a Level One terrorist alert.

There were glances all around the room, Ellis commented, "Your time away has been worthwhile. Let's keep this in house and let the big boys deal with them. Their base is in Kent and currently under surveillance. Once we can ascertain that the main players are there too, we will react and go in."

Brown was conflicted. He knew he had to try and prevent the main target from being arrested or even shot, but he also felt a duty to get rid of him.

He listened to what was being said by the others and in his own mind and decided that he would be in a better position with the authorities by supporting them. His other associates would not be overly happy, but they had to understand. He was the one on the ground and had better intel as to which way any investigations may be going.

He asked if they needed the police to assist by placing a cordon within an area and closing that down while the operations took place. He could liaise with them before taking part in the military side. Ellis replied, "That's a good idea, we need to bring in Freeman and his team and discuss the arrangements, I'll contact him now."

Brown excused himself and went over to the coffee machine and poured himself a mug. Another officer joined him at the coffee machine, and he made conversation with him about the potential operation. His mind, however, was on Conference Room 2, which seemed to be housing a lot more civilians than military. There was very little overt activity taking place, but there was a large wall map, which he saw was showing several areas of London. There were also some files on the table which were being examined in depth.

He didn't linger and went back into Room One. On the display board was a different map, this one of Kent, whereas the one in the other room was primarily concerned with London. He knew then that there were two separate operations forming, all he needed to know now, was what each one was about.

He sat through an hour of discussions and alternative plans before Ellis called for a lunch break. He went up to him and asked if Freeman was on board with the operation to which Ellis replied, "Of course and both DI James and DI King will be part of the cordon teams."

He then asked about the officials in Conference Room Two and whether it affected their operations. Ellis was guarded, but replied, "We have intel of another unit operating in UK, but seemingly based in the London area. Personalities are sketchy, some ex-military and some contractors, all courtesy of our American Allies. It's very much in its infancy, but of course as and when it firms up you will be brought into the loop, as always Kevin."

He replied, “Thank you Sir, my country has always come first, second and last. Anything I can do, however small is my pleasure, and duty.” Kevin responded immediately, with enough sincerity as he needed to make his boss smile.

He picked up a tuna mayo sandwich from the food table and sat and decided to wait until Sarah and Jason arrived before making any final decisions as they may have updated information.

CHAPTER 15

The quietness was suddenly interrupted by shouts coming from Conference Room One. He rushed over and took his seat inside. Ellis was on the phone and when he was finished, he told the assembled members that Gregerov was at the location in Kent, together with seven other males. There were three vehicles, a Mercedes SUV, a Ford panel van and a heavy lorry, with tarpaulin covers, parked to the side of the property.

He brought up an overview of the house and surrounding grounds and clearly visible were the three vehicles. Brown was impressed by the speed in which the data had been obtained and was now forming part of the forthcoming operation.

Ellis said, "Captain Brown, you and Sergeants Collins and Thompson will be situated 250 yards from the house, at here, here and here doing overwatch as normal." Ellis pointed out the spots where they would be hidden but in full view of the property. Brown looked at the overhead views and was satisfied that they would have full cover, not crossing each other's line of sight, but fully able to cover the whole site.

He continued "Team Alpha under the control of Captain Sheridan will be the lead entry team. Team Bravo will cover the rear of the property and Team Charlie will follow Team

Alpha into the premises. It is now 13:30 hours and we will commence at 15:00 hours, giving Captain Brown and his snipers plenty of time to get established and give us any feedback which may be different to what we know now."

He looked around the table, "Any questions?" he asked, Brown said, "What about the cordons?" and as he said that the doors opened, and Sarah and Jason entered the room. He smiled at them both, they stood and were introduced to the assembled room.

Ellis said, "Glad you can make it. I think that you are going to get the results all your hard work deserves. You have your teams and the other police enforcements necessary?" Sarah told him that they had enough manpower to cover all roads and pathways in a ten mile area of the house. She said, "Commander Freeman showed us the map page and we have already briefed the officers, some will be in marked cars and others will be unmarked and a variety of different models and makes."

She continued, "At least one member of each team will be armed. They will all have vests on with the wording POLICE, so as not to cause any doubt in anyone's eyes and minds." She stopped and asked if there were any questions or any updates within the last forty minutes. No one said anything and she and Jason sat down and listened to what was being said amongst the military personnel.

Brown walked over to them, sat down and said, "Glad you are both on board, didn't want this to go down and you not being there." Sarah smiled and said, "Wouldn't miss it for the world."

They were interrupted by Ellis saying, “This is highly dangerous everyone. If possible, let’s get them alive, especially Gregorov, he will be a mine of intelligence for us.” There were nods all round, but also a few comments that if they were shot at, then they’d be shooting right back.

Brown thought to himself, better dead than sorry.

At 14:00 hours Ellis shouted to all that it was time to go. Everyone vacated their seats and walked outside. Sarah saw the soldiers checking their weapons, some of which she had never seen before. Brown was with his two Sergeants in a huddle. They were carrying long rifle cases and jumped into a large Volvo SUV being driven by an unknown person. Brown waved to them both, gave them the thumbs up and the car drove away.

Sarah and Jason drove down to Canterbury and met the police officers who were going to be conducting the outer blocks. They had all been told their duties and that they were to be in situ by 14:50 hours. Unless they heard differently, they were to assume the operation was going ahead. They all had the registration numbers of the three vehicles at the property and if any tried to get away, the teams would be notified on their closed channels.

They all got into their cars and vans and drove out in different directions. Sarah and Jason met with Commander Freeman and having quickly briefed him, they left Canterbury and went to their designated spot.

They tuned their radio to the channel chosen for this operation. They sat in their car, about 5 miles from the location. At three o'clock, they heard the command for Team Alpha to go and enter the building, "Go, go go!" They waited for any input, but suddenly they saw a huge cloud of fire and smoke erupt from the site of the property, followed immediately by what can only be described as a roar and a rolling thundery noise reverberating around them.

There was complete silence until they heard the voice of Captain Brown, shouting, "Abort, abort!!" He then said over the radio that all the teams within a hundred metre area were down. He could not see any survivors.

A voice, unknown to them said, "What about the occupants, any evidence of them surviving?" Brown said, "From the blast, nothing could have lived through that. That was a huge load of C4 explosive being detonated there."

Freeman and Sarah looked at each other, wondering what had gone wrong. Was the place booby trapped so on entry it set off the explosion, or was it remote? Freeman said, "Brown are the vehicles still there?"

A few moments later they heard what they had been dreading, Brown reporting back that all three vehicles had gone in the confusion of the explosion. Sarah said, "They knew we were coming and planned it all." The next voice they heard was Ellis, telling everyone to be on alert for the vehicles, all roads to be cordoned and blocked off, no exceptions.

They were totally on high alert and as each and every vehicle that went past, they noted the registration details. A number of Mercedes and lorries went past in quick succession, while white vans were two a penny, but none had the right registrations. After about five minutes a report came through that a lorry bearing the registration number had blasted its way through a cordon and was being pursued. From the information being given it appeared that there was only one man visible. The pursuit vehicles were told to stay behind and another vehicle would employ the "stingers" ahead and a marksman team would be attending.

Everyone else was told to remain in place until the outcome of this pursuit had been resolved.

Chapter 16

Jason said out loud that he had a bad feeling about this. It was a diversion for the others to get away and whoever was in the lorry was prepared to sacrifice himself for the cause. Freeman agreed and got onto his phone and spoke with someone on the other line, presumably Ellis, and told him of the fears they had about this. They saw him frown and disconnect. "We have been told they have the situation in hand and to stay where we are and wait."

Sarah said, "Trigger happy idiots, haven't they learnt from the house?" There was a general agreement all round.

A few moments later the radio broadcast that Sgt Collins was in place with the stingers and they could see the lorry approaching followed by two police vehicles with their lights flashing. They heard "Stingers employed." followed by silence.

A sudden cry erupted, "Oh god, what happened?" then silence again. There was a lot of static on the air, and what seemed to be garbled messages and shouts made by different persons. Their car tried to establish what was being said, but what was taking place was obviously chaotic and with no radio discipline at all.

Freeman changed channels on his radio and gave his code word, and immediately he was connected, "What the hell is going on with all this? We have explosions, and something about a lorry and nothing except a load of noise and babble." he almost shouted down the radio.

The response was "We have lost contact with the two vehicles pursuing the lorry. It seems that after the stingers were deployed another explosion occurred, but this time there has been a release of some sort of toxic gas which is spreading and has taken down any one in its path. We cannot get near to establish the severity, but from initial reports it does not sound good. We are now imposing a major incident in the area and evacuating anyone within a ten mile radius."

Freeman said, "The operation is cancelled as far as I am concerned. We now concentrate on the civilians living in the vicinity of the area. I will relay this message to the military, and they are going to have to assist us with a lot more manpower."

"What is the current situation for us?" the operator asked, "We have mobilised all officers from Kent who are not on essential duty, anyone on leave is being recalled to assist. Until we get further information, we cannot give you any complete numbers, but I anticipate we have in the region of three hundred officers. We have enough safety equipment for two hundred from our own supplies. Portland Down have been informed and are sending up three teams to assist and identify the gas which has caused this disaster."

Freeman asked if the Commissioner and above had been informed and was told yes and would be giving a press conference in due course. The official line is that it was apparently a chemical lorry that overturned and spilled its load.

Freeman scoffed, "Yeah, how long is that going to stay the story. Whoever gives that line is asking for a shortened career." He then told the driver to take them back to the operations centre in Aldershot so he could find out what and how it all went wrong.

As they drove back towards Aldershot, convoys of emergency vehicles were speeding down the opposite lanes towards both sites, but more importantly, the area where the gas attack had taken place.

Freeman was thinking in his own mind how could the intelligence have been so badly misjudged, unless they had a mole inside the military. Where did they get all the explosives and how on earth were they able to manufacture enough gas to cover a whole area and cause so many casualties.

His thoughts were interrupted by Sarah who basically asked him the questions that he was thinking. She was shocked and wondered how the military, and Brown in particular, had got it so wrong about Gregerov. Far from being arrogant and careless, this had been planned to the last detail. The other two vehicles would now be miles away and probably switched or bearing new plates. God knows what was in those vehicles.

On arrival back in Aldershot they all went into the staging room and entered Conference Room One. Ellis was sitting in his chair, looking into a large tv monitor, showing both sites. The house and outbuildings were just a big crater, fires still smouldering.

Emergency vehicles were scattered around, but the scene was still too hot for any form of recovery. Nothing could have survived the carnage. On the other part of the screen was the burnt out remains of the lorry. It was a shell of twisted metal, partially melted. From the view of the drone, bodies were lying in a radius of approximately two hundred yards and a pall of toxic smoke was hanging over the scene and slowly moving in an easterly direction towards the M23 corridor and ultimately the M11 and London.

Ellis was directing teams to try and establish what the gas was. Until then they had no direct plans. In the meantime, he asked Freeman to coordinate with the various police services and arrange for any evacuation in the path of the gas. The extent of the gas was over a mile in length and increasing all the time as it dissipated from the original explosion.

Freeman rang the Commissioner and told her to contact the Prime Minister and Home Secretary plus the heads of MI5 and MI6. He would be having a zoom briefing in 30 minutes. As she tried to say something he said, "Ma'am, all our lives and millions of others depend on what you do in the next few minutes. This is not politics, this is a situation the country has never faced before, now get on with it and be ready in thirty minutes." He put the phone down, let out a big breath and said, "That's focussed a few minds!"

He moved over to the next monitor which was showing what Ellis was seeing too. He heard Ellis ask, "Can anyone give me an update, report in your locations and situation." After a moment of static, Sgt Thompson came through, "Am pinned down by trees, nothing too serious but unable to move away. Nothing in front except rubble and fires. What in hell happened?"

"Anyone from the lorry site, please come in." There was silence. "Anyone in the cordons, please respond." He heard a faint sound and clicking, but no discernible voices. He was able to pinpoint the noise to four miles east of the crash site. He looked across at Freeman, who immediately got onto his control room, gave his code and told the operators not to allow anyone within six miles of the crash site, and to report to him every 10 minutes. Had they any news from officers in protective outfits?

He was told that due to an accident on the M23 they were only just arriving at the scene, but would be able to give them a preliminary report in a short while. Freeman swore loudly, and threw the phone down, "What could go wrong, has gone wrong." he exclaimed.

The radio squawked and Captain Brown came on the air. "Sorry Sir, I have only just been able to get away from the site. There are traps all around the area, and we need the bomb boys to help us get closer." He continued, "This has all the hallmarks of a military operation, run by others much more senior than Gregorov, and with a lot more abilities at planning and statistics."

Sarah looked at Jason, the look on her face saying so much for the spooks intelligence and planning. Her private thoughts were on Brown, glad he was alright, but disconcerted by the events.

A few moments later the radio came to life, Freeman looked across at Ellis who was also getting the radio back up and running. “Sir, this is Susan Docherty, Portland Down, got some bad news, the gas is some sort of nerve gas and lots of it!”

Everyone looked aghast and the voice became almost disembodied, “From what we can see and from the Drone sightings this is going to float into London in the next 6 hours if the wind stays as it is. You need to evacuate as many as you can in order to minimise casualties. I am afraid that at this stage we have no idea of the strength of the gas, but obviously from first impressions it certainly incapacitates victims and probably kills quite a number. We will be able to tell you in a while after our scientists have completed their preliminary examinations of personnel at the scene and surrounding areas to get a representative analysis as it moves down wind.

You are going to have to be prepared for a catastrophic number of casualties, nothing in its path will be unaffected. Preliminary numbers from our computer readings give approximately two hundred and fifty thousand as a conservative estimate. Once we have identified the gas we will, hopefully, have some countermeasures which we can employ, but until then consider this as a category one terrorist strike until told otherwise.”

She rang off. A stunned silence went around the room. Everyone was thinking about their families and where they lived in relation to this terror which had been unleashed upon the public. Their silence was shattered when a phone rang. The Commissioner of Police was on the line and had the others ready for the video conference call.

Freeman just did not know what to say, but he was the point of contact and they all had to be informed and others of a lot higher pay grade will be taking overall control and taking responsibility. He did pity what Ellis was going to endure in the coming days and weeks. One by one the faces of the parties concerned appeared on the screen, Freeman Introduced everyone in the room and asked what they knew about the incidents so far. The Commissioner opened by saying that she had briefed the Prime Minister, who had in turn briefed the other Ministers of the operation at the hideout in Kent.

The Prime Minister interrupted by saying, "Who is responsible for these shambles?" Ellis responded by saying "I was the officer in charge on the ground, my operation." The Prime Minister said "You're fired, now get out of my sight. You will be dealt with later by your superiors."

Freeman interrupted, "Madam Prime Minister, before you go off playing politics, there is more to this unravelling as we speak." He looked across at Ellis, who was sitting, ashen faced, from the vitriol he had just been exposed to. "About thirty minutes ago a vehicle which had been part of the group who we had under surveillance, exploded after a short chase. It has released an unknown amount of nerve gas into the surrounding area. We have been unable to speak to any of our teams as we believe they have been caught up in the attack. Scientists from Portland Down are at the scene and trying to identify the substance and its potential danger."

The commissioner replied, “We have been receiving many calls about people collapsing in the street, multiple accidents on all roads leading into London, and we are becoming overwhelmed by the sheer numbers. We are having to get assistance from surrounding forces, but they are also under the same pressure as we are.”

The Prime Minister talked directly to the Heads of MI6 and MI5, “Did you know anything about this?” Sir Norman Graham, head of MI6 replied, “We were aware of some activities involving overseas individuals, but we had not formed any opinions as to the extent and threat level.” The Prime Minister answered “Well you know now don’t you!!

“Ellis, you are back on watch. The army is to be mobilised for the whole of Southern England and to assist the police in everything they need, which ever force requires it. Home Secretary, they are under your command for the length of the incident. Brief me in thirty minutes or earlier if you get the results of the nerve gas back.”

She closed her window and there was a silence. Freeman said to everyone, “I suggest that we all meet in person at this site. Then we can coordinate all our activities and requirements together, otherwise it’s going to get very fragmented.” There was a general agreement and Ellis said he would send them all the GPS coordinates for their location. The cameras closed and the four of them sat together around the desk, “Let’s see what the boffins can give us, then we can maybe do something positive.”

Ellis asked where Captain Brown was, Sarah told him that she had no idea. She thought he was returning to base, so that he was part of the new formations. Ellis considered this strange and picked up a phone and said to the other end, "Find out where Brown is. Just check his phone location and then report back to me."

A moment later the caller told Ellis that Brown was actually outside the Security Centre and was on his phone to an unknown number. Ellis thanked the caller and set his phone back down. He said nothing but went over to a man in civilian clothing, whispered something, and returned to the table.

They all looked at each other, not sure of what was going on. Sarah spoke out and asked, "Is there something we should know sir?" He replied in a terse manner "No." A few moments later Brown joined them and apologised for being late, saying he had been on the phone to some of his contacts. Ellis asked who and Brown replied "Gunnery Sergeant Biggs, a colleague of mine in the US Rangers. I was trying to establish any links with Gregorov and other syndicates operating. He said he will be getting back to me when he gets clearance from his Director."

Ellis said, "Oh how is Biggs, what number wife is he on now?" and laughed, Brown replied, "Three as far as I am aware, but you know he will always hanker after his first wife and daughter."

Ellis smiled and commented that life can be a bitch then as well as now. Sarah and Jason looked at each other but felt uneasy as to how this was all working out. Brown sat next to Sarah and smiled, and then said, “This is not our finest hour by a long chalk. I have not seen this amount of explosives used since the terrorist attacks in Beirut and Nairobi. Biggs was going to get me some more information on a couple of cases he has dealt with in the past.”

Ellis seemed satisfied and thanked Kevin for his input but reminded him of the importance of being punctual and attending meetings when told to do so. Kevin replied “Sorry sir, I was trying to get a lead in advance. At the moment we are just guessing on all fronts.”

The phone rang, an unknown number. Ellis signalled for the operator to check the caller ID as he picked up the phone, “Hello?” came the voice, “Dr Docherty here, we have analysed the chemical makeup at the scene. It’s a knockout nerve agent, not intended to be deadly, but will take anyone in its path down for a couple of hours. If they have underlying problems, then of course it can become deadly.”

There was a palpable sigh in the room and Suzanne continued “I am of the opinion it was a diversion, a pretty sophisticated diversion, so that your attention was distracted away from the main targets. The body that was found, or rather pieces of the body, indicate that it was male, and probably, from the ink marks and dental work on the piece of the mouth we were able to put back together, he was Eastern European. I’ll give you more information as we get it.” she commented, and Ellis thanked her, and the line went dead.

Freeman picked up his phone and asked for the Commissioner of Police and Prime Minister. He was connected within seconds. He told them of the results of the gas compound from Dr Docherty and the outcome of the effects over the next few hours. The Commissioner exclaimed that it was the only bit of good news she had these few days. The Prime Minister just said, "Your asses are still in a sling, one bit of good news, doesn't make a lady happy. Get on with what you are being paid to do, and I want another briefing in 3 hours."

The Commissioner said, "She needs to come to earth, sitting in her ivory office, doesn't she even have the slightest inkling of what is going on?" Freeman said, "Not for me to say ma'am, but I'd not disagree with a word you have said." The Commissioner chuckled and asked for a briefing in two and half hours, so at least she would have a start on the Prime Minister.

Ellis asked if there was any news of the first site. Freeman came back and said that examination of the scene was ongoing. Thirty three team members were unaccounted for. Of course, no one was able to get close to the centre of the blast and for about one hundred yards around it.

The road blocks and vehicles were still in situ where possible. Extra officers, both military and police had been drafted into the areas. Protective clothing had been issued and all affected persons were being taken out of the danger zones and taken to hospitals over the south and east of England. Now they knew what the gas was, they would be able to give an antidote quickly to aid recovery.

The biggest problem was that they had no idea where the suspects and the suspect vehicles might be. All ports, airports and private airfields were shut down, but that could not continue indefinitely.

Freeman suggested that the Police team move back to their own offices for now, but meet daily, either on zoom or in a neutral location to give their reports. If anything major developed then the Police would obviously liaise immediately with that information and he hoped the military would do the same too. Ellis concurred, but Sarah noticed Brown looking less than eager without saying a word.

As they drove back to London, Freeman queried why Ellis was being so harsh on Brown and asked Sarah to try and dig deeper into his background. If she needed, she should contact him and he would go through different channels, but he did not want to be seen being too overt at this stage.

In the meantime, back at Aldershot, the operative spoke with Ellis again. "He made three calls in the past hour, one to America, and two to another unknown number. It is taking time to get into that number, its heavily encrypted." Ellis responded, "Keep at it, just you, no one else, understand?" The caller acknowledged and cut the line.

Chapter 17

When the police team arrived back at their command post, they were met by Inspector Richard Stone. He briefed them on what was known to date. They had eleven officers confirmed dead from their unit and in total twenty five police officers had been killed or were missing since the initial blast. At the second scene, several officers were either dead or incapacitated, but nothing could be confirmed until the level of the gas toxicity had reduced, and the searchers were able to reach more officers. Other forces had also suffered casualties and again were waiting on final numbers.

They were astounded by the sheer numbers. As they entered the control room, a number of officers were seen weeping and ashen faced. They were just sitting at their desks, unable to comprehend what had taken place within the past few hours. Freeman called over to the control desk and asked if there was any news on the two vehicles outstanding. The reply came back negative, but a plain clothes vehicle near Dover had seen two vehicles of the description but different plates being driven together along the M20 away from the port.

A helicopter and two drones had been launched and were approaching the vehicles, but no closer than two miles. The registration plates were being picked up by the drones and they should be available within two minutes. It also appeared that there were three persons in the Mercedes, and an unknown number in the van, but known to be at least a driver and passenger in the front.

Freeman asked if the military command were aware of the developments and was told they were, but at this stage they had made no comments about it. He immediately contacted Ellis and asked why he had not been informed of the new developments. It seemed that all the information was going one way and the police were working with one hand tied behind their backs.

Ellis tried to tell him that he was in the process of contacting him with the updated information when he rang. Freeman knew this was a load of rubbish but bit his tongue.

He said, "We will be working together again in a short while. If what we suspect is correct, we'll have to ensure they are away from any built-up areas and I'll be getting the Prime Minister's authorisation to use whatever force is necessary. I suggest you do as well with your top brass. When you do, get back to me."

Freeman slammed the phone down and said he needed a very strong coffee. Everyone in the room was looking at him and there was a deathly silence about the place.

The phone rang in the control centre and it was put on loudspeaker. The voice said both vehicles were bearing false plates. Both sets of plates had been reported stolen five days ago in Lincoln. The registration numbers were broadcast over the airways and it seemed everyone was writing the details down.

Freeman immediately contacted the Commissioner and gave her the information. She told him to standby and she would contact the Home Secretary and the Prime Minister. Almost simultaneously Ellis was on the phone to him and gave the same information as he had received. Freeman told Ellis that the Prime Minister was being informed as they spoke. Suddenly the Red emergency phone rang and was answered by Sgt Carol Mason. She gave her name and she looked across at Freeman and said, “It’s the Prime Minister.”

He took the call and was asked a question. He called over to Sgt Mason and asked if they had a current update on the position of the vehicles. Mason replied that they were on the M22 approaching Ashford. He relayed the message to the Prime Minister, who said, “You are authorised to use whatever force you deem necessary. There are heavily armed army vehicles tracking the suspects from both ends. They will be stopped at a suitable distance, disabling the vehicles if necessary.” Freeman was surprised at the response by the PM and said, “Yes Ma’am.” She then continued, “The drones are armed with weapons and so is the helicopter. If possible, we want prisoners, but if they resist, then that’s not our worry any more, just do what is needed to get rid of the problem.”

Freeman said, “I need such authority in writing Madam Prime Minister.” She responded, “It’s on its way to you as we speak, keep me in the loop.” The line cut out. Sgt Mason called out that an email had arrived for him from Downing Street. She handed over the printed copy.

Freeman read it over to Ellis at the other end, and told Mason to forward the mail to him for their records. This was to ensure that they were safeguarded from any misconceptions or ambiguity that could arise if they had not got it in writing.

Freeman received the live footage from the drone on the large monitor and saw that the vehicles had slowed down and were both in a line across the carriageway of the motorway. At about two hundred yards distance either side of the vehicles were light armoured tanks, also in line across the highway. There was an eerie silence, but the clarity of the scene and vehicles was remarkable. Freeman told the occupants of the armoured vehicles to remain inside, under no circumstances was anyone to exit until told to do so.

From inside one of the armoured vehicles a voice could be heard saying, "This is the army. Switch off the ignition on your vehicles and step outside." There was silence and the order was again repeated, but to no avail.

Freeman heard Ellis talk to someone and tell them to immobilise the vehicles immediately. They were to shoot the engine blocks and tyres out. Immediately Freeman and the team heard gunshots through the radio of the army vehicle, and from the drone, puffs of smoke appeared at the front and sides of the two stationary vehicles. From the drone images they could not see from where the shots had come.

A few moments later three men alighted from the Mercedes, all carrying what appeared to be rifles and grenade launchers. They fired towards the armoured vehicles. Ellis gave the order to return fire and within seconds shots rang out from the large calibre gun mounted on the vehicle and other shots from various locations within the immediate vicinity. The three gunmen were shredded by the high calibre shells and holes and body parts and blood coated the Mercedes. From the viewpoint in the control room, it was over within 10 seconds. Smoke from the weapons drifted across the lane, otherwise there was silence.

A voice from the armoured vehicle called out for the occupants of the van to leave their vehicle, no weapons and face down on the floor. There was again no response and the order repeated. The control room watched as no action was taking place.

Ellis gave the order that if they did not leave the vehicle within thirty seconds they were to be fired upon. This message was relayed by the operator in the army vehicle. Both front doors opened simultaneously and the barrels of two large weapons were pointed at the armoured vehicle. Before they could be activated shots were fired from the side of the motorway and the weapons fell out of the van followed by two males One tried to stand, but was hit immediately by several rounds from the army vehicle and he evaporated in a haze of blood.

Everyone waited for a few minutes for any further sign of life, or potential danger by fire or explosion. Freeman and the team watched as eight men suddenly emerged from the greenery at the side of the road and ran towards the van. A little box was placed on the rear door of the van and a second later a puff of smoke was observed, and the doors flew of their hinges.

Two soldiers were seen pointing their weapons into the van and a voice was heard to say, "We have a live one, a male." A small cheer went up in the control room, before Freeman said, "Secure him, he is not to be left alone. Check for any possible ways he can harm himself or you."

Moments later a male with his hands behind his back was pushed out of the van and landed on his face in the road. No one showed any sympathy as he was bundled back to his feet.

He was made to stand and a photograph was taken by one of the soldiers, a copy of which was received by both Ellis and Freeman together. It was put up on the big screen and a gasp went up as they realised that the man in custody was Gregorov! Freeman heard Brown shout out, "Too much of a coward to die with the team. By the time we have finished with him, he will wish that he had."

Ellis told him to stop. He will be initially handed over to the police as it was their investigation. The military were only assisting. The army will get their chance when he had been processed and locked into the depths of Bradbury Lines later.

Freeman told Ellis he was arranging a team of specialist officers to escort Gregorov back to the station. They were to remain on alert in case any rescue attempt might be made. Also, it was important to get both vehicles back to London so they can be fully examined for any potential evidence.

After Freeman had signed off, Brown spoke to Ellis and said, "I'd like to be part of the escort team taking him back. He knows of me, and of course I know him, so he will be doubly cautious as to what he says or does." Ellis responded, "Sorry Kevin, let them do their job, they know how to handle him, but I'd like you to be present during the interviews as and when needed." Brown was hardly able to contain his anger, but said, "Yes of course sir, I am always available you know that."

CHAPTER 18

In the meantime, Freeman rang the Commissioner of Police and told her of the outcome. She was delighted to have got Gregorov and told Freeman that they would have an unrestricted path back to their station for him and the escorting detail. Sarah and Jason sat at their desks, discussing how to conduct the enquiries ahead of them, including interviewing Gregorov. They were joined by Freeman and another man in civilian clothing. The man said they were preparing the Interview Room 3 for the interrogation. It was the furthest from any external walls and the corridors were not straight but angled as they went deeper into the building. This would prevent any surprise attack, and all outside doors and shutter would be sealed.

Sarah and Jason looked at each other, surprised at the level of security. They didn't say anything as they knew this building had been used many times over the years for interviews of all sorts. He added that all recordings would be sent to a secure server away from the station immediately. The Prime Minister had signed an authorisation giving the police fourteen days grace to conduct any interrogation.

Freeman interrupted and said that Captain Brown would be allowed to sit in on some of the interviews, but only as an observer and give expert assistance when required. Sarah and Jason looked at him and Sarah said, "I am not sure about that sir. There are a few question marks hanging over Brown that I do not trust." Freeman responded, "Ellis has the same thoughts and was actively looking into Brown, and for now it was best he was kept on a short leash and available to all of us."

There was a flurry of activity within the station, and instructions given for extra security both inside and outside. Freeman consulted with the Commissioner of Police on the new arrangements and was told that Gregorov would be with them in twenty minutes.

Sarah and Jason finished their coffees and picked up the files which had been prepared for them, outlining specifically the shooting in the market, and also events proceeding until his arrest.

They heard noises outside the centre, a lot of talking and the sounds of multiple footfalls nearing and then moving away from them. They watched through the various cameras in the room as Gregorov was escorted in. He was released from his handcuffs, and as he sat down his hands were then relocked with a chain across the table, securing him fully and his ankles were chained to the floor. Sarah stood watching and thought to herself that she has only seen it in the movies before, didn't realise that it happened for real.

Two armed officers stood in the room, one in front, and the other behind him, their masked faces making them look even more threatening than normal. The room emptied of all the other personnel. Sarah saw Gregorov look up into one of the cameras. He initially just glared at the screen, but slowly he started to smile, a smile only with his mouth, his eyes were dead, he had no soul.

Sarah shivered to herself, but in her mind, she knew she was going to nail this bastard who had caused, and, was responsible for, so much death and destruction

They left the control room. Everyone was watching and nodding and a few gave them the thumbs up. They went down the corridor, past numerous armed officers until they reached the interview room. They punched in the code and entered. Gregorov sat there and looked at them both with his cold fish eyes. They sat in front of him and introduced themselves as DI James and DI King. Gregorov didn't even bother to say anything, but said, "I claim diplomatic immunity, I am a representative of the Russian government. Please call the Ambassador and arrange my release as soon as possible." Sarah and Jason sat there for a moment, until they heard "leave now" through their earpieces.

They stood and left the room, Gregorov grinning as they left and he said, "No puny government can keep me locked up."

They got back into the control room and Freeman was already on the phone to the Prime Minister. He was giving her the update and they could hear her down the phone shouting out loud and saying that he can forget it. A little Russian gangster doesn't do this to us. She then said, "Leave it with me, I know who to contact, don't let anyone near him, not even the Russian ambassador." The line cut dead and Freeman looked over to them and frowned, and said, "I really hope somebody knows what's going on somewhere, because I have got lost in all this."

Ellis rang and said, “If he was in military custody the same rules wouldn’t apply. We have enough powers to bury him and there is nothing they can do.” Freeman reminded Ellis that he was in Police custody and that every man and his dog knew that. They just couldn’t lose him to the military. Ellis reluctantly agreed, but promised that they would be available if required.

CHAPTER 19

As they sat and discussed the problems now facing them, the door to the control room opened. They were surprised to see the Prime Minister, Home Secretary and the Commissioner of Police enter with a tall slim man, who was accompanied by two other males. From their appearance they were obviously some sort of security. They introduced him as Kierov Amorich, the Russian Ambassador to the United Kingdom.

The Prime Minister said, "The ambassador has arrived to see his official. He is to be given unhindered access and will leave with Gregorov after we have finished some minor administrative details." Sarah started to say something, but Freeman looked at her and shook his head. She was devastated by this turn of events. The Ambassador was shown into the room with Gregorov and the sound system was switched off as per protocol. They saw the two men sitting and talking alone and Gregorov indicated the cameras in the room. The ambassador seemed to ignore them.

While they were in the room talking, the Home Secretary was called into another room and answered the phone. She stood still, taking in what was being said, but no one could hear it. She was seen to be writing something down on her tablet, before leaving the confines and re-joining the group gathered. She indicated that she wanted to discuss some matters with the Prime Minister and they stepped aside.

After a few moments they returned. The Prime Minister told them that one hundred and twenty eight people had died as a result of the nerve gas and over one thousand were in hospital and many more were likely to die. There was silence throughout the control room.

The Home Secretary then said, “One of the fatalities near the scene was the daughter of the Chinese Foreign Minister and the Chinese authorities have already been in contact and demanded we take the most severe action against the criminals. I told them that the main perpetrator was a diplomat from Russia. That did not go down well at all and we were told they would be hearing from them soon.

He continued, “There was a bus load of American vets going down to Folkestone to the war graves there. Unfortunately, they got caught up in it as well, of the 36 on board, there are only two survivors.” The American Embassy has been informed and we are awaiting their response”.

Freeman saw the Prime Minister and Home Secretary smiling and looking at each other. The Prime Minister said to Sarah, “Can you please ask the Ambassador to join us?”

Sarah went and knocked on the interview room door, which was opened by the Ambassador. He said, “What do you mean by disturbing a meeting with Government officials, I'll make sure that you are properly disciplined. What do you want?” Sarah replied, “The Prime Minister would be grateful if you could meet her for some urgent discussions. That's all I am aware of.”

He grunted, spoke something to Gregorov and walked with Sarah back to the control room. As they entered, the Prime Minister indicated that she would like to talk to him in a side room, no sounds, but visible to all. They went inside, closed the door and they started talking.

When the Prime Minister finished talking, the Ambassador suddenly slammed his fist onto the table and shook his head. He pointed at the Prime Minister and obviously she said something back as he went red and went and stood in a corner of the room and took his phone out. He spoke into the phone and a conversation took place. From his actions he was shouting and remonstrating over the phone to whoever he was talking to.

Suddenly he handed over the phone to the Prime Minister. She had a conversation whilst the Ambassador walked around the room in a very agitated manner. The Prime Minister gave him the phone back and they came back out of the room.

She said, "The Ambassador will speak with Gregorov and then he is leaving alone." They all looked at each other as the Ambassador shook the Prime Ministers hand and said, "I think that it is the best outcome." Sarah was asked to show the Ambassador back to the interview room and wait until he was ready to leave.

As they walked back to the interview room, the Ambassador turned to Sarah and apologised for his comments earlier and quipped "Your country certainly has its ways and means to solve any problem."

Sarah opened the door to the interview room, and he entered and closed it behind him. All of a sudden, she heard loud voices coming from inside. It went on for a few minutes, until it went silent. The door opened and Sarah saw Gregorov slumped on the table, talking to himself and glaring at her. The Ambassador shook hands with Sarah on his way out, accompanied by his security team. He said to Sarah, "Good luck, he's all yours, his diplomatic immunity has been stripped on the instructions of the Russian President no less." She looked at him, dumbstruck, he smiled and walked out of the door towards his car.

Sarah returned to the control room and everyone was seated around the conference table with the Prime Minister at the head. Sarah told her that he had left, and what he had told her. The Prime Minister said that the unfortunate deaths of the daughter of the Chinese Foreign Minister and the American vets had worked in their favour.

It was a sad episode, but she had told the Ambassador of the two incidents and that the respective Governments were incensed and demanded action be taken against Russian interests. If the Russians persisted in continuing to support Gregorov then they would be compelled to take action against a number of diplomats stationed in each other's country as a first step.

The Ambassador had immediately contacted Moscow and ultimately ended up talking to the Russian President. He was furious that such an incident had taken place and that one of his most trusted diplomats, as he termed him, was involved. When he was informed of the Chinese and

American involvement due to the deaths of the citizens, he realised that Gregorov had to be thrown to the wolves.

She continued, "That is when I spoke with him. He told me that with immediate effect Gregorov was no longer a diplomat and that his Russian status had been withdrawn. He asked that there was to be no mention of this conversation anywhere, and that he would contact the Chinese and American presidents to offer his condolences."

She further added, "He has now been detained under the Terrorism Act and he can be detained as long as we wish. He has no rights to any legal consultation or outside communications. The leaders of the other political parties have agreed to this course of action."

She stood up and she and the Home Secretary walked out. The Commissioner said, "I wish we had the support half the time from her as she has given us today, let's be thankful for small mercies." She smiled and left the room with Freeman.

CHAPTER 20

The control room was quiet. There was wonderment as to how this had happened and the complete autonomy they appeared to have been given. Freeman returned and told Sarah and Jason that they could now get back on with the interview and to ensure Gregorov was made totally aware of what his situation is now and in the future.

Sarah and Jason entered the room, this time there was no show of arrogance or bravado from the prisoner cuffed to the table. They sat in front of him, as before, and opened their files. Sarah began by saying, "You can no longer claim any form of diplomatic immunity and even Russian nationality." He looked defeated and told her that he had been told by the Russians of this and that they had abandoned him. He seemed both deflated and angry and Sarah knew that in time they would get all the information they needed and probably a lot more.

Jason told Gregorov that initially they would be interviewing him about the murder of the Albanian in the street market. Gregorov looked at him and said, "yes, what do you want to know?"

Jason said, "Did you kill him?"

Gregorov replied, "Yes."

Sarah couldn't quite believe how he had just suddenly admitted it. There must be more to this she thought to herself.

Jason said, "Why did you kill him?

Gregorov answered, "Because I was told to. I had instructions that he had to be eliminated as he was trying to take over certain interests in my country. This could not be tolerated, and we were to cleanse the Albanian filth out once and for all, starting with him."

Jason asked, "Who instructed you?" Gregorov replied, "My paymasters in the Kremlin." Jason looked at Gregorov and asked, "Exactly who in the Kremlin?"

Gregorov replied, "I don't know, but I was instructed directly by Ambassador Amorich and I have no doubt he was instructed by his mentor, the President, who has sanctioned other events before."

Jason and Sarah sat in front of Gregorov. This was unexpected. They were trying to decide in their own minds how to proceed next when the door opened and Freeman told them to leave the room.

Once outside Sarah said, "What the hell's going on boss? What are we supposed to be doing, this is way out of our league!"

Freeman replied, "He has confessed to the killing, which is what we are concerned with. We have to get the finer details of it and then we will have to consider handing it over to others who are on a much higher security clearance than we will ever be."

Sarah retorted, "We'll do what we can. Do you want to include the follow up escape and actions?"

Freeman answered, "I'll let you know. I need to make a few phone calls first." Jason answered, Yes Sir," and they returned to the room where Gregorov was sitting.

Sarah told Gregorov they wanted to concentrate on the shooting first and then they would go onto the other matters later. Gregorov nodded, and said, "I was number one choice for over ten years and now they just want to get rid of me. I have many secrets which I will share." Sarah looked at him, he was broken, confused and lost. He did not what know had happened fully and above all he was angry.

Sarah asked, "Why did you set up two snipers' nests?" He looked at her bemused and said, "Why do you say that? I had my position on the roof. Where else would I be?"

Sarah produced a photograph of the room with the glass cut out and looking along the market street. "I am showing the suspect a photograph of room 24 on the third floor of Sharp Street, where the shooting took place."

He looked at it and shook his head, "That is not me. I do not recognise that at all, although there are others who do that often. I had checked my position fully and knew that it was secure and fully capable of easy escape. In buildings it can be a lot riskier."

He continued, "I had heard rumours that there was more than one contract out on him, but I thought that was rubbish. That never happens normally unless it is a government official or someone important like that."

Sarah asked, "Any ideas who might have been the opposition?" She was fishing and she had just thrown the question in randomly to test his veracity and reactions. He looked at her and smiled "Oh, I have a very good idea. He has been at it as long as I have, for country and for his own business too. He has been playing everyone for a long time."

Sarah felt her chest tighten and her mind was reeling. "Do you know who he is?" she asked. He smiled and said "Of course, this is a very select club, but for now I'll keep that to myself, got to have some leverage for the next few days."

"You fully admit that you shot the man?" she asked. He replied ,"Oh yes, he was just vermin it meant nothing to me." He continued, "I was being paid my usual rate, five thousand dollars for a confirmed kill. In my country that's a lot of money. I am a rich man now, but I don't think I will get to enjoy it all. I have a diary of all I have done. You can have it when I am ready and then you will see what I have achieved. They are going to regret what they have done to me!" He slammed his hand on the table and looked at them both. There was an animal look in his eyes and both were glad he was chained to the desk and that there were armed guards in the room too.

Sarah said, "You were obviously not working alone, as evidenced by what happened later and from our intelligence reports." Gregorov responded, "They were allocated to me, not my choice, but they did their jobs and as you can tell, they were very efficient."

Jason asked, “Who were they? There are no survivors except you.” He answered, “They were some people who my ‘so called’ Government appointed to me. I did not have anything to do with them, except for them to give me intelligence for my kills and afterwards to clear up so no trace was left.”

“When you were tasked with the killing of Burlov, when did you receive your instructions and from whom?” asked Jason.

He replied, “I received an encrypted email from one of the men attached to me. He seemed to be in charge of the others. I was the important one. I was the one to carry out what was needed.”

“Where were you staying prior to being at the farmhouse in Kent?” asked Sarah. He just replied, “Around London, when we are in England, houses are provided. I was not concerned where as long as I could be near my target.”

He said he was tired and wanted a rest for a while, but would answer more questions later. Sarah looked up at the camera and left the room, leaving Jason and the guards sitting there.

Freeman was outside and told her that his suite had been sorted. It was in the high-risk security centre three levels down from where they were now. He would be supplied with a meal and he asked Sarah to see what Gregorov wanted.

She replied by saying that he was a madman who had killed so many of their officers and caused so much destruction. He retorted that if they are seen to be treating him well, he would respond with more information. It was vital to get as much as they could and as soon as possible.

Sarah showed her displeasure by going back into the room and slamming the door. A few minutes later she came back out and told Freeman that he wanted fish and chips and sticky toffee pudding and custard. He also wanted a double espresso coffee and a glass of water.

Freeman told her that he would arrange it and for her to take Gregorov to his suite under armed guard.

Sarah said, “I hope you are going to give us a choice of food too, we bloody well deserve it after today.” He laughed and joked, “We'll see if the budget extends that far.” He left her outside. She went inside the room and told Gregorov that his suite was ready, and his dinner would be provided as per his request.

He was escorted to his room and guards were placed outside. He showered and changed into clothing provided by the police. Only coveralls but at least better than the clothes he had been wearing for the past two days. The old clothes were removed from his room for examination by the Scenes of Crime experts to see if anything valuable could be found.

He sat and received his meal, and as he ate it, he considered his options and found them to be limited. He would try and keep as much back for as long as possible, but he knew that in the end he would be forced to reveal all.

He was angry about the way he had been let down by his employers but he would get his revenge. He knew the secrets of many of his competitors and peers and he would lead the pretty police officer to his cache in time.

He went to his bed and lay down, feeling tired and his body ached. He closed his eyes for what seemed only a few minutes, but when he opened them again, he saw that he had slept for over 6 hours and there was a knocking on the door. The door opened and an armed police officer indicated that he had to get up and would be taken to the interview room again.

CHAPTER 21

Back in Aldershot Ellis was being briefed by Freeman at regular intervals. Brown was sitting in the same room but for some reason Ellis was only supplying him with certain information, whereas in the past he would be privy to everything. He was told that Gregorov had admitted the shooting of the Bulgarian but denied having anything to do with the firing position in the building opposite. Brown said, "That might be a backup if the first shot had failed. They may have had two shooters, that does happen as you well know sir."

Ellis responded, "That's true, but from what we are being told, he was the lone shooter and all the others were back up to him, as instructed by their Russian paymasters. He is one very pissed off Russian. He has been dropped by the authorities and he has told the police that he will give them what they need to know over a period of time. He is not asking for anything in return but giving dribs and drabs just to stay safe where he is."

Brown said, "They are playing a dangerous game, the longer he is with them the more of a risk it is. He should be under our control and we'd soon get what we need from him." Ellis responded, "They have promised that when they have everything they need in respect of the shooting and the escape and subsequent events, they will hand him to us for intelligence purposes in respect of the national security aspects."

Brown said nothing but inside he was very nervous. It was imperative that he found out what Gregorov knew. He had no option to stay where he was for now. He had been told that at some stage he would be involved in interviewing Gregorov, but as he had already admitted it all, he was not sure this was going to happen.

Ellis was still collating information from the scientists as a result of the explosion and gas release. Initial findings were revealing that the explosives at the farm property originated in Bosnia around thirty years ago. They were able to establish the batch from its markers built into every explosive made since the second world war. Many countries had been involved in the chaos of the Balkans war, not least Russia. Other countries including UK forces who were part of the United Nations contingents also had their fair share.

Huge amounts of equipment, including arms and explosives had gone missing due to corruption and black market dealings. Countries had sold on stockpiles and not accounting for them, while individuals and certain politicians made their fortunes.

Preliminary examination of the nerve gas found it to be a very mild and diluted version of mustard gas that had been used during World War One. It had been banned for many years since the end of that war. Occasionally stockpiles of the gas had been found in drums and hidden in shelters and underground. It was also rumoured that China and Russia, as well as a couple of other Eastern European countries, had been experimenting with it again as a possible weapon. But all chemical weapons were outlawed, and the countries claimed that any gas they did have was for medical research in trying to find antidotes for such weapons. This was viewed with scepticism by most countries who had signed up to the different weapons agreements over the years.

Ellis had ordered Brown to do more investigation into Gregorov, anything that they might find useful as and when they had him in their custody. Brown was sat at his computer terminal and had logged into various websites and databases around the world. He had a high clearance which gave him access to many individuals, both for the benefit of the military and for himself and his other associates who paid a lot more lucratively than the army.

One of the sites he entered into looked up individuals who were basically mercenaries. He entered his password, which was accepted, and he started to browse the latest list of individuals who had been flagged. This database had been constructed by a company who were security consultants for other companies and countries to choose individuals for assignments. Although Browns' details were not on that list, he was the go-to man for any wet work that needed doing. Whenever he logged on, his details were flagged by the company and a mirror copy of what he was doing was downloaded onto their servers.

He typed in the details of Gregorov as they were known to the authorities, including his location and current situation regarding his non activity as a shooter. He typed further looking for other information from sources. He found that Gregorov was one of three brothers recruited into the Russian army, the other two had died in Afghanistan. He had been recruited by the Russian Secret service at the age of twenty.

He had disappeared off the radar for almost ten years. There were rumours circulating that there was a sniper of exceptional quality who was travelling the world and killing anyone who did not conform to the rules of the Russian president and his close circle. He did not find out anything else, but typed in a single word, which transmitted all the information to the company. He then ticked on six names, held the key on each of them for three seconds and released it. This action was all that was needed to initiate an action back at the company offices in Basingstoke.

He logged off and took the information he had obtained back to Ellis. Unbeknown to him, a remote terminal had captured his keystrokes and they were being analysed at a specialist centre near London. Since the two phone calls he made were to encrypted numbers, enquiries had been made by the Sergeant on the instructions of Ellis. They had come back as being made to a company in Basingstoke, specialising in security personnel for mercenary missions.

Ellis didn't know exactly what Brown was involved with, whether it be passing on information or much more serious, being for hire. He knew Brown was probably the best sniper in the world and that thought scared him. He knew he had to detain him at the control centre for as long as possible.

Brown for his part was relaxed, as he had supplied enough information and given his associates details of who he wanted on this assignment. They were good, experienced men but expendable in the grand scheme of events. He would be here and therefore no suspicions, or any amount of thoughts and ideas could fall on his shoulders. He went and poured himself a coffee and carefully looked into the various rooms to see what was happening. No one looked up and just concentrated on photographs sent by the police and reports being shared by both parties. He could not see anything untoward, but he knew he had to be careful at all times, and this was one of them.

CHAPTER 22

Back at the police station Freeman was informed through his contacts that there was the possibility that something big was in the offing. There appeared to be a team forming for some sort of operation. It was not known what it might be, but in light of the current situation, it was imperative that security levels be increased, and operational conditions be implemented at all levels of the building. The message was passed to other units using the building and all entrances and windows were shuttered, preventing any natural light entering. Just as important, with the ventilation and backup power systems installed any attempt at gas or liquid intrusion was impossible.

At the car park levels, one metre high solid stainless -steel stanchions rose from the concrete, forming a pattern whereby no more than 2 metres separated them from each other. Each was linked by an infra- red beam, which was shown on the control room monitors. These measures were known only to the users of the police station for obvious reasons. For security reasons there was another control room in a secure facility one hundred miles away.

Freeman informed Jason and Sarah of the situation and they both looked at each other and understood the situation they were in. “Do we know any more details yet?” asked Sarah.

He replied, “No, but the situation is being monitored very closely through our super-secret friends. We understand that there is a minimum of six ex-military servicemen as part of the team. We are presently processing their individual expertise, which may give us an indication of what might be going down.”

He continued, “We are trying to ascertain if there are others being recruited and what sort of time scale we are talking about.”

Sarah asked about the military involvement at this stage. Freeman was quiet for a moment and said that the senior staff were aware of certain matters and being kept up to date as new intelligence was gained.

Jason said, “What about Gregorov? What’s happening with him?” Freeman responded, “He is being moved. The only people who know this are us three and the four escorts that have now been assigned to him. They know where to take him and keep him safe. I am sorry but even you two don’t need to know his new location for the time being.”

Sarah said, “Of course. Maybe it is best all round. I can’t believe that anything can happen here.” Freeman retorted, “We don’t know if that is the case. We have to be ready for any eventuality. The Prime Minister and the Royal family have all been informed and all sensitive bases and offices are now having their security upgraded. Military bases are also being strengthened but in a much more discreet manner and their computer systems have been reorganised totally to block any outside interference.”

He continued, "We are not sure from where all this is originating. But we know that servers are being routed worldwide, sometimes ending in UK, other times in USA and even South Africa. We have to narrow this down. We are not working blind, one of the individuals has left his mark and the boffins are working on that. He is not as clever as he thinks he is."

They all felt the tension rising within the complex. There was more movement and shouted commands. Everyone who was in the control room was now isolated until being told otherwise. Freeman called for everyone to hand in any mobile phone they might have. They were to be deposited into a secure lead lined container in order to prevent any information as to locations being transmitted.

A call was made to the control room and was told that Gregorov had been safely conveyed to his new location. All contact with the outside world would now cease until the correct password was given to resume communications.

Freeman conveyed all the information via an encrypted phone to the Commissioner of Police, who told him that she would have a face to face meeting with the Prime Minister and brief her. Freeman then conveyed a message to Ellis, this was a prearranged message, appearing to be spontaneous. He gave Ellis details that had been previously agreed with and then said the police will continue to deal and interview Gregorov during any heightened security warning.

Ellis called all his senior officers into the conference room, Brown included. He then briefed them as to the current situation with the police. He informed them of a group of mercenaries had been contacted with a view to commit as yet, an unknown, operation against, again, unknown target or targets. He apologised for being so short on details, but the police had only recently intercepted some chatter over the internet, which involved the United Kingdom.

He instructed all his officers and their teams to try and establish more detail as to what it might be. They all returned to their posts and went into the different data bases they had been assigned to.

Brown sat with Ellis and said, “What’s going on chief, something to do with Gregorov or what?” Ellis commented, “We don’t know yet Kevin, it seems the police are getting jittery about something but from what I have been told, it’s very early and no details being given over the air.”

Brown said, “Where’s it coming from?” Ellis replied, “From the internet connections it appears to be in the middle east, possibly Syria or Iraq.” This line of information was deliberately given as per the arrangements between Ellis and Freeman.

Brown grinned and said, “Always the bloody Arabs causing trouble. Would have thought by now they would be more careful as to what they say and transmit but thankfully they are stupid and give themselves away.” Ellis looked over at him, saw his reactions and knew that this was another turn of the screw. He was still unsure of how much Brown was doing outside the military but he was getting more and more sure that whatever it was, he was somewhere in the uppermost of the organisation.

He admired the instincts of DI James and her colleague DI King. They would make good intelligence officers in the military and other organisations. For now, they were with Freeman and using their abilities to keep Brown confined. He knew he was serious about getting outside, but he would not let him. He still had access to the computer, but this of course was being monitored.

CHAPTER 23

Back in London, Sarah and Jason asked when it would be possible to resume the interview. Freeman told them to give it a couple of hours, wait and see what develops, Gregorov was as safe as they could make it. Everybody was on a state of high alert but the unknown factor, the target, that was what was concerning him.

They listened to the control room officers in an effort to see what was forthcoming, but there did not seem much chatter coming over the airwaves. Freeman was constantly on the phone, to whom they did not know, but suspected that it might be scientists or the military.

A few minutes later a phone rang in the control room, was answered and the operator said it was for Freeman. He said, "Yes?" He listened, and seemed to be surprised as to what was being told to him. He put the phone down and took Sarah and Jason aside.

He said, "There has been an assault on The Old Bailey. There is continuous gunfire and explosions within the buildings and surrounding areas. We are not sure on the number of assailants and casualties at present. Both police and military are currently proceeding to the scene."

Jason asked, "Was the Chief Justice there?" He replied, "No, he was late getting away from his office, so he was lucky, but other members of the judiciary are there as they were discussing the current security levels and policies in light of what took place yesterday."

He continued, "We are to stay locked down, no one in or no one out. How has this happened so soon and how did they know that the Chief Justice was going to be at Old Baily today? It had not been scheduled and kept very quiet for obvious reasons. We have a leak at the highest level and whatever we say, or do, must be on a need to know basis from now onwards."

The phone rang again. The operator answered, looked at Freeman with a look of shock on her face and handed him the phone. He answered and held the phone to his ear. He said, "Good god man, when will it end?"

He dropped the phone and turned and faced them. "That was the Commissioner. There has been an explosion and another release of gas, this time at Waterloo Station. Scotland Yard received a coded message, five minutes before the bomb went off. It also said that a number of bombs have also been placed at other stations and terminals around London and will be detonated at intervals unless their demands are met."

Jason, Sarah and the whole of the control room were aghast. Freeman continued, "They have not made any demands yet. They are toying with us. We are going to need as much assistance as we can muster to search and make places safe, if possible."

"What can we do?" asked Jason. Freeman responded by saying, "Nothing, this is your place here. I have a feeling all this is connected and trying to distract us from what we are supposed to be doing here. They will not succeed. Excuse me I must make a phone call."

He went into the control room and clicked on a number, and it was answered immediately by Ellis. "Have you heard what is happening?" said Freeman. Ellis retorted, "It's still coming in, but the country is now being put onto a national emergency footing and emergency laws are going to be enacted and will override all other legislation."

Freeman nodded to himself and said, "Have you received anything from anybody as to what is going on?" Ellis replied, "Nothing, as you know we have received some chatter, but nothing concrete and we have all our resources trying to find further information." Freeman knew from the phraseology that Brown was still with him and under their surveillance within the bunker.

Freeman told Ellis of the threat to detonate more bombs if demands had not been met. But to date, there had been no demands, and searches were still continuing at all main line stations, but nothing had been found. The gas had been found to be more of a side issue, not too toxic, but enough to make people panic and have some symptoms of nausea and coughing. It had dispersed quite quickly, but the station was in ruins, the central roof had collapsed and trains wrecked by the force of the blast. It was too early to give the number of casualties but it would run into hundreds.

He told Ellis that The Old Baily was in flames, most of the main building had been destroyed and had collapsed in on itself. There were many casualties amongst the judges and staff. There was still residual shooting continuing within the complex, but the police were gaining the upper hand and it was believed that at least half a dozen attackers had been killed.

When Ellis cut the line, he told the officers around the table what he had been told by Freeman. He looked at them all in turn as he said this, gauging their reactions. Some looked shocked, others had tears in their eyes, Brown had no reaction, he looked ahead, made eye contact with Ellis, but there was no emotion in them.

Brown asked, "Sir, any indications what nationalities are involved yet. Are they Muslim suicide squads or what?" Ellis knew that Brown was trying to deflect the blame onto others. He was still unable to establish too much about the calls and the company that Brown was communicating with at this stage.

Ellis replied, "We believe there is a foreign element to it all. The Middle East seems the most likely but that the moment we cannot be sure We have our guys running checks on all frequencies and IP addresses to see if there is anything more concrete."

Brown nodded his head, and said, "Let me do some checking, I have contacts in some intelligence services. Mossad and NSA are still in my contacts." Ellis said, "OK, Kevin, but be careful what you say. Let them give you the information and not the other way round. Keep me informed of everything. Use the recorder to keep a record then there will be no miscommunication."

Brown left him and went to his allocated terminal. He logged on officially and then relogged again using his other name and code. He didn't have to say anything but used his keyboard and typed what appeared to be random letters and numbers. He then reverted back to his proper typing with correct wordings and accessed the websites he needed. He wrote various emails and messages to his contacts and logged out from them. He returned to Ellis and said he was waiting for responses from both agencies and would check again in a few minutes. He sat with his boss, ate on his ham and pickle sandwich and drank his coffee. He looked around at the activity going on and said, "I am sorry sir, everyone is busy except me. It seems I have a waiting game to get my information. I just hope it is what we need to break this open and help anyone who needs it."

Ellis replied, "Be patient Kevin, you'll get your chance to do what you do best in due time, but firstly we have to know who and what we are dealing with." He looked at Brown and could see he was restless and wanting to leave the bunker under any pretext he could find. Ellis reminded him that they had to stay in the bunker until further notice except to leave for operational purposes, and then only in allocated teams.

Ellis's phone rang and when he answered he was told by Freeman that the bomb used at Waterloo was detonated when the TGV from France touched the buffers at the end of the platform. This has caused a massive explosion which had ripped through the carriages. The upward force of the blast had brought the roof down and the front of the station had blown out causing further damage and casualties in a much wider radius. It was known that the train was from Paris via Lille, with a stop at Ashford International Terminal to let passengers off. No new passengers would have been getting on for the short trip into London.

CCTV cameras were identifying passengers who had alighted at Ashford and has either left by local train or by vehicle. It would seem that around thirty individuals had got off, but from the information so far obtained, there were two hundred and sixty four passengers who were destined for London.

Ellis said, "Any more news from The Old Bailey?" Freeman answered that it appeared the attack on The Old Bailey was designed to coincide with the Supreme Court meeting, ironically on the new security laws and terrorism. He said that firing had stopped and special services and police experts were now entering the premises. both through the main building and outlying complexes, with a view to finding the attackers. Initial reports suggested that there may have been as many as twenty attackers involved and they had use of and access to a lot of high powered weapons and explosives.

Freeman continued, "We are aware of a large number of casualties, but at this stage we cannot be sure exactly who they are. We are hoping that the majority of the judges and their staff made it to the cellars and safe rooms. There are still hotspots and the fire services are dowsing them down, so progress is slow."

"I will keep you informed and maybe we will have to call on some of your expertise at some stage," he said to Ellis, "but we will have to be sure of what the situation is before doing that." Ellis replied "Yes of course, I understand fully. I'll give my staff an update now. Perhaps their various enquiries can be further extended with this information. Thanks again."

He gathered his officers back to his office and briefed them on the latest update from the police. He ensured that everyone knew what the situation was, and he deliberately mentioned the fact of the passengers disembarking at Ashford. He also told his troops that he felt that, in the not too distant future, their assistance was going to be required. There was a stirring amongst the men, some were nervous, others, like Brown, were obviously relishing the thought of being let off the leash and doing something.

Ellis cautioned them by saying, "We still need a lot more information before we get to that stage. However, with all the intelligence services and ourselves doing what we can, I am sure we will be out and about soon enough and getting whoever is responsible for all these terrible acts. We have come a long way in a very short time since the shootings in London a few days ago. I don't know if any of it is connected or that it was just the trigger for all the mayhem since."

Everyone resumed their positions at the computers scattered around the control room. Brown went to his terminal and logged in as previously. He again typed in a number of random letters and numbers, before reverting back to his role liaising with Mossad and NSA.

His logins had been recorded both times and the sequences he had given were being entered into a number of highly complex programmes and being cross referenced to any other non-sequential letters and numbers from other sources. In addition, his genuine actions on the machine were also recorded. Whatever went out and whatever was received were simultaneously being seen by both parties. No information was being stored at the bunker, everything went to a complex at Camberley, which was top secret and known only to a few people. The operator in the bunker room had been seconded at the outset of the operation from Camberley. He and Ellis were the only two within the bunker who were aware of the existence of the high-tech complex.

Two emails had arrived at Browns terminal and he printed them off and went across to Ellis. He said, "Sir, Mossad have been hearing chatter about operations in Europe. They have assets on the ground in Lebanon and Egypt and from the information given there is a particular cell operating out of both of those countries."

He showed Ellis the email confirming what was being told by Mossad. He then told Ellis that NSA had heard very little chat, only home grown groups who were advocating setting up townships for themselves and not being controlled by the US Government. There was very little overseas chatter, in fact they were saying it was the quietest it had been for many months. Perhaps that was because they didn't want to advertise what they intended to do within the UK.

Ellis thanked Brown for the information and asked him if he could get back onto his Mossad contacts to try and find some identities which might have crossed their paths and suggested that the name Gregorov aka Schmeil had come to their attention too. Brown smiled and said, “Yes sir.”

Brown smiled to himself as he went back to his terminal, confident now that he had diverted attention away from himself or his contacts and placed it firmly towards the middle east.

Ellis indicated to the operator that he needed to check into the authenticity of the emails. Something was not right but he could not put his finger on it.

CHAPTER 24

In London, the police operations room was abuzz with telephone calls. Printers were shooting out pages of information and being distributed to the appropriate officers. Freeman was continually on the phone to various individuals who either rang him or he made the initial approach. Sarah and Jason were reading the casualty reports from both locations. The bombing at Waterloo had caused a huge number of injuries and deaths. The concourse had been crowded with people waiting to board trains for both Europe and within UK.

Most harrowing was reports that amongst the casualties were two groups of school children who had been booked onto the Eurostar for a trip to Paris as part of their GCSE level examination course. It was not known that many had been killed or injured and no firm details were available. Sarah was almost in tears, she was finding this particular report very distressing.

There was a flurry of activity and the large screens showed passengers disembarking from the train at Ashford. A total of 34 people got off, eleven women and twenty three males. From first appearance they all got off in small groups, ones and twos, but further CCTV coverage showed that as they walked away from the platform, one group in particular seemed to walk closer until they got to the car park. When they got to the gate, a dark blue van bearing the name of a company based in Bradford drew up and they all got in. The vehicle drove off towards the M20.

It would seem that five males and one female were part of the group. They were obviously savvy to being seen on CCTV from their demeanour, but they were not aware of another camera which had been recently installed as a result of the motorway event involving Gregorov. This clearly showed, from the different angle, the faces of the group. Already the computers in various locations were going through facial recognition on them. It was also established that the van had been stolen from Bradford two days previously.

Sarah could see that the males were of middle eastern background, but the female was definitely Caucasian and in charge of the men from the way she was ordering them around and pointing into the vehicle.

The details of the van and occupants were immediately circulated as far as the south of England, into East Anglia and the Midlands. Thirty minutes later came a report from the Met Police that the van had been found abandoned and burnt out on an industrial estate just outside Peckham. What was interesting was the fact that a body had been found in the driver's seat of the vehicle. It was unidentifiable due to the severity of the burns. DNA would have to use if they were to have any success.

The photographs of the six wanted persons were immediately circulated to all police officers in the surrounding areas. It was arranged that a press briefing would take place at 1800 hours and then the information would be made public.

At Ashford, the details of all the passengers disembarking were noted from the CCTV and what vehicles and who they met were logged. A team from Ashford Police station had been tasked to search for and obtain the details of the remaining twenty eight individuals.

When the photographs of the six individuals were sent across to the Military, Ellis showed it to his senior staff. It was passed around each person and they shook their heads and said that they did not know or recognise any of them. When it got to Brown, he looked at it for a few moments and said, "I don't recognise any of the men, but the female is familiar. I think she is Russian and the name starts with something like Karakova, but I am not sure. She will be in the system, I am sure."

Ellis told two of his officers to check the various databases with the name Karakova or any of its combinations. Ellis asked Brown how he thought he came to know the female, and he responded by saying that during an operation in Iraq, she had been the contact for some local Shiite group and had been responsible for supplying them with information and hardware.

He further added that he thought she had been killed during a raid by US Special Forces on their camp a few days later. According to post operation intel everyone was killed inside the camp and three foreign women were among them. He was not sure if the bodies had been formally identified or just assumed it was her amongst them.

Obviously, given what he had just seen, she was not dead. He seemed genuinely surprised by it. Ellis saw the look of confusion and was a little taken aback. After all the suspicions he had on Brown, he was expecting a totally different reaction.

He rang Freeman and gave him the details of Karakova, but left out the reaction of Brown, this he would impart and confide with later. Freeman thanked him for the speedy identification. Ellis reminded him that it was just a provisional, but the thanks were appreciated, and he would pass it on to Brown. As soon as they got anything confirmed or if the police did, they would share it.

Freeman told Sarah and Jason of the updates. Sarah was sceptical, but Jason seemed pleased of the progress. There had been no recognition from any of the data bases that they had used, but then again, GCHQ had not responded. That was nothing unusual but recently, in view of the severity of all the events, they did expect some cooperation.

There had been two, unconfirmed, reports of a group of six people driving around London as if to go north on the M1. Blocks had been put in place on two lengths of the motorway, but no vehicle had been sighted or stopped. It was thought that both vehicles had left the motorway much nearer to London than anticipated.

At the Old Bailey, two live attackers had been discovered. One was badly injured. The other, a much younger youth, was found cowering behind a wall in one of the kitchens and offered no resistance when he was apprehended.

He was terrified and unable to speak or form any comprehensible words at all. He bore no identification and all the tags had been removed from his clothing. He had been examined by a doctor and found to be suffering traumatically but had no other injuries. He had been cuffed and was being sent to their station for a secure imprisonment.

In the remains of the Old Bailey, they had found twenty two bodies. Six of them were judges, eleven aides and the remaining were staff of the courts. There were still a number missing and the recovery was slow. Nine attackers' bodies had also been found in various locations. Three of which had self-inflicted wounds to the head.

It was obviously a pre-planned attack as their vehicles were found about a mile away from the scene. Inside were sleeping bags and food and ammunition wrappings. The officers on the scene found it strange that the vehicles were intact, considering what they had undertaken was inevitably a suicide mission. Bomb squad officers had examined the vehicles, both Ford Transit vans, and both bearing false plates, but found no sign of any booby traps or any other unpleasant surprises.

There were no signs of identification inside the vans but it did not seem that the vehicles had been cleaned either from the state of the insides.

The officer in charge there felt that they had been planning for the assault but for some reason it had hurriedly been brought forward, hence the state of the vehicles.

Arrangements were made to take the vehicles, under heavy guard, to the nearest police station where a detailed examination would be carried out.

All this was conveyed to both Freeman and Ellis. Both were surprised by the events at the Old Bailey and, when further explained to the others in the respective control rooms there was a general feeling of this had been something which had been conducted in a rush, with inevitable consequences. Sarah asked, "What is going to happen to the survivors? Do we keep them or hand them over to other services?"

Freeman laughed and said, "If the Prime Minister had her way, they'd be hung, drawn and quartered outside Parliament. I think she was being half serious. Which is frightening." There was laughter, which broke the atmosphere of the overbearing feeling of despair and sadness.

He carried on, "The initial interviews are going to be conducted by our secret squirrel friends first. We have enough here with Gregorov inside our premises, we don't want more complications."

Jason asked, "Why not give him to the army?" Freeman replied, "They have a number of leads resulting from the Waterloo bombings, they can deal with that. They are looking for the female who is known, plus the others who are currently on the run but not identified."

He continued, "The airports and all shipping ports are closed. Every CCTV is concentrating on facial recognitions of these people throughout the country. All services are on highest alert, so we have to find them before they go to ground too deep."

He looked at his watch It read 5:32pm. He told the teams to take an early supper, half now, half at 6:15 and then they would see what the situation was and maybe have another go at Gregorov. He was hoping that there might be more information from Brown and Ellis on Karakova and, perhaps see if there was any reaction from Gregorov on the mention of her name.

CHAPTER 25

Brown responded to a ping on his mobile. He went to his terminal and typed in one set of numbers. Immediately his screen lit up and he called Ellis over. They both looked at the information that Mossad was sending through. They looked at one another and Ellis rushed over to his terminal and dialled Freeman. Brown saw Karakova was in actual fact Brigita Gregorov, the wife of Gregorov who was in custody with the police. Brown was quite shocked. He never realised from all his studies of Gregorov that he had a wife or another member of family. At this point he could not even try to do anything untoward but just replied to his Mossad contact, thanking him and telling him that if he finds more to contact him as soon as possible.

Meanwhile Ellis was talking to Freeman, who was incredulous that this information had been found, and even more worried about the events that had taken place, if she was, as it seemed to suggest, in control of the cell on the loose. He looked across the control room, signalled for Sarah to join him and told her of the quite frankly shocking and disturbing news. Sarah looked around, seeing the faces of the staff observing them, one or two now becoming aware of the potential implications of what had been revealed.

Freeman told Sarah to call all staff back to the control room for a briefing in five minutes. He rang the Commissioner of

Police, who was stunned "What do you propose to do?" she asked. "We have to ensure that we are totally secure from air and ground as we can be. Obviously, we have an idea of what is coming down the line now."

Freeman instructed all officers to report to the armoury where they would be issued with side arms to all and automatic weapons for those who were qualified to carry them. Additionally, Kevlar vests and headgear were now to be worn until further notice. A number of officers seemed unhappy but none of them argued or even thought of saying anything with the realisation of what might be happening soon enough.

Within ten minutes the whole centre looked as if it was prepared for anything. All the other units in the building had been similarly informed and equipped. Arrangements were being made for some of the Metropolitan Police's heavy vehicles to be deployed outside the station but due to roads being gridlocked that was taking time.

In Aldershot Ellis was briefing his officers of the situation and increased security. Brown asked if he could take a detachment of men and assist. Ellis told him that he was to concentrate on the intelligence he was gathering. He had done a remarkable job through his Mossad contact and didn't want to lose the impetus taking shape.

Brown went back to his terminal, inserted his code and the second instantly behind it. He typed in his letters and numbers, paused and repeated them. He logged back out into his official sites and saw that he had received an email from the NSA. This one just said that someone with a high security clearance was to contact a number, details given, and they would be given additional information. His contact apologised and said he was sorry that Brown did not have the necessary clearance, although he had been given access to quite sensitive information at times.

Brown logged out and he had no option but to give Ellis the information that had been sent. He was wondering what could be so secretive that he was not included. He knew from the previous communications that they had not got much chatter and suspected that everything might be connected back to the Middle East, but the disclosure about Karakova had changed everything. Maybe they had some feedback about her from their contacts in Eastern Europe.

Ellis read the message, thanked Brown again and went into his office, which had facilities for blocking out any incoming interference.

He sat in his chair and dialled the number given. When it answered it was an automatic response request. He had to give his details and clearances, followed by a pre-planned sentence containing numbers and letters. He was told to stand by. He waited twenty seconds and then heard, "Hello Mr Ellis, I am General Stanford Grayson, Deputy Chief of Staff at the NSA."

"How do you do sir," responded Ellis "What is so important that we need to talk like this?"

Grayson said, "We have been receiving some very odd messages over the last few days, not only involving Karakova and her team, but other organised groups in different parts of the world. We have many contacts as you know. They are adamant that these groups are not being controlled within their own organisations but by an unknown third party based in Europe. This organisation seems to have access to unlimited funds and people. We just get bursts of code of no more than ten seconds before it stops. "

Ellis did not say anything, but then he said, "Do you have times and dates of such spikes of information. We may be able to corroborate with our computer whizz kids and see if we get the same results.

He continued, "Captain Brown, one of my most trusted officers, has been able to obtain as much information as possible from Mossad. It identified Karakova and, more importantly, her relationship with the shooter Gergorov who was responsible for the mass killings on the motorway and explosions at their safe house. We have everything on lockdown now, thanks to him. Now we have this additional information we are very grateful."

Grayson told him he was more than welcome but be careful of what information had been divulged. Ellis told him that he had two computer geeks monitoring all terminals in his bunker and at a remote site. He would be the only one to use them. Not even Brown would know what was spoken between the two of them.

They cut the communications and Ellis rejoined the officers and told them that NSA had got a potential connection with a drug cartel in Mexico. Several of the cartel members had left the area. They were enforcers and had not been seen for almost a week. They may be behind the assault at the Old Bailey, but until any of the bodies had been identified, they could not be sure. NSA were more than happy to supply "their buddies over the pond" as he put it, with anything that might assist. There was general laughing and they went about their duties in lighter spirits. Brown said to Ellis, "Never had much interaction with the cartels outside of our operations in Columbia. Quite a step up for them if they did this. Someone is paying someone an awful lot of money to get these people to attack the heart of the English Establishment."

Ellis responded, "It seems that this has become a global affair. We don't know what is going to rise up next." He knew that what he had told the officers was untrue but he had to keep the real reason for the conversation to himself for obvious reasons.

Brown made himself a marmalade sandwich from what was left on the table and sat at his terminal pondering on the turn of events. He did not know what had taken place after he had sent the codes, or who was being recruited, so it seemed a perfectly reasonable scenario.

Whatever was taking place was outside his area of concern. His only concern was Gregorov and that was complicated by Karakova, his wife, being involved and loose in London. He would have to find out who exactly had given her this task, knowing that he was in custody. Maybe they didn't know that either.

He still couldn't get away, but he felt that all was under control and nothing would get back to him. The codes were one off and discarded. As he ate his sandwich, he saw Ellis walking to other officers, having short discussions and moving on, reassuring them that their work was essential and appreciated.

He came back to Brown and told him that as soon as he could, he would release Brown and his unit to join the clear up at Waterloo and be on standby for the police at the station in case they requested backup. Brown said he would go anywhere he was ordered.

Ellis commented that, thanks to various organisations, they were getting a better picture of some of the participants and organisations they belonged to. Analysing chatter over the air and internet, there has been some developments. A number of coded messages and calls had been made recently and were being pieced together by intelligence officers at GCHQ. Brown listened impassively, not showing any reaction.

He said to Ellis, "Perhaps my friends in Mossad can work their magic again. Give me the details of the coded messages, times and dates and I'll get them to go through their systems and contacts and maybe we can get a result from either side."

Ellis said, "Sorry, that's way above our pay grade, this sort of information is known to the IT guys, and they have been told not to disclose anything in relation to it. I am sorry Kevin, our hands are tied on this, but by all means contact your man in Israel and see if they have heard of anything strange being sent out. I get the feeling that they are probably as bemused and in the dark as we are at the moment."

Brown nodded and turned away. He had to be careful. Obviously, the supercomputers at GCHQ were picking up on anything which was not standard. He was glad that his machine was not being compromised, although the coding that Ellis had mentioned was disturbing. He would be able to send one more piece of code and then have to close it down and find another secure source.

His thoughts were disturbed by Ellis, who said, “Kevin, you need to assemble your team. You are going to assist Freeman and his people. Your expertise might be invaluable if it comes to any action there.” Brown look surprised as and said, “I thought you wanted me to check with my contacts?” Ellis responded, “The situation has changed. They need more bodies on the ground. The chopper leaves in five minutes, get your gear and go.”

Brown replied, “Yes sir.” He went to his locker and opened it up, taking out his go bag which was always ready when needed, however short a notice that had been given. He was trying to think of ways that he could utilise more time so he could send that one last code. He might get the chance when he got to London but not through his official phone or tablet.

He left five minutes later. Ellis picked up the phone and told Freeman. He told him to keep him busy but under no circumstances, at this stage, allow him any confidential or secret information. Freeman indicated to Ellis that he would be deployed on an upper level floor looking down on the street, he and his team covering the four angles of the station.

Ellis thanked him, and said he hoped he was very wrong about what has been discovered but they were preparing for the worst and hoping for the best.

In London Freeman briefed Sarah and Jason and then went and spoke with the Prime Minister on the secure phone. He came back and told them that Brown will be in the south east corner of the building, while his team members would be placed around the roof top. Unknown to Brown there would be a team of watchers from another building two hundred yards away and looking down on his every move. His phone and tablet had already been synchronised with their equipment, so any communications would be immediately in their view too.

Within twenty minutes Brown and his team arrived at the station. They were granted access before the place was locked down again. He arrived at the control room and shook hands with them all. Sarah smiled and said, "Nice to see you again Kevin. We are grateful for all the help we can get right now." He replied, "Thanks Sarah and thank you all. Now where do you want us, we need to set up as soon as possible and get organised between us."

Jason said he would show them their positions on the building plan, deliberately positioning Brown in the south east corner. Brown traced around the plans and said, "That's a good position for me, I can see clearly down two junctions for any incoming vehicles or persons."

Two armed officers joined them. They led the way upstairs to the roof, using their id cards to move through each level of floor. On reaching the roof, they were shown where to go and each of the six man team went to their allocated positions and laid out their equipment. Brown had his specialist rifle. This time he had standard army issue bullets. He had to just wait before he could do anything. He set his sights, made himself comfortable and used his spotter, Sergeant Jed Frith, to check the streets and buildings around them. The watchers had a perfect observation of them both, hidden as they were in the nearby block.

CHAPTER 26

The first signs of anything untoward happening was a slight tremor felt on the rooftop. It was as though there was a low level earthquake shaking the building. It lasted no more than ten seconds but was felt by everyone. Brown radioed down to the control room and asked what had happened. They responded by corroborating what they had felt but that it was very mild. People were checking throughout the building for damage or disruption.

All communications were checked and found to be working normally. Two of the terminals had briefly gone offline but had been reconnected within three seconds and working after diagnostic checks.

Freeman asked Jason to check with the metrological office and ascertain if there had been any such quakes recorded on their equipment. He came back and said they had nothing on their records to date, but would check locally as sometimes the information took a few minutes to be collected. Freeman rang down to the prisoner suite and was told they had felt a very minor tremor but literally for only a few seconds. Everything was normal there.

Freeman was unsettled by the occurrence. The last thing they needed was a natural problem on top of all the manufactured incidents over the past few days.

Suddenly gunshots were heard from somewhere about the building. Everyone went to their stations and took up their weapons and positions. Freeman suddenly heard Brown shouting down his radio that his team were under sustained attack from gunmen in different buildings around the station.

They seemed to have a perfect sight on all the teams and from what he had been told by his teams, four of his team were down. Three spotters including Sgt Frith had been killed and he was pinned down behind a concrete vent and being fired upon from at least two different positions.

From inside their positions the watchers had seen what had transpired. Calls were made to several different locations and units. Within a few minutes, sirens could be heard from a distance and getting closer. Brown looked up from his position and above him there were three drones moving around the shell of the building, then turning away and scouring surrounding premises, a short burst of cannon fire followed by the breaking of glass and concrete. It felt reminiscent of his days in Afghanistan, and where his girlfriend was stationed now.

Cannon fire, the only way to describe it, and automatic weapon fire reverberated around the block for a few minutes. He suddenly saw a missile going overhead and hitting a drone which disintegrated in a big explosion, pieces of the drone scattering over a large area with some landing on the top of the station.

The heavy firing slowed down after a few minutes and Brown was able to contact his team members. There were not many left. They had been picked off by the snipers and he had been lucky to have been so close to one of the concrete vents or he would have been one of the statistics. Two shooters, including himself and one spotter left and he had been shot and badly wounded.

The watchers relayed all the information back to their headquarters. They had been surprised by the organisation and methodical way the attackers had gone about the shooting, picking the snipers off easily, but more so the spotters, the eyes of the shooters. Everything had been recorded and this had been transmitted back to the backup teams. Those teams were already making their way into the various buildings to trace any of the assailants. They were confident they would find some, but not all.

Ellis had been brought up to date with the events and he was appalled. He wondered how it could have happened, he knew Brown nor any of his team had not contacted anyone. Also, only a few people were aware of the positions his team were going to assume. Brown was the exception and his location had been mapped out beforehand by the watchers.

Brown had sent him his current situation. He was still locked down but the firing had ceased and he was waiting for the all clear. He told Ellis of the tremors and the assault. The use of the rockets to take down a drone had helped to lessen the assault. However, the sheer firepower from all angles that had erupted simultaneously had shaken Brown. He had lost many of his team and also the ferocity of the attack had completely surprised him.

Ellis wondered what else was going to happen in the near future, whether this was just a diversionary strike or the start of another major incident. He thought to himself what the hell is so important about Gregorov that so much bloodshed and chaos was being used across the country. There had to be so much more to all this, and his suspicions of Brown were being overtaken by today's events.

In London, there was an eerie silence after all the ear shattering noise of the gunfire outside. They knew that there were many casualties from the reports being transmitted. A few minutes later they heard doors opening and closing and a large number of persons moving in the corridors. There was muffled talking and few exchanges. A knock on the door, it was opened, and Brown was given admission. They were shocked by his appearance. Gone was the confident, almost arrogant, attitude of a man in charge of his own destiny. He was shell shocked, wide eyed and pale. His whole demeanour was one of defeat and despair.

He could hardly walk one foot in front of the other. He almost staggered across to where the three of them were standing. He muttered, "I have lost my men, who did this?" He was in tears, a whole unit wiped out in minutes.

He sat with his head between his knees, looked up and said, "Is he still here? We haven't lost him, have we?" He was told they were still secure for now but everyone was on high alert and they needed him to get back his mojo and think about what might happen in the future. They had no idea if it would be soon or whether the terrorists were just trying to scare them and make them do something stupid.

He drank his coffee slowly and asked for a sandwich. He felt as though all his energy had been drained from him, like nothing he had ever felt during all his years of service. Even in the bad old days in Iraq and Afghanistan, where horrors were common place, did anything come close to the suddenness and ferocity of this assault.

“How the hell did they know our positions and how did they manage to have so many shooters and such equipment in place in such a short time?” he asked Freeman. “We didn’t know where we were going to be until we reached the roof and we were totally exposed on all areas. I was lucky I was near a concrete air vent. I was able to get into a corner where there was no line of sight.” He spoke slowly and carefully. He was trying to formulate the events in his mind as they occurred. “Frith never had chance. They seemed to be targeting the spotters first, a method we always used when we went after snipers.”

He continued, “Do we have any CCTV in the area? At least give us some indication of where they came from, who they were and how secure are we?” He was still shaking and asked if he could report back to his commanding officer and give him a full update and his take on what had happened.

He went into the control room with Sarah and talked to Ellis for around five minutes, giving him as much detail as he could, including the drones and the missile that destroyed one of them. He finished and gave the phone over to Sarah. She said, Yes?” and he replied “Captain Brown will remain with the police for the foreseeable future and the army will cover his position with someone else.” She replied, “Yes sir, I understand, we will ensure he gets a role here.”

The phone went dead. She smiled at Brown and said, "Well looks as though you are one of us now, welcome to the lockdown." They returned to the main room where everyone were at their terminals, trying to obtain information from as many sources as possible. London Transport Authority was uploading all the CCTV information for a perimeter of 300 yards round the station. Freeman asked Brown if would take charge of analysing it, he realised that it was a big job, but with the help of a couple of the analysts in the room they would be able to use their magical fingers and make things a lot quicker and easier.

Brown was not happy, but he knew he had no choice. He was with them for the duration and by looking at the CCTV he might be able to recognise someone who might be involved. It would make him look good and take more attention away from him.

Ellis received the reports from the watchers. It basically confirmed what Brown had told him. They were shocked by the ferocity of the assault and how it developed. They had their films of the events and would pass them to him. How he used it was up to him, but he had to be careful because initially it was all aimed at Brown. They said that if it was not for the vent where Brown was actually placed, he would be dead too. He was showered in bullets from all angles and it was only by genuine luck that he was not hit.

A few minutes later the feeds from the watchers was downloaded onto their system and his `nerds' got onto sorting out any useful information arising from the assault.

One of his researchers, who had been looking into the activities of Brown, approached Ellis and told him that they had been able to decipher enough of the code in the phone calls. They were able to say they had gone to Afghanistan. Now they had that information they could narrow down the internet codes and letters too, probably to a similar location. Ellis was amazed as to why he would be calling there. Had he gone across to the Taliban, or another faction who were paying him to cause as much trouble as possible, while they spread their propaganda?

He told his officer to keep this secret and find out more. It was too early to get Brown back yet. He was safer and under more control where he was. He rang Freeman and told him of the situation and was told that he would not give out that info to anyone else for the time being.

As Freeman put the phone down, he felt another rumbling. This time stronger and louder. It continued for thirty seconds and various electrical circuits went down before automatically kicking back in. This time it seemed that the noise was coming from the south east corner of the building, which was housing the more secure files and occupants, of which there were currently eighteen belonging to various organisations.

He gave instructions to all his staff to remain in position and rang the various departments to ascertain what damage had been caused or for any other problems. They reported back and told him of the shaking and noise they had experienced and how close it was but then it had stopped. They likened it to the underground railway with a train passing by. Everyone knew that something was happening, but the way it was being conducted was strange, as if they were preparing for something big, but unable to finalise it yet.

He rang the Commissioner of Police with this information and asked her to be discreet and send officials from the London Authority around the area and see if they could discover anything untoward. They were not to concentrate on the station itself but be general. He also advised her to have armed officers on standby within a suitable distance for any quick reaction.

He had the maintenance staff check all systems including entrances and windows. The computers were shut down and then rebooted. All with different passwords and operating systems but still able to access their current data and work. Everything coming into the building was shut down, water, electricity and gas. Phone lines were rerouted to the underground cabling system that had been installed when the station was made a maximum security holding centre for the United Kingdom.

Unbeknown to Freeman and his officers, a complete security ring was being placed around London. There were no major indications of mass transporting of men to different locations, no extra uniformed officers on the streets. Instead, many vans and cars of all descriptions left car parks, railway stations and even from within a royal residence and fanned out in a large circle. In every vehicle were heavily armed officers, all wearing civilian clothing so as to not draw any attention to themselves. At the same time two helicopters had lifted off from Bradbury Lines and would be in the capital in forty five minutes.

At his terminal Brown was looking through various images which were being isolated from each camera. He suddenly shouted for his operator to stop. "Wind back," he shouted. Several images went back. "There, it's him, I know him." They gathered around and looked at a man in his 30's wearing glasses, and walking slowly, as if he had a limp. He said, "He is Herman Goetze. He was a mercenary working out of Lebanon the last time I came across him. He was one of the team leaders who were responsible for the outrage in Bali a few years ago. We were never able to track him down. It was believed he had links to a cartel in Columbia and was their cleaner when any disputes arose."

The team kept their eyes on him. Brown told the operator to keep the tracking image on Goetze. Various images of Goetze came on screen and walking down various streets. He stopped to talk to a female for a few moments and then carried on.

The image of the female was on screen and immediately identified by Brown and his team as Karakova. A stunned silence went around the room knowing the implications of them meeting and what might have been said. Brown then said, "Change target to Karakova. Let's follow her for a while and see where she goes and who she sees."

Her image was brought up several times. She was also walking around the area in a seemingly random pattern. She did not speak to anyone but looked up and down a street before crossing and going out of sight. She was less than 100 yards from the station.

Brown said, "Go back to Goetze, he won't be far away I bet." His image was picked up and this time there was no limp but he was carrying a brief case whereas before he wasn't. "Can we go back and find out where he got the case?" he asked. They tried to find where he had obtained it but with no luck. "Ok let's continue with his movements and see where that leads us." They sat around watching images of Goetze coming into view, walking and then moving out before appearing in a new screen. He appeared in several places, all of them in the vicinity of the station, but not too close. He seemed to be very aware of the normal CCTV cameras but oblivious to the more discreet cameras hidden in recesses and other shop entrances.

He stopped twice and spoke to others, once showing something to a man and apparently asking for directions. On closer examination it was a map and he was pointing to a building which was next to the underground. The person nodded and left. Another monitor picked up his contact and followed him into a Newsagents next to the station. The camera kept on him for fifteen minutes, but he did not appear to come back out.

They finally lost Goetze entering a shopping arcade about two hundred yards from the station and despite all angles did not see him again.

They sat down and started to compile what intelligence they had gleaned from the sightings. It was now certain that at some stage an attempt was going to be made to free Gregorov. They knew that there were going to be a number of assailants because Karakova and Goezte were involved, and their access to manpower and equipment.

There were telephone calls being made to Interpol and the German authorities concerning Goetze and any possible links to others he might have and their whereabouts. Everything was being done as a matter of urgency. No one knew what the next stage might be.

CHAPTER 27

A few moments later there came a report like a clap of thunder, followed by two more in quick succession. The room shook violently and tables and chairs went flying. Some of the terminals crashed to the floor and the walls cracked and windows buckled out. The lights flickered but stayed on. The place filled with dust. Everyone was totally transfixed with the sudden event. Freeman told everyone to stay at their posts and make sure all entrances were covered in case of unauthorised entry. If they need to, they were to shoot to kill, any questions would be addressed later.

Freeman looked at Brown. He was sitting looking much more relaxed than earlier. He went to his desk and issued him with a pistol and five spare magazines. He then said, "I think you might feel more at home with this." He handed him his rifle and rucksack containing his spare ammunition. Brown replied, "Thank you Sir," and checked his weapons and asked what he could do next.

Further rolling explosions were heard in the building, but no gunfire at all. Freeman was a little bemused by this factor and telephoned down to the custody suites. It was answered by one of the close protection officers guarding Gregorov. He said, "They are trying to blow the walls open. They have just rocked us. We are reinforced enough to stave off any sustained attack for at least 30 minutes."

Freeman asked if all the manpower was there and he replied in the affirmative. He further said that he thought the explosions were coming from beneath the building. He further explained that the foundations and security protocols had demanded that there was a minimum of fifteen feet of reinforced concrete below them, so he was not sure why they were trying to enter that way. Freeman said, “It's another diversion, stay at your posts and I'll get some men to you as soon as possible.”

He got onto the phone to Ellis and told him of the situation. Ellis replied that two teams from the SAS had arrived and were available. They would be outside in two transit vans bearing the name of a butcher's company. If someone met them, they would be with them and into position in the security block within moments. Ellis informed Freeman he would brief the squad leader and let them formulate their plans.

Freeman had to trust Brown and told him to go and meet the teams outside. He was to be escorted by one of the police team to the doors. He was then to assist them in any way he could when they set themselves up in the cells block. Brown felt a little surprised and pleased by this turn of events and told him that he would do whatever they wanted and report back to him regularly.

Freeman told him that the only communications to be used were the ones being used on secure channels with the guards in the cell block and the SAS comms. This would be coordinated as they were totally secure and off the grid. He apologised and told him that he had no idea if their normal communications had been compromised or not, but they had to assume that they were.

Brown left the control room and went to the entrance with his escort, opened the door and saw the two vans as described on the other side of the road. He indicated for them to join him. They left their vehicles and ran across the road. Brown greeted them and led them inside and locked the doors down. The armed officers taking up their positions once again.

The leader of the SAS team introduced himself and his men to Brown, who was aware of a couple of them because of training courses he had conducted for the SAS over the years as part of their training. One of the men said, "Good to see you again Gunny. Thought they had put you out grass." There was a general laugh among the teams and he responded, "Not yet and that's what makes it so hard for others to deal with when they know it's me. The first they know it's Captain Brown is when their brains spill out onto the ground and their last thought too!"

They all walked down corridors, silent now except for the whirring of air-conditioners and dust still falling from walls and ceilings. They went down several flights of stairs, all guarded and the necessary security rules were followed at each stage. None of them had any doubt that if they failed to comply the other party would not hesitate to shoot them.

They arrived in the secure centre and found that there were sixteen heavily armed police officers, all alert and very much itching for action. The nervous tension could be cut with a knife. They were not happy that their kingdom could be the centre of attention now or at any time. The individuals they had in the cells were the scum of the earth and deserved to be where they were and even taken out to other places and never heard of again.

Each guard was allocated an SAS buddy and they were to be together until this was all over, one way or another. Brown and the SAS leader, who had introduced himself finally as Sergeant Allan Drake, would be in support between the various pairs. Anything they required would be communicated by Drake to the control room and action taken

Several distinct noises started up, continuous and loud. It was concentrated in an area near to where Gregorov was being kept. Drake reported this back to Freeman who instructed that Gregorov be taken from his cell and taken to a confinement area adjacent to the entrance of the secure cell complex. Freeman did not know whether this was a ploy by the attackers to move him and let them gain better access or they were being outsmarted. Either way, the confinement area was electronically and hermetically sealed against any interference and was around fifty feet from where the noise was emanating.

Brown and Drake organised the removal of Gregorov to his new location. He was sullen as ever, but he moved with confidence. They looked at him and both knew that this was a contingency plan that had been worked out well in advance. They went to where the centre of the perceived activity was taking place. Drake said, "I know that noise." Brown replied "Yeah, thermal lances. They are cutting through the concrete and metal bars. It will be like slicing through hot butter. It will take a while, but they will get in. We need to pinpoint exactly where they are cutting."

Drake radioed to Freeman, who told them he would be sending down some experts who had the equipment to pinpoint the exact location, and the infra-red imagers might give some idea of the number of individuals too. Additionally, a team from the Military had arrived and were doing an exterior sweep of the building and surrounding areas together with ground radar equipment.

Drake asked Freeman to give them regular updates and he instructed the teams to be on high alert and to keep themselves out of the way. There was noise from the other cells and the officers told them to be quiet or the first bullets would be for them. That stopped any more talk from the cells.

They listened to the thermal drilling, not sure how far they were cutting into the concrete, but they estimated there were 4-5 drills working together. Enough to remove quite a sizeable chunk of concrete and metal. From a distance they heard what sounded to be like automatic gun fire for a few minutes before that ceased and just the drilling pierced the quietness.

The radio went and Freeman told them that the outside team had come under fire from a number of persons. Several had been hit but fortunately there had been plain clothes backups in close proximity and they had taken out that particular problem and so the team were resuming their ground investigations.

Drake asked “How have they been able to amass such manpower? I have never seen anything like this in all my service. We had large scale frontal attacks by fanatics in the Middle East, it was like a chicken shoot, but these people have access to all sorts of equipment and expertise.”

Freeman replied, “Our intelligence searches have only just started to get results. The identities of everyone we have eliminated or captured are being processed around the world. Many countries are more than happy to assist us. They don’t want it happening on their own soil.”

Brown could not help but wonder if any of the mercenaries were connected to his company at all. He doubted it, but he could not be sure that some of them were doubling up with other groups, money talked loudly in this field. There was nothing he could do about it now, his main preoccupation now was to survive the next few hours and protect himself and everyone inside the station.

He felt very confused about his feelings. He liked Sarah James and respected Jason King and even Freeman. He certainly didn’t want anything to happen to them, but he also knew they’d probably kill him if the circumstances were right, as he would them.

He needed to let everyone see that he was a professional in all senses. Certainly not give anyone the slightest indication that he was anything other than what he was displaying to his boss and the police. He held his rifle closer and looked at Drake, satisfied they would be able to defeat any asshole who tried to gain access to their home turf.

They patrolled the corridors housing the prisoners and more particularly near the cell that Gregorov was now being detained in. There were the two normal guards, plus their two SAS minders. They looked grim and determined as they stood in their allotted place. Even Drake said to Brown, "From the look on their faces, they are not in the mood to be trifled with." Brown laughed and replied, "Are any of us?"

There was commotion in one of the cells down the corridor, the sound of a wall crumbling, followed by several shots and then silence. This was suddenly repeated several times in quick succession. All the men went into their defensive roles, to the side of each of the cells where the noises had originated. They knew what to expect, another explosion and the doors to be blown outwards.

Blinding flashes and cracker bangs filled the corridor as the doors were blown out. Dust filled the corridor and volleys of gun fire echoed down the corridor as two men each with automatic weapons stepped out. The SAS and police were too well organised for that to cause any problem and short bursts with their weapons soon disabled the incomers.

As they stopped, suddenly flashbangs were thrown out of the cells, followed by another two from each room. Their fire was concentrated on the closest officers and they soon had a number down. Retaliation gunfire from officers further away was deadly and quickly took out the attackers.

Brown and Drake moved amongst the teams. Out of the thirty two there, eight were dead and nine injured. All the sixteen attackers were dead. “A good day’s work.” remarked Drake as he took photos of all the dead terrorists. These were then uploaded to both Freeman and Ellis simultaneously.

They went into the cells which had been breached from outside. A large hole had been cut out of the wall. The occupants of the cells were dead, seemingly executed as they cowered in the corners. They stepped out of the cells and Drake radioed Freeman of the present situation, including the breaches of the walls and the need to follow the route backwards to where it had commenced.

Freeman said he would get more reinforcements to assist them. He could not release any officers from their present positions and he, Drake, was to remain in situ too in case of any further attempts. Freeman commented that he thought that it had been too easy to defend the station and the attack was too simplistic, noisy and ill directed.

Brown agreed and told Freeman that Goetze and Karakova were much too involved to just do that. From his experience with them, they were both very dedicated and detailed in any operation they were involved in. They checked on Gregorov and saw him just sitting in his cell, seemingly care free. He looked at them as they peered through the observation window and waved. Brown could hardly restrain himself, “Cheeky bastard.” he muttered, “There is no way on this earth is he going to get out of here.”

In the aftermath of the onslaught, a meeting was hastily convened. Together with a conference call including the Commissioner and Ellis, it was agreed, that Gregorov was to remain where he was. A number of drones were in the air and an enhanced deployment of police and military would stay in the area for a couple of hours before being gradually withdrawn. This would give the impression that the authorities were satisfied that the attacks were over and that they still had Gregorov safe and secure.

This would enable everyone to regroup and casualties moved out into hospitals and morgues. In addition, all prisoners were also to be removed and transported to other secure sites in the vicinity of London.

Refreshments were handed out as the kitchen had not been touched, so food and drinks were passed around. Brown had his usual sandwich. This time corned beef and tomato with a dash of mustard. Sarah had a cheese pasta dish, Jason a hot curry and Freeman a pork pie with HP sauce!

The corridor which had been attacked was secured with high tensile iron shutters and explosive charges placed at regular intervals should ingress be made through the walls. The holes in the walls had been similarly protected but everyone was sure that anyone would be foolish to try and make entrance the same way in the next wave.

They all drank coffee, hot and black, to give them more energy before settling down to discuss what they were going to do later. They knew that Goetze and Karakova would not give up easily. The area had been scoured for any sightings of them but, until now, they were like ghosts, invisible, but no doubt plotting and organising.

CHAPTER 28

Back in Aldershot, Ellis was getting an update on the calls made to Afghanistan and, more importantly, and interestingly, the coded messages which Brown had sent were all found to have been received in the same location. The calls had been made to an encrypted phone which was, in fact, allocated to a UK military unit based in Helmand Province. The coded messages were logged into a laptop issued to the British intelligence services, again in Helmand. Ellis had arranged for one of the senior officers in the camp to discover where the phone and laptop actually was and who might have access to it.

He contacted Freeman with the news, who said, “He is being kept busy right now. He doesn’t have access to any phones or electrical equipment at the moment because of the situation at the station.” He further added, “There is an SAS Sergeant with him at all times, and he is the one with the communications. Do you want Brown to return to you?”

Ellis responded, “No not yet. We haven’t identified exactly who he has been communicating with and, until we do, it’s better he is well away from here.” Freeman said, “Agreed If we survive this shit, he will be all yours.”

“Do you know where Goetze and Karakova are?” asked Ellis. Freeman responded by saying “Not far from us I can be sure, but they are keeping out of sight for now.”

Ellis told Freeman that if he needed anything, he only needed to ask. Freeman thanked him and the line was cut.

Drake and Brown went around the perimeter of the station checking on all the security aspects, making sure everything was locked down. There didn't seem to be any weak spots. There were sufficient men inside the station to defend it. They surmised that there were enough police and soldiers outside too. They knew that the Prime Minister didn't want to attract too much attention as to what was happening here, but it had gone way beyond that in their eyes.

They met up with Freeman and the two Inspectors. Sarah asked, "Have we heard anything from Ellis yet? Any more identifications or communications over the airwaves?"

Freeman replied, "He has a few irons in the fire, some developments in Asia and the Middle East, but no positive ID's yet or where the communication was pinpointed." He did not look at anyone in particular, just turned his head to each of them as he spoke. Brown kept quiet, trying to read anything into what Freeman had said but he felt that if there was anything more positive, then Freeman would have said so. He seemed an upfront person.

Their discussions were interrupted by a number of whistling sounds and the heavy percussion of explosions on the roof and upper floors. They all looked at each other and shouted "mortars!" and took cover behind tables and chairs. The noises were shattering and they knew that the mortar shells were landing in different places in the station, weakening the structure.

"Where in hell did they come from?" shouted Drake. Freeman was already on the phone to the outside and shouting instructions "Find those infernal mortars. Get the drones higher and see where they are being launched from!"

The incoming shells were ceaseless for a few minutes before they slowly fizzled out. Sarah called out to see if anyone was injured. Fortunately, there were no casualties, but from other areas, notably the higher floors, they had sustained extensive damage and injuries.

The roof and top floor had caved in onto the lower floor. A large number of fires were burning. Efforts were being made to trace and rescue officers who had been on the different levels.

The Commissioner came on line and told Freeman that six different mortar sites had been identified. What was most worryingly was that some of the mortars were multi shelled and were the latest in weaponry. They had now been neutralised. There were a lot of civilian casualties too.

Freeman said, "They are just pushing us a bit at a time. How can we fight back this enemy when we have no idea who they are and how many there are." The Commissioner responded, "The Prime Minister has every confidence in you." and closed the line.

"Bloody women sitting back there in their ivory towers while everyone is getting the crap kicked out of them. Of course, we will beat these animals but we need the backing of the bosses. I don't intend to be hung out to dry if this goes wrong." Freeman said probably a bit too loud, as everyone turned and looked at him. "Sorry folks," he said, Sometimes she really gets up my back."

A report came through that the facilities holding Gregorov was still holding firm. There was minor damage to some walls being cracked but overall, the superstructure was intact.

Freeman gathered his senior officials around him and said, "We have to do something quickly or it's going to end up in a blood bath, both in here and in the streets. Does anyone have any ideas, sensible ones please!"

They all laughed. Over the next twenty minutes a number of ideas were thrown out, the pros and cons debated, and dismissed for a variety of reasons. Eventually Drake came up with a solution which made sense.

It was proposed that the building would be evacuated in its entirety. All personnel would leave through the underground car park in any vehicle available and still useable. Gregorov would be changed into a police officer's uniform and taken out as one of the injured first. He would be on a stretcher. He would be tied down and his face covered in blood as to prevent any possible recognition. He would, of course, be tranquilised too. Several officers would be in the same position so as to show anyone watching that there were serious casualties being taken out.

Mid-way through the evacuation there would be seen to be a prisoner, under a heavy blanket, being taken out of the facility and placed into a heavy armoured carrier and whisked away at speed. In reality the person being removed under the blanket would be Drake. That vehicle would be escorted by several polices vehicles, front and rear, with all lights and sirens working. They would head out of London and make their way towards Aldershot. On route, they were to be met by armoured personnel carriers and escorted into Aldershot, where they would convene at the tank range and assault wing. There they would be protected by several columns of soldiers in the event of any attempt to secure the release of the prisoner there.

In the meantime, the actual prisoner would be taken firstly to a hospital so as to not give any suspicion that it was not genuine. There would be minimal police presence in the form of armed guards. The injured would be accompanied into the hospital by two armed officers from the station. Once in the hospital, Gregorov would be removed from his stretcher and uniform and given hospital clothing. He would be taken to the mortuary in the basement of the hospital and kept there for a few hours. He would then be placed in a coffin and taken out of the hospital in a hearse, which was common practice for the area.

He would then be taken to an undertaker. Again, from there he would be kept until the next day when a funeral had been arranged for him at a local crematorium. A service would be held. He would be dispatched through the curtains, looking for all intents and purposes that he was being cremated.

He would remain there until it was dark and then he would be transported to Bradbury Lines by helicopter. There would be enough false trails interconnected that would make it impossible for anyone to track.

They all agreed with that proposal. Freeman phoned the Commissioner of the intended plan and told her to make the necessary arrangements for it to occur within the next two hours.

He rang Ellis and got his approval. He said he would contact Bradbury Lines and make the arrangements there. He thought it would make a good exercise for the garrison and keep them on their toes

Over the course of the next hour everyone was gathered together from all floors and with whom they were dealing with. All computers were wiped clean and electrical equipment destroyed. There would be no electronic footprints left behind.

At 4pm, as planned the gates opened and the first convoy of vehicles carrying the injured officers sped out of the station. They were soon out of sight and nothing untoward was happening, which was a relief to all inside.

Ten minute later the next squad of heavily armed officers left the floor and went down to the car park area. In the midst was a man with a blanket over his head. He was hurried into an armoured carrier which then accompanied by a convoy of cars, shot out of the building and into the surrounding streets. Roads were cleared in advance for them and soon they were on the M4 and then the M3 as they sped towards Aldershot.

Freeman suddenly heard the encrypted radio come to life. Someone was shouting, "We are under attack from the air and road. We are taking heavy fire, but we have not been stopped yet."

A response came back, "We will be with you in thirty seconds Two helicopters have been sighted and firing on the convoy. Our people have been told to take them out immediately. The road vehicles will be intercepted this minute and the occupants captured if possible. Otherwise, the order is for them to be killed if they resist, which we hope they do."

Freeman called back, "We need prisoners! Keep a few breathings so we can get at them."

"Will do Sir." came the retort. Freeman was doubtful that his words would mean much in the present situation. There was radio silence for a few minutes and then the man on the other end said "Two choppers down, no survivors. Four vehicles stopped and taken out, three survivors, one of whom is injured." Freeman smiled and replied "Good work. Now get to your destination quickly before anything else happens. How is Drake?"

"Pissed off sir," came the reply and laughter. Stuck under a blanket while all the others were enjoying themselves, he'll be expecting some of your best whisky later!!"

"Tell him fine, he deserves a bottle to himself having put himself through that." The radio went quiet, and Freeman told the rest of the officers to be ready to leave.

"Are the charges in place?" He asked. The reply was affirmative and all placed where they would cause maximum impact. Freeman said, "Set the timer for ten minutes. We'll be far enough away from here, and the cordon around the building fixed and safe enough."

As he got into the lead vehicle to leave the battered station, a blonde woman walked from the side and stood in front of his car. "What the hell!" Freeman exclaimed as he saw Brigita Karakova standing in front of him with her arms outstretched to signify she was not armed. He stopped, turned to his passenger and said, "Disarm the explosives immediately. We don't all want to go up in a big bang." The passenger flicked a few buttons and told Freeman all was secure.

She approached the car and said to him "This has gone on long enough, we need to end it now, peacefully." Freeman was shocked and said, "How do you propose to do that?"

She replied, "I have contacts and we shall have a conference. The Russian Ambassador, Kierov Amorich, is willing to host the meeting. At that level I think both the Prime Minister and Commissioner of Police should attend along with yourself. You can nominate the time of meeting. I do want my husband, Viktor Gregorov there too."

She further added that she was not opposed to it being recorded and filmed if it made them more comfortable.

Freeman told her to get into the vehicle as he wanted to leave the station as soon as possible. He would be consulting the Commissioner of Police in the terms Karakova had described. As the convoy drove out, he nodded to his passenger who then reset the timer for the explosives. He was immediately on the phone to the Commissioner and told her of what had transpired. She told Freeman to keep Karakova with him and she would talk to the Prime Minister. The line was cut.

Freeman asked why she wanted Gregorov to be present She responded "He is my husband I'd like to see him one last time before we are separated for good. The Russian Ambassador is happy with the arrangements. Of course, he is still your prisoner, like I am now. There have been too many lives lost and damage caused. We are at an impasse and I don't want to it to go on."

Freeman was satisfied that she was being honest with him but, for the life of him, could not understand the change of heart.

As they drove away from the station, they heard a series of muffled explosions and as he looked into the driver's mirror saw puffs of smoke rising and the building collapsing in on itself. She looked at him and said, "Lucky we didn't pursue our efforts to enter the building to get Viktor." He smiled to himself and thought an even bigger pity she didn't.

His phone rang and he saw it was the Commissioner. She said, "The PM has agreed to this. She will speak with him directly to sort a time and place convenient, but it will be on our terms, make no mistake about it."

He replied, "Yes ma'am, I'll pass on the information."

He told Karakova of what had been discussed, and said, "We just wait until it's all organised and can get everyone together, including your husband." She replied, "Thank you, that will be special."

Freeman asked where Goetze was and how he fitted into all this? She replied, "I will give you his location at the meeting. He has done his work well, but he has let us all down, so I have no loyalty to him."

They drove in silence to a barracks in London where they dismounted and went in and showered and had a meal. It was a waiting game now. When Karakova came out from her changing room, Freeman was amazed at the difference in her. Now she was smart, her hair done up in a bun, with make up on and nice clothes. He thought to himself, he didn't think Gregorov will be half as smart as that.

As they finished their meal. The Commissioner rang and told him that the meeting was arranged for 6pm that evening. It was to be held in the basement of Cambridge House, the headquarters of MI5 and MI6. Freeman was told that neither Ellis nor his staff would be present as they were dealing with another matter which may have a reflection on the talks later.

Freeman was not overly surprised by her comments, having been in constant communication with Ellis, so he kept silent when she told him. He told Sarah and Jason to remain at the barracks until he called them, and meet up with him at an address, which he would give to them at the time.

CHAPTER 29

At 5:45pm they left the barracks and took the short drive to Cambridge House, where they were met by several officials and escorted to a room which had no windows. Down the centre of the room was a long table with seating set out for four persons on one side and another four on the other side.

The Prime Minister, together with the Commissioner of Police entered the room, with the Ambassador and another man. As they all stood in their respective places, they were all introduced to one another. The other individual was the Head of Security at the Russian Embassy. They took their places at the table and a few moments later Gregorov was escorted into the room and placed in a chair next to the Head of Security, who had identified himself as Boris Chenkov. Gregorov looked around and asked why he was there. He looked over at Freeman, recognising him, but not the others. He twisted and saw the Ambassador and said under his breath, "You snake, what are you doing to me?"

At that moment Karakova entered. She looked at him and smiled, "Finally back together my love." she said. He looked at her stunned, and just whispered, "My love, I have missed you so much." She replied, "We are together now, that's all that matters."

Freeman said, "Ok, you wanted the meeting, now let's get on with it. What do you want or expect out of it, bearing in mind you are prisoners within the United Kingdom. Even your own country has disavowed you."

Karakova said, "I understand what you are saying and the crimes we have committed against your people were needless and got out of control. All we intended was the assassination of that butcher, Constantine Burlov. He was the target given to us by our superiors, the details of who I will not give you until later. We didn't know about the other killings at that stage. From then onwards it just went crazy. We put men and equipment into place. Personally, neither myself or Viktor had anything to do with the placing of the explosives or the gas. This was down to Goetze and his cleanup crew."

She continued, "The Old Bailey was not us, not that I know of, nor was the Waterloo bombing. I admit we had been on the train and got off at Ashford, but were returning to UK to see what was happening about Viktor."

She looked across at the Ambassador, who felt obliged to respond. He commented, "What she has said is true. She has been in contact with the Embassy from the outset for very personal reasons."

Viktor continued, "Brigita and myself have been part of an undercover team for the past four years. We have been following and taking out certain individuals who were identified as being either a threat to the Russian State or their criminal actions were undermining the economic stability of our country. I am responsible for the attempted assassination of your Morgan. I was instructed to remove him as he knew to many details concerning the leadership within Russia. My superiors were getting worried that he was going to disclose some operations which were being discussed with other parties."

He continued, "Unfortunately, we were not prepared for his vehicle to have bullet proof glass, so we had to abort that and of course all the other events took over. But a word of warning, make sure Morgan is still kept safe. The contract will still be valid until fulfilled. Look closer to home to see who that is, they are not here today I notice."

He continued, "I have used many aliases over the years and been associated with several countries, Germany included. My real name is Viktor, but not Gregorov, it is Tsarin. For our operations we are told the target and given staff who coordinate with the people involved in weapons, identities and transport. Goetze was one such person. He had been recruited three years ago for an operation in Latvia. He was excellent at his work and we did not question his capabilities as to how he obtained backups and hardware."

Brigita then said, "He became part of the team and was sanctioned at the highest level to do what was necessary to support us. Everything was fine until this time. Viktor was taken to the safe house as per instructions but for some reason the normal security was compromised. In order to protect him, Goetze, for reasons unknown, did what he did at the safe house and on the motorway.

Obviously, we knew there was going to be this outcry and although Viktor did have diplomatic status, but it was not what you think. It was decided that he would lose that protection in order to maintain the covers we had built. As you know the Ambassador spoke with Viktor and explained the situation. It was agreed between them that this was the best course of action."

The Ambassador looked over to the Prime Minister and told her that everything Viktor had said was true to the best of his knowledge.

The Prime Minister said, "If you maintain that you were not involved in the attacks on The Old Bailey nor Waterloo station, which I find hard to believe, then who was it? What do you know about it?"

Karakova said, "You need to look a lot closer to home. They arranged it all with plenty of money and assistance. You have traitors in your midst as much as we do."

There was a silence on the part of the British participants, until Freeman said, "We are exploring different avenues on that score and hopefully we will come to a fruitful conclusion."

The Commissioner and Prime Minister looked at him in a bemused manner but said nothing further.

"Then why did you find it necessary to try and release Gregorov or Tsarin, whatever his name is?" asked the Commissioner. "If you are now so against this bloodshed, what has made you suddenly change your mind. You have destroyed a police station, killed a large number of officers, as well as men on your own side. What was the rationale?"

Karakova responded, “We were told by Goetze that there was easy access into the station. He then organised it all. I spoke with him on several occasions and warned him of the dangers involved. I said that Viktor might get killed himself and that was the last thing I wanted to happen. So, when all of Goetze’s plans failed, as I knew they surely would, and you were about to leave the building, then that’s when I made my approach to you.”

“You might not like it, but we are professionals too and what had happened was not good for our country or for any decent persons who have lost loved ones. We only removed the bad apples, as do you of course, with your operatives. I specifically know Captain Brown as being particularly effective at the disposing of people on behalf of your Government.”

The Prime Minister remained quiet but looked across at the Commissioner and Freeman, acknowledging the fact.

Viktor looked across at Brigita and gave a subtle nod. She then said, “You can get Goetze right now. He is at Rose Cottage in Bromley, with his team. As far as he is concerned, he is being evacuated out of the country this evening.” The ambassador handed Freeman a phone and said, “I know for a fact he is there. I won’t say from what sources obviously, but he is yours for the taking. Send in your men.”

The Commissioner looked over to Freeman and told him to contact SO19 but to leave the local police out of it. This was to be a covert operation and she did not want any screw ups. Lethal force was authorised if any resistance was made.

Whilst Freeman made the call, the Prime Minister and the ambassador spoke together and agreed that there was to be no identification of either Gregorov or Karakova. It would be preferable if all blame was placed on Goetze and who ever this other group was.

Freeman was unhappy with the politics being played and said, “But aren’t we charging these two with their involvement in crimes too?”

Karakova replied quickly, “Viktor and me will accept all responsibilities for our actions in your country. It will mean that we will never see each other again after today but at least we will feel that we have achieved peace together.”

Viktor said, “We have more sets of disclosures to make. No one, not even the Ambassador is aware of this, and I believe once we have told you it will be too important ever to be disclosed.”

All eyes were on them and Brigita said, “My real name is Brigita Tsurin. I am the daughter of the Russian President.” There was a stunned silence around the table before she added, “Viktor is my husband and we met when we were both sent to the operations wing of the Russian Secret Service. We will never say anything against my father. We request that you respect our wishes, in view of how we have brought this meeting about and told you everything.”

The Ambassador was stunned. He whispered to his Security chief. The Prime Minister did the same with the Commissioner. Freeman felt the odd one out in this almost surreal experience.

The Ambassador said, "Yes we will respect your wishes, but I am not sure how the President will take all this."

Brigita said, "He knows about this and sanctioned our meeting. Don't worry, after all this is over you will be well looked after for all your troubles."

She then said, "Viktor and myself do have one favour to request and hope that it is granted. We have been together for so many years and we have truly only loved each other. Before each operation we remove all jewellery including our wedding bands and, after the conclusion, we return them to our fingers. We are asking you all that you grant this request. It will be the last time they are removed as we will never be involved in any actions from today."

The Prime Minister replied, "Under the circumstances I do not have any objections, does anyone else?" Nobody said anything. Freeman was a little surprised at such a request, but it seemed trivial to refuse them.

Brigita took two rings out of her pocket. Viktor took one and placed it on her finger and she placed the other on his finger. Matching rings in every way. They touched hands and sat back. They smiled at each other and rubbed the rings gently. A few moments later, Brigita's eyes rolled back and she slumped to the table, quickly followed by Viktor.

"Oh god what has happened?" Shouted the Ambassador. Freeman quickly went to Viktor while the Security Chief went to Brigita. They both felt for any pulse but looked at each other and shook their heads.

No one seemed to move for what appeared to be minutes but was in fact only seconds. The Commissioner and Prime Minister, both sat stunned and the Ambassador appeared to be in tears "What can I tell the President, her father." he cried.

Freeman asked if either Viktor or Brigita had been searched prior to arrival. From his personal knowledge he knew that Viktor had been in police uniform when taken to the hospital and then given his clothes by one of the SAS men. His main concern was Brigita. He was unsure how she had been dealt with from the time of her appearance to her death. Was she searched when they were in the Barracks? How had she concealed the rings on her body? These were questions still to be asked in depth, and in the very near future.

The Prime Minister and the Ambassador rose and told them to remain where they were as they had calls to make and left the room, leaving the others sitting with the two bodies. Chenkov said to the Commissioner, "What do we do now? Who has jurisdiction over the bodies?"

She replied, "At the risk of avoiding a major political row between our two countries, I think we are going to have to make this a joint effort but with certain boundaries between each party."

Freeman thought to himself, that was typical political double talk and blame shifting. I'm the most junior officer here and responsible for bringing Karakova, or whoever she might be, to this room.

Chenkov nodded and said, "We will wait until my Ambassador and your Prime Minister return. They are undoubtedly on a face-saving mission as we speak. I would not like to be in their shoes telling the President that his daughter is dead, having committed suicide while talking to the British Authorities."

The Commissioner responded, "She will be getting advice as to who is going to get shafted and it won't be her if she has her way, that's for sure." They all laughed at that to break the sombre mood prevailing in the room.

"What are we going to do about the bodies?" asked Chenkov. Freeman replied, "We have a very good and discreet team of forensic scientists and pathologists. We can certainly get them here. Of course, you would have total access to all that's going on. But I think we will have to wait until our seniors arrive back."

They sat and looked at the bodies. Both their heads laying on the table, looking at each other through unseeing eyes. It was like a surreal exhibition of two figures, showing no signs of injuries, but smiling at each other in the face of death. It was macabre to say the least, but they could not do anything until they were further instructed.

Chenkov went to the bureau and poured himself a drink, "Anyone else need a booster after this?" he asked. "Do you have coffee?" said the Commissioner. Chenkov nodded and poured her a cup. He looked over at Freeman who also indicated yes. He poured the coffees and handed them out.

They all sat in silence, each in their own thoughts. Freeman was of course aware that the meeting had been recorded and in all probability was still being recorded. He knew that Chenkov would have also been aware but was not sure how much notice the Commissioner had taken when the details were announced.

After a few minutes the Prime Minister and the Ambassador walked in together, both looking very sombre, but also were not as worried as when they left earlier.

He commenced "I have spoken to my President. He is very perturbed at the circumstances of their deaths, particularly his daughter. He is most concerned that it had occurred on British soil and expects the full cooperation of the British authorities in this matter."

The Prime Minister followed this up by saying, "I have given him my full assurance that whatever is decided in respect of this incident, it will be carried out according to his wishes. On behalf of the British Government, I sent him our sincerest condolences. He said thank you, but she got what she deserved and now we have clear up this mess."

They all looked at one another on this information. Freeman knew a cover up was in the making, but he was going to keep that to himself.

The Prime minister said "The Ambassador and myself want you to come up with a solution to this problem now. Their bodies will be taken to the mortuary at St Georges Hospital where they will be entered as a Jane and John Doe.

From there it depends on what solution you can come up with. Be careful who you talk to. Their true identities are never to be revealed. The Ambassador and myself will remain in the building until we get a solution. If you have any questions of a national matter, please ask us, otherwise we will leave it to you."

Freeman looked across at the Prime Minister and said, "Plausible liability by any chance Prime Minister?" She glared at him and went to leave the room. Before she got to the door, Freeman said, "I assume all the information they gave us can be kept and used by our authorities, in a discreet manner, of course?"

The Prime Minister looked to the Ambassador who shrugged and nodded. She told Freeman that as long as the sources did not become known then yes it could be. She and the Ambassador then left the room.

Chenkov started by saying that they had two unidentified bodies of two apparently healthy persons, one male and one female. No sign of injuries, suggesting a possible overdose of drugs.

Freeman continued that they had been found in an old warehouse facility by the edge of the Thames, which was notorious for being used by druggies and homeless people.

Chenkov responded by saying that they were not malnourished or unkempt as if they were drug users, so that would possibly draw suspicion in an investigation. Freeman agreed with his opinion.

Freeman countered by saying they had been found at the rear of a club in downtown London. It would mean changing their clothes into a trendier set but that would help with their overall condition.

They would be discovered by an anonymous passerby who rang the police. They would discover them and report it in and enforce a cordon around the scene. The control room would send a CID unit, who were in actual fact specialist officers, and they would conduct an enquiry. The bodies would be taken to St Georges, as it had the least bodies after all the trauma of the past few days.

The Post-mortem would be conducted by Dr Graham Webster, who had dealings with the incidents that had taken place. He would establish the cause of death and, most importantly the source of the poison which killed the two individuals. He would then give cause of death as a drug overdose.

From the post-mortem, the identity of the two bodies would be ascertained, both being English. A next of kin would claim them and the bodies handed over for a funeral. They would be cremated. The ashes would then be taken to the Russian Embassy and conveyed to Russia for a service and burial there.

The Prime Minister and the Ambassador were asked to join them and the situation outlined to them. They both agreed in principal and again left to make the arrangements for such actions to be carried out.

No one felt comfortable with what was to take place and both Freeman and the Commissioner felt cheated that due process had not been carried out but, being the pragmatists, knew that this was the only course that could be taken bearing in mind the political implications.

About 15 minutes later, the two re-entered the room and the Prime Minister said, “All arrangements are in hand. The Home Secretary has spoken with Doctor Webster and given him a full update. He will do it as he is asked to because of the international undertones but under protest. “

She went on to say, “A couple have been told and they know what to do They belong to the Services and will act accordingly. The funeral home and crematorium do not need to know the background.”

The Ambassador continued, “Once the proceedings at the crematorium are completed the couple can claim the ashes. From there they will be transported to the Embassy where they will be flown to Moscow. The President will meet the plane himself and the ashes of both of them will be taken to the family vault outside Moscow where they will be interred. As far as the Russian public are concerned, they will have died in a tragic accident whilst driving.”

As they were talking there was a knock on the door and on opening it four paramedics wearing hazmat suits entered the room to remove the bodies to the mortuary. They zipped up the two bodies into bags, being careful not to touch their hands, which were then loaded on to trollies and taken from the room.

The team regrouped around the table. The Ambassador spoke first. He said, "Thank you for doing what you can. I am sorry that what they did has caused so much misery to your country and individuals. My knowledge of their operations was kept deliberately from me. Chenkov, being head of security obviously was aware, but please don't blame him, he was acting on orders from Russia and you don't refuse them."

The Prime Minister replied, "Mr Ambassador, if there is anything we have learnt today it's that we have to be on higher alert for any future incidents."

The Ambassador responded, "Yes, and you have access to all the tapes and recordings of today, use them wisely. I ask that you supply me with a copy of the transcript at some time in the future. There is absolutely no hurry I can assure you. Not even Moscow is aware that we recorded any of this, and neither of us are likely to say anything.

Chenkov nodded his agreement and the Ambassador went on to say, "Chenkov will be available as a liaison officer for as long as the British want. He will be available twenty fours a day and provide his personal number, and he will report only to me and no one else."

The Prime Minister concluded by saying, "All arrangements for the bodies are outside your areas of operations from now. I am overseeing all the aspects within the United Kingdom until the ashes are handed over to the Ambassador. From there he will take charge of the Russian side of the affair. Does anyone have any questions?"

Freeman had many questions still unanswered but he kept his thoughts to himself for another day, when it would be more appropriate to ask them.

The meeting broke up and everyone left except Freeman and Chenkov. Freeman said, "Let's get the tapes and go through them at our pace and time. In the quiet light of day there will be many matters which were forgotten in the heat of the moment."

He added, "I have two officers who have been involved in every aspect of this case, who I trust implicitly and would give us further insight into some of the comments made."

Chenkov nodded and said, "Sure, I welcome any further expertise, but I do want to be with you. I am fearful of being left out of the loop if you get my meaning."

Freeman made a call and, within seconds, a number of officials in coveralls were in the room, undoing cabling and unplugging cameras and microphones. So much stuff that even Freeman and Chenkov were impressed by the sheer magnitude of what was available for them to look at and listen to.

Whilst the equipment was being removed, Freeman asked Chenkov if he would be prepared to be seconded to his team, given a new identity of course, and assist in their enquiries. Chenkov was amazed at such an offer and said "Of course, we have to trust each other in times like this.

What accent would you like me to use?" He laughed and said, "I can be from anywhere you want me to be from."

Freeman said, "How about South African? Their language would meld into your accent. I'll get you fixed with an ID now. Chenkov smiled and said, in a very passable south African accent "Yes boss."

Freeman rang Sarah and Jason and told them to meet him at Cambridge House. They would be met there and taken to where he was currently situated. He also reminded them not to carry any arms. The occupants of the building would provide enough security for them all.

Twenty minutes later they arrived at the building and were escorted to a room in which Freeman was seated together with another man they had never seen before. Freeman shook their hands and said that they had a lot to catch up on. Of course, neither Sarah nor Jason were yet aware of what had transpired.

Chenkov was introduced to them both, firstly by his correct name and title, then they were told that in future he was to be known as Fredrick Steenson. Sarah and Jason looked over to Freeman who said, "It will all become very clear soon enough, but he can and will be trusted as an equal for the duration of this case."

He continued "In the meantime, the four of us will be going through all of the recordings and audios, to try and find anything, however small, that may help make sense of the last few weeks."

Freeman and Chenkov explained what had transpired since the early evening and what was going to happen over the next few days. Sarah and Jason sat there incredulously and kept trying to take in everything that had taken place.

Freeman said, "It will become a lot clearer when you watch the interviews and listen to the audio. Whatever you see and whatever you hear will not and I repeat will not, be mentioned outside this room unless authorised at the very highest level, do you understand?"

Sarah replied, "Of course sir." She looked across to Chenkov and said, "Welcome Fredrick Steenson to the team." He smiled back and said, "It is an honour to be working with you and Jason. I hope that we can complete this mission as soon as possible."

CHAPTER 30

Back at the tank range in Aldershot, everything was being stood down. All personnel had been briefed and told that both Gregorov and the female suspect who had also been arrested, were currently being interviewed in London. There was a general backslapping and congratulations of each other, but tinged with sadness that some of their members had not made it to safety.

Drake was smiling, the fact that the diversion had worked was a good military move and one he had done a few times in the past too. Brown said, “That went down well.” But there was no cheer in his voice or eyes. He was concerned at what Gregorov and Karakova might have said, not necessarily about him alone, but on his organisation too.

Their thoughts were interrupted by Ellis as he walked into the hangar. He congratulated them all on the duties they had performed and said, “Both prisoners were being interviewed at length. Hopefully in the not too distant future, tangible results would be forthcoming and follow up measures taken, which would entail the military. In the meantime, relax, get some food into yourselves and await new instructions.”

Unbeknown to either Drake, and, more importantly Brown, Ellis had already been in contact with Freeman and the basic outline of what had occurred had been transmitted. The most sensitive issues, including their deaths had not been disclosed, but comments about looking closer to home had been mentioned by both Gregorov and Karakova. Ellis briefed him as what he had ascertained so far about the codes, and it was agreed that they would meet in the next day or so and discuss what further paths could be taken. In the meantime, Brown would stay with Ellis and in the control room and see what transpired from there.

Ellis went back to the control room and obtained the final information in respect of the coded messages to Afghanistan. The operator told him that both the phone and the laptop had been allocated to a Sergeant Joan Williams, aged 32 years old. She had been serving in the intelligence corps in Helmand since 2018. She was responsible for translating documents seized from the Taliban and other rebel groups.

She had a degree in languages from Oxford and had been in the army for four years. Prior to being posted to Afghanistan she had been posted to the Ministry of Defence and to GCHQ near Cheltenham. There were no blemishes on her service record and she had received complimentary reports from all her supervising officers.

According to her file she was single and lived in barrack accommodation, wherever she was posted. Her parents lived in Diss and she was an only child. They were still obtaining information discreetly on her but so far, they had found nothing toward.

The messages were all incoming and there had been no outgoing communications from any devices, or from any computers that she had access too. Her billet at Helmand had been searched, but again, with nothing found.

Ellis did not want to jump the gun on any of this and told the operator to continue to monitor any communications now that the army personnel were back at the site. In his mind there would be a coordinated operation on Brown and Williams, but first he needed to understand what Freeman and his team had discovered during their interviews.

Drake and Brown joined him after a while. Brown still finishing yet another sandwich. Ellis joked, "Do you ever eat anything else Kevin?" He laughed and said, "Always room for a sandwich, any time of the day or night."

Brown asked if there had been any further news from London to which Ellis responded, "From what I have been told, they are giving us dribs and drabs, prolonging it all. It's going to take time to put it all together. They are both talking, they seem to have accepted their fate, but testing them, I think that Freeman is getting a bit hot under the collar with them."

Brown looked at Drake and said, "Give us ten minutes with them sir, they'll wish they had never been born!" Ellis smiled, "I have no doubt that with your combined skills they would be singing like canaries and hung up by their toenails. Unfortunately, in view of everything that has occurred they are playing this by the book. The only leeway they have is that they are being treated as terrorists. That means they do not have access to lawyers, and they have unlimited time."

He added, “One note of interest is that they have forgone any request for lawyers and made a promise that the interviewers will have full access to their records and operations.”

Brown mused out loud, “Why have they suddenly decided to spill everything? They must know they are going to prison for the rest of their lives. Gregorov can’t rely on the Russian authorities to bail him out, and goodness knows where Karakova fits into all this, she is a bit player as far as my sources told me.”

Ellis answered, “I am sure we are going to find out soon enough. I have a feeling that there are many threads to this story which are only just being told. I think that the next few days are going to get very interesting indeed.”

Brown said he was going to see if any further information had been received from either his Mossad or NSA contacts. He had not been in the room and in contact since the previous day. He went across to his terminal, Ellis nodded to the operator who opened his terminal and sat back.

Drake stood and watched with Ellis. He didn’t say anything, but from the outset of him being with Brown, there was obviously something that Ellis was not telling him directly, just subtle hints, like the radio back in the police station. He kept his silence and watched how Ellis reacted to what was going on.

Brown dialled into his login code and password, and immediately logged again into his other site. He made a number of keystrokes on his computer, then logged out again. He then went to his emails and found that he has received one new one from each of the two agencies. He read them and had them printed. He approached Ellis, who had received the indication from his operator that Brown had in fact double logged in as before.

Brown handed Ellis the first email which confirmed that Gregorov had been ostracised by the Russian Government on the instructions of the President himself. They wondered why it was the direct involvement of the President that had led to that course of action. Brown said, "How the hell did Gregorov get to be in such a position that it took the President himself to disavow him."

Ellis replied, "Perhaps the interviews will tell us, they know that information obviously." Brown went on to say that there was little information on Karakova that was not already known. She was an enigma, but so far Mossad, for all their resources, could not find anything deeper.

The second email from the NSA, which he handed to Ellis, referred to Gregorov and an operation he had undertaken in Germany some years previous and how Goetze has come to be involved in their group. The email gave some insight into the workings of the organisation but did not give any leads as to who was in control of them and why they were targeting specific individuals.

Ellis said to Brown, "Good work Kevin, do you think we will get much more from our sources?"

Brown replied, “I’ll keep trying, maybe try others, but they are not so well placed as the two I have been in regular contact with.” Ellis responded by saying, “Good man, keep at it. We need to give whatever assistance we can to the police, which will then get us involved. We want a piece of the action too!” He laughed and turned and went back into his office.

Once in his office, he rang Freeman and told him of the developments at his end. Freeman told him that they were going through the interviews and there were references to individuals “closer to home” involved in various terrorist activities.

Ellis said, “I hate to admit it, but I think we know who it is, don’t you?” Freeman replied, “Its looking more and more like it. What we need is the details of the organisation he is with. I think the Sergeant is just another cog in the wheel.” Ellis agreed and said he would be in touch, Freeman said, “We can meet at 10:00am tomorrow and we’ll have a full scale discussion. Just you and Drake from your end. I’ll text the location to you, delete it when you have read it.”

Ellis went back out and called Brown and Drake over. He said to Drake, “I need you to drive me up to Bradbury Lines tomorrow, be ready to leave here at 0600 hours. Kevin, you will be in charge of the control room until I get back. I anticipate it will be sometime later in the afternoon”. They both acknowledged the orders, both for very different reasons.”

During the rest of the day Ellis kept to himself. He did not talk to Drake any more than he did with Brown. He spoke with his operator and told him that he would be out of the area the next day, and perhaps at some stage, the IT system might crash for a few hours and he and the other geeks will have to repair and reboot the system.

The operator understood immediately and said that will be arranged overnight when it was quieter. He would personally make the system crash and be part of the team that repaired it.

At around 2100 hours, Ellis told all personnel to stand down fully, they were confined to barracks, but be ready at short notice, if the circumstances warranted it. Brown asked if he could leave and go and get new clothes. Ellis reminded him that as his senior officer he had to remain and take control if need be. Brown knew he could not argue with that and reluctantly nodded and replied, “Yes Sir”.

CHAPTER 31

In London, the interviews and audios had been seen and listened to several times by the four of them, both as a group and individually. Notes had been taken by them and were being collated and written up. They were all amazed as to what had been revealed during the interviews. The majority of it was too sensitive for any form of public disclosure, and probably most it will ultimately get buried in the depths of some underground bunker, never to see the light of day again.

Freeman had spoken with the Commissioner of Police several times during the evening to update her. He finally said that he had invited Ellis and Sgt Drake to attend a meeting tomorrow. He asked if she would chair the meeting, given the seriousness of the situation. She replied, "I will talk to the Prime Minister, she needs to know, but I am sure she will be ok with it, and you can vouch for the two army personnel?" Freeman replied, "They can be trusted 100% Ellis is looking at the problem from their side and Drake, being an SAS Sgt, I would trust with my life, he is no fool."

The Commissioner answered, "I'll ring her and tell what you have got so far and what you plan to do." She rang off.

They waited for about ten minutes and when the Commissioner rang back, she said, "Now that's a surprise, she must have nothing better to do, like running the country. She will be in attendance too and sit in on it all. She had said you, Freeman, will chair the meeting, but we will all have input."

Freeman was surprised at the turn of events, but said, "Yes Commissioner."

The Commissioner replied, "We will meet you there at 9:30am and you can brief us before the army people arrive." He replied "Of course, everything will be ready on your arrival."

He turned to the others and said, "What's her game? She never does anything without a reason and everything to deflect any criticism from herself."

Chenkov shrugged his shoulders and just said, "It is politics." They all laughed and continued their research in preparation for the next day.

At 0600 hours the next day Ellis entered his control room, only to find that there had been a power surge during the night and that it had taken over an hour to get it fixed. Brown and Drake both arrived together and were told what had happened.

Ellis said he had been briefed but the cause was as yet unknown. It seemed that all the power had gone down. The computer system had crashed, and for some unknown reason, the backup had not kicked in. As of 0600 hours, there were no computers up and running and a limited telephone system.

He said to Brown, "Kevin, I want you to take charge of this, this is your priority, nothing else matters. I have left instructions for the two IT guys to give you as much assistance as they can. The Sergeant is the man to go to and let him go through it all and get it up and running."

He responded, "Do we have any outside communications up and running at all?" Ellis said, "Sadly no, but until we know what has happened fully, I want you to consider us in a lockdown situation."

He continued, "We don't know if there had been any outside actions with this. My information so far is scratchy, no one had seen anything or anybody close by."

Brown said, "I'll make sure it's repaired and up and running as soon as possible. Is there any way we can be in touch?"

Ellis gave him a phone, and commented, "It's a secure line, only to my phone. There is no possibility of any calls either coming in or going out, except to my number." Brown just answered, "Very good sir, I'll keep you informed."

Ellis turned to Drake and told him it was time to go. He wanted to be in Bradbury Lines by 0930 hours, so he will need to get a move on. Drake said, "You haven't seen my driving, keep the sick bag handy!" Ellis looked at him, but kept his thoughts to himself and told him that he was ready to leave.

They left Brown in the control room and went to their car. Ellis told Drake to drive out of the barracks and stop when they reached the corner of the road leading down to the motorway. When he reached the layby, he pulled in and looked across to Ellis, and said, "Ok sir, what's going on? I am not stupid! You have something going on with Captain Brown and you are not sharing it with me." He continued, "With all due respects, it's hard to keep him close, and keep everything tight. He is a fellow soldier and a damned good one."

Ellis said, "I am sorry, but there have been events taking place which have given us cause to consider the loyalty of Brown. I promise it will all be revealed today. The control room crash was engineered by me, and it will keep Brown out of circulation and contact for the time we need".

Drake nodded and said, "Well done sir, it has certainly worked, and the phone was a clever move too." Ellis then told him "The phone he has is being monitored by my staff and everything he has done in the past week has been logged. Where other parties have been contacted, they too are under surveillance and being monitored 24/7.

Sgt Drake make your way to London. Here are the coordinates, enter them into your system and destroy the paperwork. When we get to where we are going, wipe your sat nav clean. You will find that soon enough the route to Bradbury Lines will be inputted, with times, stops and arrival."

Drake did as he was instructed and drove away, taking the M3 towards London and whatever the day may bring. Ellis sat next to him and read some papers he had. He then went to his phone and made a call. All he said was "We have him in place. Be with you in 30 minutes, and we are starving, so plenty of eggs and bacon if you please."

He looked to Drake and smiled and said, "Rank does have its privileges at times." They continued until they reached Cambridge House. Neither of them had been there before and so drove up to the barrier, manned by a soldier in full battle gear. They showed him their identifications. The soldier saluted and said to wait. They would be met and taken to where they were expected.

A few minutes later two other soldiers told them to leave their car and any weapons they might be carrying with the man at the gate and to follow them. They got out of the car, handed over their service side arms and walked into Cambridge House. The time was 0900 hours.

On the second floor they were met by Commander Freeman. They shook hands and he said, "Good to see you both again, I hope everything is going to plan back there?" Ellis replied, "Oh yes, but Sergeant Drake has not been fully brought up to speed just yet. I am sure he will be soon enough." Freeman replied, "We have someone who is not fully aware of your side of events either, so it will be a learning curve for both of them." He walked them into the conference room where Sarah, Jason and Chenkov were sat. They stood, and introductions made including Frederick Steenson. He said, "Good to meet you." Drake said, "A good attempt my friend, but doesn't quite ring true with me." He smiled and looked over at Freeman who told him that he was Chenkov, the head of security at the Russian Embassy, but as far as anyone else was concerned he was Frederick Steenson. He was part of the team who will be processing the events of the last few days. Chenkov whispered to Drake, "Me and you will get on fine methinks, birds of a feather."

For the next fifteen minutes, Freeman and his team briefed Ellis. They saw clips of the interviews and heard the audio bites. When the discussions came to that point in the interviews with the rings, Ellis and Drake were shocked when they saw what had happened to Gregorov and Karakova, especially when their true identities had been revealed.

Ellis commented, "Wonder why Brown didn't know this?" Freeman looked at him and said, "Maybe this was just too deep for him and his contacts." Ellis responded, "This may throw some light on it all for you."

Ellis then proceeded to tell Freeman what they had found as regards Brown. It included the phone calls, internet connections and the Sergeant Williams presence, presently in Afghanistan, but not for much longer. He said, "That seems to be confirming what the two prisoners have said about being closer to home." Sarah commented, "What on earth has made him cross over, he is such a hero to everyone in the British army." Ellis and Freeman said, virtually in unison "Money."

Freeman updated them on who would be in attendance at the meeting and that it was a top secret meeting. Any subsequent actions as a result of the meeting would be under the auspices of the Prime Minister. The record of this meeting would be kept for only as long as was necessary for the completion of the operations and any legal proceedings and then destroyed. They will not be part of any archives ever.

The Russians, more importantly the President, had agreed to this course of action and did not need any documentation unless it affected Russian individuals. He would be meeting with the Prime Minister tomorrow evening, at a destination to be decided and he will be briefed then.

There was a sense of disquiet around the table. It was broken only by the sounds of mugs of coffee being lifted, drunk and placed back on the polished table. There were eight files placed on the long table. All were numbered and boldly printed on the cover "For your eyes only" and a sheet for the signature of the reader.

At precisely 9:30am the Prime Minister and Commissioner entered the room and took their places at the table. Freeman sat at the head to show he was chairman, but no one was fooled that the real power was sitting further down on his right.

Freeman told everyone to sign for the files in front of them. The Prime Minister hesitated and looked at him, but he said to her, "Yes, even you and the Commissioner both need to sign for the record please. These files will be collected at the end of the meeting, no one will take them from this room."

She replied, "I am talking to the Russian President tomorrow, how do you expect me to communicate with him if I don't have a file?"

Freeman answered, "He is aware of the circumstances, he only needs to be given a verbal briefing by you, the less paperwork the better, as you indicated about the archives.

She smiled, “You are right, I’ll have to listen more carefully.” She signed the form on the file and opened it.

Freeman began by welcoming all of them to the meeting. He continued by saying that for the purposes of the operation, the two bodies would be known and Gregorov and Karakova.

He said, “They admitted the killing of the Bulgarian and the attempted assassination of Sir Jeremy Morgan. They were adamant they had nothing to do with the killings in the park, nor the explosions at The Old Bailey or Waterloo. Gregorov had said that they were supposed to just leave London, and make their way to Europe again, leaving on the shuttle at Ashford. They had been at their safe house and Goetze was making all the arrangements. He had been recruited in Germany after an operation there.”

The others listened as he continued, “Goetze was the one who set the explosives and caused the gas attack. Karakova said she had no idea that he was going to do what he did, it was not authorised, and was against their principals.” That brought up a snort from the Prime Minister. They looked at her as she responded, “Can we believe these killers?”

Freeman answered, “As you see the interviews, you can make your own decisions Prime Minister. For now, I am just giving you an overview of the events and initial comments by them.” She glared at him but kept quiet as he continued.

“They had planned to create the diversion so that Gregorov would not be caught. After he left the house in the van, he had heard the explosions and tried to contact Goetze, but without any luck. He had continued for around 30 minutes when it stopped. He had heard gunfire and then a terrible silence. He stayed hidden until he was arrested. That was when he was taken to the station in London."

He continued, "Karakova was identified by Captain Brown, as being a known terrorist. She was seen by the station talking with Goetze, prior to the attack on the concourse. She was not seen again until she surrendered at the gates when the building was being evacuated. As you will see, we were as shocked and surprised as anyone when they were together and disclosed their relationship. More importantly were her connections to the President of Russia. The Russian Ambassador and Mr Steenson have been of great help in assisting this meeting and taking our enquiries forward."

The Commissioner asked, "What has happened to Goetze?" Freeman replied, "From the information that Karakova supplied, a raid was conducted and he has been detained. He is presently in the bowels of the earth and awaiting our attention later. As you all know, Gregorov and Karakova committed suicide whilst being interviewed. The circumstances and the fallout will come later, but for now, as far as the world is concerned, they died in a road accident and their remains cremated and disposed of."

He went on further, "The recordings of the interview will be shown on the big screen now, then Major Ellis will brief you with his update on what has been taking place within the Military. Again, events there are at pace, and we hope that we will have a much more concrete scenario in the next few hours."

They sat back in their chairs and watched as the interviews of Gregorov and Karakova unfolded. There was complete attention being paid to all the talking. Sarah and Jason were particularly interested in the body language of the two individuals. They were all surprised as how open the two were, volunteering the information. Whether it was genuine remorse, or the fact that they knew they would never be free again, it was difficult to tell, but they were giving the interviewers what was needed.

As they watched and listened, they became aware that twice the comment of watching others closer at home had been mentioned. The Prime Minister went to say something, but Freeman put his hand up, as if to say later.

The final act of the interview was the request by Karakova and Gregorov to wear their rings, as they were a married couple and would never be physically together again, but always together. They watched as Karakova took the rings from a pocket and placed them on each other's fingers, before holding hands together.

For all, even the ones who had witnessed it all first-hand, it was shocking to relive it. This time it was almost in slow motion, from her taking the rings out, placing on fingers, looking at each other and then both collapsing whilst holding hands. There was a deep silence for a few moments. Ellis and Drake were stunned by the revelations, both by the fact that they were married and that they had died in this manner. After a few moments Freeman stood and switched the screen off.

He then said, "The cameras kept rolling for a further 30 minutes, but what's on there is all about the events following their deaths and decisions made. It is of the highest secrecy and the Prime Minister and a few others are the only ones who are privy to that. I am sorry that it cannot be played until its conclusion, but I can assure you that what we are interested in has been and always will be, the attacks themselves, by the two dead and their associates. Now you have heard that there seems to be another cell operating within the United Kingdom, and seemingly within the structure of the country I will hand you over to Major Ellis for his briefing."

He sat down and Ellis stood He looked around and said, "We have been monitoring the telephone calls and internet use of one of our officers, Captain Kevin Brown."

Sarah and Jason, both looked at Ellis, shocked at the news. They had known and trusted Brown since the start of these incidents.

Ellis continued, "I have had Brown's phones and computer cloned and have found that when he logged on, he double logged on to another IP address immediately trying to mask that login. He made several keyboard entries and then logged back off. Our operators made extensive searches as to the login address, finally narrowing it down to an area in Afghanistan."

The Prime Minister said, "Why am I only hearing this now?" Ellis responded, "Ma'am, we have only recently been able to identify this. We do not want to ruin anything. This is why we are meeting now."

He went on, "From the logins, which numbered six over the past few days, we were able to narrow it down to a laptop in Helmand Province, Afghanistan. We established that it belonged to a member of our armed services."

They all looked at him, not knowing how this could be happening. Was Brown in communication with an enemy within the army? The Prime Minister was getting more and more incensed with what she was hearing, but sensibly didn't say anything. She would keep her comments until after Ellis had finished.

He continued, "We traced the laptop to a Sergeant Joan Williams, who is in the intelligence corps based in Helmand Province. We know that the keystrokes were sent to her machine, but nothing was ever sent back to Brown. Despite our efforts, we have not yet found out how Brown and Williams are communicating."

Ellis then went on to give a detailed background on Williams, including the fact that there had been nothing to alert them of her activities. He concluded by adding that today, the control room at Aldershot had been shut down on his instructions, so that Brown, who was remaining at the camp, was unable to communicate outside. The only phone in the control room was one which was directly linked into Ellis himself. As far as Brown was concerned, Ellis and Drake were in Bradbury Lines until later today. Ellis handed each of the attendees a small file containing the full military details of Brown and Williams.

It was read in silence. Everyone could see what Brown had achieved in his career and Williams had an unblemished record.

Freeman asked, “Do you know if they have ever met, or crossed paths during their service?” He replied, “No we have no official records of them being connected in any way, through postings, conferences or social events but of course, within the army there are always possibilities to meet.”

The Prime Minister stood, looked at everyone and almost snarled, “What are you going to do about it? Isn’t it time we stopped talking and finally did some work for which you are all being paid handsomely.”

She sat and Chenkov/Steenson responded, “What do you think we have been doing? Sitting and drinking tea, like some of you in your posh offices. We have been at this for twenty four hours. No sleep and getting this meeting ready and formulating any plans which might need enacting. You will not be getting your hands dirty, so please, give us some respect.”

She looked at him, mouth open, unable to make any response, then nodded and said, “I am sorry, I know you are all working hard, and I appreciate it, but I get so frightened when I hear that our own people might be traitors.”

He smiled and said, “We are all aware of what might be, and we will do our best to bring all this madness to an end.”

Sarah looked over at Ellis, and told him, “We have that shooting in the park still under investigation, do you think that Brown might have had a role in that? He is certainly skilled enough to be able to do it, three shots in five seconds, all kill shots.”

Ellis replied, "With his skills of course. He was considered to be the premier sniper in the British Army, and his kills in operations confirm his reputation. I cannot go into them because of National Security, even the Prime Minister would be unhappy if she knew what goes on in the name of security."

He looked across at her, smiled and said, "It's for your own good ma'am". She shrugged and commented, "I just don't know what to believe, my Ministers have never been as forthright as you have, thank you for your honesty and briefing."

Freeman took over and said, "We are going to interview Goetze later today. It doesn't really matter what he claims, we have the evidence against him. What would be beneficial to all of us would be the names of his handlers and persons behind him that seem so important to various people."

He continued, "I will brief the Commissioner on our plan of action. At the same time Major Ellis will be conducting his operation in the apprehension of Brown and Williams."

Ellis countered, "I have had a SAS team fly out to Afghanistan, and on command will extract Sergeant Williams, gather all her belongings and equipment and fly her back to the United Kingdom. We have not informed the officer in charge at the camp, but we will brief him after the operation has been concluded. Simultaneously, another SAS team will arrest Brown, together with his equipment and vehicles. A search team will hit his house and search it from top to bottom. He will be detained and taken to Bradbury Lines and kept there until Williams arrives. They will then be interviewed by our interrogators."

He ended by saying, "Unlike the civilian authorities, we are not time constrained, nor do we have to comply with your rules of interview. They do not deserve any such niceties."

The Prime Ministers laughed and said, "I did not hear that from a serving British Officer but go ahead and do it. There is no sympathy from here."

The Commissioner asked, "What time do you propose conducting these ops?" Ellis replied, "We aim to arrest Williams at 0300 Afghan time, that's when people are at their lowest ebb. Brown will be arrested at 19:00 hours, commensurate times as in Helmand."

Freeman then said, "It's now midday. We have seven hours before Brown is arrested, then all three of them will be detained at Bradbury Lines. There will be a lockdown in place at the camp from 1800 hours. All the personnel there are being told that it is part of an exercise. By 1000 hours tomorrow they all will be in their cells, awaiting our arrival. None of them will know that the others are also being kept. The cells are scattered around the camp."

The Prime Minister suggested that everyone had a break for an hour, have lunch and reconvene at one thirty pm. They could then ask questions of each other and finalise plans. There was a welcome murmuring, and everyone moved into the next room where food and refreshments awaited.

Drake reminded Ellis that they were supposed to be in Bradbury Lines and to contact Brown and tell him that there had been a delay and would not be back in the office until 1800 hours.

Ellis phoned Brown, who told him that most of the problems with the IT had been resolved to a large degree, but the phone lines were still down. Ellis said to Brown, "Good work Kevin. Unfortunately, we have been delayed and won't be back in the office until 1800 hours. Please remain in charge. When we return, we will give you an update on what we have ascertained and what we intend to do."

Brown said, "Anything we can do now sir. It's pretty boring here and maybe I can help in some way?" Ellis said, "Its fine, just do what you are doing now, if there is any change, I'll ring you on the phone."

Brown replied, "I hope we get something positive soon, I am so wanting to get those murderers and terrorists." Ellis smiled to himself and responded, "Be confident that we are getting on top of it."

He rang off and said to Drake, "That will keep him interested until we get back." Drake said, "I'd better not get close to him, I might kill him before anyone gets a chance to interview him."

Ellis just said to him, "Get in the queue. Let's go and eat."

They all sat comfortably together, even the Prime Minister had thawed out enough to sit around and engage in conversation with Steenson. Others sat and went over the events of the morning and the implications of what had taken place over the past few days.

Sarah and Jason were saddened about Brown, but also angry that he had fooled them into believing he was one of the good guys. They knew that he was out of bounds as regards being interviewed, that was a military operation. They both knew that it would not necessarily be subtle or gentle on either him or Williams.

Sarah said to Jason, "How on earth has this Williams woman got involved in all this. She seems an intelligent woman, spotless record, and yet she is prepared to betray her country with Brown. There must be a huge incentive for her to do it and who found her weakness?"

After lunch they reassembled and discussed the events of the morning, but there was very little anyone could add further at this stage. The next phase in the operation was approaching and they all wanted to get it moving. Freeman and his team were going to Hereford, whilst Ellis and Drake were returning to Aldershot.

At 3:30pm the Prime Minister wished all the teams good luck and to get the treasonous sons of bitches. The Commissioner of Police took Freeman aside, wished him luck but reminded him that he was a police officer and the rules of prisoners and interviews were in force for them. He replied, "Don't worry, despite whatever he deserves, the rules will be followed by us, can't say the same for the military."

She looked up at the heavens and said, "I don't want to know, just stay away from it."

CHAPTER 32

Ellis and Freeman got together and wished each other good hunting and they would see each other again at Bradbury Lines. Freeman and his group had initially booked into the Green Dragon Hotel in downtown Hereford.

They left in their vehicles, Freeman and Steenson in one car and Sarah and Jason in the other. After leaving London, drove along the M4, then the M5, until they reached the M50 where they turned off and drove the short distance to the A49 from Ross on Wye to Hereford. Both sets of officials felt a nervous excitement about it all.

They had gone over all the recordings in their minds many times, making sure that they were totally conversant with the facts. They did not want to miss anything out when they spoke with Goetze the next day.

They arrived at their hotel, checked in and then went to Bradbury Lines where they were met by Colonel Brace, who showed them around the camp. most of it was heavily fortified and with armed soldiers patrolling the grounds. He told them that Goetze was in a cell, detained under army regulations until they formally interviewed him, when the civilian rules applied including times and conditions.

Freeman said, "Thank you, we appreciate that assistance as well as anything else you have provided. Major Ellis and his people will be with you in the morning with their prisoners."

Colonel Brace commented "I cannot believe Brown would have gone over to the other side. Only a very limited number of personnel are aware of what is happening, but they all want their five minutes with him. They guarantee he would not come out of it alive."

They all smiled and Sarah commented, "I agree, but we have to get the information before we let your guys loose. As much as I'd like to do it myself, we have to ascertain who is behind all this and what Brown's actual role is, besides being a sniper of some ability."

Brace replied, "He is the principal trainer for all our snipers. He has never been bested in any training sessions prior to others graduating." Sarah informed him of the killings in the park in London and how that had been carried out.

Brace thought about it for a few seconds and said, "He is more than capable of bringing that about, any specialist force in the world would want him. He is unique, that's why this is such a betrayal to us all."

Meanwhile Ellis and Drake were driving back down to Aldershot. They were also going over the events of the day, and, more importantly, what was going to be carried out in the next few hours, both in Aldershot and in Afghanistan.

They drove as far as Ash Vale and stopped at one of the barracks leading into Aldershot itself. On entry they were met by a Corporal Steven Watt. He shook hands with Drake and was introduced to Ellis. He saluted and told him that his squad were on standby and ready for their briefing.

They all went into the small office to the side of the guardroom and Ellis nodded to Drake that he was to give the briefing. He said, "At 1900 hours we will be entering the control room in the basement of the Command Centre based in the centre of Elizabeth Way. Once we have entered, courtesy of Major Ellis, we will arrest our target, Captain Kevin Brown". There was a sharp intake of breath from the squad, and one said, "The Captain Brown?" Drake replied "Yes, he is unaware of anything that has taken place over the past few hours. This part of the operation will be held in conjunction with another operation in Afghanistan."

He continued, "The Control Centre has been effectively kept incommunicado since this morning. Brown has been placed in charge there, so we were kept aware of his location at all times. Corporal Watt and one of your team will detain him, Major Ellis will give the reasons why and then any property he has, including phones, computers and what is in his locker, will be seized. Any questions?"

Corporal Watt asked, "What if he resists?" Drake replied, "He will be taken down, but not lethally. You have tasers and in the last resort, he can be immobilised that way."

Watt nodded and then said, "What are we detaining him for?"

Ellis intervened and said, "I am sorry at this stage we cannot tell you, but rest assured you will know all when I actually tell him the reason for his detention."

He continued, “In addition to your squad, there is another team who will raid his property at exactly the same time as he is being detained. There are civilian Scenes of Crimes Officers who will also be there conducting their searches. They have a lot more expertise than we do.”

He concluded, “Is everyone clear on what they will be doing. I will leave it to Sgt Drake to give you your final duties. We meet back here at 1845 hours.”

Drake spoke with his men quietly. They were a little awed by what they were about to do, but their professionalism was taking over and whatever needed to be done, would be done. Corporal Watt was given the taser in case of any resistance, but they all hoped it would not be necessary, even if they did not know what he had done yet.

At 1845 hours they reassembled and left their barracks for the short drive to the Command Centre.

CHAPTER 33

At 1900 hours Ellis walked into the control room, followed by the squad, who were all in black and carrying fully loaded arms. Brown looked across, saw them and approached Ellis. He was told to stand still, the soldiers moved around him, he looked around and said, "What is going on?"

Ellis said, "Captain Kevin Brown, I am arresting you for treason, in that you have committed multiple acts of treason and terrorism against the United Kingdom. You are being further detained for the murders of Mr and Mrs Jacobs and their daughter."

Brown shouted, "This is rubbish. What evidence do you have, what have I supposed to have done? You know me, I could not do this under any circumstances."

Ellis replied, "Kevin Brown, you are being relieved of your rank and position. You will now be taken to a site where you will be interviewed, and the evidence put forward. Currently your property is being searched by specialist officers. I would advise you not to try and resist. I have given the officers instructions to immobilise you in the event that you do try."

He kept quiet but was stunned to hear that he was suspected of the murders of the family. How in hell had they found that out. He was also concerned of what they might find at his house. He had hidden everything as normal, but it was always possible that someone would be lucky and discover his clothing and rifle.

He was told to put his hands behind his back. He was cuffed and lead out of the main room to a side room under guard.

The SAS squad and the others in the control room were shocked to hear what Ellis had disclosed. Everyone, except of course, the senior computer operator, who had been involved from the outset and he would never be identified under any circumstances.

Simultaneously in Afghanistan, a squad of SAS troops entered the sleeping quarters of Sergeant Joan Williams. The first she was aware of anything untoward was when a bright light was shown in her face and she was hauled out of her bed.

She was told to stand to attention and a voice told her she was being arrested on suspicion of treason and an accessory to crimes against the United Kingdom. Her legs crumpled beneath her and she cried out, "I don't know what you are talking about, I am just a sergeant doing my job. Please tell me this is all a terrible mistake."

A hood was placed over her head and she was forced to kneel. She was cuffed and told not to move. The squad removed all her personal belongings and one of the team brought the commanding officer to the tent.

The leader of the team said, "I am Corporal X, Sergeant Williams has been arrested on suspicion of treason and will be taken from here to a place to be interviewed. Where are all the communications equipment kept that she has been using since she was stationed here?"

Captain Jonathon Richards, her commanding officer, exclaimed, "What right have you got to come here in the middle of the night and subject one of my troops to such humiliation without contacting me first?"

The Corporal said nothing, looked at him and produced a document from his pocket and handed it to him. He opened it and read it, the colour draining from his face as he did so. He kept looking at the document and the Sergeant on her knees and hooded.

He then said, "All the equipment she uses, phones, computers and tablets are kept in store. Each officer has their own locker for the equipment, and it is signed out and in every day. If you come with me, you can gain access through the duty officer, who will give you what you want."

The Corporal then said, "We will also take all your logs for the last month with us as well. You can make copies for your own records, but we insist on having the originals."

Captain Richards nodded and showed him the way to the store. There they collected all the equipment that Sergeant Williams had access to, as evidenced by the logs maintained by the duty officers.

Copies of all the logs were made and handed back to the Captain. Corporal X said, "As you have read, you are commanded not to give any information to anyone about

Williams. If anyone asks, she has been given compassionate leave due to an illness in the family which necessitated her leaving suddenly. Do you understand?"

He replied, "Yes completely". They returned to the cabin where Williams was still kneeling. She was hauled up and taken out of the cabin by the squad. She said, "Please tell me what I am supposed to have done wrong, is this an exercise, a bad joke? Please tell me something."

She was walked across the quad, where she was placed into a helicopter which immediately took off for the air base within Helmand camp itself. Within ten minutes she had been transferred to an aircraft where she was sat down and confined to a section at the rear of the plane. Two soldiers maintained a vigil of her as the plane left Afghanistan air space and made its way to the United Kingdom.

Sergeant Samuels, aka Sgt X, used his satellite phone and dialled to Ellis. He reported that their end of the operation had been successful and that she and all the equipment was on its way to him.

Ellis said, "Any problems your end?" He replied, "None at all Sir, after Richards saw the letter and nearly had a heart attack, everything went fine. Williams is still protesting her innocence, but that's to be expected."

Ellis responded, "Job well done. See you in the morning as planned."

In the meantime, Brown had been taken by helicopter to Bradbury Lines and detained in one of the interview pods scattered around the camp. He was kept cuffed and hooded, except when given food. No one spoke with him. When he was unhooded, a light was shone into his face so he could not see anyone.

Several times he called out as to why he had been detained like this and demanded to speak to Major Ellis. His comments were not answered and after a while, he lay on his bed and started to analyse what had taken place.

His mind went over what he had done for the last several days and thought to himself that nobody could have suspected him of the shooting. He had been with the Police long enough to know that they had no clues as to who was involved. He was also sure that they would not find anything at his home either. He has always been very careful as to where he kept his equipment.

He had left his phones in a safe box which was not registered in his name and outside of London. He always wiped the satnav GPS signal from his car after every journey and never left a paper trail. He was confident that any communications to his company were untraceable, as they had gone through pay phones and the cards, he used for the calls were always destroyed after the single use.

His computer terminal had been used sparingly. He had learnt to use computers and their inner workings by one of his mentors in the company. Unless someone was literally watching, there was not a chance that he would be seen double logging on even for such a short time. Besides, no one in the control room was clever enough to check on the usage by him and others at any one time.

He had no idea what the time was, but from his own internal clock he surmised it was around 0200 hours. He turned over and went to sleep, having worked out all the angles that could be used against him.

CHAPTER 34

As Williams was being flown out of Afghanistan, she was terrified. She knew she was in a large transport plane. She was cocooned into a small space, where she was unable to move. She had got over the shock of being detained when she had been dragged from her bed, humiliated by unknown soldiers, and now being flown somewhere in a plane.

She could not think of anything she had done wrong. She hadn't caused any problems at the camp or fraternised with anyone. She had made no telephone calls at all since her posting and her computer terminal was only calibrated for inward communications. Any outward information had to be done through the main central terminal, under the auspices of the day officers, who were constantly rotating shifts.

She thought of home, her parents and boyfriend and wondered if she would ever see any of them again. She knew that there had been times when treasonous soldiers just disappeared and never heard of again.

She dozed off several times, her mind in a turmoil. The drone of the plane kept her drifting in and out of the sleep, even more than the nightmares she was suffering.

After what seemed an eternity, she sensed a different tone to the plane and a few minutes later felt the plane bumping down onto a runway. She felt a rush of optimism as the plane came to a halt and she felt the tail gate opening. The coolness of the morning air felt fresh on her body but unable to see anything she could only sense it as being sunny and dry.

Before she could gather her thoughts, she felt two pairs of arms take hold of her and drag her down the tailgate and on to the ground. She stood shaking, hearing many different sounds. She said, "Is this an exercise, I know what happens, please give me a clue."

Nothing was said and she was marched across the tarmac and thrown into a helicopter and belted in. She sat there a few minutes, heard other sounds and then the distinct sound of a helicopter started up.

She felt herself rising and then a forward motion of the helicopter forced her back into her seat. She had no idea where she was. All she could tell was that she was not in a hot, desert country.

She had no concept of time as she sat and listened to the helicopter flying to god knows where. After some indeterminate period of time she felt the helicopter descending, slowing down and finally felt the wheels hit the ground.

She felt the jolt, the engines being switched off and the speed of the rotor blades slowing down until they ceased completely. The doors opened and again she was lifted out of her seat. This time however, she was walked for a few minutes before she heard a door open. No one had said a word to her for the whole journey and this was sending her crazy.

A door opened and she was pushed inside. A light was shining, her hood was removed and in front of her stood two men completely in black and hooded themselves. She screamed involuntarily and they pointed out a tray of food and drink on a table in the corner, together with a bed and a toilet and sink in the opposite corner. The door was closed, and she sat in the room, alone, confused and wondering what was going to happen next.

CHAPTER 35

At 1030 hours, Freeman and Ellis and their teams met in the Officers Mess at Bradbury Lines. In addition to them, there were four other men, who were introduced as Kenneth, Brian, Sandy and Mark respectively. Surnames were not mentioned. No one said anything about it, just accepted it, but they all knew they were military officers, experts at interrogation in their own right.

It was agreed that for the moment, Freeman, Sarah and Jason would concentrate on Goetze, whilst Kenneth and Brian interviewed Brown. Williams was to be interviewed by Sandy and Mark.

It was confirmed that none of them would be told of the location they were being held and also there was to be no mention of any of the others until the initial interviews had been concluded and discussed amongst themselves in their teams.

It was further agreed that Ellis and Steenson would listen in on the interview of Brown and Williams but take no part. They would provide any intelligence needed as a result of the individual interviews.

They each had their files and a preliminary set of questions. They would lead in slowly, waiting for the responses, and repeating if necessary. During the initial interviews there would be no physical evidence introduced into any of the questioning.

They placed a time limit of 3 hours initially, then they would take a break and meet back at the Mess and compare any notes that might cross reference each other.

The interview rooms were all placed one hundred yards apart, sound proofed and furnished with a table, two chairs, and a camera to record the entirety of the interview. Their cells were situated adjacent to the interview rooms. Whilst there were no physical guards present inside the pods, at all times four SAS officers would be present outside.

Freeman asked if they were ready. They all nodded, picked up their files and left the Mess to commence their tasks, some more pleasurable than others, knowing the details of the individuals being detained.

As they walked over to their pod, Sarah said to Jason, "This man will never see the light of day again and he knows it. I am not sure if we will get anything from him. I think Sandy and Mark have the best chance with Williams. I hate to admit it, but she is probably the weakest link of them all."

Freeman interjected, "Yes, you are probably right, unless she is so clever that she has fooled everyone so far, but I cannot see that. We will let her talk and see where and how she implicates Brown."

He continued, "Brown is SAS, he knows all the techniques and tricks, he is not going to be easy. They will just interview him at first over the park killing and see where that progresses. He does not need to know what we know about Williams at this stage. Have we heard anything from the house search yet?"

Jason said, "No, there are nooks and crannies everywhere, they will need at least until the end of today."

They arrived at the site, showed their credentials to the officers guarding the entrance and went inside. It was cool and bright. At one end of the complex there was the cell in which Goetze was being held, then the interview room and closest to the door was the observation and recording room.

Sarah and Jason entered the interview room, whilst Freeman and Steenson went into the observation room. Goetze was already in the interview room, seated behind the table and he was shackled by his feet and wrists. Currently two armed soldiers were on guard, but as the two police officers entered, they left.

Sarah and Jason sat opposite him. They identified themselves to him and he made no comment. They studied him as he sat there, early 30's, dark brown hair, his eyes were dark and his skin pale. He had several days growth of beard. He wore a white pair of overalls and white flat slippers.

Sarah opened the proceedings by telling Goetze that the interview would be recorded and that he was under caution. He did not have to say anything unless he wished to do so and that whatever he did say could be used in court as evidence against him.

He said "Whatever, just get on with it, ask your questions. The quicker I can get this over with I can go back to my bed."

Sarah said, "Tell me about your relationship with Gregorov and Karakova."

He said, "Gregorov was my leader, he recruited me. I did what was expected. I have not seen him since he was arrested by your people on the motorway. I don't suppose he will tell you very much. He is too well connected in various organisations to let on anything. Karakova is just another member of the team that does work for Gregorov. He likes her that's for sure. I think he even sleeps with her, but that's for his pleasure. She is a nothing like me."

Jason said, "How long have you been with him and how did it start?"

He replied, "For almost four years. He was doing an operation in Germany, and I was told to help him. I was a cleaner. After he had finished, I went in and cleaned up. We had a backup crew of four of us, so where he went, we followed. If there were bigger operations, like the one in London, then we could request more manpower and it was provided."

Jason continued, "Who did you receive your instructions from?"

He answered, "I never knew who, it was all done on burner, single use phones that were picked up and stored in designated places. Gregorov had our numbers and all he had to do was call us and we'd respond. Ask him and see if he will give you who his contacts were."

Sarah asked, "Where does Karakova fit into all this, you were observed talking to her prior to the assault on the police station?"

He commented, "We would discuss what equipment and manpower was needed. I gave her the requirements and she supplied them as far as possible. We always seemed to be in the same location for every operation that Gregorov did."

He continued, "I was more the undertaker, if you get my drift, and she was the grocer. She had her own team with her. They kept very much in the background, but sometimes I noticed her with a few others I did not recognise. I asked Gregorov about her and he told me to concentrate on my efforts and she will do hers. Work as a team and be ready at all times."

Sarah said, "Lead us through to the killing of the Bulgarian and subsequent events."

Goetze replied, "He had been assigned to his killing, it was just another contract as far as we were concerned. We had done possibly a dozen others in the past few years, not just here but all over the world. As far as we were concerned, we were just getting rid of the scum of the earth."

He continued "That went smooth as you now know, a perfect shot, and clearance from the scene. Unfortunately, we didn't know about the other shooting in the park, so we had to take some immediate actions to get away from the police activities. We took over a flat, Gregorov had to eliminate the occupants, we were called in and disposed of the bodies. They were taken to the lakes outside Frimley and dumped in there. They are wrapped in carpet and clingfilm, should be easy to find."

Sarah and Jason sat there and took in what he was saying, it was surreal. He was volunteering this without even having to be pressed. In the control room Freeman was already on the phone, making arrangements for the lakes to be searched immediately to confirm his story.

Goetze continued, "Gregorov was given another assignment, a high- level English Civil servant. We did the initial assessment but was given a very limited time slot. He did his work, but with the extra security that was in place and him having a bullet proof car, this was never planned for. He was lucky to escape from it. We had not properly planned it.

Gregorov later told us that it was on the instructions of someone high up in his organisation and that the man had crossed him, and he wanted him taken out. It was a personal and not a business killing. Gregorov said he would deal with the matter direct. He would ensure it would never happen again.

We had to get Gegorov out of the area, that was a priority dictated from on high. We drove out to the farm, which had been pinpointed as our exit point and then from there we were to get a ferry from Dover and back into Europe."

He continued, "We heard what was happening on various police frequencies and through our resources. I told

Gregorov that we will create the diversion while he escaped. He told me to leave it with him and he made some calls. In about an hour a team arrived in a large van loaded with various sorts of equipment."

He carried on, "We unloaded boxes from the van and Gregorov told us to lay the explosives all around the building. There was almost a ton of high quality C4. I wondered where they had been able to acquire so much in such a short time, but I didn't query it. I and my team then laid all the boxes in strategic positions around the house if there was any kind of operation to take us out."

Sarah and Jason did not say anything. They were happy to let him ramble on.

Goetze asked for a coffee, and it was agreed that a short break was in order. He was given a coffee whilst Sarah and Jason went next door. They were also given coffee and Sarah said, "What are you making of all this? It's almost too good to be true. Why is he admitting all this so easily?"

Freeman responded, "He has been telling the truth so far. The police found the two bodies at the site he indicated. He had no reason to tell us. We'd have never found them until it was much too late to associate them with Gregorov. Keep on with him, let him say what he wants, then we can go back later and pin him down more.

They finished their coffees and re-entered the room.

Meanwhile in the next pod, Sandy and Mark walked into the interview room where Williams was seated, shackled to her seat and guarded by two soldiers who left on their entry.

They sat opposite her but did not identify themselves. Mark said, "Are you Sergeant Joan Williams?" she nodded and said, "Yes."

He said, "Speak up Williams and sit straight, when we ask you something you will answer it truthfully, do you understand?"

She replied, "Yes sir". She looked down, her eyes were dark and red from crying. Her hair was lank and greasy, she was shivering and kept sniffling while she tried to concentrate on the two men in front of her. She was wearing the white overalls afforded to all detained persons.

Sandy then said, "You are under military jurisdiction, therefore we are not obliged to follow the rules of English law. You can and will be detained for as long as is necessary. You are not entitled to legal representation. Do you understand?" She cried out, "What have I done, tell me please, I am just a Sergeant doing my job."

Mark leant across so that his face was only inches from her and said, "You have been arrested for treason, in that you have conspired with a person or persons known and unknown to commit terrorist acts against the United Kingdom. Do you understand what I have just said?"

She recoiled, and gasped, "What are you saying? How can this be? I have never met anyone who I didn't know, you can ask anybody. I never leave the base or meet with others."

Sandy said, "Don't be so stupid Sergeant Williams, you don't think that we don't keep tracks on our soldiers, especially in the Intelligence Section where you work? You are not that thick, even though you seem to have been over time."

She looked at him, "If you tell me what I am supposed to have done, then I can answer you, but I have no idea what you want."

She burst into tears, and sobbed to herself, tears running down her face and on to the flimsy overalls she was wearing.

Mark said, "Take us through your daily routines at work. Don't leave anything out or that will confirm to us you are hiding something and guilty of treason."

She said, "I am usually on duty from 1400 hours to 2000 hours daily, my leave day is Mondays, you can check the rota. I work those hours because that is when we get most of our information from our outlying stations or incoming troops. The information is given to my three assistants and that is then entered into my computer."

She continued, "I check the veracity of it and decide what further action might be required by either the informants, who sent me the information, or by the section chief who oversees the data."

Sandy said, "Do you receive data directly from any source?"

She replied "No, it all comes through my teams, I just assemble the data and pass it on. You can check my computers if you want to."

He responded, "Your computers and phones are being examined as we speak to see if you have received any unauthorised transmission whilst on duty."

Mark said, "Who do you communicate with when you are online. Send messages and talk to others when on duty or in your own time?"

She replied, "Nobody, how can I? We are not allowed outside access on any of our electronic equipment. My section is very secretive, and we cannot risk any lapses in security. Our equipment is not set up for outside contacts, the firewalls are strong. We are not allowed to use our own equipment for outside contact."

Sandy asked, "How do you communicate with the outside world?"

She responded, "I am there on a six month tour of duty as you are no doubt aware. I have been there just over one month. We are allowed to contact home once a week at designated times in the office of Captain Richards

Sandy said, "Who do you contact?"

She answered, "My parents, my mother is not well, so I talk to them every week for 15 minutes, which is our allotted time. We cannot send out any written communications from there, so they are my contact whilst there. This is why I just don't understand what is going on."

Mark asked, "You speak to no one else at all?"

She responded, "No, our calls are all made in front of the Captain. We are not allowed to make private calls on our own. We don't even have mobiles or pads while there."

Sandy moved closer to her and said, "Listen carefully, Sergeant Williams, your very future depends on what you are telling us. Think about who you are in contact with, the officers in the field, anyone you can think of."

She sat for a few moments, her eyes closed, her body tense and shaking. She suddenly opened her eyes, put her hands to her face, and said, "Oh no, but we never spoke."

Mark said, "Who?"

She whispered, "My boyfriend sends me texts every few days, so I know he is all right. I can't answer him back, but he knows that it gets through. But it's nothing, just letters that he sends telling me his feelings. I cannot believe that it would cause this. I am so sorry, but we wanted it as a secret. I can give you all the stuff he sent if you let me."

She sagged in her chair, weeping, and not knowing what to say.

Mark said, "Who is the boyfriend. Where can we contact him?"

She replied, "I never know where he is, that's why we communicate like we do. I know he is in England and his name is Kevin Brown. He is a Captain in the army."

Nothing was said but Mark and Sandy looked at each other. Mark said to Sergeant Williams, "Captain Kevin Brown, how long have you known him?"

She answered, “A little over a year, but he is away so often that we can only take short breaks together. He is an instructor in one of the regiments and goes all over the place. When he is away, we let each other know we are alright. But since my posting I have not been able to talk to him, so we arranged that he would send me letters which I could understand.”

She hung her head, saying over, “I am sorry, I am sorry, but I didn’t know we were doing anything wrong.”

At that stage, Mark and Sandy decided it was time for a break after hearing what had just been said. They stood and left the room. They were met outside by Ellis and Steenson, who seemed as shocked by the news as they were.

“Either Williams is the cleverest liar I have ever met, or she is telling the truth. We were not prepared for this, we need to examine everything again and, if necessary, she can show us.” said Mark.

Ellis said, “Hold on, let’s find out more about the procedures in Helmand first. Work from there, follow the trail back to Brown. I’ll get on to my people in Aldershot and go through the transcripts of his usage. Do you know where her computers and phones are?”

Mark replied, “They are here and kept in the secure lockup. We’ll get some guys over to go through them. We can get assistance from GCHQ as always, and they are only just over an hour away. If they can’t get into them, nobody can.”

Ellis responded, "I'll get on to them right now, we need to clarify this before we get too involved with Brown. I don't want him wriggling off any hooks. I'll speak with the others and get a delay, but this is a matter of importance and can change everything."

He further added, "I need to speak to Freeman and his team and find out what is going on there. I hope there are no surprises with them, otherwise we are all going to look silly."

Mark and Sandy sat in the observation room looking across at Williams. She was pale, sobbing and shaking her head. Every so often she lifted her eyes up and looked into the camera and mumbled something which they could not make out.

Ellis made his call to GCHQ and they told him they had a helicopter there and would be to them in less than 30 minutes. He made arrangements with the camp commandant and then spoke with Freeman.

He said, "We have got a problem here, Williams claims to be the girlfriend of Brown."

There was silence and then Freeman replied, "You have to be joking. How was this never picked up? Is she for real? What has Brown got to say about it?"

Ellis answered, "We have not spoken with Brown yet, and we are not going to until we get answers from Williams. We are going through her equipment. She admits to being in contact with Brown through some sort of coded messaging. It's going to take a while. We have our people in Aldershot and here going through her stuff and should get an answer in a couple of hours. Sorry it can't be done any quicker."

Freeman sighed and said, "Better this way, you are not under the same rules as we are. If we can get more information from what she has given you, then so much the better. Goetze is singing like a canary, he is just admitting to everything. There must be a catch, but so far, everything he has told us matches up with what we knew in advance. He has even given up two bodies that no one knew about. We are having a break. He is having a coffee and we are gathering our thoughts for the next stage. He does not know about Gregorov and Karakova, we don't intend to enlighten him."

Ellis replied, "This is going to take longer than we first thought. Carry on with Goetze and we will continue with Williams and hope we get something from the techies quickly enough."

Freeman went back to his team and gave them the information he had received from Ellis. Sarah said there had never been any mention of this woman. He had never said anything, and the records indicated that she had never been part of any contacts he might have had.

Freeman said, "She insists she is just his girlfriend. She has not known him for too long, but they kept in touch through the coded letters on their machines. These are being gone through with a fine tooth comb, but it does mean we cannot get at Brown until we have all the facts. We cannot afford to go in half prepared, he is much too savvy for that."

Sarah felt disconsolate. The end result was not getting any closer, and if anything, slipping further away. All they could do now was continue with Goetze and hope that he could provide something. She was doubtful as she didn't think he was high enough in the chain to have access to all the secrets that might open this case.

They returned to where Goetze was seated. He had finished his coffee and sat quite relaxed. Sarah Said, "Tell us what happened at the escape house and on the motorway."

He looked up and said, "I told you, we had set explosives around the property. The priority was getting Gregorov out of any danger, by whatever means needed doing. We had three vehicles available to us. We intended to use the Mercedes for the getaway, but Gregorov himself said that that would be the decoy and he would go in the Transit van. There were many on the roads and less liable to be looked at.

I told him that the Transit was packed with some gas cylinders. I was not told what was in them, but they had been loaded into the van a few days previous when we stole it. I thought they were oxygen bottles or for cutting equipment in case it was needed on our operation."

Sarah asked, "What happened at the house? How did you know the police would be arriving?"

He responded, "We had an anonymous call on Gregorovs phone. It was decided that we would all leave the house together in the vehicles and set off in different directions. I was in the Mercedes and stopped about 300 yards from the house. We could see the police teams getting into position, moving forward. I waited until most of them were close enough and used the remote to detonate the explosives. Even if I say myself, it was pretty spectacular."

He sat back and smiled, it was all that Sarah and Jason could do to stop themselves from hitting him. They sat and glared at him and Jason said, "You animal! you killed over 20 police officers that day. Don't you have any remorse?"

He replied, "It was just business, I am sorry that it happened. It was us or them, we could not leave anything behind in the house. I saw your army guy settling in, far enough away from the blast, but lost him in the explosion. I thought we might have finally got rid of him."

Sarah looked up and said, "Do you know who it was?"

He replied, "That snake Brown, I am surprised he is still in the army and not dead or locked up with what he does".

Jason asked casually, "What has he done?"

He replied, "You have not heard the rumours about the sniper who has two paymasters? From our sources it is Brown. No one has found out who the people are, except that they pay him big money to carry out their wishes. He has never failed yet. He has made over twenty kills for them. Most of them are in England, so check your records, but some in Germany and France too."

Sarah continued, "Why has nothing been done about it already?"

Goetze answered, "He is protected. Gregorov would have loved to have taken him out, and nearly did a couple of times, but was told to leave him in place. Did we get him at the house? It would be a real coup if we had."

Sarah replied, "We don't know all the details yet, so I cannot answer your questions. But we hope to have the answers soon. Do you know what identities he has been using over time? That way we can check and find out more. Until we confirm that Brown is dead, we are looking at all possibilities."

Goetze seemed happy with the response and said, "I'll give you some names and locations when we are finished. I am not trying to get out of what I have done. I know that I deserve everything and am not going to get the protection that the others get."

He continued, "I got away from the scene and drove down towards Dover. Then I heard that the transit had been stopped and that there was a gun battle taking place. I didn't know what to do, I had not received instructions so carried on with the rest of the team to Dover and took the ferry to Dunkirk and waited over there for further instructions.

The next thing we heard was about the explosions and gas release on the news. Believe me, I did not know anything about it. I may be many things but not a mass murderer, I had no idea what it was for. I haven't seen Gregorov since he was arrested at the scene. As you know I saw Karakova and asked her about it, and she told me to mind my own business and that it was in the past. All she was concerned about was getting Gregorov out of the cells.

We came back over to try and release Gregorov, but it was a suicide mission. There was no way we could have got him out without destroying the whole building with him in it."

He sat back and yawned. He said, "I am tired, I need to have a rest for a while. If you give me some paper and a pencil, I will give you the names he uses and where he has been. I cannot give you everything, but this might help get the snake."

Sarah said one moment and left the room, she was met outside by Freeman who queried the honesty. Sarah agreed, but under the circumstances she told him that they had no choice to go with it and then check out his story as soon as possible. All it needed was a couple of the names to be recorded and they would have so much more on Brown.

Freeman handed over a sheet of paper to her and gave her a pencil, warning her not to let that pencil out of her sight at any time. She looked at him as if to say I know what I am doing and turned around and re-entered the room.

She passed over the pencil and paper to Geotze, who started to write onto the sheet. She reminded him that he was to write in English, he nodded and started to make a list.

He wrote a list of names and dates, and places, almost one side of the paper. He put the pencil down, Sarah got hold of it. He said, "I cannot be sure 100% of the dates, but the places and names, yes. We have tried to get close to him for a long time now. Please say we got him in the explosion. I can die a happy man and many of my friends and peers will celebrate long into the night with the news."

Sarah told him they would take a break and let him rest for a few hours whilst they looked into the information he had supplied. He was escorted out of the room, and they sat in silence for a few moments digesting what had just taken place.

They went and joined Freeman and Steenson. He organised several copies of the list so they could all see what was there and attempt to link anything they knew into it.

Freeman sent a copy by courier to the control room and told the officer that this was of the highest priority and that he was not to give it to anyone except The Commissioner of Police herself.

The Commissioner herself, was thrilled with the news and was arranging specialist officers to sift through records and instances mentioned in the list. She told Freeman, "This is what we have been waiting for, well done."

CHAPTER 36

They all sat in the observation room, and went down the list, none of the names seemed familiar, but a few dates and places came to the mind of Freeman as being terrorist events. He would do the research and if Brown was responsible for any of them, he would be there when Brown was dealt with for the act of treason and murder. Treason was an offence which, in the British army, still carried the death penalty.

Freeman left the room and rang Ellis and told him of the news. He was told to wait and that he, Ellis, would be over to him in a few minutes.

On his arrival he was shown into the room where the others were all seated. He was flushed and as soon as he saw the list, he said "I know that name, and that one, they are soldiers who died a long time ago, but the dates and places are not where it happened."

Freeman said, "Are you sure?"

Ellis replied, "They were my men, and yes, I am sure. The bastard has been using the names of dead heroes to carry out his treason. What sort of man would do that? I bet all the others are names of dead soldiers too, he'd have no difficulty in getting their names from the various databases and registers."

He asked, "Do you mind me sending a copy to my trusted operator? He will be able to find out a lot more than we can through the military records?"

Freeman responded, "As long as he is on a secure server, and only him, and no one else has access to the list. I have to trust you on this, and I know he has come up trumps before, so yes. Can you ask him how the tracing is going with the computers and internet too?"

Ellis smiled and made the necessary calls to his Sergeant and forwarded the list to him. He also established that there had been a total of nine communications between Brown and Williams, but the coding had not yet been broken. Additionally, nothing had been sent by Williams to Brown at any stage.

Ellis relayed the information to Freeman, who thanked him and said they will wait for whatever the list brings and to give Goetze a rest. They were keeping him sweet and on their side by granting him the requests.

Ellis and Mark and Sandy spoke together. They decided that they would continue with Williams while she was still vulnerable, tired, and confused. They would ask her about the messages between her and Brown and see her response.

They went back into the interview room, and sat in front of Williams, who looked totally defeated and a shadow of her former self. Mark said, "We know that Brown has sent nine messages to you in the past few months, why send them that way?"

She looked at him, "They were personal, it was our way of keeping in touch. He arranged it, he wanted me to know he was safe at all times."

Sandy interjected and said, "If he wanted to let you know that he was safe why all the secrecy, don't just tell us it was the rule at Helmand about personal calls. You could have contacted him during the weekly call to the family, yet you persisted in this charade of it being personal. You knew exactly what you were doing and that was betraying your country."

She screamed out, "They were our way of saying we loved each other for god sake. Please let me tell you, I have nothing to hide. It was just a simple few letters each one saying something. I'll show you, let me have my computer and I can do it, please I'll do anything to help you."

She sagged forward in her chair and tears fell as she tried to contain her emotions. There was a knock on the door and Mark went and answered it.

Ellis was outside with a sheath of papers. He said, "This is the raw list from her machine. Let's see what she says. Show her the first one and let her tell us what it says, but don't believe a word until we get more confirmation from the other messages."

Mark went back in and placed the first message from Brown to her on the table. She ran her fingers over it, and then said, "Each letter represents a word, we never used the same sequence twice. That was part of the fun for us, scrambled and then I'd put it together. He said I was the intelligent one." She smiled a little, and then said, "Maybe not so intelligent after all, but I thought he really meant it."

She then pointed out the letters, "L is for love, M is for miss, K is for kiss, I think you get the hint now. You can guess what some of the letters mean, I am not saying them."

She put her head down while Mark and Sandy went over the note, writing down the words fitting to the letters, they showed it to her, she nodded, and changed a few words and said, "That's what was sent, every message contained the same letters, just jumbled around for fun and to make it bit sexier. There was no hidden code, it was fun at the time, relieved the boredom. I thought it was sweet and very personal, how wrong could I be."

Mark picked up the paper, and together with the other sheets in his hand he took them out of the room and gave them to Ellis. He showed him the sequencing of letters and smiled and said, "That should help the codebreakers." and laughed.

He continued, "We'll give her a short break now, give her some food, let her shower. Make her think we are on her side, until we fully transcribe the wordings. We can then decide if she is being truthful or not."

Ellis agreed. It was something so simple, yet so difficult. Why hadn't it been picked up before. His men would now have to go through everything again, hindsight is a wonderful thing.

He relayed the message over to Freeman, who was somewhat taken aback. They were going to have to get together for another meeting and possibly use different tactics in future, bearing in mind what information they now had.

The two interviewers went back to Williams. They told her she could have a shower, rest for a while and get something to eat. They would be verifying what she had told them. Mark said, “This doesn’t mean you are off the hook Sergeant, but it is in everyone’s interests that we establish the truth.”

She replied, “Why don’t you talk to Brown, he started all this. I just felt as though I meant something to him, and while I was away, his letters to me were special.”

Mark replied, “All in good time, get some food and rest, we will be back soon enough.” They left her and she was taken back to her cell where food and clean clothes were waiting for her.

Ellis was sitting in the observation room when he received the call from Aldershot that he had been waiting for. His Sergeant told him that the letters that Williams had provided, was correct in all aspects. He had found no underlying meanings in any of the words when decoded, but that wasn’t to say that it was not possible, but on the balance of probabilities she was being truthful.

Ellis asked about the list he had sent over. The Sergeant told him that all the names related to soldiers who had died in hostile situations. Brown had been involved in the operations with every one of them. The locations and dates, however, did not match, and they were conducting further checks on those.

Ellis said, "Check with the passport office for any passports issued in those names in the years since the deaths of the personnel. Also do financial checks and property checks in those names too. I am beginning to think that we might find a mine of information when you do." His Sergeant responded positively and logged out.

Ellis rang Freeman and said that they needed to have a meeting soon, as more information had become available. They agreed to meet in the Officers Mess within ten minutes.

They all met in the Mess and served coffee by the orderly. Ellis told Freeman what had transpired with Williams. He said, "She gave us the lettering for the code that Brown sent to her. From her point of view they were love letters, she even gave us the converted words from the letter. I have had them analysed and on first viewing seem genuine, but we are still going over them."

Freeman asked, "Was she able to transmit anything back to Brown or send on to anywhere or anyone else?"

Ellis retorted, "No, her machine and any communications were strictly controlled and internal. I think that it's possible that Williams is the only innocent in all this. Even if she is, she is still facing military charges of unauthorised use of equipment. It means the end to her career as a soldier."

Sarah said, "That's a bit unfair, it's that monster Brown who needs sorting out."

Ellis commented, "Sergeant Williams is very good at her job, maybe a civilian appointment might happen for her." He smiled and left it at that. He then continued, "Have you found out anything about the names on the list and the dates and locations?"

Freeman said, "The names don't match with the dates. They don't match locations of incidents. I think that we are missing something vital which has happened in Browns other roles."

Ellis answered, "All the names mentioned are of service personnel who have died within the past few years, when Brown was on official duty. We are going through our files to match up the names with any documentation taken out since their deaths. Maybe that way we will be able to connect that with the places and dates."

Freeman responded, "We will do the same." Steenson interjected and said, "We have many records, I will get my people to cross analyse all these facts too."

Ellis looked across at Freeman, who said, "It's all right, he has the ear of the Prime Minister and access to certain records even I am not able to gain access to."

Ellis asked how Goetze was cooperating. Freeman told him that he was being very obliging so far. Everything he had told them had been confirmed by their follow up enquiries. He confirmed that they had not yet gone as far as the attack on the police station, but that will be brought up shortly. Goetze was unaware of the relationship between Gregorov and Karakova, nor the fact they were dead.

Sarah said, "We will keep him unaware of all that is coming to light. We will thank him for the list and tell him that he has provided us with valuable information in relation to Brown and anything else he can think of we'd very much appreciate it."

Freeman replied, "Good idea, keep him on our side, he might disclose information valuable to us that he might not realise he knows."

They returned to the room and sat in front of Goetze. He appeared relaxed and any tensions he showed earlier had gone.

Jason said, "What was your involvement in the attack on the police station, we know that you were present during it."

He replied, "I met Karakova twice during that time, I was surprised to see her. I thought she had gone to Europe out of the way. But she said she had returned to get Gregorov out and had brought with her a team of sappers and tunnellers. I had not been informed this was going to happen and told her that it would be impossible to get through, it was a high security building.

He continued, "She told me that they had the equipment to get through the shell of the building. I didn't argue with her because I knew it was futile. Some lorries brought in some huge digging equipment and she set the sappers to work.

The noise was horrendous. I told her that you'd know immediately what was going on. She was determined, and I had no option to stay close in case she required any assistance. They were drilling in several spots. I kept telling her it was useless but then there seemed to be a breakthrough and then a whole load of shooting. I decided to leave then, I wasn't going to die for a suicide mission."

He looked across at them, and said, "Its sounds cowardly, but I have been around long enough to know what is safe and what is stupid, and this was stupid in the extreme. I don't know what possessed her. She will have to tell you what went on in her mind herself when you interview her."

They showed no response and he continued, "I went to the house, where we were going to be evacuated from.

However, not one of them returned and obviously somebody had given them the address and you caught me there."

He said, "Karakova had access to high places, and so does Gregorov. They were in separate teams when we operated in the Balkans and Eastern Europe. When we moved around, she seemed to show up and talk with him more and more. It was almost as though she was becoming his main point of contact. Gregorov would not tell me why, he just told me to do my job and she will do hers."

He continued, "I have no family. I am not even sure who would miss me, if anyone at all. I think that all of our team have been killed or arrested, and they will not shed a tear for me that's for certain."

He commented, "I don't know if I can tell you much more now, Gregorov and Karakova will have all the inside knowledge. They might take some time to give it up, but I think they will, they are not stupid."

Sarah said, "Let's take a rest now. We need to do some checking and will get back to you then. In the meantime, have a meal and rest. You have been helpful, and it is appreciated. You know we cannot promise you anything, but I am sure the authorities will show their appreciation too."

He left the room and they sat for a few minutes. Freeman entered and sat with them and said, "I don't think that we will get much more out of him unless we start probing his operations prior to these. I think that other intelligence agencies will be more successful in getting any information."

They agreed with him and collected all their notes and tapes of the interview and went to update themselves on what Goetze had disclosed on the list.

In the other interview room, Williams was shown back in. She looked much more awake and fresher, her hair was combed, and her clothes were clean and tidy.

Mark opened with the question, "Did you ever meet Brown at his house?"

She replied "Of course, we spent time with each other, I lived in barracks, but he had this house. He was supposed to be in barracks too, but he said he was senior enough to live in a house off the base. At weekends and a few nights in the week we would go there and then return to work next morning."

Sandy said asked, "What was the address?" She looked at him and said, "Don't you know, I thought he had registered it with his superiors, another lie I suppose."

She continued "15 Horseshoe Lane, Mychett. It's just outside Aldershot, but far enough away for us to have privacy, that was what I thought anyway."

Mark left the room with the address and gave it to Freeman. He looked and said he did not recognise it but would send a team over immediately and get the place searched. He felt this was another, important, breakthrough in their investigation.

He returned to the room and said to Williams, "Any other locations he took you when you were together, or that he mentioned?"

She sat and thought and then said, "We went to a building in Basingstoke once. I had to stay in the car while he went inside. He was there for about 30 minutes, and when he came out, he was carrying a briefcase. I asked him what it was, and he told me he had left it there on a previous occasion. I thought it odd as he was meticulous in what he did, but I didn't ask any further."

Mark responded, "Would you be able to identify the building if it was shown to you?" She responded, "Sure, it was the biggest building there, probably eight to ten storeys high and not far from the marketplace."

In the observation room, Ellis directed that a full list of all properties in the building be obtained immediately. If there was resistance, tell the individuals it is a matter of National Security and arrest them if they fail to comply.

In the interview room Sandy asked, "Did Brown meet with others when he was with you? She replied, "One or two. One I know was in the army because of his uniform. The other man, he never told me about him nor introduced me to him. He did go out a few times and told me he was going to see a friend. When I asked if I could go with him, he said no, they were not nice people."

She continued, "You must think I am stupid, but I really liked him, and he seemed genuine, not like some of the other squaddies around, I still don't know what he has done, can I see him?"

Mark replied, "No you can't, we are interviewing him. He is not to be interrupted. We are getting information from him, which may have a bearing on what you are saying and may be prejudicial to you."

She gasped out loud, "Prejudicial to me? I have done nothing wrong. I have told you what I know, I don't know what else I can tell you. You have to believe me."

She broke down sobbing and kept repeating that she had done nothing wrong. She was his girlfriend, nothing else and she didn't know what he had been doing while they were dating and, more importantly, when she was in Afghanistan.

At this point, Ellis entered and said, "Ok Sergeant Williams we are finished for the moment. You are confined to barracks. A room has been set aside for you. You will of course, be taken under blindfold and remain guarded. At least it's a decent room, and you will stay there until further notice, do you understand?"

She smiled and replied, "Yes Sir, of course, anything, I really am just an ordinary soldier." Ellis nodded and she was led out of the room. Mark said, "I think she is telling us all she knows. He has taken her for a ride, but we have got some information which may prove useful."

They left the interview area and met with Freeman and his team in the Mess. They sat and discussed what had been said, by both Goetze and Williams.

Sarah was impressed that Williams had given them an address where they had stayed and the details of the building she had visited, although not the actual office.

Ellis said that a team had already arrived at the house and were searching it for anything that may shed light on Browns activities. Additionally, the details of all the companies registered at the building in Basingstoke had been obtained. Most of them were local, but several were registered through nominee companies. This would take longer, but with the National Security tag being played, he was confident of quick results.

Freeman asked about the names and details on the list supplied by Goetze. He was told that of the seven names on the list, birth certificates and passport requests for all of them had been made within the past few years.

Ellis further added that a number of bank accounts and credit cards had been attributed to those names. The addresses and details were in the process of being confirmed. None of the addresses corresponded with the Horseshoe Lane address.

Freeman said, "We can do discreet observations on all the properties immediately. We can then see what is going on in each other them, or whether they are just a front for other premises."

Ellis said, "We have only found two addresses where a driving licence or a vehicle has been mentioned. These two are the most promising. One is in Guilford and the other in Fleet, neither are too far from each other. Both are definitely accessible to Basingstoke and London."

Freeman said, "Give me the details and we'll set up a surveillance on the premises and if you can supply a couple of your guys as backups that will be appreciated a lot." Ellis agreed and made a phone call, then said, "The teams will be in Aldershot in one hour and will move out from there. The other properties can be checked as well, we'll supply the necessary backup."

Freeman moved next door and liaised with the Commissioner of Police. Between them they organised more watches on all the premises.

On his return, Ellis showed him two driving licences, one in the name of Gordon Lamb and the other in the name of Stephen Grey. Freeman grinned and said, "Yes, now are getting somewhere." He was looking at the photo of Brown on both the licences.

He added, "Those properties have got to be turned upside down. I don't care who is or is not in there. This has given us what we need to go to town on him." He again rang the Commissioner, told her of the information, and repeated his instructions to go through the house with a fine-tooth comb.

CHAPTER 37

They all sat around the table with a growing sense of anticipation. News came through that all the passports had been used in the last 3 years. They included overseas trips to places diverse as the Philippines and Columbia, as well as numerous times within Europe and only once to the United States.

Twenty minutes later came the news they were all waiting for, the photographs on all the passports belonged to Brown.

After the initial euphoria, Ellis said to Freeman, "We now need to obtain all the times he was overseas on any of the passports."

Freeman said, "Leave that to me. We can correlate all the dates he has been outside the country on any of the passports with any known incidents in those places."

They both got onto their phones and gave out instructions to their respective offices. Within twenty minutes responses came back showing the trips out of the country that Brown had made over the past three years. Many of them were for a few days only, but several were for up to a week.

After obtaining the passport details in the names which Brown was using, they had also established the details of the credit and debit cards he had obtained in those names. These were being checked too, establishing locations used, places visited and stayed.

They were satisfied that they were now establishing a pattern of Brown's movements. His activities and all the information they had obtained so far were being entered into the computers and then onto a large screen. Slowly but surely, a picture of his life started to emerge.

Each of the names being used by Brown was entered into the spreadsheet. All corresponding personal details were entered in chronological order.

Their concentration on the screens was interrupted by a shrill ring of the phone, and Ellis picked it up and said "Ellis."

He listened to the phone for a few moments and then put it on speaker. They heard "We have found five passports and other different papers in bags hidden in the pipework in the garage. We have also seized a large number of guns, specifically rifles and ammunition making material."

The speaker continued, "We will send you the details in the next few minutes. We are now going to go through everything, the place is not booby trapped but did have an alarm system, which we disabled before entering the premises. It is going to take us several hours before we can complete all this. Do we need experts who can make proper records evidence wise?"

Freeman interjected and said, "Yes, we have a team of experts who can assist your men there. They are fully trained Scenes of Crimes officers who will catalogue everything for the chain of evidence in the event of a trial."

The reply came back, "Thanks, it will be much appreciated." The line went dead, and Freeman picked up his phone and called the control room at Scotland Yard and asked to be put through to DS Grace Meadows.

Within a few seconds she answered the phone and said, "Hello Sir, what can I do for you today?"

Freeman responded, "Afternoon Grace, I have a crime scene just perfect for your skills. We have a breakthrough on the park shootings and its connected to Captain Brown. I need you and your team to go immediately to near Aldershot and conduct a forensic examination of the premises. I'll give you the details on your mobile. Take as long as you like, there is already a lot there, but I am sure we will find the golden pot somewhere there. You might need ground radar too, he is a devious bastard."

She replied, "No problems I'll get my team together now. It's been pretty quiet theses past couple of days, wondered what you and Sarah were getting up to. Thought you had gone to ground, if it means getting Brown then I'll rip the place apart myself."

She laughed and said, "Send me the address and I'll be back to you as soon as possible. Are there time constraints on this or is it military and to hell with the rules?"

Freeman smiled and said, "Enough Grace, we are all in this together. You will be met by Corporal Sheila Malone. She will brief you and supply you with what you need. You'll get plenty of pleasure out of this I am sure, go get him." He disconnected and then immediately sent the address to Grace for her to search.

It soon became apparent that the address in Mychett was his primary address. Another address he was renting just outside Wimbledon was in regular use, according to neighbours. All other addresses checked out as being rented to other military staff or were on long term rental to university students.

Freeman contacted the Commissioner and told her of the developments. She sounded pleased and would pass the information to the Prime Minister, who might just be grateful for all the work everyone was doing. Freeman smiled inwardly, thinking that was the pot calling the kettle black after some of her recent comments.

He then said, "I have sent DS Meadows to Mychett where it appears that the house is the main base for Brown. We think he has been using an address in Wimbledon for his daily use. The neighbours all know him from his comings and goings over the past couple of years. Can you get another DS and SOCO team over to Wimbledon and get them to do a fingertip search of the whole premises."

She informed him that she would arrange a Serious Crime Squad team out there immediately and they were to report to him direct.

She then asked, "Have you started interviewing Brown yet"? He responded, "No, we are getting everything we need before going head-to-head with him. I don't want there to be any weaknesses in our investigations and results."

She then asked about Goetze and was told that they believed they had obtained as much evidence from him as they were going to get. They were getting an eight day extension order under the Terrorism Act to cover themselves. She seemed pleased with that and then asked about Williams.

Freeman said, "We all believe she has been a pawn in this. She was the one who told us about Mychett, and another location which we are sorting out. She will be court marshalled out of the army, but I believe Ellis is impressed with her intelligence skills, notwithstanding her problems with Brown. She will be offered a position somewhere suitable."

The Commissioner told Freeman to stay with it. Not to rush it, but don't leave yourself open to criticism in the long term. With that she said she would sort out the Wimbledon address and clicked off.

They all returned to their seats. They looked at the screens and decided that different intelligence agencies would be needed to track Browns movements while in the different countries.

Ellis said he had a number of agencies around the globe who could provide instant information. He was wary of using Mossad and the NSA because of their connections to Brown. It was agreed that Ellis would liaise with the FBI and the CIA and get the information through them and not mention Brown per se.

Freeman would work with GCHQ and the two MI's, five and six, through his opposite number in MI6.

Steenson then said he will use his contacts in his country. It was apparent that Brown had been operating in the different areas. He didn't specifically say what agency, but as far as Freeman, Sarah and Jason were concerned it would be through the Russian embassy. Freeman said that Steenson had complicated relationships with different authorities, but he was totally trusted by him and his team since they had met him when with Gregorov and Karakova.

Ellis commented, "The more information we can get, the deeper we can bury this son of a bitch. He is a disgrace to the uniform and country."

They all went to different parts of the Mess, leaving Sarah and Jason together with Mark and Sandy sitting in the middle, feeling somewhat left out. Mark said, "I believe you are the ones investigating the park shootings of the 3 family members."

Jason said, "Yes and ironically Brown was asked to help us due to his knowledge of the manner of the killing and, even more ironically, assisting with the Bulgarian's shooting." Sarah said, "I'd seen him cycling in the street even, he looked good." They all laughed, and she joked, "All the good ones are either married or terrorists."

Mark said, "Brown has always been a hero, we looked up to him. He was extra special. He was one of the best shots in the world. What possessed him to do this. I know, money!"

Jason commented, "His ego got too much, he made this reputation in the military and needed to prove himself outside. Worked for the highest bidder I think, but we will know soon enough."

Sandy said, "You know the worst part, he is using the names of our dead comrades for his evil life. I cannot forgive him for that. He deserves the firing squad just for that."

They sat in silence for a few moments until Freeman, Ellis and Steenton returned. They gave them updates as to what they had done and with whom and said that all they could do now was wait for any connections to turn up.

They heard the helicopter with Williams on board taking off for another military establishment nearby. She would never know that she had been at Bradbury Lines. Sarah felt sorry for her. She remembered the times when she was younger, and things had not turned out good for her.

All she cared about now was ensuring they had everything they needed to take to Brown. It had not yet been decided who would be conducting the interviews, but she hoped that it would be a joint matter, so she could have him for the park murders.

Within thirty minutes phones started to ring and the three officials started making notes on their pads and passing them on to the main computer where it was transferred on to the large screens.

A pattern soon emerged that within thirty-six hours of his entering a country there had been a high profile killing which always involving shootings. The majority of cases were one on one shootings, but three were double killings, and according to the authorities a high degree of difficulty had been needed and used to accomplish them.

They all looked at the screen as the information was updated, he was a prolific killer. Jason said to no one in particular, "Who the hell is running this man? This is a costly international operation, there must be people all over the world doing this."

Freeman said, "We think the answers lie in Basingstoke and Mychett. Once we have finished there, I am sure we are going to find out all the figures behind this."

He continued, "All the killings seem to relate to either Government or high-ranking officials in banking or industry. We will have to get our friends to enquire with all of the victim's employers and ascertain a common link between them."

Freeman's phone rang and on answering it said, "Hello Grace, what have you got for us? She replied, "Sorry Sir, we have a problem. Ground radar has picked up a body in the garden behind the house in Mychett. I have called Doctor Webster, and he is attending now. Until he arrives, we cannot do anything outside, but we are still examining inside the house and there is a whole load of papers and stuff here."

She continued, "There is also what appears to be a trapdoor leading into a basement in the garage too. We have not got into that yet, the bomb squad are checking to make sure its secure. We don't want a repeat of the other times. He has a safe in the floor in his lounge which was covered by flooring and carpets. A locksmith is on his way now to open that. We have no idea what we are going to find. There are iron filing cabinets, boxes and trunks all around. Unfortunately, we have detected residue of C4 and other equipment for making ammunition and bombs."

She rang off, and Freeman said, "Well you heard that, just when we thought it couldn't get worse, it does."

Sarah said, "What about the address in Wimbledon, any news from there yet"?

Freeman responded, "They have a car which they have impounded and going through that. There are also false cavities in many of the walls, but again they are being careful with them and going through bomb detection protocols with each one."

They all felt frustrated that they had got so much information and were getting closer all the time to pinning Brown down to all the atrocities he was now suspected of committing. All that was missing was a few more details to confirm his involvement in the treason and murderous acts they suspected him of.

Whilst they waited, they received details of the offices in Basingstoke. They discovered that two of them were connected by proxy partners, and ultimately registered in Luxembourg. A quick analysis revealed that the owners and chief operating officers were ex-military from the United Kingdom, America and South Africa.

Ellis said, “Leave them to me. We have our resources and will see what they are up to. Our friends will dig into their operations and see what they can drag up. I’ll also arrange for the individuals to be subject to surveillance orders wherever they are maybe.”

Freeman looked at him and said, “You can do that?” He replied, “We have many more powers and abilities that you can never have. “

At that moment, Freeman's phone rang, and he said, “Yes, Grace what have you got for me?”

She answered, “The body is a male, between 10 and 15 years of age and has been in the ground for at least twenty years as far as Doc Webster can tell. He is taking it back to the morgue and will give us more from there. There was no clothing with it and the bones are pretty well chewed up.”

She then continued, “The cellar has been opened, there was nothing to protect it. The guys are going through it now and there are loads of guns and ammunition in there, enough to start a small war! A lot of it was manufactured in south Africa.”

Freeman and Ellis looked at each other but said nothing. “Freeman said, “Carry on Grace, log everything and please let us know if you find anything that needs our immediate attention. What about the safe?”

Grace commented that the safe was of a top-grade construction. The safe engineer was drilling out the locks, but no x-rays could permeate into the safe, such was the high grade of metal. She said her goodbyes and disconnected. Freeman just said, "We are going to have to wait a little longer, but we are almost there."

By the end of the afternoon, all the details of the known passports, credit cards and travel locations, hotels and length of visits associated with Brown were up and running on the large screens.

They sat discussing them and worked on a matrix to be presented to the interviewers when Brown was ready to be interviewed. Freeman received a call from Doc Webster, the pathologist, who confirmed the age of the male as being approximately 13 years old. He did not show any signs of injury leading to cause of death. He was able to say however, that the body bore signs of long-term illnesses and disease. He had been able to obtain a few DNA samples and would send them for analysis against all known databases.

Freeman thanked him and told Jason to check on the property in Horseshoe Lane as to the ownership over the past twenty years and see there is any connection with Brown. In addition, do property searches on all the properties in the lane, that may be helpful too.

A short while later, as Sarah and Jason were processing the property in Horseshoe Lane, Ellis received a report from his team at the address in Wimbledon. They had found different files on individuals from around the world. Most had "completed" in red ink written on the cover. They had found these in the garage inside a stand which had been hollowed out. In total there were twenty-six such files.

Ellis exhaled loudly and said, "I need those immediately. Copy them all and send them by email to my email address now. Anything else of note?"

He responded, "Several pistols, non-military issue and other equipment including camouflage netting and scopes. There are no rifles here though. But we are still looking and finishing off."

Ellis told him that once they had finished, there was to be an armed guard of at least 6 men on duty twenty fours a day at the house until further notice. The officer replied in the affirmative and rang off.

Ellis told the assembled group of the findings of the twenty-six files. They looked up at the board and realised that was three times as many kills down to Brown than was previously known.

Ellis said, "They are being sent by email as we speak. Log them and cross index them all with what we know so far." He added, without mirth, "How did he ever manage to do any proper soldier work?"

Jason reported that Brown had only owned the property in Horseshoe Lane for the past five years. There was no record of him living in the vicinity before that. According to the records, the owners around the time of the death were a Rita and Victor Heath. Freeman said, "Pass it on to the local police, they can carry on with investigating it. We don't have the time to continue with it. Jason, you contact the Senior Investigating Officer down in Aldershot and liaise with him."

Jason left and made his phone call, coming back a few minutes later and saying that they will conduct the enquiries. They want us to hand everything over for evidential purposes. I told him that it was a case of National Security and that the body aspect was surplus to that. He was not happy, but I told him if he had any complaints contact the Prime Minister, that shut him up."

They all laughed, and the tension was lifted a little. They settled back and within a few minutes Ellis's email buzzed and he opened it and saw that it was the files he had requested.

He started to download them, and they continued the downloading for several minutes. He arranged for them to be printed but in the meantime forwarded the files to the members onto their own pads and laptops.

As they opened the different files it became apparent that they had only scratched the surface. The detailing in the files was extensive - from receiving the instructions to finalising them and carrying it all out. There were notes on airlines, hotels, and very importantly, initials and names of persons who he had met during his overseas trips.

Freeman told everyone to stop and allocated each of them three files. He told them to examine them and get as much information as possible and then paste them onto the screen. He recognised a few from the existing list but not many, which worried him.

They spent the next ninety minutes assembling the details on the large screens. They were all amazed at the complexity of the information received and the amount of intelligence which they were now compiling. Ellis made an off the cuff remark that they don't need to interview him, just shoot him and get it done with. There were no objections to those remarks.

Finally, Grace made the call they had all been waiting for, they had gained access into the floor safe. She said, excitedly, "We have found over seventy passports in different names and bearing different photographs, together with other forms of Identification from several countries."

She continued, "There are also some documents relating to a number of companies, including the ones in Luxembourg. His name appears as an official of those companies, but I cannot read the details. I am going to need our Commercial Crime guys to look at them. There are also bank accounts for five banks, two here and the others in South Africa and America.

She said, "Millions of pounds have gone in and out of those accounts over the past few years. It will take our guys ages to go through them, but interestingly Brown is a signatory to both the United Kingdom accounts and one in South Africa."

Freeman and Ellis looked at each other and both said, "Got him!" They shook hands, and Freeman said to Grace, "Brilliant work, make copies of what you have. Send the originals to us by helicopter as soon as you can, time we fixed Brown once and for all."

He gave Grace their location, there was silence for a few moments, then she said, "Wow, you certainly get around. I'll bring the originals myself to observe the chain of evidence, and I can get to ride in a chopper and see the camp, double winner for me."

Freeman looked at Ellis who nodded and said, "We'll be pleased to see you DS Meadows, with all the work you have done it's the least we can do for you."

She responded, "Thank you both, will be with you in a couple of hours by the time we have finished copying everything." She rang off.

They sat in their group, taking in what Grace had just told them. They were still finishing their other enquiries regarding the passports and the locations they had been used in. Freeman told Jason to take charge of those enquiries and finish those as soon as possible. They needed to clear their desks for all the new information they had received and was about to receive through Grace.

Freeman left the group to give the Commissioner an update on all the events. She was shocked at the extent of the criminal enterprise that seemed to have taken place. She asked, "What is the reasoning behind it all. Surely our Intelligence Services should have picked up something, even a few snippets, but this is far bigger than normal."

Freeman commented, "We have Brown now for certain. Goetze is also done and dusted, and Williams has been released into Military custody for the time being. But, and it's a big but, we need to find out why Brown shot those poor souls and their connection with any of this."

Ellis responded that their names had not emerged from any of the files they had seen so far. They were either not who they seemed to be, and that was a long shot, or they were in the wrong place at the wrong time for one of Brown's shooting experiments. Freeman opined that he thought they had been the innocent victims who had set off the trail of events leading to where they were today.

Sarah and Steenson agreed with him. Steenson admitted he did not know as much as everyone else involved in the investigation. To him, the mistake was made when both Gregorov and Brown were given the same contract and Brown did not finish it. He asked if there were any records of Gregorov and Karakova appearing anywhere.

Sarah replied, "I haven't seen anything, but there will be records somewhere, he is too organised not to have secreted some form of paperwork in a hole."

They all agreed. The started by looking at the dates of both shootings and worked back for a week, analysing any bank transfers, emails and travel details of all the names they had so far on display.

Steenson picked up on an email giving details of an Eastern European who was causing trouble and needed to be eliminated. He said, "There was no name, but a place and time for a meet was suggested. That was two days before the killing by Gregorov. The fee for that operation was £100,000 and payable into his nominated bank account. There is no record of the accounts, but we should be able to find out when we get the information from DS Meadows."

He posted the information onto the big screen for future reference. It appeared that the more intelligence they were gathering, the more the gaps were being filled and it was all coming to a conclusion.

They all went about their tasks quietly and efficiently. They all felt the need to complete as much as they could before Grace arrived with the rest of the documents and evidence. Every few minutes they would gather and discuss a point somebody had found which needed an explanation. Then it would be inserted into the relevant onscreen file.

About an hour later, Freeman received a call from Grace saying she had landed and needed escorting to the Mess as she was not allowed to move anywhere. Freeman told her to wait and arranged for someone to go and meet her and bring her to them.

A few minutes later Grace entered the room carrying a box which contained a large number of plastic bags. She put them down and smiled broadly as Jason went over to her, gave her a huge smile, and kissed her on her head. He whispered, “Missed you.” She looked up and said, “Missed you too.”

They all looked at them, Sarah was wide eyed. and Jason said, “Got to keep some secrets from you Sarah, you don’t hold the monopoly on them.”

Grace just said, “Hi folks, thanks for letting me come here, it’s good to be among friends again.” Freeman responded, “A good one Grace, never saw that one coming, I’ll have to be more careful in future.”

They all laughed. Grace opened the box and reminded them that she was the exhibits officer. Everyone, no matter what rank, had to make sure proper entries were made when they opened each bag.

Jason and Sarah split the passports between them and searched for any link in the documentation. Steenson and Freeman started to go through the financial records, the bank statements, and credit card details. Ellis concentrated on the company files they had unearthed.

Over the next few hours, they all had their pads and were typing into them and the information was then entered onto the big screens. The photographs on the twenty-six passports were scanned into the computers and sent to GCHQ where they were examined and, where possible, names were linked to the photographs.

Contact was made with the passport office for the application forms in relation to the passports, to be sent to them. From there any form of identification used in support of the forms would be checked and addresses confirmed.

Freeman and Steenson started to go through the banking records and saw that vast sums of money had flowed in and out of the accounts over a number of years. Brown was signatory on two, the other signatories on the accounts were not known. Immediately the banks concerned were contacted and their records demanded.

The two UK banks told them they would not provide anything without warrants. Freeman told them to wait, put the phone down. He contacted the Commissioner of Police and asked that she contact the Prime Minister and for her to emphasise to the bankers the importance of the request. She said she would and put the phone down.

Ten minutes later, Freeman rang the banks again and was told that the information they required was being sent by secure email to them immediately. The officials apologised for any misunderstanding.

When Freeman told the others, they all wondered what pressure the Prime Minister had put on the banks to get the information. However, they were all glad that she had done so and that it had made their jobs so much easier.

They found that the complexity of the bank documentation was above their capabilities. They would have to contact the Commercial Crime Office, to find out what they could come up with. The other problem was the cooperation of the overseas banks. They were unsure how they could arrange for the necessary cooperation and get the transaction details they needed.

They decided to concentrate on the UK accounts first. As and when they had sufficient information, they would contact the relevant authorities.

In the meantime, Ellis was going over the company documents and finding the backgrounds to them. It appeared at first sighting that they had all been formed at around the same time. Brown was a founding signatory to three of the companies. However, their details had been hidden by proxy companies and secretarial directors in overseas countries like Hong Kong and Singapore. Over time directors had changed with the exception of Brown. Ellis said to himself that he must find out the circumstances of the others leaving the companies, whether voluntary or removed one way or another.

He set out the listings in his pad and sent them to the large screen and opened up a new area of investigation.

Grace sat at her desk and watched as all the information was displayed. She followed each new entry and looked over the screen as quickly as she could to try and match entries with peoples, times, and places.

After an hour of inputting, Freeman said, “OK, time to take a break. I don’t know about you, but my brain is befuddled, and my eyes are aching with so much concentration. We’ll take an hour and I’ll arrange for meals to be brought up and we can eat and relax for a while.”

They put everything down and went and sat in their chairs. Jason and grace sat together, holding hands, and just talking softly. Sarah looked across and realised that she had missed being close to anyone for the past few months. She had concentrated on her career and put that before her happiness. She made a promise there and then not to let that happen again. She closed her eyes and within a few minutes fell asleep.

The others settled down into a relaxed mood, all deep in thought, but grateful for the break. Steenson felt that he had not stopped since he had joined the team. He wondered if he would be able to continue with them in the future. He had never felt so much a part of a team before and it surprised him.

They ate a meal of chicken curry and rice, with naans all prepared by the Gurkha chefs in the Mess. They sat and collected their thoughts and discussed how they could proceed. They had a mountain of evidence now, and more than enough to implicate Brown in the running of various companies which both financed and were financed by others to commit assassinations.

CHAPTER 38

Freeman and Ellis then went into the merits of interviewing Brown early. They would supply the basic information, for example his use of the internet and phone where he logged on twice in quick succession. Why he had done it, and why the speed of each transmission? Maybe they would not disclose their knowledge of his relationship with Sergeant Williams for the time being unless he told them himself. They would go over his postings and whereabouts over the last twelve months.

Ellis said, "We have his record, it covers his service from officer cadet through to his present rank and posting, his previous postings and travels are all here. We can pin him down on the dates we know he was out of the country and see his reactions."

Freeman responded, "We need some samples of writing from him, or at least something he has written lately. Preferable in person now, and to get a sample of his DNA. I notice there is no mention of it on his file."

Ellis said, "We get DNA from all the other ranks, but it was felt to be bad taste to ask our officers to supply theirs. There has been this culture within the military that some of us are trying to change but have met a lot of resistance."

Freeman replied, "We have a few hours of today left still. Let's get it started, we can see how it goes, and by then we will be having more information coming in and available."

Ellis said, I'll lead, and you can interject as and when. Sarah and Steenson, you have the earpieces and mikes and feed us information and facts as we go on."

Freeman continued and said, "Jason, you and Grace can carry on inputting the information into the computers and passing it on to Sarah. We will try and get back here within three hours. I think by then we will have had enough and hopefully we will have made some inroads with him. If we find we are achieving too much and haven't got any backups we will just halt it and start again tomorrow."

They finished their desserts and drank their coffee before printing off what they needed for the first part of the interviews. They split up into their pairs and left the Mess to travel the short distance to where Brown was being held.

Jason and Grace sat for a few minutes in silence before Grace said, "Did I come across a bit strong when I entered, it seemed to shock them all, you hadn't told them anything?"

He replied, "No, I have never said anything to anyone, not even Sarah. She will be giving me the third degree after all this I know. But I am glad they saw us. I have hated keeping us in the shadows."

Grace smiled and said, "Yes me too, now let's get to work before they think we are shirking."

Ellis and Freeman entered the interview room where Brown was seated. He looked up at them both and said, "You have kept me here long enough and not told me what is happening. I deserve some respect for my rank."

Ellis responded, "At the moment Mr Brown you are being held on various charges involving National Security. Under military law you can be held indefinitely and denied any legal representation whilst being investigated. You know the rules as well as I do, so don't pretend you are ignorant of the facts."

Brown commented, "Why is Commander Freeman present when this is supposed to be a military matter, of which I have no knowledge as nothing has been explained to me."

Ellis replied, "As you know, we have been conducting a joint operation from the outset, and you have been part of that. Your expertise was invaluable to the Commander and his team. However, over time, certain incidents have occurred which have caused great concern to him and me, especially."

Brown said, "What are you talking about?" looking at Ellis with a frown.

Ellis continued, "There is the matter of you logging on twice on your terminal, the second time for only a few seconds before logging off. That is against all rules and regulations to have more than one connection open at any one time."

Brown said, "That was a mistake, sometimes I am concentrating on what I am going to say to my contacts and log in again, realise my mistake and close it immediately. I have never left it open."

Ellis said, "How many times has that happened?"

Brown responded, "I think two or three times, I am not sure. I can check my computer for you if you let me."

Ellis commented, "No need, it has happened twelve times over a three month period, can you explain that?"

Brown replied, "I cannot explain it any more than what I have just said. It was an accident made in the heat of events."

Ellis looked at him and said, "No, Brown, they weren't accidents. You deliberately logged on a second time, you were online for twelve seconds on each occasion before logging off. That is no accident."

Brown shuffled in his seat and responded, "I had no idea of how long I was on, but as soon as I realised, I logged off."

Ellis continued, "Then how do you explain these random letters which were transmitted before you logged out." He showed Brown the printout of the logs he had made.

Brown looked at them and replied, "They are obviously just keyboard letters that I must have hit. They don't signify anything. As far as I am concerned, they were errors which stopped when I logged out."

Ellis then said, "Think very carefully about your next answers Mr Brown, they are going to have a large bearing on how we are going to deal with you."

Brown looked at them both and said, "What do you expect me to say? I made mistakes, so discipline me, kick me out I don't care. But for something so small I don't know why we have had all this cloak and dagger rubbish."

Freeman said, "When you logged in, where did you log into, what site?"

Brown replied, "I don't know, I didn't go into any site, like I said they are just letters to me.

Ellis commented, "Strange that they are exactly the same letters on all occasions, except they are in a different order. Any comments you care to make?"

He shrugged and said, "I am sure you have your theories, I'll be interested to hear what you have to say."

Ellis reminded him of his position and situation and said, "We don't have theories. We have evidence of the times you were online and typed those letters. We also know where you sent the messages too, care to elaborate?"

Brown looked surprised and said, "Well if you know so much tell me, I am not going to roll over and play dumb for you."

Ellis said, "All the calls were made to one computer in Helmand Province in Afghanistan. That person is in the British Army and currently in custody as a suspected terrorist. Does that help to jog your memory?"

Brown said, "Whoever it is must be a traitor, why would they pass on letters which make no sense. I know my computers have never been hacked, so I don't know the reasoning behind it."

Ellis shook his head and said, "Perhaps the name Sergeant Joan Williams might ring a bell?"

Brown closed his eyes, put his head down, and finally said, "Yes, I know Joan, we have been friends for a while. Since she went on deployment to Afghanistan, she has been unable to communicate with the outside world. We decided that we could still be in touch, at least a few times. I knew what I did was wrong, and no blame can be placed on her. She did as I suggested, don't be hard on her."

Ellis said, "Now we have cut through the rubbish of the last thirty minutes, tell me what you did, and don't leave anything out. You have seen the paperwork, tell me how and why."

Brown sat back, looked up at nothing in particular and said, "Once I logged in properly on my machine, I'd immediately log in again with another password. As soon as I was connected, I sent the letters to Joan. We had decided on the letters before she went to Helmand, ones that could be used every time in a different order. There was nothing untoward in it. Yes, it was against the rules, but we weren't hurting anyone, I was just letting her know that I still cared for her. Just my luck that with all these cases involving Gregorov, I was being looked at too. I suppose that is a compliment to my skills that you were looking at me. But the computer nerds beat me in the end. I thought that one of your guys had been hanging around my station a bit recently."

Ellis said, "Now you know that you cannot pull the wool over our eyes anymore, let's move on to other matters which are of a much more serious nature."

Brown looked at Ellis across the table, the room felt constricted, no windows, and only the fan from the cooling system disturbed the silence. Ellis opened a file, not close enough for Brown to read the details, but he was aware, of course, that it related to him. Ellis deliberately took his time, going through the various pages, looking up at him, then resuming reading.

Freeman just looked relaxed, as if he was expecting something dramatic to happen, but Brown kept his silence.

Ellis said, "From our investigations it appears that you have been on a number of overseas journeys in the past few years which are not connected with your duties. According to your file you were on overseas duty eight times in the past three years for a combined time of twenty weeks."

Brown replied, "I cannot give you exact dates, but that's correct. I was sent overseas on various operations for the army. I don't see what I might have done anything wrong. What are you insinuating?"

Ellis replied, "Insinuating nothing Brown, it's the other trips you have been making outside your official duties which interest me most. Of course, none of them have been under your name, have they?"

Brown looked surprised, “What do you mean? Where have you got this information, who has been trying to set me up?”

Ellis responded, “Since your arrest we have carried out searches at your address in Wimbledon and found various documents hidden in different locations which all relate to you, care to comment?”

Brown answered, “Not now, I need a break, can you get me a coffee and make me a club sandwich, no one would make me one since my arrest as you put it. Can you make it with seeded loaf, ham and tomato on one layer and cheese lettuce with salad cream on the upper layer, I’ll be very grateful.”

Ellis commented, “I’ll arrange for your sandwich, you’ll have a fifteen minutes break and we’ll resume. When we do you had better come up with some answers to our questions, time is not on your side.”

They left the room while Brown’s break was being prepared. Freeman said, “That killed him, he is desperately trying to think of what to say. The more we keep him on the back foot, the quicker he will make a mistake”.

Ellis replied, “We’ll just concentrate on his place in Wimbledon first. I am almost certain he doesn’t know about our knowledge of Horseshoe Lane, so he will keep away from that as much as he can.

If we are lucky, he will give us some snippets and think that we will be satisfied with all that. He has a superiority complex and that will drop his guard too. He knows what he has at his house and will try and give plausible explanations for everything."

They returned to the room, Brown was finishing off his sandwich and said that it was a good one, on a par with any fine restaurant. They ignored his sarcasm and Ellis opened the new file with the details of all the passports found in his garage struts.

Ellis started by saying "We found the forms for passport applications tucked inside one of the struts ". He laid out the documents in alphabetical order and said, "These are 26 applications for passports, what is this about?"

Brown responded, "They are all for military operations involving myself and my team members when we have to go undercover".

Ellis countered, "There is nothing in any records of you being involved in such operations, using these passports. Six of these forms bear your photograph but with different names, did you ever get the passports or what?"

Brown replied, "No, they are insurance and for a quick requirement if we ever needed them, but fortunately it was not necessary. I just kept them out of the way in case we had to go live."

Ellis said, "Who were the others, who were the applications made out to?"

Brown replied, "Colleagues from different teams within the Special Boats Unit and SAS. We have trained together for several years, and I have carte blanche to choose my men if needed."

Ellis said, "Who is the senior officer who sanctioned all these actions? There is nothing in your records to suggest anything like this. I have known you for twelve months now and I have seen that two of the applications have been filled out in the last six months."

Brown replied, "I am sorry sir, I am sworn to secrecy about him. I am sure he would vouch for me, but I will not disclose who he is."

Ellis looked at Brown straight in the eye and said, "You had your chance to tell us the truth. You have chosen to lie and cover yourself with a ridiculous story that doesn't add up one little bit."

He continued, "We are not just hanging around, we have checked every one of the applications and found out that passports have been issued in respect of everyone who's names are on the forms, including the six with your photograph displayed. Anything you'd like to say now?"

Brown just said, "They are for use military wise, that's all I need to say."

Ellis countered, "We have checked the identities of the other applicants against all databases and nowhere do any of them appear as serving soldiers. In fact, from our investigations and liaisons with other countries, none of them have ever served in the UK army and most have criminal records, the majority of whom are associated with

South Africa and America. They are better described as soldiers for hire."

He went on, "Seems to me that you are a soldier for hire too in your spare time. You keep company with killers and other undesirables, and what other secrets are you hiding?"

Brown commented, "I have been infiltrating these people for a couple of years now and need to know who they are. I have been a facilitator for them in getting passports, but I don't know what happens after that. I am told what to do, do the jobs and gain their confidence."

Freeman interjected and said, "Who is your point of contact? Surely if you are above board and doing what you say then you have no reason not to tell us, whether he is army or another government branch."

Brown shrugged and said, "Official Secrets Act."

Ellis said, "Where are the passports now, the ones in the names of the true soldiers who died fighting for our country, that is as low as a man can go and try and dishonour their names and the others which were supplied?"

He replied, "After using them once I threw them away as I didn't want the other side to find out too much about me. The others I have no idea, you will have to ask them and good luck with that."

He sat back, seemingly satisfied with his answers. He knew that they would never find any documents linking him to anyone else. If this was all they had on him then he'd be out soon enough and although have to leave the army, a much more rewarding life awaited him.

Ellis then asked, "We found traces of military grade explosives at your property too, there was also some ammunition making equipment there too, what is that about?"

Brown responded, "As a sniper we often make our bullets to our own specifications. That goes on everywhere, and nobody ever asks about it. As long as the shot is good, and the target is taken out that is all that matters."

He continued "I work with explosives when training troops or using them under fighting conditions so that they will not panic. I probably have got some on my clothes and transferred it when changing. It's very light and no doubt was no more than dust circulating."

Ellis said, "Wrong answer, there were traceable amounts found in the garage and in your car. We identified it as C4 explosives which had been manufactured in South Africa. Every batch of explosives ever made has their own identifying features and the stuff found at your house, was from two different batches, and none of it had ever been assigned to the British Military."

Brown said nothing at first, he looked across at both Ellis and Freeman, realising that they obviously knew what was at the house in Wimbledon, but not the other location.

He then answered, "Ok yes, the explosive is not ours. But I like to experiment with explosives when on operations. When

I find a few grams during the ops, then I collect it, bring it home and try to analyse and work things out by making little devices which would assist the work of the army."

Ellis responded, "You realise that you have committed serious offences by having such explosives in your possession? By your own admission you have conducted yourself in an unworthy manner befitting an officer in the British Army."

He replied, "I have given my life to the country, so I made some mistakes, I'll have to accept my punishment and get on with life."

Ellis continued, "You seem to have forgotten about the passport applications, the fake passports, and other little details. They are also criminal offences and that makes us wonder what else you might be hiding."

He countered, "The passports were just throwaways. Part of the grand scheme of things if ever needed and I knew it would be easy to obtain one and even use it. Gave them to others, they thought it was a buzz me getting them documents when they would be banned from getting them."

Freeman said, "Do you realise the potential harm your actions could have caused by doing that? What did you think would happen, they would say thanks and hand them back over to you?"

Brown replied, "That was not my problem, they paid me enough so I did it, didn't take a lot of working out what could be done."

Ellis asked, "How did you contact them, or they contact you?"

He answered, "Through some mates in other special forces in different countries. They were also doing the same and when they spoke to me, I agreed. The money was more than I could ever earn here, and the risks were minimal if careful."

Ellis smiled and said, "Not careful enough, were you? You never thought about the consequences of what you were doing with Sergeant Williams. That has come back and bitten you in so many ways you have no idea of what is going to befall you in the next few days."

Ellis reminded Brown that for the moment he was still technically an officer in the army. All of his actions could be construed as potential terrorist acts. He conceded that his actions with Sergeant Williams were a criminal use of military equipment, but in view of all the circumstances and her statement, he was satisfied that there was no ulterior motive in it.

Brown stared at Ellis and said, "Thank you, she had no idea of what I was doing, I kept her away from it. She would not have understood anyway, and it was too much of a risk. I hope you go gently with her, we did it for each other. Everything else is on my shoulders."

Ellis said, "Is there anything else at the house you wish to tell us about, obviously you know we are stripping it completely. Your car has been impounded and is being searched too. We have obtained the records of calls made to and from that address as well."

Brown said, “No, you have wrecked my life, you have ruined it, there is nothing left for me to say or do. I am cooperating with you, so that must count for something.”

Ellis retorted, “As far as we are concerned, nothing counts in your favour. You have ruined your own life and reputation for money and arrogance. You have become a disgrace to everyone. You only admitted matters when you saw that there was no way out, not because you thought it best to assist us.”

He continued, “You created ideas in your own mind, in any attempt to lead us way from your treacherous activities. What about the arms you have at the house they are not military issue, how do you explain that?”

Brown appeared surprised and said, “Just stuff I collected when on overseas duties, I suppose they are trophies. I put them out of the way in case anyone came across them and stole them from me.”

Ellis said, “We have examined all of them, and they are all pretty modern. Many of them have never been found overseas in terrorist hands or enclaves. We have the records of your overseas operations and we have never had one of them from those jurisdictions.”

Brown stayed silent. Ellis said, “More lies, if we can link any of those guns to killings over the past few years, you'll be facing murder charges as well as all the other offences.”

He added, “Is there anything you'd like to disclose voluntarily or are we going to play cat and mouse all night and drag everything out of you?”

Brown looked him and said, "What else is there? You have got everything you need from the house. You have found all the hidden stuff, either charge me or send me back to my cell."

Freeman interjected, "Mr Brown, we have only just started with you. We have enough information to keep going for a lot longer on you and your associates. There are too many discrepancies in your story, you might have been a hero at some time in the past, but now you are nothing other than a common criminal who has no regard for his fellow men and country."

Brown responded, "Perhaps if you give me details, then I might be able to answer your questions. But I am not going to say anything to you just for the sake of saying something."

In the control room Grace and Jason were trawling through all the paperwork which was being sent to them by the various departments and agencies. They had excellent response from the Commercial Crimes Section. They had called in their forensic accounts staff and had gone through hundreds of entries in the bank accounts and deeds which had been uncovered from Horseshoe Lane.

As they entered all the information onto the screen and into their computers one name started to appear quite often. He was a signatory on several proxy forms, the companies having been formed in Hong Kong through secretarial companies.

Following the paper trail back and forth through several jurisdictions, the ultimately company, or more correctly two companies were found to be registered in Luxemburg and South Africa, but with offices in Basingstoke.

When Jason spoke with the accountants, he discovered that the same person was a signatory on several numbered accounts held either in England or Europe. On most of the signatory cards, three names were entered and any two could sign.

Browns signature appeared on five accounts, three of which bore the signature of the individual they were now finding out about.

Jason and Grace stopped what they were doing and tried to rationalise what they had found. This was way above their understanding so far of all that had taken place. The seemingly random attacks were now linked in with Brown and Gregorov and their activities. They were going to have to pass this further up the line and let the senior staff decide what to do next.

In the interim they would compile the report and attach the relevant documents and email them to Freeman and Ellis for their attention. They would remain where they were and continue to sift through the information. At last, they were more in control now they knew who else was involved.

As they sat and discussed the developments, Jason said, "When is it all going to end? Who is going to conduct the overseas enquiries, are we having to form a worldwide task force?"

Grace immediately shouted out, “I’ll do it, count me in.” They both laughed and drank their coffee, before returning back to the ever-increasing pile of papers which were being churned out like a blizzard.

Jason rang Freeman and told him that he was sending an email through to him with a number of attachments. He told him he would not disclose the names of anyone over the phone, but it would be apparent who they were referring to when it arrived. He further asked how the interview with Brown was going and Freeman responded that it was like drawing teeth. He was not volunteering anything but realised that what we had on him was significant.

He continued that when cornered he acknowledged the fact that he was totally blown and gave what was needed, but no more.

Jason said, “What has he said about Mychett?”

Freeman said, “We haven’t gone into that yet, he thinks he is in the clear with just Wimbledon. He doesn’t know what we have or what we know. I’ll let him stew for a while before we drop that on him. I want to see what you have got for me. How’s Grace doing?”

Jason said, “Busy, busy and she is volunteering for the next task force, so she keeps out of mischief.”

Freeman laughed and said, “Keep up the good work, keep me informed with any further developments.” He rang off.

Grace said, “Some people have all the fun, but we get to

know first." as she entered some new information into her computer and displayed it on the big screen.

Jason spent the next thirty minutes compiling his report and attaching the relevant documents to it. As he was ending, he found that he was still getting more and more information on the new man and Brown. He ended his report by telling Freeman that he would need more time in order create new reports to keep him updated. What he had now would have to serve the purpose.

He finished the file and clicked the send button and sent it on its way to Freeman and Ellis. He thought to himself that will put the cat among the pigeons that's for sure.

CHAPTER 39

Freeman and Ellis received the email from Jason simultaneously. They left Brown in the interview room and joined Sarah and Steenson. They opened their laptops and downloaded the mail onto the screen in the viewing room. As it appeared on the big screen, there was a complete silence. The screen rolled down giving details of Jason's report and they could hardly believe their eyes.

As the attachments were displayed in chronological order, they could see quite clearly the course of the criminal activities. They were reluctant to use the word terrorists, but that is what these people were.

Freeman said, "We are going to have to brief the Commissioner and the Prime Minister on this. They will have to come here to be briefed. This is much too sensitive to be discussed over the air, and very top secret for eyes only."

Ellis agreed saying, "Go and arrange it now, we'll put Brown back in his cell until we need him again, he can rot in hell."

Freeman drew aside and made his call to the Commissioner of Police but didn't give her the full details. He said that she had to be here and to include the Prime Minister too. No one else was to know. It was even more imperative that secrecy be maintained.

He said, "You must go to Downing Street personally, talk to her privately without any of her Ministers or officials present. Just say she has to travel with you to see myself and Major Ellis on a matter of urgency. I am sorry that I cannot give you any further information, but you will understand when we meet."

She replied, "You had better be certain about all this because if it is not, she will have your guts for garters and probably mine too. But she has said she wanted to be kept in the loop and I'll do it".

Freeman said, "Thank you. There will be a helicopter in Horse Guards Parade waiting, it will convey you both to us. Take your car, don't use her official transport."

He rang off and went back to the others who were assembled around the table reading off the screen and making notes on their pads and then trying to cross examine the new information with any evidence they already had.

Twenty minutes later Freeman had a call from the Commissioner who said she had persuaded the Prime Minister to go with her. They were now boarding the helicopter and would be with them in ninety minutes.

Freeman told the others of the developments. He told them to finalise what they were doing and wait for them to arrive. He would brief them and then they would decide on any future course of action.

He rang Jason and asked him if they had found any more documents and other intelligence relating to the new suspect. Jason informed him that a passport in the name of Johnathon Smith had been unearthed, but the photograph was that of their target. They were in the process of liaising with Immigration and Port Authorities as to the usage of the passport. As soon as they found anything, they would contact him immediately.

During the next hour, they all discussed the repercussions and how they could proceed with everything that had taken place. There were links to Brown and Gregorov and by implication with Karakova. It appeared that even the shooting in the park was somehow connected to the overall scheme of things.

They realised that whatever they did next would mean some very heavy manpower and time would be of the essence. The Prime Minister and the Commissioner of Police would be the ultimate decision makers, and even heads of other agencies.

There was a knocking on the control room door. The Prime Minister strode into where they were standing. She said, "I do not approve of being taken from my office like this and even my phone has been discontinued, do not under-estimate my feelings on this."

She looked over at Freeman and Ellis and continued, "So what is so important you could not tell me over the usual channels."

Freeman smiled and handed over the file without saying a word. She opened it. As soon as she saw the contents, she sat down, looked at him and said, “Is this true”?

He replied, “Yes ma’am, keep on reading and find the attachments relating to the report. You will see that he is totally involved in all that has taken place and he and Brown are two of the major players. There are others who we have identified, but they are not so important as them.”

She was pale. “I trusted him. He is one of my closest advisers. He has the secrets of so many aspects of our day to day running of the country. How could this have happened. When did you find out?”

Freeman responded, “After we arrested Brown, we had information from a source that he had a property unknown to anyone previously. There were all found in a safe, and other hiding places in that property. There are many passports and banking documents relating to The United Kingdom and overseas banks accounts, together with company registrations.”

He continued, “Once we started piecing it all together, his name came up on quite a few occasions. All in connection with bank accounts, company ownerships and again many of them as co signatory or as co-director with Brown.”

“We have also found a passport with his photograph on it but in another name. We are currently finding out where and when he has used it.”

She finished reading the file and its contents and put it down as if it was poison. She said, “You have my full authority to do whatever you like with his man. Thank you for disclosing it in this manner. You know I was upset, but you are all vindicated thank you. Sir Jeremy Morgan is officially a wanted man. You must do what you need to do. I will not say anything or do anything which may cause him to suspect anything. As soon as he is arrested, then I'll make provisions for his replacement.”

Freeman said, “Madam Prime Minister, if I can ask a favour, don't say anything for the time being until we have been able to round up all the others and take them out of circulation. We are having to go through many departments around the world to facilitate this. It is our aim to coordinate everything so that none of them get the chance to disappear or get rid of evidence.”

She responded, “Of course, under the circumstances we have to get rid of this cancer in our midst, once and for all. Do we know who did the park shootings and why it took place now?”

Freeman commented it appears that Simon Jacobs had been doing some financial work for the group and had uncovered some discrepancies. He said he would report it, but before he did, Brown took him out on the instructions of Morgan, and to make it look more innocent, his wife and daughter had to die too.

The Prime Minister looked shocked, “But what about the attempt on Morgan's life, I wish they had succeeded now.” she commented. bitterly.

Freeman said, “At the moment it is just conjecture, but we believe that the faction that contained Gregorov and Karakova were acting under instructions from a section within their own organisation, who were being taken over by Morgan and his sections. They certainly were conducting operations in eastern Europe from the travel documents we have unearthed.

He continued, “Mr Steenson, who you know of course, is liaising with his counterparts in Russia and the surrounding areas to establish what incidents have taken place when these overseas individuals carrying the passports we know to exist were in those countries.”

The Prime Minister replied, “How far does their organisation extend for goodness sake. I see him every single day. He is always at the office and attending meeting with me. He has the trust of all my Ministers, what do I say to them?”

Freeman said, “For now, nothing. We cannot afford to give him any indication that we suspect him. We have Brown in custody, and he might be nervous about that. We are working on a cover story that Brown had been in a serious accident and was taken to hospital, and its only recently that we have discovered who he is. He is currently in a coma and in intensive care in Cambridge.

He continued, “Major Ellis will pass the news on to his senior officers. Telling them that he will be out of action for some considerable time. I think that this will ultimately get to Morgan.”

She smiled, “Remind me never to get on your bad side Commander. I'd hate to end up anywhere near you. This weekend is a Ministers weekend at Chequers and Morgan will be there. Do you think you have enough time to arrest him before that?”

Ellis said, “We are trying to arrange an international Task Force to arrest all the individuals known to us. At the same time, we have isolated nearly one hundred bank accounts and companies around the world. With the best will in the world, I cannot see us being able to undertake such an operation until the beginning of next week.”

The Commissioner said, “From our perspective, all the Intelligence agencies together with GCHQ have been working with their counterparts around the world, the cooperation has been brilliant. Of course, everything has to be done in secrecy, so its slower than we would normally like.”

The Prime Minister replied, “All of you have done an incredible job I have to admit. I was sceptical about all this, even when we were with the Russian ambassador and when Gregorov and Karakova killed themselves. I thought that we would end up getting the minnows and the sharks getting away with it all as they often do.”

She continued, “What do you have to do this evening, are you interviewing Brown?”

Ellis said, “Not at this point, we have him with enough evidence already from just his property in Wimbledon. He can remain where he is for as long as we deem it necessary. My rules don't apply to civilian rules." and he smiled.

She responded, "Well ladies and gentlemen I am hungry, I suggest that we take a break and get the chefs to cook us dinner, I think we deserve it. I missed lunch, so let's get them to cook up a decent meal, with all the trimmings and courses."

She removed her jacket and shoes and made herself comfortable, she looked at the Commissioner and said, "Amy, don't be such a fuddy duddy, get that uniform top off and relax."

The Commissioner sighed but did as she was told, and everyone sat around the large table in the middle of the Mess.

The Prime Minister asked Freeman and Ellis if they had a phone she could use. She said that her own phone was on constant surveillance for obvious reasons and if she used it the information might fall into the wrong hands.

Freeman said, "Sorry Ma'am, who will you be contacting?" She replied, "My PA, just to let her know I am in a conference with the United States Ambassador and not to be disturbed under any circumstances." She smiled and said, "I can be as sneaky as you too."

Freeman directed her to a phone in the Mess and told her that it was secure, but only be on it for under thirty seconds. She looked at him and said, "This is worse than being in school, but I know."

He said he would arrange the meal and asked her if she had any preferences. She thought about and said, "A good curry with all the bits and pieces, followed by Rum and Raison ice cream. I can never get this back at home, not good for me they say. Oh, and cold beers, even the non-alcoholic is good, as long as they are cold."

Freeman said, "We dragged you out into the sticks, so the least we can do is look after you for a few hours. We never know what new information will arise as well, so you are in the loop for that as well."

Freeman remained close by while the Prime Minister made her call. Once it was over, he escorted her back to her seat and went to the kitchens where he ordered their evening meal.

He returned with a trayful of cold beers, all alcohol free, due to them still being on duty. They were passed around and even the Commissioner smiled as she drank her beer.

She retorted, "Anything else we need to know or do for the time being. If not lets enjoy our meal and then we have to get back to London and resume our different lives and duties, but as I have said before, thank you all for what you have done."

They all sat talking, it was quite surreal with the Prime Minister of the United Kingdom, senior army and police officers together with a known security officer of an Eastern Bloc country, all relaxed in each other's company.

After a while they were served their curries and more cold beers. When they finished their meals and coffees the two visitors left the Mess and departed for London. The others all returned to their seats and went over the next few days tactics and summed up what they had and how far down the line they were with regards to the forthcoming operations.

Freeman called Jason and Grace and told them to finish for the night. They would all resume again the next day. He was told they had made as much preparation as was possible with all agencies and supplied the relevant documents to each country without disclosing which other countries and their involvement was about. He thanked them for their work and said he hoped they had a good night. Grace interjected and told him they would.

The next morning Freeman told Ellis he was going to see Brown. He would be asking him about his relationship with Morgan and gauge his reaction to his questions.

Ellis said, “Just keep it simple to start, how he knows him. What meetings and discussions they have had over the past couple of years. If he is as smart as I think he is, he will realise that we know a lot and might just give us something in return.”

Freeman told the others to liaise with Jason and Grace and log in whatever new information that had been received overnight onto the screens. He told then he was hoping that the list of countries offering their assistance was growing and making the forthcoming operation easier and smoother.

As they entered the interview room, Brown was eating a ham and cheese toasted sandwich and had a cup of cappuccino in front of him. Ellis asked if he was being looked after and Brown replied, "Would be better if you let me go, but I guess that is out of the question I presume?"

Ellis said simply, "You presume right."

Freeman and he sat opposite Brown and Ellis asked, "What is your relationship with Sir Jeremy Morgan?"

Browns eyes gave the game away as they opened wide before he could control himself. He said, "I don't have a relationship with this man. All I know is that Gregorov made an attempt on his life when I was working with the police on the London murders."

Ellis looked at him and said "Are we going to play games again? Why do you think we asked you the question? We are not playing guess the name in the hope that you might have heard of him. I'll ask you again, what is your relationship with Sir Jeremy Morgan?"

Brown sat in silence for a full minute before answering. He said, "I have known Sir Jeremy for a number of years, since he was a civil servant in the Ministry of Defence. We used to meet on occasions when it was deemed necessary for policy decisions or training matters. We got on well, he seemed a nice guy, but above my pay grade since he was posted into Whitehall."

Ellis countered, "How about your current relationship with him, personal and professional?"

Brown looked over at them, "You obviously know that we have connections nowadays. We never stopped, just didn't inform anyone. Jeremy has the business acumen and I have the contacts and between us we have formed an alliance with others for our mutual benefit."

Ellis exploded, "Do you realise what you are responsible for? Countless acts of terrorism and killings all over the world. Many of the deaths have been innocents, just for your blood lust! And for what? Money, no honour, you have no scruples or morals."

He continued, "Are you going to tell us everything about your connection with Morgan or are we going to have to drag it out of you?"

He replied, "I don't know very much of course. I just do as I am told and get it done. He and his inner circle are the ones who make the decisions, collect the monies and pay me when I have completed an assignment."

Freeman said, "Wrong answer again. You are making a fool of yourself. What do you think Morgan is saying right now? He is saying whatever he can to save his scrawny neck and not get a life sentence here or a trip to Guantanamo Bay, which is where you will be heading if you keep this up."

He continued, "Why don't you tell us about some of the companies that you and Morgan are partners in and the bank accounts you both control as signatories. You didn't think we knew about them, did you?"

Brown seemed taken aback by what Freeman said and he sat back and looked at both of them.

He said, “If you know so much, then why do you need to talk to me? just get on with it and charge me. Morgan is not the sort of man to say anything unless he is forced to. I wouldn’t put anything past some of the interviewers who are used. I have seen enough of them over the years.”

He continued, “Sir Jeremy approached me and asked if I’d like to join him and some others doing undercover black ops work for the benefit of the country. He said it was all off the record, but he had been sanctioned to be the head of it due to his background in Defence.”

He continued, “It soon became obvious that there was a lot more going on than just doing special operations. He started to confide in me. We discussed how we could both benefit from our association. I have contacts through my specialist training, and he has his contacts in business and banking.

I couldn’t be seen to be away from my duties too often, so I created some identities from mates I had known and used them. It was easy to get passports, just filled in the forms, and hey presto a brand new passport. When I told Morgan about how easy it was, he got me to get more for him. He paid me one thousand pounds per document. I was not going to turn that down.”

Freeman said, “How many passports did you get for Morgan?”

He replied “Not sure, but I think around twenty five or so. I used the ones with my identity once only and then ditched them and handed over the rest to Morgan. I don’t know what he did with them.”

Freeman ignored his answer and continued, "Who's idea was it to form those companies and open bank accounts. What was the reasoning behind that?"

He responded, "His really, he was getting more and more associates and the finances were increasing considerably. We decided that if the money could be hidden away from the Inland Revenue here, then accounts would have to be set up in safe countries. To do that, companies had to be formed so that everything looked as though there was income and expenditure flowing naturally."

Ellis commented, "So you were just his gopher and did as you were told?"

Brown laughed, "There you go, trying to rile me, of course not. He may have been in overall control, but I was also a decision maker. I made appropriate suggestions as to how and when events would happen. He relied on my expertise as much as I relied on his business acumen."

Freeman said, "So that goes as far as being co-directors and co signatories on a large number of bank accounts spread across the world?"

Brown said, "Morgan would give me the forms to sign, and I did. I checked to make sure everything appeared legal and had no problems with it."

Freeman, said, "Where did he give you these forms, where are they now? What about the cheque books and credit cards which were issued with every bank account, where are they?"

Brown responded, “You’ll have to ask Morgan those questions, I just got them and he took care of them. When I went overseas with the alternate identity, I had cards which I used, but like the passports I disposed of them when I didn’t require them anymore.”

Ellis said, “Did you or any companies you are associated with ever purchase or acquire arms and explosives from anywhere in the world?”

Brown commented, “I know that some trade was done by a few of the companies in different countries. I have never handled any of the transactions or the payments, you need to ask Morgan those questions.”

Freeman looked at Brown and said, “Why do you think we are asking you the questions. He said you have the armament expertise and did all the sourcing and purchasing. He is the money man. You tell him what it costs and who provided it and he makes sure they are paid.”

Brown just shrugged and said, “He can say what he likes. He is digging his own grave that’s for sure. He must realise that he is never going to get out of what he has done. I know that I am looking at serious charges, and you seem to know everything about me. You certainly have done your homework on me and got what you needed from my house.”

Ellis added, “We have also been searching for records from all over the world. Far from being a lacky for Morgan, you have been, at least equal to him. From the details given to us by many international security offices and having looked into the overseas operations under your various guises you were probably the instigator in several illegal transactions around the globe."

Brown smiled and said, "My reputation proceeds me, some of it real, some of it exaggerated, I am sure."

Freeman looked across at Ellis with an increasing sense of frustration and anger towards Brown and said, "We will stop here for a while. When we come back, we will focus our attention on Horseshoe Lane shall we?"

Brown went pale and said, "You know about there? How did you ever find that out? It's not listed in my name or any of the companies registered."

Ellis said, "Not so clever now, are you? Have a good think of what you have told us. When we come back, start again with what has really happened and this time the full facts."

CHAPTER 40

They left Brown as he was returned to his cell. When they entered the Mess, Sarah told them that she had heard from the Prime Minister, and she wanted to talk with either Freeman or Ellis.

It was decided that Freeman would contact her as he had spoken with her more than Ellis and trusted his judgement. He rang her and she answered immediately.

She said, “I have had a thought of how to get rid of Morgan without causing to many questions. When he arrives with me at Chequers, we will go into the Oak Room well before any of the others arrive. Once there your men can take him away.”

“I will tell the others that he had a heart attack and was taken to hospital. Unfortunately, he died before getting there, such a terrible waste of a gifted civil servant. I'll make sure it is announced to all the Ministers and their staff. As far as everyone is concerned, he is dead, and you can bury him in whatever hole he deserves to be flung.”

Freeman said, “What about his family”?

She replied, “They will be told he died of a heart attack. I'll meet them at some stage to offer my condolences. The family will receive his pension and other benefits accorded to his position.”

Freeman said, “You have been with us too long Madam Prime Minister.” and they both laughed.

He continued, “I’ll make all the necessary arrangements, just be there early. There will be an ambulance attending the scene immediately and he will be seen to be stretchered out in case there are any witnesses around.

He will end up here with Brown. Is his home a government property or his own?”

She replied, “It’s a Grace and Favour home for senior officials, why?”

He replied, “We will need to get in there and find out what he has got inside. We don’t want his family to do anything drastic. We don’t know if they know of his activities.”

She replied, “As far as I am concerned, you can enter immediately, you don’t need to tell them exactly what the reason is. The security services are checking and making safe any documents and files that might be in his possession. They can be told its normal procedure whenever a senior government Official like Morgan dies. There is a need for continuation at the highest levels and therefore files and documents have to be handed over.”

Freeman was quite surprised at her manner and knew he had underestimated her abilities when required in cases of emergency. He said “Of course, we will enter within the hour.”

The Prime Minister then said, "When you have Morgan locked up there, I want to visit him and give him a piece of my mind and let him know exactly what life will hold for him in the future."

Ellis said, "We will ensure that he looks dead, if and when his family want to see him. We have ways of making someone look very dead for the time that anyone wants to pay their last respects."

The Prime Minister said, "I'd personally make him dead, not just looking dead. I'll will leave it to you, and I have kept my diary free for the first few days of next week." She rang off as he smiled at her new found attitude.

Jason reported back to Freeman that the body found at Horseshoe Lane was probably buried there in the late 1990's. There was insufficient DNA to be able to trace anyone. In the late 1980's Horseshoe Lane was part of an estate where travellers lived, so it could have been anyone. The local police have ceased any enquiries and are taking no further action.

Freeman felt sorry that someone would go unnoticed, but he thought of the many hundreds that go missing and are never found.

Jason then said, "We have liaised with all the relevant authorities, they are on board, and we have scheduled all raids and arrests for seven am UK time on Monday. The Commissioner has arranged that Gold Command will be the central focal point for all nations. With your permission I'd like to be there and assist them."

Freeman said, "Of course, you have been the point of contact for so many and its essential you be there if there are questions raised. I suggest Grace is there too. I am sure she has been just as busy as you. I'll tell the Commissioner that you have my authorisation to attend and to have an active role in the operation. We might be back then as well. It will depend on events here."

He continued, "Morgan will be arrested on Saturday, the first you will hear of it will be the obituary announcement of his tragic death from a heart attack. He will end up here. It might be necessary for Grace and her team to search his house on Saturday. I'll give you the reasons and details by email."

Jason replied, "Thank you Sir, I'll pass on the message, she'll enjoy getting her hands dirty again."

They returned to Sarah and Steenson, and they discussed how the next few days were going to work out. Freeman told them that Jason had liaised with the relevant authorities, and everything was on plan to carry out the raids on Monday morning.

He continued, "Morgan is being dealt with on Saturday in rather unconventional terms. He will die from a severe heart attack at Chequers and be taken to a local hospital. From there he will be brought here where he will be like Jesus, and the miracle of Easter Sunday, when he comes back to life. He will probably wish he had died by the time we have finished with him."

They laughed and Ellis said, “Grace and her team will be going through Morgan’s home after he has died, official government business of course.”

Freeman continued, “He is bound to have stuff hidden there, and Grace is just the girl to find it. Once she gets her nose on the trail, nothing stops her. We have a good idea of his involvement, but it would be nice to see who else is in his sphere of influence.”

Freeman decided to end the days proceedings saying that they would start again with Brown next morning. They would start to work on what was found at Horseshoe Lane, beginning with the arms in the cellar. The safe discovery would come later.

Steenson said, “He has never mentioned anyone else except Morgan. Perhaps you can mention some of the individuals named on the passports, his ex-military buddies, who died in service.”

He continued, “He would have had to do research to get all their details from various sources. The passport office contains details of millions of people who apply, their life histories almost. He must have done his homework or got someone else to do it. It was not Morgan that’s for sure.”

Freeman nodded and agreed with him.

Steenson said, “Go at him in a different direction, upset his train of thought. If he gets too comfortable, he needs taking out of it. Talk for a few minutes about the weapons, then suddenly change to the passports, then to Morgan and accounts. Don't let him get settled into one form of questioning."

Freeman smiled and said, "Why don't you and Major Ellis interview him this time around, a new face will put him off his stride in any case."

Ellis laughed and commented, "Good cop, bad cop. I think I know who is going to be the bad cop." Steenson simply said, "Years of practise my friend," and laughed.

They entered the interview room where Brown was seated. He looked at them and asked where the nice Mr Freeman was.

Steenson said, "Don't be such a sarcastic jerk, you need to show respect. You are already looking at enough serious charges as it is. Tell us about the cellar in Horseshoe Lane and what was inside it".

Brown looked agog at Steenson and said, "You saw what was in there, somebody must have put whatever it was in there without my knowledge. What was in there? Obviously, something that you think I had something to do with."

Steenson leaned forward and said, "Yes, I do think that, and in fact I know you do. You never thought that anyone would find your hidey hole, did you? You have been rather careless Mr Brown. Our people have found an absolute treasure trove of evidence to connect you to every item in there."

He continued, "Let's start with the various arms and ammunitions stacked in the cellar, the majority of which seems to have been shipped from South Africa."

Brown commented, “I have no idea what you are talking about.”

Steenson just looked at Brown, slid a file across to him and said, “Would you like to read the first few pages, and then stop giving us this crap you are spewing out.”

Brown opened the file, read the first page slowly, and then turned over to page two. He closed the file and sent it back to Steenson, who said, “What now? Are you going to be straight with us, or are we going to continue to play games all night? We have all the time in the world. We can keep putting you back in your cell, go for a nice meal, and then return at our leisure to continue this charade.”

Brown said, “Can I have a snack please, and I’ll tell you what I know about it.”

Ellis said, “What do you want?”

He said, “I want a Coronation Chicken sandwich on Sourdough bread, with a side order of chips and salad cream.” Ellis looked at him and shook his head but said, “And to drink?”

Brown said, “Cloudy lemonade.”

Ellis said, “It will take a few minutes, so in the meantime, think carefully of what you are going to say. Mr Steenson is not a patient man, he has a family to go home to, and he hates to be late.”

As the food for Brown was being prepared, they observed him through the observation window as they drank their coffee. Gone was the arrogance of earlier days. He looked around nervously and drummed his fingers on the desk. His whole persona was one of resignation, mixed with the shock that he had been found out as much as he had.

Ellis turned to Steenson and said, “Wait till we tell him that we have found his safe, that will blow his mind.”

Steenson grinned, “Plenty to keep going for now. Let's finish our coffee and see if he is anymore disposed to telling the truth.”

They entered the room as he was finishing his sandwich and dipping his chips into the salad cream. He smiled, said thanks, and pushed the plate away.

Steenson immediately said, “Are you going to tell us about the cellar now?”

He replied, “I did it as a favour for some associates I know. I let them use the cellar on condition they moved it all quickly. I don’t know what was there. I have tried to contact them but unable to get hold of any of them.”

Steenson responded, “Give me their details, I am sure I can find them for you. I don’t suppose you tried very hard at all”.

Brown said, “Sorry, I lost my contact book some while ago and I can’t think of their numbers offhand.”

Steenson laughed, “Just give me their names and I’ll find them for you, and you can tell them direct what I need to know.”

Brown responded, "I didn't know them that well, so cannot really remember their names fully."

Steenson leaned forward and whispered, "That's a real pity for you. It seems that we are going to have to put all the responsibility for all the illegal and banned weapons onto you. Your fingerprints are all over the cases in the cellar, and lo and behold, guess what?"

Brown looked at him, "What?"

Steenson smiled and said, "Your fingerprints are all over the actual weapons and explosives inside the cases, so there goes your innocent explanation. Of course, there is also the documentation with each box, goodness gracious, they belong to companies you are associated with as a director or executive."

Brown said, "I had to make sure they were safe. They might have come from a company I am named in, but I wanted them got rid of. I usually wore gloves but sometimes forgot, never thought that they would stay at the house for so long".

Ellis opened a file and took out a blue hard backed book and said to Brown, "Recognise this?"

Brown looked at it and his head dropped, saying, "Where did you find it. It was nowhere near to the arms boxes. I hid it inside the support legs of the workbench."

Ellis grinned at Brown and said, "Oh dear, more lies, your court martial is not going to take long, is it? But I can guarantee that you are going to spend the rest of your days locked up in a special cell reserved for men like you and Morgan."

He continued, "Perhaps you can now identify the men who you said brought the weapons to your house." He slid the book across to Brown who opened it and flipped through the pages.

He pointed to several names, ones that both Steenson and Ellis recognised.

Steenson said, "Do you know where they are now?"

Brown said, "No, they move about a bit in the organisation, but you have their contact details now. They will confirm what I have said to you."

Steenson replied, "No need to, they are all in custody and have told us exactly what the situation is with you and the arms. They have no intention of spending the rest of their lives locked away. Three of them handed over their passports too. Funny how you said that you had thrown them all away."

Brown just shrugged, "Looks as though you have everything you need, I admit to the weapons and the address book. You know about my companies, and obviously some guys can't keep their mouths shut."

Ellis asked, "Why have you betrayed your country like this? You were a very respected officer. One of the finest marksmen in the world who is in demand with the top military institutions around the globe. We have spoken to many of them and they are shocked and appalled at the allegations being made against you."

Brown replied, "Its simple, money. The potential for making money outside of my captaincy was enormous. I have made a fair amount of money from what I have done but it could have been a lot higher. I had to be careful. My work in the military has taken me all over the world and enabled me to make contacts in all of the countries and most have provided me with opportunities in my own right."

Steenson said, "How much money have you made out of others miseries?"

He replied, "Not sure, probably a few thousands. It was going to go to my retirement fund, think that's gone now too."

Steenson said, "Where are the bank accounts where that money was deposited into?"

Brown responded, "The main one is in Luxembourg, secrecy laws are strong there. I only use that one to deposit the funds. They are then transferred to some of the companies which I am involved with, basically money laundering."

Ellis asked, "Where does all the money come from to pay for the operations, the manpower and equipment and planning?"

He replied, "The sponsors pay us upfront in total. The money is in different accounts around the world and its kept in escrow until the job is finished. If it doesn't work out, they get refunded. If it's successful then everyone involved gets their portion."

Steenson said, "What is the pay-off for you and Morgan?" He replied, "I get a percentage of the funds. Morgan always has ten per cent as he is the overall head of the organisation."

Steenson retorted, "That's a bit unfair, you seem to take all the risks and do the hard work. He gets the money and stays under the radar. I am sure you get more ill-gotten gains than you are admitting to."

Brown looked at him and said, "Some are bosses, some are workers, bit like you and him really."

Steenson leaned over and said through gritted teeth, "You and me never were and never will be the same. You are just a lying sociopath who has only one goal in life, make as much money as you can and to make other lives miserable."

Brown sat and said nothing. Ellis opened another file from the pile he had brought in with him. He looked Brown over and said, "The reality is that you are the signatory to thirty four bank accounts around the world. Thirteen are companies you and Morgan are co signatories to. Nine in your own name and twelve in names you have used through false identities you have created for yourself."

He continued, "These of course are just the ones we have uncovered so far, every country and bank throughout the globe has assisted us and have indicated that there are a number of others, details of which they are compiling and sending over to us".

Brown looked devastated. He looked over at Ellis and then to Steenson who just smiled and said, "Wait till he gets to the good part."

Ellis said, "From the records, in the personal accounts in your name you had amassed slightly over twelve million pounds sterling and sixteen million in United States currency, a far cry from the little you said you had in your account."

He added, "Under your false names, it gets even better, almost twice as much in each currency, you are a very wealthy man Brown, or should I say was a wealthy man. All your accounts have been frozen and awaiting court decisions as to how they will be distributed."

He smiled and continued, "All the company bank accounts have been frozen too. Accountants have been employed to examine the books of each company. Despite your story that you are not a major element in those organisations, the records and reports reveal that you were as much a part of the companies as Morgan. He is saying that, in fact, you made many of the decisions and not him."

Brown looked straight ahead and said, "Morgan is weak, I should never have got involved with him. He made it too easy for me. I'd have been better off with the likes of Gregorov and his woman. At least he'd never have given me up."

Steenson laughed and said, "Where do you think we got the information from? He might not have known everything, but he started us on this road. He told us about the park shootings, and the irony of you assisting the police. He was another one who did not want to face a lifetime in a Stulag back in Mother Russia."

He finished by saying, "Even Sergeant Williams has been of assistance. She was the one that led us to Horseshoe Lane. She was mightily impressed by that house, and thought she had a chance of something with you. There is nothing like the wrath of a scorned woman."

He replied, "She was the one female in my life who I really liked. I still do. I can't blame her for what I have done, and she is being honest. I hope that she doesn't suffer too much because of me."

Ellis answered, "She will be fine. She will get disciplined for breaking army regulations and have to leave. But under the circumstances, I think they will not be too harsh on her."

Brown relaxed and said, "You have basically everything you need to know. I do not have the records of all the operations and did what and who were the targets. Morgan had most of the sensitive files at his home in a safe, in the dining room, behind the painting of himself and his wife. I don't know the combination, but at least it's a start for you and drop him in it with me."

Ellis looked at him and said, "Thank you, that's a start, but let's get back to you. You must have kept records of the business and contacts, financial affairs. You didn't just leave it all to Morgan. What about the passport applications you organised and obtained for the members of your group?"

He replied, "Yes, I made all the applications out, part of my commitment, and collected them when they were ready and distributed them as and when they were needed. I didn't keep any of them, as far as I was concerned, the ones I used, I destroyed after use. The others were supposed to get rid of theirs too, but as you know they gave me them back. I put them in the cellar out of the way. I should have destroyed them."

Steenson said, "You are a very organised man, and yet you say you made some mistakes, important ones, that's not like you. I think that if we continued searching long enough at Horseshoe Lane, we would find some more items, am I right?"

Brown said, "Haven't you got enough, seems to me that you have ruined my house. If I had any more, I'd tell you."

Ellis said, "Two things Mister Brown, firstly, the property has been seized as proceeds of crime, and secondly, you did have more, and we found it."

Brown stared and barely whispered, "Found what?"

Steenson, said, "Don't be so coy, the safe of course, cram packed with so much stuff, it felt like our birthday and Christmas all in one. We found passports piled together, application forms for all of them. Cheque books and statements, company registration forms, you name it we found them."

He continued, "Strange how they got there when you said you had got rid of them all or never had them in the first place. Your life was in that safe, payments for contracts completed, names and dates and locations."

Brown shook his head and said, "Never thought you'd find that. I had at least thought that I could keep something to myself. However, seems I can't even do that now."

CHAPTER 41

Sir Jeremy Morgan arrived at the Prime Minister's office at 8:00am in preparation for the forthcoming cabinet meeting at Chequers later that day. He was shown into the room and was surprised to see the home Secretary there too. The Prime Minister indicated for Morgan to take a seat and said to the Home secretary in a serious tone, "Thank for you the news, I will see you later and perhaps you can have some more information for everyone then."

The Home Secretary nodded to Morgan on her way out and said to the Prime Minister, "Of course, as soon as I have any, I'll let you know."

After she left, the Prime Minister said to Morgan, "Sorry, but the Home Secretary has just delivered some sad news. I am not sure, but do you remember Captain Kevin Brown?"

He looked over at her, trying not to display too much emotion and said, "Yes I think you told me that he had been helping the police in some murder enquiry?"

He sat and said, "Yes, I remember a bit of that, he was also a highly decorated soldier as well if I have the right man. Why, what's the problem?"

She sat back behind her desk and said, "The Home Secretary has just told me that he was killed on Wednesday evening. It appears he was cycling home when he was hit by a lorry and killed instantly."

She continued, “He was badly disfigured and had no identity on him and so they had to take DNA and were able to identify him that way.”

Morgan looked shocked, thinking to himself, no wonder I have not heard anything from him for the past few days. Instead, he said, “That’s awful, poor man, he will be sorely missed, I am sure. The police will miss his assistance too. He seemed to be the right person for them.”

The Prime Minister looked at him with a sorrowful face and thought to herself, you sanctimonious bastard, you will be getting your dues in the not too distant future.

She said, “I have spoken with the Commissioner of Police and sent my condolences to them. I don’t think we can do much more now. Their enquiries into the attack on you have come to a conclusion. I cannot go into too much detail, even with you Jeremy, it’s all sub judice at the moment.”

He was relieved about the information she was telling him and said, “Of course Ma’am I understand.”

She then said, “Can you meet me back here in thirty minutes, I want to go over all the files with you as I am relying on you to assist today. My PPA has gone sick and I cannot read anyone else into today at such short notice.”

He responded saying, “Be my pleasure Ma’am, this is what I do.”

He left the room and went to his office and sat a bit stunned. He was unsure of what to do next. He decided that he would attend the meeting at Chequers and see if any further information was forthcoming before doing anything else. He felt secure in himself but would need to extract some contact details from his files back at his home, those could wait until later.

He made himself a coffee, and then collected the requisite files from the security office at Number Ten before re-joining the Prime Minister.

For the next three hours, they went over the schedule for the cabinet meeting. The Prime Minister was deliberately pedantic over all the files and Sir Jeremy took notes when directed by her. At around 1pm, she said she was ready to leave. She wanted to be there before any of her ministers and he should distribute the files in the conference room.

The drive to Chequers took around thirty minutes, and after they went inside, the Prime Minister turned and went into her private office and closed the door. Inside was an SAS officer, who nodded his head. She sat down, welcoming the moment when Morgan was going to be taken out of her life once and for all. He spoke briefly into his radio and left the room.

As Morgan entered the conference room, he tried the light switch but it didn't work. With the curtains already closed the room was dark until suddenly, three beams of light exploded into his face. He was blinded, and then felt arms on him and pushing him to the floor.

He felt his arms pinned behind his back and he shouted out, "What's happening?" the response came back, "Shut up, keep your mouth closed." He was hauled to his feet and as his eyes became accustomed to the light saw four men all in black facing him with automatic weapons.

He felt his legs give way and was roughly pulled up again. As he stood there, he saw the Prime Minister enter the room. He said, "Ma'am these men have attacked us, be careful."

She smiled for the first time that day and said, "Far from it, they are protecting this country, which is more that I can say the same for you. You are a traitor. You are never ever going to be free again. By the time this country has finished with you, you will wish you were never born. Your family will be looked after, as far as they are concerned you died whilst working."

Morgan said, "What about Brown?"

She answered with a wide smile, "Oh, don't worry about him, you'll be joining him in the next few hours, in the deepest cells we have. He has been our guest for a while now and what we haven't got out of him wouldn't cover a stamp."

She continued, "We have some very good interrogators and you will be meeting them soon enough. I suggest you think about what you might want to say, rather than us dragging it out of you, that might hurt."

He answered, "So all that stuff you told me this morning was a load of rubbish. What was the Home Secretary doing there?"

She answered, "Oh yes, it was giving me great delight telling you that your friend was dead. I imagined you nearly having a heart attack when I told you about him. It stopped you doing anything. Not that you could have done very much, because your every move and noise you made was being recorded and the phone lines in your office were out of order."

She continued, "She was there on another matter, and has no idea of what you have done. But it was good fortune and added to the atmosphere which was created."

Morgan responded, "You can't do this to me, I know my rights and I demand to see a lawyer."

She looked at him saying, "See who is here with me, they are military and your actions have been treasonous and against the country and therefore falls under their jurisdiction. They can detain you for as long as they wish and definitely no access to a lawyer."

She continued, "There is an ambulance waiting for you to take you to a hospital where you will be declared dead. Your funeral will take place in a few days for all to see. For my own satisfaction I will have it recorded and played back to you at some stage. Let you see how everyone felt so sorry that you died. You will wish you really had died."

Morgan laughed and said, "What are you talking about I am fine I am probably fitter than most men my age."

He suddenly felt a sharp pain in his neck, and he looked around and as he did so he felt himself falling and everything went dark.

The Prime Minister said, "Ok gentlemen get him out of here. The ambulance is out the back, load him up and take him to King Georges Hospital where you will be met by Doctor Graham Webster. He will take you down to the mortuary and take over from there."

He was loaded onto a stretcher and carried out by the team, leaving her alone in the conference room. She took out her mobile and pressed a number on her speed dial. It was answered immediately, and she said, "Dr Webster, your client is now on its way, you know what is needed."

He replied, "Of course Ma'am," and disconnected.

She sat back in her chair, waiting for the Ministers to arrive.

Thirty minutes later with all her cabinet ministers seated she entered the room. She sat at the head of the table and said, "Dear Colleagues I have some sad new to tell you. This morning myself and Sir Jeremy Morgan arrived early to prepare for this meeting. Unfortunately, a little after getting here he suffered a massive heart attack and died immediately."

There was a collective gasp around the table and the Home Secretary said, "He seemed in such good health when he arrived at your office this morning."

The Prime Minister retorted, "I know, he was in fine fettle all the way here It was awful. he just collapsed in front of me, there was nothing I could do. I called 999, and an ambulance arrived really quickly. They examined him but said there was nothing they could do for him. I believe he was taken to King Georges Hospital."

The Cabinet Minister responded, "On behalf of all of us here, we are truly sorry for his demise. He will be missed by many and a respected man as well as a Government official."

She had to control herself from nearly bursting laughing from what she had just heard, but said, in as grave a voice as possible, "Thank you for those kind words, I have to arrange for his wife to be told now and let her see him one more time."

She rose and left the room, pressed a button on her phone and dialled her Chief Government civil Servant, Sir Colin Harris. He answered within a few seconds and she told him of the news about Morgan and asked that he visit his widow and give her the news as he was his Senior in the Cabinet Office. It would show the respect that Morgan deserved for all his service.

He replied in the affirmative. She then said, "As is the procedure with all deaths involving senior officials, the Government is obliged to remove any documents and files found at his house. He will have an office there for sure, that will need to be secured. I suggest you ask Lady Morgan if she would like to go to the hospital and see his body, whilst we have a small team of searchers who will remove what is needed. I think it will save her any more pain and sorrow if she is not around."

He replied "Of course, she will know the procedures in any case. I will take her personally. We have known each other for many years since we joined the civil service together."

The Prime Minister responded, "The team will wait outside the gates until you have left. Please lock the room as soon as you can, and they will take care of the rest."

She curtailed the call, knowing her instructions would be carried efficiently and effectively by Sir Colin. What he didn't know and was never going to know, was the location of the secret safe, given up by Brown during his interview. The team would be led by Sgt Grace Meadows, and she would be the lead evidence officer once again.

She returned to the conference room where the others were gathered and told them what had been put in place. She again omitted to tell them about the safe. They conducted their business in a subdued frame of mind, with the exception of her, as she kept thinking of how the next stages were progressing.

Sir Colin Harris arrived at the home of Morgan, and as soon as Lady Morgan opened the door, she knew something was very wrong. He entered the house and gave her the sad news. She sat on the sofa and broke down in tears. He told her that he was presently at King Georges Hospital and perhaps she might like to go and see him. He told her of the rules governing senior civil servants and she replied that she was aware and thanked him for being so discreet and sensitive about it.

She gathered a number of articles from her room. Then, she and Sir Colin left the house in his official car. As they left the gates, DS Meadows phoned to Dr Webster and told him they were on their way. They would be with him within thirty minutes. She also informed Freeman and Ellis at their base too.

As the car drove away, Grace and her team entered the house of Sir Jeremy Morgan. It was a well maintained, period property and she could see that Lady Morgan had been proud of her husband with the number of photographs scattered about the place. Some were well dated, seeing them as young couple and others up to date, more formal in nature as befitting his position within the government.

Grace walked through to his office, feeling no remorse for the man at all. She was determined to find as much as possible about him and his activities over the past few years. She knew that his study would contain mostly official papers, and she had an assistant from the civil servant with her in the room as they went through those files. He tied them up and boxed them before they were taken away.

She found a strong box behind his bookcase. It was locked, but she was able to prise it open. Inside she found a large number of company seals and articles of Association. She closed that up and boxed it for her own evidence.

She then entered the dining room and went to the safe, where it was hidden behind the painting. She took the painting down and saw what she was looking for. She noticed that it was a combination lock together with a key lock too.

She called out to her locksmith and told him to open the safe as soon as possible. If not, they would take it all out and open it when they got back to base.

Grace rang Freeman and told what she had found, and that the safe was solid. She thought it would be opened without too much trouble. When she had finished, they would tidy up and leave the house for when Lady Morgan returned.

She looked around the house, searching for any spots where he might have hidden anything, but she was satisfied that the safe held all the dirty secrets of him and Brown.

CHAPTER 42

Sir Colin Harris and Lady Morgan arrived at King George Hospital where they were met by Inspector Craig Hallam.

He introduced himself and said, "Lady Morgan, I am sorry for your loss. In all cases of sudden death, we are obliged to look into the cause and satisfy ourselves there are no suspicious circumstances."

He continued, "I need to be present when you make a formal identification. I know it is difficult, but I have to follow rules like everyone else."

She nodded, and said, "Thank you for your kind words. I understand you have to do your job."

He led them down the corridor where they were met by Doctor Webster. He shook hands with them all and said to Lady Morgan, "He is behind the curtain, when you are ready, we will pull it back and you can see him and identify him for the police."

She looked over at the window and tears formed in her eyes as she nodded and said, "Yes I am ready."

Webster nodded to a colleague who pulled a switch and the curtains opened. Once open, they revealed Morgan lying on a stainless steel stretcher, covered in a green sheet except for his head and shoulders. She gasped and put her hand to her mouth and looked away. She nodded at Webster who had the curtains closed again.

Inspector Hallam said, "Lady Morgan is that your husband?" She replied, "Yes." and burst into tears. Sir Colin put his arm around her shoulders and led her away from the room and Inspector Hallam followed.

Webster sat at his desk, filled out the death certificate, giving the cause of death as heart failure, and gave it to his assistant who passed it on to the administration section of the Mortuary.

He then went back into the mortuary and took out a syringe and injected Morgan in the neck again. Within a few seconds Morgan's eyes opened wide and he gasped loudly. He looked around and saw Webster standing in front of him with a syringe. He shouted out, "What just happened?"

Webster replied, "Simple, you died, your wife identified you, she left, and I have brought you back to life." Morgan sat up and realised he was only covered in a sheet. He shouted, "What the hell is going on?"

Webster answered, "You are no longer anybody, you are now under the authority of the Army and Metropolitan Police. As such I have nothing more to do with you, get dressed. Your clothes are on the chair next to you."

He walked out of the room and in his place two men dressed completely in black and carrying firearms stood at the door.

One of them told him to get dressed immediately and he would be taken away to a secure facility.

He got off the bed, and dressed himself and said, "I am Sir Jeremy Morgan, I want a lawyer, you cannot treat me this way." The man replied, "I don't care who you are, I have my orders and you will obey them."

Morgan stood and he was immediately hand-cuffed, and a hood placed over his head. He felt himself being marched down a corridor and heard a door open and he was bundled into the back seat of a large vehicle. He lay on his side as he felt the vehicle drawing away. He tried to move but when he did so he felt something hard and metallic hitting him in the ribs.

Back at the hospital, Lady Morgan sat with Harris and she said, "What will I do now? I need to make arrangements and let people know."

Harris responded, "Leave it to me Lady Morgan, I'll make the necessary arrangement and will do the paperwork for you. You will just need to see it and confirm that its ok for you."

He continued, "Unless you have someone in mind, I can get an undertaker to handle that side of the arrangements. We can discuss details later."

She replied, "Thank you, I really don't know anything. I'll be very grateful if you would do that for me. It sounds silly but

I left everything up to Jeremy to do, I was there at his side when needed really." He smiled at her, and said, "Do you have anyone you can call and stay with for the moment?"

She shook her head replying, “We had no children. I do have a sister, but she is in America at the moment, but I will be alright I promise. I have been used to being on my own over the years.” He said, “Come home with me, and you can stay for as long as you feel comfortable. I don’t think you should be alone at this terrible time.”

She smiled and said, “Thank you, I do appreciate it. I know that the house is being checked for any Government files he had in his office. Its procedure for them to be removed, especially when they have been kept by someone so senior as Jeremy.”

He took her arm and they left the hospital and got into his Government vehicle. He telephoned the Prime minister and told her of what had taken place since he had met with Lady Morgan. He told her she would be going to his home and probably stay there overnight.

The Prime Minister thanked him and told him to take care of her. He responded by saying that he had told her he would take personal charge of any arrangements that needed doing. He rang off.

She immediately dialled Grace Meadows and told her of the present circumstances, and Grace replied, “Thank you Ma’am, we have just got the safe open and its full of treasure. We will keep you informed through Commander Freeman.”

The Prime Minister returned to her meeting and gave them an update on the death of Morgan. She told them that Downing Street will be putting out a press release later that evening and highlighting his achievements during his Government Service. They all nodded, and a few said that it was the least the Government could do.

In the meantime, Grace and her team had opened the safe, and found a large number of files inside. She thought, typical civil servant, always keeps stuff in files and making it easier for her. She quickly scanned the files and found many reports and financial records of a large number of companies. There were references to individuals and several referring to Captain Brown.

She bagged the files and then looked further into the safe, where she found several pages of type written letters in Russian and Chinese. She could read that they were addressed to Jeremy Morgan at this address, but nothing else. She bagged the letters and after ensuring it was all empty, replaced the door and picture as if nothing had been disturbed.

At the same time this was happening, Morgan felt the car stop and he was pulled out and walked a few paces. He could feel the wind given off by propellers and the noise he recognised as being a helicopter. He felt himself being pushed up a few steps and then buckled into a seat. Within a few seconds he felt the craft rise. He shouted out, "Where are you taking me, what do you want?"

He received no response and he sat back contemplating his fate, particularly after what the Prime Minister had said to him. He was starting to feel frightened for his health and life. He was not sure who his captors were, other than they spoke English to him. He thought about his overseas contacts and shivered at the thought of what might happen if it was one of them.

He sat in fear, listening to the noise of the helicopter, trying to hear if the men were saying anything but they remained silent.

He called out, “Hey, I need to use the toilet.” He heard one laugh and say, “Then you’ll be making a mess then won’t you, nothing like that on here. We are not flying you first class. You are lucky to be flying economy.”

Tears filled his eyes, he was not used to being spoken to like this, but he had a feeling that at some time in the future, it was going to get a lot worse. He thought of his wife and wondered how she was taking it all. Had anyone told her what was happening and if so, could she contact someone in the Government to help him.

He shook his head, realising that it was the Prime Minister herself who had got him into this situation. He thought of the alleged death of Captain Brown and what had really happened to him. Perhaps he was being held like him and being tortured somewhere trying to get information. He knew Brown would never let him down or disclose anything that would incriminate himself.

His mind was a jumble and he felt he was nearing his end.

After a while he felt the helicopter slow down and with a hard bump, landed and switched off its engines. A few minutes later he was lifted out of his seat and down a set of steps. As soon as he left the helicopter, he felt the cold wind and the rain saturating him. He was marched over a hard surface before he heard a door being opened.

Another set of hands took hold of him and walked him along what seemed to be a corridor from the sound of the footprints. Nobody had said a word to him, and he was totally disorientated. He was pulled to a stop and he heard another door open and he was pushed into what he presumed was a room. His hands were uncuffed and his hood removed.

It took him a few moments to get used to the low density light but he soon recognised that he was in a room with a table and chair in the middle. There were no windows. In the corner was a low flat bed and in the opposite corner a rudimentary toilet next to a wash basin.

He looked at the two men standing either side of him. They were dressed in black with masks over their faces. He could not tell if they were the same ones from the hospital or another pair. Neither of them said a word and turned and left the room locking the door behind them.

He went over to the chair and sat down looking around, the room was no more than a prison cell. He thought to himself, that whoever has done this will suffer for what they have done. As soon as he was free, he would make contact with some friends who would do his bidding. For the moment he would be patient and wait and see who would be talking to him.

CHAPTER 43

Freeman had Brown returned to the interview room. He and Ellis sat before him. Freeman said, “Have you had time to think on what we said to you and what you are going to tell us?”

Brown replied, “I have told you what I can, have you spoken to Morgan yet?”

Ellis answered him, “Oh, of course you don’t know. He was told you had died in a road traffic accident a few days ago. He was present when the news was announced by the Prime Minister. He said what a wonderful soldier you had been and a good friend, but he said that you had been in control of everything.”

Brown said out loud, “He is a lying bastard, I had the operational experience, but it was him that had all the contacts in the business and banking sectors initially. You have all my records and I told you where he kept all his secret stuff. That alone should tell that I am telling you the truth here.”

Freeman said, “He is currently being held in a secure facility and all his papers have been discovered and being researched. So, before he gets to give his full version, perhaps there are other things you might want to get in first, so we can decide who is lying or otherwise.”

Brown went quiet for a few minutes, before saying, "Get him talking about a company in China. I don't know the name of it, but that is where he has received large amounts of finance recently and he seems on good terms with the head guy, who is also a senior communist leader. I have seen some letters in his safe."

He continued, "One time he had a visit from two Chinese guys, they were picked up at Heathrow and conveyed to the office in Basingstoke. I was there, but not party to the meeting which lasted an hour or so. After it finished, we went for a meal to a local restaurant. They spoke good English and talked about their wish to spend more time in England working with Morgan. Later I asked him about that conversation, but he didn't elaborate. I never followed it up, but the letters arrived shortly afterwards."

He then said, "Personally I have never used any Chinese or even Russian guys in my teams. I do not trust them and never know where their loyalties truly lie. I know that anyone who does my sort of work is only in it for the money and have no real loyalty. I know the men, and they know me and also know if they do a good job they get paid well and will be used again."

He then said, "Any chance of a couple of bacon and egg sandwiches, I get hungry quickly. While I am having them, they help me think properly as to what else you might find useful on that jerk Morgan?"

Freeman sighed and looked at him and said, "Do you eat anything else except sandwiches?"

Steenson entered the interview room and sat in front of Morgan. He placed a file on the table in front of him and as Morgan looked at him, he said, "Your obituary is being written as we speak. You had a wonderful career and will be missed by your colleagues, friends and above all your devoted wife, who says you will be forever in her heart.

The media will be doing a good expose on your life. You will be a two day wonder before it all goes quiet and you will be forgotten like everyone else. But you don't worry yourself, you will never be forgotten by us.

We are going to give you a life as you have never known before. When we have finished with you, you will be joining your friends from around the world in the deepest darkest holes mankind has ever built."

Morgan said, "You can't do this to me. We are a civilised society, there are rules, I demand to see my lawyer."

Steenson smiled and said, "Weren't you listening? You are dead as far as the world is concerned. You belong to us and all that counts now is how you answer our questions in the coming hours. Answer right and at least you will have a modicum of comfort, don't talk and you will wish you had really died."

He continued, "Your friend Brown has decided he would like a little bit of comfort for the rest of his miserable life. He has been telling us how you have set it all up and he assisted you in the operational side. It seems both of you made a lot of money. You don't need to worry about money any more. All your assets have been seized, and more pertinent, where you are going you never need to think about money again."

Morgan blanched and started to say something when Freeman entered the room. He said, "We have opened your safe, what a bagful of secrets and treasures we have discovered."

Morgan shouted, "How did you find that? I bet it was Brown who told you, saving his own scrawny neck and dropping me into it."

Freeman just answered, "We searched your house and we came across the safe, wasn't hard to get into it. But it was like winning a lottery, all the numbers were coming up in sequence."

Steenson said, "Now is your chance to tell us your side, and for every bonus point you give us, the easier it will be for you. If you leave anything out, then back to square one, a bit like snakes and ladders."

Morgan said, "There are documents showing all the companies we have formed around the world. As you have no doubt seen, me and Brown are the main signatories to them and have signing powers on the bank accounts."

He continued, "I have kept all of them recorded since we began. Identities, meetings, you have them all, so you know what I am talking about."

Freeman then said, "For your information Morgan, on Monday there is an operation being mounted all around the world, based on the information we have retrieved from yourself, Brown and others who are either properly dead or in custody. We expect that we will have over one hundred arrests and over two hundred companies closed down and their assets seized by the close of play. I can tell you this as you are a dead man, that everyone in the different organisations you are associated with are aware that both you and Brown are dead."

Morgan looked at him and smirked, saying "You will never know everything. You just think you know what is happening, but people like you will always be pawns in the game."

Freeman said, "That's not helping your cause, is it? being so belligerent and trying to be smug. I bet there will be many others who will be only too happy to disclose their roles in what they have been doing once they have been arrested and the evidence is before them."

He continued, "Talking of which, you have not been very forthcoming with the truth have you? You have only conceded what you have had to, like Brown did initially until he saw the error of his ways."

Morgan said, "What are you talking about? You have got the files, you know about me and Brown in the United Kingdom, what more could you possibly have?"

Freeman sat back and smiled, "Have a guess? You might surprise yourself even."

Morgan sat up, closed his eyes and the reopened them and said, "You found them, didn't you?"

Freeman said, “Found what? What are you talking about? Give me some details and I can give you an answer. What you have asked makes no sense to me at the moment.”

Morgan responded, “Were there some letters in the safe which were not in the files?”

Freeman looked at him and said, “Where in the safe might they be and what are they about? Give me a clue here and perhaps we can sort that out and find them and see what they are.”

Morgan said, “Maybe you are fishing, sounds as though you are trying to get me to say things which are not necessary. I’ll let that go and put it down to your bravado and desperation.” He sat back and smiled and stared at both of them.

Steenson stood up and put his face in front of Morgan and said, “You are a stupid, arrogant man. You have no idea what we are going to do with you. If you continue lying to us, your wife is suddenly going to find that all the bank accounts you share with her are empty. All the other stuff like shares and your two safety deposit boxes will be empty and she will be destitute. She will even lose your pension as well.”

He continued, “It might even come out in the press about your criminal activities and the treasonous acts you have committed against this country. Think of the effect it will have on her and any friends she might have.”

He sat back down again and watched the reaction on Morgan's face. He was ashen. He whispered, "Please don't do this to her, she had nothing to do with any of this. It will break her."

Freeman responded, "Tell us everything and she will keep everything, including the pension and will never be any the wiser, you have my promise."

Morgan said, "There are some papers inside the safe, either in Russian or Chinese. They are our recent paymasters and they have been more and more active in the operations. They have committed millions of pounds to our organisation and we have allowed them to be in contact with some of our members."

He continued, "We don't trust them fully, so we have not allowed them into our inner circle meetings."

Freeman said, "Tell me about the meeting you had with the Chinese guy at your offices in Basingstoke."

Morgan gasped and said, "Brown really is trying to save his sorry ass, suppose I had better do the same. The Chinese wanted more of a stake in our organisations. It seemed to me they wanted to take it over and use the existing arrangements for their own purpose."

He carried on, "We only met for about an hour, it was not that comfortable a meeting, they left a letter with me signed by a very senior Chinese Official and was told that if we changed our minds, he was the man who would be in charge."

Freeman opened a file and pushed a letter towards Morgan saying, "Do you recognise that?"

Morgan smiled and said, "You are not so daft after all. Of course, that's the letter of introduction from the Chinese authorities. I am sure you have had it translated already and so know the contents. You can see why we did not choose to take them up on their offer, although the finances were pretty tempting."

Freeman said, "Who knew of this letter?" Morgan replied, "Brown of course, he met him at the airport and took him to meet me. Later we had a quick lunch before he flew back to China. I also spoke to a few other people about the misgivings and was told that they supported me in not taking them on."

Freeman said, "Thank you, but it took me to talk about your wife before you said anything. As I said earlier, you need to be volunteering, not having it dragged out of you."

He continued, "Is there anything more you are hiding from us, think before you answer, everyone's future depends on what you have to say."

Morgan said, "If you have found the Chinese letter then you must have found the one from the Russians too. As it says in the letter, they were requesting that one of their top snipers be left alone and not pursued by our organisation."

Freeman said, "Yes we have it, but it does not mention any name, so how did you know to leave alone?"

Morgan replied, "I was handed the letter personally, and the envoy gave me the name in confidence and that it should never be said openly or written down. I passed the details onto Brown."

Freeman said, "Yes Gregorov, we know of him and that Brown was trying to eliminate him as well. He never did of course, and in fact Gregorov got closer to removing Brown than vice versa."

Morgan looked surprised, "He knew better than that. He only has himself to blame if he broke the rules. Do you know where Gregorov and his woman are now? Her name has been mentioned a few times over the past few years and as being part of a team, but we have never been able to find out the connections."

Freeman replied, "Well it's something we know, and you will never know. A very interesting couple who supplied a mine of information to us over a period of time."

He continued, "It was partly due to them that we discovered the connection between you and Brown. From there it was pretty easy to establish what we know now. Every law enforcement agency in the world has been assisting us as well. Our own intelligence organisations have been working twenty-four hours a day collating all the evidence required for our operation tomorrow."

He continued, "Your boss, the Prime Minister has been aware of everything from the beginning, and she sanctioned and organised your arrest at Chequers yesterday."

Morgan closed his eyes, grimaced and said, "Never did trust that woman, the previous one was much easier to control. No love lost between us, but I am sure she is gloating about how clever she is."

Freeman said, "No, she is not, just very sad at your treachery and furious that you thought you could get away with it for so long. She has said that at some stage she will visit here and talk to you for a few moments, which is much more than you deserve. She also said she will give the eulogy at your funeral, if she can bear the disgust she has for you."

Freeman concluded by saying, "You will be kept in your cell for the next twenty four hours. Once we have started to obtain information regarding the operations you will be interviewed again. You will be fed as with all prisoners. No special treats for you ever again."

CHAPTER 44

Freeman and Steenson left Morgan, who was led out of the interview room and returned to his cell. They returned to the Mess and were both delighted to see Grace Meadows and Jason King sitting in their chairs with Sarah. Next to them were a couple of large boxes and Grace informed them that they were the full contents of Morgan's safe and they had compiled a report giving details of each file pertinent to the enquiry.

She passed the report around and they perused it. The information was extensive and gave new insights into the workings of the various companies and details of the main instigators and finances.

Freeman said after going through them, "Jason and Grace, its brilliant you are back with us and at the right time too. This report is tremendous and the fact you have done it in such a short time is amazing. It's enough for me tonight, I am going to have to call it a day. Let's all meet back at 7am tomorrow morning. We'll all be refreshed, and we can prioritise what needs to be done. At the same time the warrants and arrests are being made up. We have set up the command Post here. There are several satellite centres around the country in case of problems, but I don't envisage any now."

After Freeman, Ellis and Steenson left, the three sat together and caught up on the news. Sarah was particularly interested in the romance between Grace and Jason, calling them crafty and knew she should have never left them alone!

Grace laughed and said, "You have no idea what you have missed." as she cuddled next him and kissed him softly. Sarah smiled and thought to herself, I am missing out on a lot. I have let myself become too involved in work and not left enough time to relax and find the right friends.

They sat and drank as they talked, all comfortable with each other, Grace regaling her work at both Browns and Morgan's houses. They all laughed and shared their time together knowing that tomorrow everything was going to change, how it would, nobody knew.

In their respective cells, Brown and Morgan were contemplating their own futures and neither of them were looking forward to it.

Morgan thought about his wife, she was alone now, thinking he was dead. She would have to live her life in such a different way to what she was used to when he was still alive. He believed that she would be looked after. He had tried to make it go that way, but of course, what he himself had done could never make up for anything else.

He hoped that whatever was said about him publicly would make her feel proud, and his departure was made easier that way.

Brown on the other hand, was bemoaning his stupidity with Williams, it was a silly error made in the heat of the moment. He had liked her ever since they had met, but he had got carried away. He had devised the calls, never believing they would get discovered. He knew that from those silly actions everything else had transpired.

He had thought that by helping the police into a shooting, he himself had committed, he would be able to mask his own actions and blame it onto others. He was the author of his own misfortune, and he would live with it for the rest of his life. At least she would be left alone.

He considered what Morgan had told the authorities, but he told himself that it didn't matter. He had told them about Morgan and no doubt Morgan had disclosed details about him. He just shrugged it off mentally and thought that this was his lot and there was nothing no one could do about it and his fate was already sealed.

At 5am, the alarms went off and they all showered, dressed and met back in the Mess. As they helped themselves to food off the buffet table, they discussed how the day might work out. Freeman told them that he had teams around the country supplementing this office and analysts would be passing on any information in real time.

He said, "The analysts here are some of the bests in the world and they are a mix of us and the military thanks to Major Ellis. We have complete trust in them. They had no idea they would be here until picked up two hours ago and flown here under cover of darkness."

He continued, "Steenson will take charge of events in Africa and the middle East, Major Ellis will take on Europe and Asia and I will be doing America and China and Russia. Anything related to these areas goes through us. Sarah you are with me, Jason you are with Steenson and Grace you are with Major Ellis. We have to work together on this to gain maximum impact."

He finished off by saying, "Read the reports that Grace and Jason have compiled from the stuff they found at Morgan's house, they will give you new insights into what we are aiming to achieve today. The operations will start at 0700 hours so be prepared for a long and demanding day."

Just before their allotted time, they all went and sat behind their consoles and waited for the commencement of the operation. As they sat and drank coffee and tea from their mugs, the different monitors started to show green lights all over the screens. They had been divided into continents and then down to cities and towns.

Within a few minutes, over 90 per cent of the target locations had been entered. Over the next twenty minutes, more and more green lights flashed up and showed that virtually all premises had now been entered and the waiting game for information was just starting.

Ellis spoke up and said, "The Edinburgh team have arrested an individual in an office within Morgan's group. He was in contact with a person in New York, do we have any idea who that might be yet?"

Freeman said, "Nothing yet, but that might be due to lag, I'll let you know."

Ellis came back and said, "It appears that the man detained had false particulars, his passport and driving licence were false and going under the name of Alexander Jackson. This is his photograph just sent, anyone recognise him?"

Freeman said, "That's an MP, from the Party north of the border. He is Bruce Johnstone, what the hell is his involvement? He needs to be isolated immediately and taken to a secure site."

Ellis got onto the phone and instructed the officer in charge of the search team in Edinburgh to remove him immediately. He was to taken under full security lockdown to the Naval base at Rosyth where he would then be taken to another location. Any documents and files were to be sent with him under armed guard.

Sarah said, "Were we aware of his involvement before today?"

Freeman reported, "We had the name Jackson, but of course, in view of the time constraints we had not done any background work on anyone. We might find that there are others around the world who hold political positions and using false details."

He spoke to his operator and told him to send a message to all that the identities of all persons detained, however minor they might appear to be, are to be double checked before they removed from their present locations.

Over the next few hours, several individuals were identified as using false particulars and when their proper names were found, it was shown that they held either senior positions in government, or para military forces in different regions. All these persons were isolated immediately and taken to secure locations within the territories they were detained.

It soon became apparent that the searching officers had found mountains of material in virtually every location they had entered. Banks had been cooperative and had given the investigating officers full access and all the financial records were being forward to the control room for analysis and forensic auditing.

The Control Room and satellite centres were receiving information constantly. From the data being received, it soon became apparent that many countries had fallen under the influence of a few organisations. It seems that they all led back to the United Kingdom and an office in Basingstoke, through a myriad of companies, and proxy bank accounts.

A total of one hundred and sixty four persons had been detained in premises raided. Of that total, nine had given false particulars and were now being removed and taken to other secure facilities for processing.

Bank accounts revealed sums running into the billions had been laundered through the various companies under investigation and the authorities had frozen all accounts. Additionally, they had taken action on seizing many properties listed either under the names of the companies or individuals and their proxies.

Freeman, Ellis and Steenson spent most of the day answering queries from the various locations they had been allocated. They gave advice when possible and responded as and when they had collated the answers to questions raised.

Sarah, Jason and Grace moved around the control room, helping each of the three as they called out for assistance. They moved to different consoles and typed in their commands and within moments facts were shown on screen, collated, and reports printed which were constantly being updated within minutes as more and more information came into the control room.

After a couple of hours, the flow of information slowed down and they gathered around the main table, with mugs of coffee or tea, and went over the enormity of what they had witnessed.

Freeman said, “That was spectacular, I think we have achieved something today that has never been done before. The criminal world is going to take a while to get back into any semblance of order and at present they are weakened. It is up to the various authorities to keep on at them while they can.

Ellis responded, “What are we going to do with our Scottish friend? I don’t think we can do the same as with Morgan and Brown, but I think we need to have some time with him. I’ll have him detained under one of our military laws which gives us fourteen days and without access to a lawyer."

Freeman replied, "We'll have him brought here, usual method, cuffed and hooded and kept in the same area as our other two."

Sarah said, "We need to have all the documents he has access to, and that will include his parliamentary office. That could be a problem if the First Minister plays up. The Prime Minister can authorise a search of his office in Westminster, I am sure."

Ellis replied, "Under military law she cannot oppose his offices being searched there. If she resists, she can be arrested for complicity in a crime against the State. I am sure she won't want to go down that path."

Jason laughed and said, "Shame, be nice to see her go head to head with the Prime Minister on this issue."

Behind him a voice called out, "Go head-to-head with whom young man?"

They all turned around and saw the Prime Minister, together with The Home Secretary and Commissioner of Police standing at the entrance to the control room. Jason went red and said, "I am so sorry Ma'am, didn't expect you there, just a bit of humour with the others."

She smiled and said, "Don't worry Jason, who is going to make me annoyed?"

Freeman told the Prime Minister about the detention of the Scottish MP and she grinned and said, “Good, let her try it, I'll wipe the floor with her annoying voice and make sure that the press hear of his treachery and suggest it goes further into her party.”

She continued, “Apologies, for not letting you know of our arrival, but in the circumstances, I thought it better if we just had a ladies day out.” she laughed and continued “Seriously we wanted to keep it quiet, we are having a conference with the Chiefs of Staff of the Armed Services and so it is very hush hush. Please brief us on the new developments, we have plenty of time.”

Coffee was brought to everyone and the three of them were briefed on the current situation. Most of the information they were given was dominated by overseas raids and arrests, but even then, there were connections back to Morgan and Brown.

The Prime Minister said, “Its ok, I have briefed them.” They looked at her questioningly and she responded, “If anything happens to me, then certain protocols have to be put in place. They have been told of who but not where as yet.”

Ellis said, “As far as I am concerned their names are sponged from any records. Browns details of his military service and personal particulars have been wiped clean and he is buried in an unmarked grave in the middle of nowhere.”

They looked at him and took in his comments, The Prime Minister said, “Morgan is having his funeral in two days time. There will be a good turn out and the usual platitudes given. He will then be cremated and his ashes scattered in the English Channel".

She continued, "He is too high a profile Government Servant to just disappear, although we all know what the true story is. His wife will scatter his ashes in a private ceremony. While I am giving the Eulogy at the main service, I'll try not to gag or cringe while I say such nice things about him."

They all laughed and relaxed, Sarah and Grace both felt a little strange being in such company, but everyone was acting as informal as they could be given the circumstances.

Information continued to pour into the control room and the analysts and data operators compiled a running figure of the time lines and what had been achieved. A list of who had been detained and the companies involved were given to the three visitors. The Prime Minister took one look at who had been implicated and said, "There are some very well-known people in this lot, this is almost like a film script and the good guys win in the end."

She continued, "I'd like to think that what we have achieved will bring about changes for a long while, but that's me being optimistic. I'll be having meetings and calls with a number of leaders over the next few days. They will get the abridged version of course, but I'll make sure we get all the kudos for the original hard work."

Freeman smiled and said, "Thank you Ma'am, but if it was not for the original hard work of Sarah and Jason and Grace, we would never have got to this position. They are the ones who saw the connections and acted up on them. Steenson also deserves a special mention, I am sure you will relate that to the necessary authorities when you speak with them."

He continued, "I think we are going to be here for a while getting everything analysed and into report form. We have already started to get interim reports from other agencies, We will be giving them details of what we have achieved. Again, I must add it will not be everything, as I am sure they are holding stuff back too."

They split into different groups conversing and reading reports as they were produced.

After a while a report came into the Control Room that the Scottish MP, Bruce Johnstone, had arrived and was being taken to the cells. Freeman told the group he wanted to go and see him and told Jason to accompany him.

The Prime Minister rose and said, "I will join you I want to see the look on his fat face when he sees me entering with you."

Freeman laughed and said, "You have a sadistic streak, don't you? She responded, "You don't know the half of it. In this job you need to have a hide as thick as a rhinoceros and a mind like a steel trap. Let's go and greet him in his new home."

Freeman looked at the others, who shrugged and nodded as they left the room and made the short walk across the ground to where the interview rooms and cells were kept.

As they walked across, she said, "Go in first, and then I'll knock and walk in, that should knock him out of his stride."

They entered the cell block and Freeman walked into the cell holding Johnstone. He sat down in front of him and told him who he was and why he, Johnstone was here.

Johnstone sneered, "Where is here, and what am I doing here. Talk to my party leader and she will have your guts for garters and I can be on my way home."

Freeman said, "Here is where you are going to be for a while. You don't need to know the details but, the more you tell us about your dealings with organised crime, then the shorter it will be."

Johnstone said. "No comment, I want a lawyer now."

Freeman said, "You have been arrested under the Terrorism Act and you know what that means, we can detain you for as long as we like and with no legal advice."

He responded, "Get my party leader, she is a solicitor, she will know what to do."

At that moment, the door opened and in walked the Prime Minister. Johnstone immediately said, "Get me out of here, these animals are keeping me locked up and without telling me my rights. You are the Prime Minister, you tell them what to do."

She sat in front of him and said, "Shut up and listen, you are part of a worldwide criminal organisation operating in every major city. You gave false details to the officers who entered your premises, further implicating you."

She continued, "I have spoken to your party leader and told her of the background to your detention. Initially she was disgusted that the UK Government had arrested one of her MP's and she would immediately be taking out a court order for your release."

Johnstone retorted, "You had no rights to detain me at all. This will cost you your job."

The Prime Minister just said, "Just listen will you. I explained a few home truths to her about her party and the future, especially if the public were to hear the full details of your treason. She suddenly saw the error of her support for you and told me that as far as she is concerned you are finished, and I can do whatever I want with you. No loyalty there it seems."

He looked over at Freeman and the Prime Minister and said, "If I go down from this and I expect to do so, then all her dirty political secrets will find their way into the public domain."

The Prime Minister said, "Go ahead, that will solve a lot of problems for me." and she laughed and continued, "Whatever you do, you are finished. Just tell our people what they want to know, and your name will not appear in an obituary in the Scottish papers as a result of a tragic road accident."

He looked at her with astonishment and said, "You are joking of course, aren't you?"

She didn't flinch and said, "I am not here to make idle threats Johnstone. You could end up as a footnote in history, soon forgotten."

She stood up and said to Freeman, "He is all yours, do what you need to do with him. I'll speak with you later." She walked out of the room.

Johnstone said, "Where am I exactly? I don't remember much since the men walked into my office and found me going through my files."

Freeman said, "You don't need to know where you are, in fact you will never need to know, this is your home right now."

He continued, "Why did you give the officers a false name when they asked you or your details. Surely you must have known they would recognise you?"

Johnstone responded by saying, "I was told that if anyone entered unannounced that was what I had to do. The documents are in the other name and so it was natural to give that name."

Jason said, "Who told you to say that?"

He replied, "I am not sure to be honest. I met a few people in London when down there on parliamentary business. One of them was a Senior Civil Servant and the others I cannot recall. There were several meetings and I admit I was attracted to the rewards. I felt that there was something not quite right about it all, but I didn't go into it. I did as I was asked to and opened the office in Edinburgh.

They paid for everything and I just forwarded documents to a place in Basingstoke when they arrived to me."

Freeman asked, "Did you not read what was in those documents? Surely a man of your standing must have seen that the information contained inside was not legitimate by any form of imagination."

He answered, "I only did it part time, I was in London most of the time. You were lucky, and I was unlucky that you caught me there before I travelled back down to London."

Freeman said, "You have committed crimes against the United Kingdom, which in effect is treason. You will be dealt with under military law as that is the most effective way of keeping you in custody. Of course, any court hearings, if there are to be any, will be held in secret."

Johnstone sat with his head down, and said, "What about my family, will they know what has happened?"

Freeman said, "They cannot for security reasons know the true reason for your arrest. You can tell them anything else, but if you try to say anything untoward you will be disconnected, do you understand?"

He replied, "Yes, give me a few minutes and I'll think of something."

Jason said, "In the meantime, we have seized all your personal records from your office in London. We will be going to your home too and conducting a search there too. That is part of normal procedures. Make sure what you say to your wife coincides with our enquiries, albeit in a minor way as far she is concerned."

Johnstone said, "You don't leave me with much choice as to what I can say. I'll have to tell her that I have been arrested in connection with a fraud matter. That I have allowed myself to be taken in by some scammers and used my name and position to defraud a large number of people overseas."

Jason said, "As you wish, but you will tell her that you are being detained in a secure location and maybe detained for an unknown period of time."

He answered, "Yes, and I'll tell her that the First Minister is aware of the situation and she has no comment to make. She should not worry about contacting her at this stage until it's all sorted out."

Freeman nodded his agreement and gave Johnstone a phone. He dialled a number and after a few rings it was answered. Johnstone then told the other party of what had happened and what was going to happen for the foreseeable future. He ended the call to his wife with the words that everything would be fine.

Freeman then said, "Are you prepared to give a full statement as to your involvement in this matter? It needs to be from start to finish and include names and details of all the companies and individuals involved."

Johnstone nodded and said, "Yes, I'll tell you everything I know, I am not one of the high rollers. I was greedy and thought it was fool proof, I am the fool as it turns out."

Freeman turned to Jason and told him to take a statement from Johnstone in written form and under caution. Jason nodded and said, "Yes sir, it will be a pleasure."

CHAPTER 45

Freeman then stood up and left the room and walked across to the Mess where he met the three senior officials together with Sarah and Grace. He told them what had happened with Johnstone. He told the others he was going to see Morgan and Brown to pass on the good news of the operation and their impending confinement

The Prime Minister asked if she could accompany them to see both men as it would be the last opportunity she would ever get to set eyes on either of them again. She said, "I don't get many moments of such satisfaction in my job as I am at the moment, I want it to last." she laughed and started out of her chair.

They walked out of the room and back into the cell block, the Prime Minister and the Commissioner of Police walking together with Freeman and Sarah.

They walked into the cell of Brown. He stood as they entered and was shocked to see who they all were. Freeman said, "The whole operation that you and Morgan set up has now been dismantled. We have arrested well over two hundred individuals worldwide. All the companies are closed down and there are huge funds which you and your criminal friends will never get their hands on."

He continued, "We have accumulated enough evidence to convict many of those arrested. Of course, it does not apply to you as you are officially dead to the outside world. Your crimes will be marked down as detected and no further action required due to the death of perpetrator."

Brown looked across at them and knew that he was never going to be free. He said, "It was good while it lasted and at least I have the thought of screwing Morgan who didn't hesitate to drop me into this hole."

The Prime Minister said, "If it was up to me, you'd be hanging right now. However, what's going to be your life from now on will be a hell of a lot worse. You went from being someone who was admired and respected to a traitor who sold out his country for money. Not even any nationalistic reasons, purely money."

She walked out of the room without looking at him. Freeman told him that the only times he would be seeing anyone now was in further interviews to clarify certain matters, but he did not expect that to happen much.

With that he and the others walked out of his cell, which was then locked. They joined the Prime Minister who was shaking with anger, who said, "Let me see Morgan."

They walked the few paces to where Morgan was kept. The door was opened, and she saw Morgan sitting on a bunk bed. She was shocked by the change in his demeanour. He was pale, unshaven and had a haggard, defeated look in his eyes.

When she entered, his eyes flew open and he almost fell of his bunk. He asked why she was there, and she replied, "So

I can see you one last time you treacherous bastard. You were my trusted confidante and all the time you were conspiring against your own country. Everything you did was a lie, nothing was truthful. How could you?"

Morgan said, "That's life, cannot win them all, but we did a good job doing what we did, we had good friends everywhere. Pity it has to stop sometime, but I'll live with it."

Freeman told him what had happened. He seemed shocked and asked if Brown had assisted them in finding out the people and companies.

Freeman just said, "We had our means to get you and Brown. Now you are nothing anymore, not even officially alive."

The Prime Minister followed it up by saying, "Even if I say it myself your eulogy was pretty convincing, hardly a dry eye in the house. You were cremated and your wife is having your ashes scattered."

She smiled at him and said, "Besides, I saw her talking with a gentleman at the service. They gave me the impression they were on more than just speaking terms, I think she might be thankful you died when you did."

Morgan shouted, "You bitch! You loved telling me that didn't you?"

She looked at him straight in the eye and said, "Very much so, but to a dead man like you, it makes no difference what she does now and you can spend the rest of your miserable life thinking about that."

She turned around and walked out, the others were silent until Freeman told Morgan, “Your friend Bruce Johnstone is also enjoying his time in a nearby cell too. He has been surprisingly forthcoming as to his involvement, you could have chosen someone more discreet.”

He then said the same as he told Brown about any future possible interviews. It not likely to be often as they were not directly involved any more being dead.

As they walked back to the Mess, Sarah looked at Freeman and raised her eyebrows, he shook his head and smiled. Sarah was amazed by the intensity of the Prime Ministers anger. She also understood how she, and the country had been betrayed by them both. Particularly Brown, as she herself had been having taken him in as part of her investigation team not so long ago.

On arrival back at the Mess the mood was quiet, everyone was mulling over the mood of the Prime Minister, but she turned around and said, “That got them going, didn’t it? The look on their faces and reactions were pictures. I shall sleep happy tonight thinking of them rotting in their cells.” She laughed and said, “Come on, it was an act, I have many roles on a daily basis, that one will keep me amused for ever.”

Over the next few hours, more information was received by the control rooms and reports prepared. They were read and passed to each other. Towards the evening the three visitors declared their intention to return to London.

As they were escorted to their helicopter by Ellis and Freeman, the Prime Minister said, “Please keep me informed of everything that you think needs my attention, especially matters involving potential governmental problems overseas."

Freeman replied, "Of course, Ma'am, wouldn't dream of leaving you out of the loop." They shook hands and as they boarded the helicopter the Prime Minister said, "If nothing else, give me the good news of the actual deaths of our two subjects as and when it happens."

Ellis laughed and said, "The pleasure will be all ours, believe me."

They returned to the Control Room and, as the day was winding down, they conferred around the large conference room table as to how their respective areas had managed during the first day of the operation. It appeared that, with few exceptions, most of the aims of the operation had been achieved.

There were a few objectives in each region that would not be completed until the next day and from the intelligence that had been received, follow up actions might take several days to complete, depending on what each team had discovered.

As they talked, teams of analysts and writers came into the Control Room and took their places at the various consoles. They all had current reports on-screen, and their roles were to consolidate all the information available, make assessments and any possible further enquiries that would be needed to be taken.

After dinner, they all separated and went to their respective rooms. Sarah noticed Grace and Jason going together into Grace's room. She smiled and felt pangs of envy as she went into her own room.

CHAPTER 46

Overnight, the administration and results of the previous day were updated and files for each of the six officers were complied. Images as well as the written words were indexed and formatted in order.

At 0600 hours the next day, Freeman and Ellis walked into the Control Room and were amazed at the huge number of bound files sitting on the tables. The staff were sitting at their consoles almost in a state of exhaustion. Freeman thanked them for all their hard work and efforts, and told them all to go off duty, and go to their accommodation and he would see them all again that night.

In the next thirty minutes they were joined by all the others, as well as the day shift operators, most of them carrying coffee mugs and breakfast rolls. They looked at the files and collectively groaned and Jason said, "How can we possibly get through all this in the next few hours? it's going to take days."

Ellis broke in and said, "Have faith young man, the first few pages in each file has a summary of what the whole contains. Every important file and images are numbered in the synopsis and found in the main file."

Jason muttered, "Thank goodness, thought I was back at school for a minute." They all laughed and as they were served coffee, looked at the screens for updated arrests, properties searched, and evidence seized. Additionally, the details of all bank accounts associated with the arrested persons were on screen and formed part of the reports.

The amount of money that had been seized was staggering. In some instances, the amounts seized from the organisations were more the Gross National Product of many smaller nations.

As they read the summaries of the files it soon became apparent that the centre of everything criminal was the small unassuming office in Basingstoke. Sarah said, "Have we missed anything there? It seems that an awful lot of the locations and reports refer to that address."

Grace said, "There was nothing there, I stripped the place bare. Whatever was there, we have, and you saw what we got. I even did the offices next door and one level up and down to make sure we had not missed anything."

She continued, "We did the post office, Royal Mail sorting office and the three courier companies for anything relating to the companies. The local banks were visited and what we found we have here. To me, most of the activities were almost certainly franchised out, with just the essential elements referring to Basingstoke and Morgan."

Freeman answered, "I agree with Grace. Morgan and his close associates kept it as simple as they could. However, it ended up growing out of control. Even Brown was unable to stop it. He ended up just being interested in killing anyone who had the highest bounty on their head. He kept in with Morgan because it suited him. The business with Gregorov was very unsettling for him and he was never in control of the running of the companies after that."

Sarah nodded, and said, "I agree, he thought he could get something over on Morgan by being with us, but in the end, he was not careful enough with his own personal life and that screwed him totally. One bad move and the whole damn circus toppled because of it. Major Ellis deserves all the praise for that, without him none of us would be any the wiser."

Freeman said, "All the jurisdictions will now be compiling case files for court cases or warrants of arrest for wanted persons. We have to also compile prosecution files for the CPS in respect of the activities conducted on British soil and conspiracies with other countries and individuals who are overseas."

He continued, "Of course, as far as anyone is concerned the two main protagonists are already dead, but we do need to conclude the killings and all subsequent events legally. The compilation of the files will be your responsibilities Sarah and Jason. I will, of course sign them off through the Commissioner of Police to CPS."

He continued, "I think we will be more or less finished here within a few days, and so it's time we wrapped up as much as we can between now and then. We will have to vacate here soon in any case. We have Major Ellis to thank for our facilities here and in other locations."

Ellis said, "We have our own reports to write too, again factoring in the demise of Brown, but we need to finalise what the military has taken in this role."

Sarah said, "What about Sergeant Williams?"

Ellis replied, "She is being released. She will resign from the army as part of a conversation between myself and her. She will then re-join my staff in a civilian role, and the indiscretion she committed has been wiped clean. She is a good officer and her intelligence capabilities will fit perfectly into the Department I oversee."

Sarah smiled and said, "Thank you sir, she was helpful in all this and an unwitting pawn. Browns mistake was our stroke of fortune. I liked Brown, he seemed a good man, not romantically of course, but he was proficient, now of course we know why."

Freeman told his teams to collate all the files relating to the activities in the UK. They were to separate what they needed, and then make a list of what other statements would be required in the future. From the events that had taken place there would still be many.

He said, "Divide yourself up into the groups that need statements to be taken either civilian, or police as well as military. Ensure that all physical evidence is included, as well as copies of documents relating to everything in the attached files."

He continued, "It's going to be complex and slow, but you all know everything from day one, so it should make things easier. If you have any problems let any one of us three know and we will assist you. Remember anything that took place at the Russian Embassy does not include the Prime Minister nor the Ambassador in any way at all, not even their presence."

He concluded by saying, "We will have to be careful as to how we submit the files, they have to be exact in their contents. Pool your resources with the techies and I think we will be ok. I am sorry it has ended this way, but in the circumstances, we have no choice."

Jason asked, "What about Johnstone? What do we do about him?"

Freeman said, "He will be dealt with. He will be charged with offences relating to fraud, to which he will plead guilty. He will get a suspended prison sentence and resign as an MP. The full facts will not be read out in court. But if he ever tries to bring up the subject in the future, he will find he will be in a deep dark hole too."

They all split up and started to read the files in front of them. They made notes in their laptops, including names and particulars of witnesses and others who had been at the various scenes. Phone calls were made, and appointments made for the next few weeks.

Sarah went over the initial investigation into the park shooting and highlighted several new aspects which she had not connected with originally. She set out a timeline for every event and was stunned by the sheer volume of what had happened. Although it was less than a month since the shooting, it seemed a lifetime ago. They were all totally exhausted. Not just with the hours of duty, but also from the events, the killings, the wholesale slaughter and the scale of the deceptions and persons involved at all levels.

She felt tears welling up in her eyes. As she looked around, she saw the looks on the others faces as they grasped the magnitude of what they were expected to do. There was silence in the room, broken only by the whirring of printers when documents were being printed. Even the operators at the consoles were quiet, there was no banter between them, just the soft clicking of the keyboards at their consoles.

Over the course of the day, various persons rang the direct lines. Freeman and Ellis, together with Steenson, were able to provide the necessary information to all the queries directly or through the three officers sitting at their desks.

Slowly files started to accumulate. But given the case substance, it would take days before all the statements were taken and sent to them. In the meantime, lawyers from the CPS were being sent the reports and associated paperwork in order to assist in the legal aspects of the case. No one knew, of course, the current location of the team.

Without there being any particular reason to interview their prisoners, the teams worked quickly, talking with each other as they put together an ever-increasing file of evidence. They were methodical as they searched every document and image. They found that they had quite large references to overseas countries. On the advice of Freeman, subsidiary files were created off the main files. These files would be subject to scrutiny at the highest levels of Government.

CHAPTER 47

At around 5pm the second evening, Freeman approached Sarah and said that Brown wanted to talk to her.

Sarah said, "Did he say what about? I have nothing to say to him."

Freeman replied, "He sent the message and said he had something to say, but would only talk to you."

She responded, "If he is wasting my time, he will wish he really was dead and buried for real." She got up and walked down the corridor to where Brown was seated in the interview room.

She sat in front of him and said, "I am busy, what do you want? Don't waste my time or you'll regret it."

Brown looked at her and said, "Don't be so angry, I have told you what I know but there is something that obviously none of you have found out, and I will give that up."

Sarah frowned, and wondered what they didn't know about Brown? His whole life history had been laid bare over the past few weeks.

She said, "Go on, tell me what you think I don't know."

She continued, "And why me? why not Commander Freeman or Major Ellis?"

He answered, "Because I trust you, you have always been fair with me. Even when you knew what I had done, from the outset, you were a professional and I appreciated that."

She replied, "Look what happened, you betrayed me, us and more to the point our country, just for greed."

He commented, "Yes you are right I have. I am very sorry to you on a personal basis."

He then said, "Before I go any further, can you please get me a Ham and Camembert sandwich with piccalilli please. It might be last one I'll ever get to have, after that I will let you into everything."

She smiled, "You and your sandwiches, don't you eat anything else?"

He laughed and said, "Saves on the washing up and over the years been the easiest to eat. I can eat them all day in preference to anything else."

She shook her head and opened the door and asked the guard to get him a sandwich and said, "Get one for me too, have to see what the attraction is."

As they sat and waited for their food, he started to explain to Sarah as to why and how he had started his path into the criminal life. Before he got too far, Sarah said, "I am not interested to be truthful, you did what you did and that was your choice. I don't need to hear this. I need to know what you are going to tell me and then I can get back to my work."

They didn't speak again until the sandwiches arrived. As they ate them Sarah remarked, "Not bad, I'll have to try this at home sometime."

Brown just smiled and continued eating and drinking his coffee. After a few minutes they finished their food, the plates were cleared away and Brown sat opposite to Sarah. He looked at her and said, "There is one more thing I do need to tell you. It is important that you know as it might affect the outcome of your enquiries."

Sarah sat back in her chair and said, "The floor is yours. You have my attention, but it had better be worthwhile."

Brown sat up straight and said, "Did you find a body in Horseshoe Lane? I am surely the lovely Grace didn't miss it, but just tell me you did."

Sarah was momentarily shocked at his remark and it showed on her face. He continued, "From your reaction, obviously you did. I don't suppose you have identified the young man, have you?"

Sarah said, "Excuse me for one moment, I need to get some advice before answering you." She left the room and met Freeman in the observation area. He appeared as confused as she was and told Sarah that that information had never been released to anyone.

Sarah asked what she should do, and he answered that she should go with it, admit about the body and see where it leads. She looked at him and shrugged and then returned to the interview room.

She said, "Yes, we found a body and no, it has not been identified. What can you tell me about it?"

He said, "He was a homeless youth, he hung around the barracks in Aldershot for a while. He did a few odd jobs for some of the guys, he was thirteen. His name was Kevin Brown."

Sarah sat there hardly believing her ears. She responded, "Repeat that again, did I hear you right?"

Brown said, "Yes, his name was Kevin Brown, he had been with a travelling family since he was a child. His mother had dumped him with them and then they got fed up and one day upped and left and left him alone."

Sarah was trying to assimilate this news and said, "So there are two Kevin Browns?"

He laughed and said, "Don't be silly, I took his name, my real name is Goran Medinkov. I came to England when I was sixteen as an illegal. I am originally from Bosnia but escaped during the fighting there. I was living rough and when I was moving around, I met Brown one day. We started to go around together. I had no papers, but he kept showing me his birth certificate saying that he could do anything having that which gave him some recognition with the authorities."

He continued, "He was quite big for his age, and we had talked a lot and I remembered everything I could about him. He helped me with my English. I was a quick learner and knew that I could stay in this country if I tried harder."

Sarah was shocked by the revelations but tried to stay calm realising how it was all going to end. She was determined to let him finish what he wanted to say. She was unsure how much it was affecting the investigation. She looked through the glass towards Freeman, but not receiving any knock or movement she let him carry on.

Sarah said, "What should I call you now, Brown or Medinkov?"

He answered, "Medinkov from now onwards please. I have carried the name Brown around for far too long and have neglected my real self."

Sarah then commented, "How did you get to assume the name Brown?"

He answered, "Not as you think, he got ill, and I tried to get him to a hospital, but he said no and wanted to go back to where he lived when the traveling family were in Horseshoe Lane. We went there and he knew exactly where he had lived with them."

He continued, "We were in the garden for nearly two days and then he died. He just lay down and died, that was New Year's Eve 1999. I didn't really know what to do. I knew he had his certificate, so I took that and was going to leave him but decided to bury him and nobody could ask any questions if he couldn't be found. I thought that he would be discovered one day, but there wouldn't be much of him."

Sarah gathered her thoughts and said, "So how did you become Brown? You had no education or other official recognition?"

He responded, "I just went into a doctor's surgery, showed them my certificate and told them that I had been a traveller, but now I needed to be checked for a pain in my chest. It was easy. They registered me to an address in Aldershot, where other immigrants lived. They didn't check anything."

"From there I went to the dole office, showed them my forms, and they just accepted it and over a few weeks my new identity was born, bank account and National Insurance number, once I got a little job."

Sarah shook her head and then said, "What has this got to do with the investigation?"

He said, "Well I joined the army and got into some training camps, and that it is where I met Morgan. He was giving a talk at a camp in Wiltshire. I had only just joined this training base, but it was different to what I knew of other camps.

I was intrigued and stayed behind after the presentation. He was talking to two other officers, both senior in one particular regiment. He spoke for around ten minutes before they left. I approached him and told him how I had found his presentation different and quite stimulating. I had been in the army for around four years and was still a lieutenant.

He asked me for my details, and I gave them to him. He said he would be in touch and if I felt like meeting him and some others to discuss the meeting they had just held, then I'd be very welcome.

Over the next few months, I attended meetings at his home and other locations, where there were up to twenty people present. It was intense, but I got drawn to it, my background felt as though it was to become the life for me."

Sarah wondered where all this was going, he seemed to be just rambling on. She knew that his story was being checked as he spoke, but she could not see where it was leading to. He had obviously got close to Morgan and his cohorts, but nothing important was being disclosed.

Medinkov continued, "Morgan knew about my sniper capabilities through some contacts in the army. He told me that if I was willing, I could put them to good use. He said he was in government and he had contacts in many places. He said a man of my talents could be useful and it would be lucrative to both of us. I was a bit unsure at the beginning and told him I would think about it.

We met several more times, he even came to my barracks one time. He kept on about me helping him in some projects. I was going nowhere, got lots of awards, but no further promotion beyond Captain for a shooter like me, so in the end I agreed."

Sarah was getting impatient with Medinkov and said, "Get to the point, we know that you and Morgan ended up as partners, both traitors and criminals. What do I need to know further?"

Medinkov retorted, "What Morgan didn't know was that I had recorded every single meeting with him. A diary, if you wish, of my life from the day I met him until I was arrested."

Sarah sat up and said, "We never found anything at any of your premises to suggest that you did that, are you just trying it on?"

He smiled and said, "No, but I am not going to just give it up now. I want a favour from the British Government in view of my tragic accident. I want to be buried in my home country. "

Sarah said, "You know what the situation is don't you? you are here for the rest of your life, and then you will be buried in an unmarked grave."

He replied, "Yes, I know, but I am sure you can arrange a burial in my name in Bosnia, using an excuse of my death in the United Kingdom. I don't care, I want my name to die with me in my home country. With all your resources I know you can do it, please grant this one last wish."

Sarah was unsure of what to say and said, "Let me speak to someone and see if it is possible, but you have to give us what you have or you will never leave here, whatever your name may be."

She left the room and was met by Freeman and Ellis. She said, "What do you make of that?" Ellis said, "I think we could accommodate him, it's not going to be nice, but his body could end up back in his homeland. Not this body, but I am sure we can acquire one which corresponds to his age and can be quietly buried in his hometown."

They both looked at him and Freeman said, "Are you serious a burial in Bosnia? but the real Medinkov stays in his cell for all time?"

Ellis replied, "Its unusual, but this whole case is unusual. Run it past the Prime Minister and if she approves, I'll sort the mechanics out, the least I can do for you, and we get all of his secrets."

Freeman left the room to make the call. Sarah returned to Medinkov and told him that they were talking to people at the highest level as to the possibility of his request being met. Medinkov said, "Thank you, at least you have tried, even if it doesn't happen."

They sat silently, Sarah not really at peace with what had been suggested, and the fact that something of this order might even be sanctioned. She just considered herself a Detective Inspector investigating crimes in London, not part of a huge international organisation toppling worldwide crime syndicates.

Freeman returned to the side room, knocked on the window and Sarah got up and left. Once there, Freeman said, "That woman never surprises me, she has given the go ahead. She will give her consent in writing to his request on the condition of him handing over what he has."

Ellis said, "I'll leave you guys for a bit, it will take a short while to organise it all. Sarah, can you get his full particulars for the casket and for the cemetery?"

Sarah shook her head but left and went and saw Medinkov and gave him the information he wanted to know. She told him that written confirmation to his request was being signed off by the Prime Minister and he would receive it.

Not that it would do anything for him except he would know he could trust her at all times.

He smiled and then gave her his full name, date and place of birth. He asked that his cause of death be an accident and that his coffin was not to be opened at any stage. She took all the details and handed it all over to Freeman, who then said, "I know you are not happy Sarah, but the greater good is what we need to do and that comes first."

She responded, "You are not kidding, but with everything else that's gone on, this just seems another development in the scheme of things."

A few minutes later, an email arrived directly from the Prime Minister accepting what Medinkov had requested. It was signed by her and time stamped too.

Sarah took hold it and went and saw Medinkov, she gave him the document. He burst into tears and read it over and over before saying thank you to her with tears in his eyes.

She said, "Arrangements are being made for a body to be returned to Bosnia, where there will be a short ceremony and a burial will take place. As far as the authorities are concerned Goran Stefan Medinkov, a resident of England, died in a tragic accident when the cycle he was riding was in collision with a lorry."

She continued, "A search of his home found a letter, requesting that in the event of his death, he wished to be buried in his homeland. His request was forwarded to the Foreign Office and the necessary arrangements made between Bosnia and the United Kingdom were made."

He looked at her and replied, "That's more than I could have hoped for, thank you. If you look in the shoulder grip of my rifle, you will find a package wrapped in bubble wrap. In there you will find a key to a safety deposit box in the name of Goran Medinkov in Lloyds Bank, Station Road, Aldershot. It's a numbered box, the number is with the package and inside you will find everything you need to know, which is a lot more than you think you know now."

She said, "Thank you, no wonder we never found the deposit box when we asked all the banks to give the details. We will talk again when we have obtained the contents of the box, and the update on your burial in Bosnia."

Sarah left the room and said to Freeman, "Let's find out what is so important. Where is his rifle?"

Grace interrupted and said, "It is in the armoury here as an exhibit. It has not been touched since we seized it when he was arrested. I'll go and get it as exhibit officer and give to it Medinkov as part of the chain of evidence. He can give you the key as part of the investigation which will give his story some credence."

She left the room and Freeman said to Sarah, "She is a real smart cookie, you have a good team going. Her and Jason seem to be getting along very well too."

Sarah laughed and said, "Yes very well. I like my team. We work well both together and independently. It will be hard going back to the station routine again after this."

Freeman said nothing but waited for Grace to return. When she came back carrying the rifle bag, she and Sarah went into the interview room and said to Medinkov, "Please remove the contents of the rifle and hand them over to me please, its necessary for legal matters."

Medinkov unzipped the bag, removed the rifle and twisted the end of the butt. After a few twists he opened it and removed a brown paper parcel. He handed it over to Grace and said, "That is the key you are wanting so you can get into the deposit box."

Grace thanked him and took back the rifle and zipped the bag up again and left the room.

Sarah said, "Thank you, and to let you know a death certificate has been issued concerning the death of Goran Stephan Medinkov and that will accompany the remains back to Bosnia."

He thanked her and she returned to the observation room where she saw Grace holding a key in her hand and a piece of paper with a series of numbers on official Lloyds Bank note paper.

Freeman said to Jason, "You and Grace get to the bank now and bring back whatever is in that box. There is a helicopter waiting outside and should get you there in plenty of time before it closes. If there are any problems, let me know and I'll ensure that they will cooperate fully."

They then left. Freeman and Sarah sat in front of the bank of terminals which were still being updated as more information was discovered and entered into the system. The operators were sifting through the multitude of files and even as they sat and watched, more files were placed on their desks for analysis and evidential purposes.

Sarah said, "What will truly happen to them, can we really bury them in such a way that they will never be heard of again, or that they ever see the light of day?"

Freeman remarked, "Of course, ironically, they will be costing the taxpayers a fortune for their betrayal but the money we seized will go towards their upkeep. There are secure facilities in places you do not need to know about that house these people. It's no less than what they deserve, unfortunately judicial execution was banned a few years back under a previous Prime Minister, otherwise we would have simply eliminated the problem."

Sarah was amazed but said nothing. This was a whole new world she had got involved in and she was not prepared for it. She understood the reasoning behind it but could not get her head around the consequences for these two men.

She said, "When this is all over, are we are just going to forget what happens to these men? God knows I have no sympathy with what they have done. They fully deserve to spend the rest of their lives in prison, but to do what is being suggested is something I cannot fathom."

Freeman replied, "We cannot afford any more similar incidents like the assault on the police station when they tried to release Gregorov. If word gets out that they are alive and in prison I, and the Prime minister, fear it will result in another round of atrocities."

He continued, "We have facilities for such people. It is used sparingly, but if needed then we can and do use them. Only the Prime minister and the Home Secretary can authorise such confinements, and both have to be in agreement. To my knowledge it has only been acted up on four times in the past twenty years."

Sarah responded, "Where are they now, what happened with them?"

He answered, "I don't know exactly, and if I did, I cannot tell you under the Official Secrets Act, which you all will be signing in a short while."

Sarah retorted, "Have any of them ever been released?"

Freeman commented, "There was never a risk that they would."

Sarah pondered his comment and just said, "Let's get this all over and we can get back to ordinary crimes." They laughed. She felt as though she deserved a holiday after what they had gone through over the past few weeks.

CHAPTER 48

As they were sitting and discussing the impending change in the life of Medinkov and Morgan, Grace and Jason were arriving at the Lloyds Branch in Aldershot. As they entered the building they were met by the Manager. They introduced themselves and he asked for the key and code to open the deposit box.

He explained how they could open the box. They had three attempts with the combination numbers. If they made any mistakes after the third attempt it would lock down and they would not be able to access it.

Grace looked at him, smiled and said, "For your sake, I hope we do get it right, otherwise by the time we do get access the safety box this room will not be fit for the purpose."

His eyes opened wide, looked at them and saw they were both smiling at him. He led them into the room, where he took out his key, inserted the key supplied, twisted them into position and then Grace dialled in the numbers into the locker. As she dialled in the last number, they all heard the click and the door opened slightly.

The look on the managers face was one of extreme relief. Grace saying, "We were never going to fail, we have done these many times before." The manager was shaking and gave a wry smile to them both.

They took out the box from within the locker and placed it on the table to the side of the room. Jason opened it as Grace took the photographs for evidential purposes. Inside were at least ten notebooks, and a number of CDs and a large number of USB sticks.

As they took them out, Jason saw that the notebooks were in chronological order. He opened the first one and started to read it. He looked over to Grace and said, "We need to bag this immediately and get it back to our people, they need to see it as a matter of urgency."

She logged everything they had taken from the deposit box. She gave the manager the receipt and left the bank. On the way back to the helicopter Jason said, "They are going to have a field day with this. Even the little I saw is explosive. I am not sure how they are going to react to this. If the rest is the same as the beginning, then we have only touched the tip of the iceberg."

Grace said, "Let the bosses see what we have got. They can have their big meetings and decide what to do. We have done what was asked of us and we still have to finish the files for CPS, although that's a paper exercise as far as I am concerned."

Jason said, "I know, but look what we have achieved. I don't care what happens to any of them, they can rot in hell as far as I am concerned. Medinkov has fulfilled his part of the bargain, so his remains will get shipped to Bosnia. Some unknown body will suffice and Medinkov will die happy in the knowledge that somebody in his hometown thinks he has come back after all the years away as a good patriot."

He continued, "What will happen with Johnstone?" Grace said, "He is finished. I have no idea what they have in store for him, but I hope he lives to regret every minute of it."

After an hour or so, their helicopter started to reduce height and soon they felt the jolt of the wheels as it landed. They both carried the boxes back into the control room. Both were grinning and Grace shouted "Bingo!"

The others turned around on hearing Grace and, seeing their reactions as they carried in the large box. Jason said, "I don't know what is going to happen with this lot, but even the Crown Jewels won't need the security all this will need."

Freeman approached and took hold of the box and looked inside, he opened the first journal, read it for a few minutes then closed it and said to Grace, "Book in each document, CD and USB as soon as you can. I'll decide who has access to them after I have made a few phone calls. Until then they are not to opened by anyone else, do you understand?"

She nodded and went to her desk where she entered everything into the exhibit logs, both in written form and digitally. She then sealed the box and placed it into the large safe in the corner of the room.

Whilst Freeman was away. They sat together, looked at the monitors in front of them and saw that there was only a trickle of information now being sent back to the centre. Telephone calls were still being made back and forth to the different agencies. All of it was being coordinated through this central control room.

More and more authorities were compiling their prosecution files, issuing Interpol Red Notices and arranging for court appearances or extended detentions for the ones who had been arrested. It seemed for now that there was a lull in the activities. But they all sensed that they had not even scratched the surface of what was taking place around the world.

Sarah sat and watched as the list grew slowly. She felt proud of what her and her teams had initiated and achieved with the worldwide investigations. She went over in her mind as to what triggered each event, but she could not get it out of her mind that there was a missing link in each incident.

She wandered over to the screens and whiteboards, which were related to all the events in the United Kingdom, from the shooting in the park, to the arrests of Brown/Medinkov and Morgan. She looked from each board to the next trying to find a link or a hint of somebody who was involved but was presently unknown. It was gnawing at her, but she was reluctant to tell anyone in case they thought she was being paranoid. She stared at the screens, lost in her own thoughts when it was disturbed by Freeman returning.

She looked up and turned around and faced him. He sat down at the head of the table with all the others, and said, "Following discussions with the Prime Minister, it has been decided that we will assimilate the information contained in the box and prepare reports as required. Once we know what the whole picture is, then it will be decided what action will be taken and by whom."

Jason said, "Who will be doing all that? We still have the prosecution files to finish."

Freeman responded, "I am afraid it will have to be everyone here. It will be all hands on deck. We cannot afford to give any of this out until we know what and who we are dealing with. I did tell her that we would not be in a position to start this for another week or so. She was quite happy about that saying we had waited this long that another few days would not make much difference."

There was a silence and a look of resignation on their faces. Sarah said, "We all need a couple of days break Sir. I am happy to do it, but my mind is so full of all this as it is. I am worried that we might get confused and mixed up if we go straight from one to the other."

Freeman said, "Of course, I think that the current files can be wrapped up in the next few days. Then we close shop, go home to families or whoever you are with and just relax. I have made arrangements for the camp commandant to ensure the premises are always secure, day and night."

Ellis commented, "Will you still need the services of myself and Steenson when you start the new stuff?"

Freeman replied, "Of course, the Prime Minister made it very clear that she wanted you both to stay as part of the team until its natural conclusion. She has already or, will soon, be speaking to your respective offices and telling them of her decision. I don't think there will be any objections in the circumstances."

Everyone in the control nodded and the mood lightened immediately. There was a new sense of purpose and energy with their work. Jason asked, "What about the other control rooms which we have been making use of? Will we be closing them down now?"

Freeman didn't answer immediately, then said, "I don't think so, we'll have to keep a skeleton crew with each control room. We are not going to be conducting any proactive investigations until we know the full extent of what we have uncovered. We can always bring them back up to speed at a later stage if required."

Grace then said, "Sir, why can't we second some of the ops from the other control rooms to here? They know virtually as much as we do. They are completely trustworthy, and they can help with the admin and stuff which we will have to plough through."

Freeman replied, "That's a good suggestion Grace."

He turned to Ellis and said, "Would you mind some of your best guys coming across to our side too? They have been really helpful when dealing with Williams and Brown as they knew him."

Ellis smiled and said, "Of course, they will be happy to be still part of it. These are probably the most exciting times they will ever have in their lifetime."

Freeman said, "Thanks, its much appreciated. I know who I want to be part of the backup team when we start the examination."

Sarah went back over to the whiteboards, feeling more alert and confident than a short while ago. As she searched through the different links, she kept reminding herself of the timelines of the incidents and more importantly, what gaps between events. She traced the personalities and their connections through all the scenarios, but elements were missing and that frustrated her but she thought that perhaps the missing links would be in the next batch of evidence they would be uncovering after the break.

She knew that deep down she was not going to be finished with this case, and its attendant side issues, for a long while yet. She was glad she had her friends with her and that reassured her.

CHAPTER 49

She looked across at Freeman who beckoned her over. He said, "In view of what we have, I do believe Medinkov. The Prime Minister has signed all the necessary papers for a body to be repatriated to Bosnia for burial."

He continued, "Do you want to tell him the good news? It might be the last time you will ever have to speak with him, subject to anything we find on any of the new stuff we have obtained, courtesy of him."

She said, "Why not? I need to close this once and for all. I just want to see the look on his face as I leave for the last time."

Freeman smiled and said, "That's something we all want to see."

Sarah entered Medinkov's cell and sat before him. She said, "What you provided us was correct. We have taken everything from the deposit box, and we are currently analysing the contents. Once we have done that there may well be occasions when you will be interviewed again. I don't know at this stage whether it will be me or someone else."

He replied, "I am glad that I have finally been able to be of some assistance. I have no excuses for what I have done to this country and the people in it. I am particularly sorry for the hurt I have caused to people who meant something to me. I allowed myself to be get greedy and betray everything that I had stood for." He continued, "I'd much rather it be you if anyone is going to question me. I don't think I'd like it be anyone else."

She said, "You know I cannot promise that at all. There are many considerations to be taken into account, including timings and other matters which might not be within my powers or technical abilities. It will be decided by my senior officers. I can say though, that whoever it is will take into account both your treachery and assistance in equal measures."

He replied, "Too bad. Can I ask for one last favour if that is the case. Can you get me a prawn sandwich with a seafood sauce on a slice of sourdough bread please? Our last meal together."

She responded, "Of course. You will always be the Sandwich Man to me and no doubt you will to all the others you have come into contact with."

She went out and ordered it and then re-joined him, saying, "The body will be sent back to Bosnia as promised. This will happen within the next seven days. Once that is done, then both of us will have fulfilled our promises. Of course, as far as the world is concerned you are dead, and you will remain in isolation whilst you still live." He replied, "I deserve no less under the circumstances."

The sandwiches arrived and Medinkov took them and started eating immediately. He finished the first one as if there was no tomorrow and said to Sarah, “Delicious, thank you.” He then ate into the second part of it when he suddenly stopped.

He went red, his eyes bulged, and he started shaking. Sarah pressed the alarm bell and went to give him the Heimlich manoeuvre believing he was choking.

He pushed her away and in a rasping voice, “There is nothing you can do, I am highly allergic to prawns and you, of all people, has given me my way out of here, thank you.”

He continued, “Now the real Medinkov can go back to Bosnia once and for all.”

He slumped to the floor gasping out loud, then quickly his breathing becoming shallower and shallower. Several officers including Freeman, rushed into the room to give assistance, while Sarah stood aghast at what had happened and the shock, she felt knowing she had helped him do it.

A doctor entered the room, stabbed an Epipen into his thigh immediately and placed an oxygen mask over his face. He felt for a pulse and found none. He commenced CPR and with the use of a defibrillator worked on him for several minutes as he lay on the floor. The doctor looked up at Sarah and shook his head. He pronounced Medinkov dead. She felt devastated and tears started to fall.

Freeman came to her and put his arm around her and said, “There was nothing you could have done or anticipated about this. There is nothing on his file to show that he had any allergies whatsoever. He did this on purpose, he knew he had come to the end.”

Sarah sat in the chair and was unable to do anything. She felt as though her whole world had just collapsed. She had tried to do the right thing, keep his trust and be open and fair with him. He had committed the ultimate betrayal and she had nothing left to give.

She said to Freeman, "I know what you are saying, but he sat there, cool as a cucumber, knowing he was going to die. He asked me for the sandwich knowing I would get him it, like every time before. I couldn't do anything, no one could, now we have nothing to help us with the stuff we are looking at. We are back to square one all over again. I hate this bloody world at times."

She stood up and walked out of the room, while the medical staff made arrangements to remove the body. She went outside and sat on a bench. She held her head in her hands and burst into tears. She was used to death, but this was personal, she had helped him die, even if she did not know it. She felt a loss, and that shocked her, as Medinkov really didn't mean anything to her on a personal level. When he was Brown, he had been eye candy on his bike, but that had soon worn off. He had been instrumental in her being where she was now and everything that had taken place in recent times.

She became aware of someone sitting down beside her, it was Grace who said, "Damn that man!! I was looking forward to a good prawn sandwich later, and he went and took it, selfish bastard."

She laughed out loud, and said, "He served his usefulness like all the others and took the cowards way out. That is what makes us different to them."

Sarah smiled and said, "You are right, in the end, we carry on and make the world a safer place. But it still sticks in my craw what he did."

She looked at Grace and said, "Tonight, I am going to get totally bombed, wake up tomorrow with an awful hangover and start all over again. Want to join me? A lady's drunken night, the men can wait. I don't feel like facing men for the moment."

Grace giggled and said, "Ok girl, I'll get the first round in, we'll use your room. Jason is too settled into my room to kick him out."

Sarah laughed and said, "I knew I could rely on you. I need a good long shower after this and then we can start. Let the guys finish off for today and in the meantime, I'll go grab some snacks and the booze. Later you can give me the lowdown on Jason."

They both went back into the main room where Freeman told them that everyone was finished for today in view of the events surrounding Medinkov. There was a collective round of applause. Everyone picked up their files and bags and left the room. Sarah and Grace went to their respective rooms and Sarah noticed Jason following Grace along the corridor.

She went into her room, undressed, and threw her clothes into the washing machine, still shaking at the sight of Medinkov dead on the ground. She got into the shower and turned it on as high as she could possibly bear it and scrubbed herself until she felt as though she had scraped all her skin off and any remaining trace of him.

She stood under the shower and let the hot water take away the tension in her body. Her muscles relaxed with the power of the water and her thoughts moved on to when this was all over. She promised to herself that she would have some proper time for herself. She was determined to catch up on what she had been missing out on for what seemed for ever since she joined CID.

She dried herself off and dressed herself in a blue one-piece soft trouser outfit, which was warm and casual and just what she needed for the evening. She rang the Mess and ordered food. It was all junk food with lots of sweet sugary chocolates, tonight was not a night for being sensible about food or drink. She ordered several bottles of Pinot Grigio, vodka and orange juice.

When the food and drink arrived, she opened the wine and filled her glass as she waited for Grace. She sat back and had nearly finished it when there was a knock on the door and Grace walked in.

She was wearing her black polo top and jeans. Sarah laughed and said she looked like a ninja and they both laughed. Grace poured her drink into a tall glass and said, "Cheers, here's to an evening neither of us will remember in the morning."

Whilst Sarah and Grace were away, Freeman spoke with the Prime Minister and told her of the death of Medinkov. She said, "Damn, wish I had been the one to give him the sandwich, but at least it gets rid of one problem."

She continued, "With your agreement, we can put him in the coffin and send him back to Bosnia where he belongs. We have the documentation all ready and he is the genuine article. We can close the file on him once and for all and it's not going to cost the taxpayers any money."

Freeman said, "That's by far the best way forward. We will send the body to where it needs to be for administrative purposes and then it can be flown to Bosnia and handed over to the authorities for burial and we can have it signed off."

The Prime Minister rang off and Freeman made the necessary calls for the body to leave the camp and go to the place of embarkment.

CHAPTER 50

Next morning everyone assembled at the usual time of seven o'clock. The last two to arrive were Sarah and Grace, who both looked like death warmed up. They were in the same clothes as they wore the previous evening. They both gave sheepish grins, apologised for their state, and promised that they were ready to start work immediately, which everyone doubted!!

Freeman laughed and said, "Its traditional that you have a full English to start the day, its ready for you on the table." Grace looked over and went a shade of green and sat down immediately. Sarah just turned round and walked out, returning a few minutes later, rubbing her face with her hands.

Sarah grabbed a mug of coffee and sat at her desk, trying to assimilate what had come into the room during the night. Fortunately, it seemed that it had been very quiet, except for a log between Freeman and the Prime Minister.

She looked over at Freeman who responded, "We have made arrangements for Medinkov to be in the coffin which will be sent to Bosnia. We will have then cleared any outstanding issues with him in this country. The records show he died in an accident and there is no reason to change that at all. His body left here two hours ago and taken to a base in Surrey where he will be transferred to a civilian plane and flown out of the country."

Sarah nodded and felt strangely at ease with that. She felt better knowing that there was a finality to his life. It was a chapter of her life that she never wanted to repeat.

As the coffee took effect, work started to pick up again within the control room. The new evidence took on a new sense of urgency and everyone concentrated on the contents.

As the contents were being analysed and reports compiled, a number of queries and comments were made and there were calls for assistance within the room. What was surprising was the total lack of passwords and encryptions on the USB sticks. The operators were able to access the contents instantly, the files all on the screen for them to open.

The analysts copied the files as they were opened. They were then sent to the printers which churned out copies for the groups to read and prioritise for later enquiries.

During the day, Freeman and Ellis signed off on the original investigation files for the CPS. Of the other case files, one was going direct to the Prime Minister, another specifically for Ellis, and another for Steenson. Everyone stopped what they were doing, gathered around and clapped when they were placed into the large crates which were sealed and moved out to the transport department.

Sarah watched as the operators' terminals began to close down. It was as if a part of their lives were switching off. She sat back and reflected on what they had done over the past weeks. The sights she had seen, the horrendous events that she had accepted as part of her work were now in boxes. The number of people either dead or as good as dead, she didn't want to think about that too much.

Grace and Jason came over and sat with her, Grace saying, "Feeling better? You were hammered last night! I have never seen you like that before. Your secrets are safe with me." and she laughed loudly. Sarah closed her eyes and said, "Oh no, not on the table again, was I?"

Grace smiled, "That's the least of it, but don't worry my lips are sealed." They both laughed, and Jason looked at the two of them and wondered what they had got up to last night.

After their coffee break everyone went back to their tables and started to read over the new information contained in the files. As they read more and more into it all they saw the extent of the data and potential leads. Sarah and Jason looked at each other and both suspected, that in time they, or another team, would be back delving into the darkness of what was being uncovered.

Sarah wondered how Brown/Medinkov could have amassed this amount of information and kept it secret from the likes of Morgan. The teams weren't in a position yet to make such presumptions but had no doubt all would be revealed.

As the day wound down, so did their time at Bradbury Lines. They emptied their desks packed their personal files away into boxes. They left the Control Room for the last time and went to their allocated rooms They found their personal cases waiting outside. Sarah reflected on the mess her room was in when she left it earlier that day but chose not to say anything. They all met up in the Control room and as more analysts arrived, they said their goodbyes.

As they walked out, they saw yet another growing list of files on the desks but carried on. No one looked back and were certainly not thinking about the contents. All any of them wanted to do was to enjoy the break they so richly deserved.

Over the next few weeks, all the information contained in the USBs, DVDs and diaries which Medinkov had so painstakingly kept, were downloaded into a format that everyone could understand. It was then entered into the new, larger, computers which had been allocated to the four groups of analysts and investigators, both Police and Military. All the information was printed out and prioritised for future in depth investigation.

CHAPTER 51

Work was the last thing on Sarah's mind as she drove down the motorway in France towards Biarritz, one of her favourite places. She was in her beloved and ancient Renault 4 and she just took her time admiring the scenery and getting the mood into her veins the closer she got to her hotel. She loved the rugged coastline near St Jean de Luz and the hotel overlooking the cliff where the waves crashed over the rocks. At night she could hear them from her room as she drifted off to sleep.

Since that day two weeks ago, when she, Grace and Jason had boarded the helicopter back to London, she had felt a great weight lift from her shoulders. Her sadness and betrayal of what had taken place, from that fateful morning in the park right up to Medinkov killing himself in front of her had been overbearing but ebbed away the further she flew from what had been her home for so long.

Her first few days had been a blur, most of it spent sleeping, doing her laundry and, inevitably, in the evenings a few glasses of wine to help her unwind and forget the horrors of the past few months. She had spoken to Grace every day and given reports of her romance with Jason, including some information that should have been keep to herself, but they laughed and joked about it all and Sarah felt good about them. She knew Grace had only told her those little secrets knowing it helped Sarah get over her sense of guilt and responsibility for Medinkov. It seemed the world was a paradox. One where death and greed and corruption ruled many countries. Where individuals, including heads of State and other evil gang lords instilled fear and mayhem wherever they went.

The world where Sarah was now could not be any more different. She was laying out by a pool, in a bikini, the sun caressing her body and relaxing her both mentally and physically, a couple of drinks next to her. As she looked across the pool at the local male talent, she thought to herself of how much she had missed out on. Much too much, perhaps it was time to change that.

As she watched them, she could not help but think back to her last relationship and how that had ended badly, purely down to her own constant need for work and promotions. He had been patient for long enough but there had come a time when even he had had enough of her being out all hours, working, and when she got home, too tired for them to spend any quality time together. One day, late at night as always, she got home and found the flat empty of all his things and a note expressing regret.

She vowed that from now on she would put her own life first and work second, even though it would mean missing out on promotion and a higher pension which she would be getting in a few years. She settled back, sipped a glass of wine and wondered who the lucky guy might be later, looking at one fit guy, and she laughed to herself.

EPILOGUE

Freeman and Ellis spent most days still at Bradbury Lines sifting through the information and reading the reports. It soon became obvious that there was a considerable amount of evidence that neither Morgan nor Medinkov had divulged. There was nothing they could do about Medinkov now, but Morgan in particular, had not been at all forthcoming with his involvement, despite his claims that he had told them everything. Freeman made a note to personally interview him again and remind him of the public disclosure that the Prime Minister had mentioned and that the benefits his wife now had could just as easily be taken away.

Once a week, the Prime Minister, the Commissioner of Police and the Home Secretary travelled to Hereford for an update on the information and to discuss future tactics. If the truth be known, they were also there for the curries which they had grown increasingly fond of over the months of visits. There was a general agreement that, again, there would have to be at least three dedicated teams within the United Kingdom and more cooperation with authorities around the world, although most were already on standby for any future developments.

Three weeks later in Scotland, Bruce Johnstone, the disgraced MP, pleaded guilty to several counts of Fraud. He was sentenced at Glasgow Crown Court to three years imprisonment. This had all been agreed between the Prosecutors and the Defence and only the basic details had been read out in court.

He was escorted from the court and placed into the prison van waiting to transport him and the other convicted persons to Peterhead Jail, sixty miles away. As with all the prisoners, he was handcuffed and placed into his cell within the prison van.

The van with the prisoners and guards left the court area and drove out of Glasgow onto the motorway leading to Peterhead. Overhead at one thousand feet, a Police Scotland helicopter maintained a constant vigil as the van drove along the motorway.

They had gone about thirty miles. The traffic had started to thin out when the observer in the helicopter pointed out what appeared to be a large drone approaching in the opposite direction at a distance of almost three miles. The pilot radioed into the control room and requested information on the unknown drone.

The response came back that there was no information at all on it. The occupants of the helicopter suddenly saw a flash and then the white trail of what they thought to be a rocket leaving the dark grey object. They shouted out to the control room that they had seen movement from the drone but, before they could even finish the message, there was a blinding flash on the road below and the van containing the prisoners erupted into a mass of white flame and smoke.

Within seconds the smoke billowed hundreds of feet into the air, the helicopter having to swerve to avoid it, and although they tried to find the offending machine when they stabilised, there was no sign of it. It had seemingly vanished into thin air. The pilot sent a distress signal to the control room informing them of the suspected attack on the van and dropped from its present height and hovered over the scene.

From their position there was nothing left of the van. Instead in its place was a crater several feet deep and wide. A number of other vehicles had been damaged, but not critically.

Within a few minutes they saw a convoy of emergency vehicles descending on the scene. They both knew nothing could be done but the motorway was going to be a crime scene for many hours. They gave an update to their control room and left the scene as another helicopter joined them overhead.

At Police Scotland, the names of all the dead at the scene were entered into their database. One name in particular came up on screen, Bruce Johnstone, and against the name was a telephone number that should be contacted in the event that anything untoward happened to him. The details were passed to the Watch Commander who made the call, and it was answered by Commander Freeman at Scotland yard.

After the call, Freeman sat at his desk wondering who had been responsible for the attack. It had obviously been well planned and carried out.

Freeman hit the speed dial numbers on his phone and simultaneously three phones rang out. No peace for the wicked he thought to himself, here we go again.

Two miles away in the penthouse of another tall building overlooking London, three men looked out and the Chairman said, “That will show that stupid woman we are not dead and buried. Inform the others to prepare themselves.” He dialled a number and within a few seconds it was answered, and the recipient gave a code, agreed by all parties, and said, “We will be in Hereford within 24 hours”. He rang off. The chairman said, “They have no chance of getting anywhere near the camp, just cannon fodder. They are expendable but shows our intent to everyone.”

Made in the USA
Columbia, SC
21 August 2024

e34f8fef-8d6e-4b5d-aa09-111767d7aa77R02